Praise for *New Yor[k]*
MICHE[LLE]
and The Chron[icles]

"No one provides an emotional payoff like Michelle Sagara. Combine that with a fast-paced police procedural, deadly magics, five very different races and a wickedly dry sense of humor—well, it doesn't get any better than this."
—Bestselling author Tanya Huff on The Chronicles of Elantra series

"Readers will embrace this compelling, strong-willed heroine with her often sarcastic voice."
—*Publishers Weekly* on *Cast in Courtlight*

"The impressively detailed setting and the book's spirited heroine are sure to charm romance readers, as well as fantasy fans who like some mystery with their magic."
—*Publishers Weekly* on *Cast in Secret*

"Along with the exquisitely detailed world building, Sagara's character development is mesmerizing. She expertly breathes life into a stubborn yet evolving heroine. A true master of her craft!"
—*RT Book Reviews* (4½ stars) on *Cast in Fury*

"Each visit to this amazing world, with its ri[ch] character, is one to relish."
—*RT Bo[ok Reviews]* [on Cast in S]*ilence*

"Another satisfying addition to a[n] [entertai]ning fantasy series."
—[*Publish*]*ers Weekly* on *Cast in Chaos*

"Sagara does an amazing job continuing to flesh out her large cast of characters, but keeps the unsinkable Kaylin at the center."
—*RT Book Reviews* (4½ stars) on *Cast in Peril*

"Über-awesome Sagara picks up the intense action right where she left off… While Kaylin is the heart of this amazing series, the terrific characters keep the story moving. An autobuy for sure!"
—*RT Book Reviews* (4½ stars) on *Cast in Sorrow*

The Chronicles of Elantra
by
New York Times bestselling author

Michelle Sagara

MICHELLE SAGARA

CAST IN DECEPTION

mira

mira

Recycling programs
for this product may
not exist in your area.

ISBN-13: 978-0-7783-3110-0

Cast in Deception

MIRABooks.com

BookClubbish.com

Printed in U.S.A.

With thanks to

HexaDoken
Ijon
Jenova
Medicris
Mifu
Popsoap
Sgt. Shivers
Team NoD
TehVappy50
TerminusEst13
The Stronghold Team
Torr Samaho
WaTaKiD
Yholl

CAST IN DECEPTION

CHAPTER 1

"*You* wake her up."

Kaylin's eyelids felt glued shut. She opened them anyway. Above her head, a tiny dragon appeared to be running in place.

"Why me? It's not my decision that's causing the difficulty!" That was definitely Mandoran.

She didn't immediately reach for the dagger under her pillow. She did, however, push herself into something that resembled a sitting position. Her familiar leapt up on her shoulder, where he squawked at the hair that then fell into his face.

"You were the one who said we should warn her." Annarion.

Kaylin knew that the two Barrani men could argue with their mouths shut. They knew each other's True Names, and had their miniature version of telepathy. Grimly—morning was her best time of day only if you made a list and turned it upside down—she slid off her bed and toward a night robe, determined to remind them that they could argue *silently*.

"If the two of you could shut up for five minutes, *I'll* wake her up." That was Tain. Kaylin froze and changed clothing direction; there was no way she was going back to sleep.

"I think she's awake now," Helen, her sentient house, said, with just a hint of disapproval.

"Good."

Say that in five minutes, Kaylin thought, shoving her arms into her shirt. The buttons were on the inside, which was not where they were supposed to be. "Helen, can I have some light?"

Light immediately flooded the room. The familiar squawked his resentment. Kaylin was saving hers for possible future need, but she was now worried. "Is Teela here?"

"Not yet, dear."

Tain didn't drop by for a random social visit. Not without Teela.

"What's happened?"

"It's not an emergency," was Helen's gentle reply. "Or at least not yet."

"Don't give me that look," Tain said, before Kaylin could open her mouth.

"Why are you here?"

"Ask Mandoran." Tain looked about as happy as Kaylin felt, which was unreasonable given that Barrani didn't need sleep unless they were badly injured.

Kaylin, however, swiveled in Mandoran's direction.

"Teela's coming over," he said.

"What happened?"

"Nothing yet."

"Why is she coming over?"

The two younger Barrani exchanged a glance. To Kaylin's surprise, it was Annarion who answered. "She's coming to ask Helen if she can move in for a while."

Kaylin turned to Tain.

"I haven't spoken to her yet," Teela's partner replied. His eyes were blue.

"I believe," Helen said, interrupting them before Kaylin

could speak, "you can ask her yourself. She's almost at the front door."

"Don't look at me like that," Mandoran told Kaylin. "This has nothing to do with me. I voted against it."

"Against what?"

When Mandoran failed to answer, she passed the frown on to Annarion, who looked both defiant and uncomfortable. "I'm taking the Test of Name."

Tain's eyes darkened to a midnight blue, and if Kaylin hadn't been human, hers would have joined them. "You're *what*?"

"I'm going to the High Halls to take the Test of Name."

Kaylin was not stupid, in spite of what many of her early teachers had believed. She could put two plus two together and end up with four. "If Teela is coming over to ask if she can stay for a while," Kaylin said out loud, "does that mean the *rest* of the cohort are coming to visit as well?"

"Not without your permission," Annarion replied, guilt shifting the corners of his eyes and mouth.

"Look, some of us think it's an *incredibly stupid* decision. But we know it's dangerous, and none of the rest of us have taken the Test, either. If he goes, we're not going to let him go on his own."

"Teela's taken the Test."

Mandoran exhaled. "Yes. We know. That's part of the problem. She can't come with us." He stared, quite deliberately, at his feet. Since this meant—to Kaylin—that he was trying not to look at anyone else, she frowned.

"She can't go with you."

"No. Not if she follows the customs and laws of the High Halls."

Kaylin did look up then. "But Tain hasn't taken the Test of Name."

Silence.

Kaylin said, "Oh, no. *No.* I am *not* getting between the two of you while you're arguing. You won't kill each other, but the collateral damage will probably kill anyone who isn't Barrani!"

"We are not arguing," Tain replied. His voice was chilly, his eyes the same dark blue.

Annarion apparently also found his feet interesting.

Tain was not a Lord of the High Court. He was Teela's partner, and Teela was. But the other Barrani Hawks were like Tain. A second class of citizen, a lesser class, in the eyes of most Barrani Lords. He'd never seemed to give a damn. But clearly, he did now.

She wondered who, among the cohort, had voted against Annarion taking the Test. Mandoran and Teela, certainly. But had any of the others?

"Yes," she said, out loud. "The cohort can stay here as our guests. Given what happened with the two of you," she added, looking at the Barrani who were still staring at their feet, "I want *some* of the city to remain standing."

"They've been taking the same lessons we have," Mandoran offered. "They learn what we learn."

"Are they like you or like Annarion?"

"...We're not sure yet."

"Then they are *definitely* staying where Helen can keep an eye on them."

By the time Teela arrived at the front door, Tain, Annarion and Kaylin were standing in front of it. Mandoran hung back, but not with any real hope of avoiding a face full of blue-eyed, angry Teela, which is what greeted them when Helen opened the front door.

Her eyes shifted into indigo when she saw Tain. Tain didn't appear to notice, but he wasn't one of the cohort, and he'd lived in the real world—near Teela—for much longer than anyone else had.

"What are you doing here?" she demanded, with no grace whatsoever.

Tain didn't throw Mandoran to the wolves, which is clearly what Mandoran had been dreading. "I've heard that the cohort, as Kaylin calls them, is coming to stay."

That wouldn't have been Kaylin's choice of opening words, but Kaylin was not Teela's partner.

"Please come in," Helen said, before Teela could respond. "Kaylin hasn't eaten yet."

No one had eaten yet. No one really felt like eating, either, as far as Kaylin could tell.

Teela and Tain quit what might have devolved into a staring contest as Helen ushered everyone into the dining room. They took their chairs as if chairs were weapons or armor. Teela even turned hers around so the back faced the table and she could fold her arms over it.

"Why," she said again, "are you here?"

"I told you."

"My friends are not your problem."

"No."

Teela's eyes narrowed; she turned to glare at Mandoran, who shrugged. Her words, however, continued to be aimed at Tain. "I don't want you to endanger yourself needlessly."

"I'm not. I've always been far more cautious than you are."

This was arguably true, but Kaylin was not nearly suicidal enough to make the argument. She looked at breakfast as it appeared on her plate, and wondered if it would be safer if breakfast for everyone else—or at least the Barrani—could be finger foods for just one day. Teela was giving the cutlery a side-eye that suggested she might use it for something other than food.

"You are not taking the Test with them."

"I haven't taken the Test. I *can*."

"You've never wanted to be a Lord of the High Court. And babysitting—"

"Hey!"

"—is not nearly a good enough reason to change your mind."

"No. It's not."

"Tain—"

"The cohort are coming to Elantra. *Sedarias* is coming to Elantra. The High Court has maintained the polite fiction of joy at the rescue of the cohort."

Teela said nothing.

"How long do you think that joy is going to last? Annarion is the bloodline heir. Karian is the bloodline heir. Mandoran is—god help his family—the bloodline heir. And Sedarias is the bloodline heir."

Kaylin turned to Tain. "Wait, what do you mean?"

"Annarion is not the only person present who intends to take back what Nightshade lost. Sedarias, however, *would have* been the Lord of her line had she not been sent to the green. The others are technically heirs because of politics or deaths due to the wars." He exhaled and turned to her.

"Is this really the time for a teachable moment?" Kaylin demanded. Tain continued to stare at her, which was his answer. "Fine. Their family lines—what are they, anyway?—have been ruled just fine since they were sent to the green. The Lords of those lines probably have no interest at all in being displaced."

"I have no interest in reclaiming my family holdings," Mandoran said.

"You said your family was gone!"

Mandoran shrugged. "As far as I'm concerned, they are."

"The High Court would not agree," Teela said, her voice dry as tinder.

Mandoran made clear what he thought the High Court could do with its disagreement.

"You are correct," Tain continued, speaking to Kaylin as if there had been no interruption. "Those families have held power for centuries. The children of the green were a myth—a sorrowful myth, perhaps—one that could be safely used. Now they are a very real fact.

"Teela is Lord of her line. She has had centuries to establish her rule. She is secure enough in that rule to be a Hawk—an Imperial Hawk. But the alliances she's built to maintain that power are going to shift."

"There is no guarantee of that," Teela said.

Tain didn't bother to reply, but his expression made clear just how little he thought of her counterargument. And he took his life in his hands by continuing to address his words to Kaylin. "Teela will, therefore, be drawn into the drama of the Test of Name. As long as none of the cohort are Lords of the High Court, everything remains academic. If they are not Lords of that court, they cannot claim their inheritance. It's *possible*," he said, his emphasis bordering on sarcasm, "that the High Court could be talked into believing that Mandoran, Eddorian, and Karian have no interest in ruling. There is nothing in the Empire that could induce the High Court to believe that Sedarias does not."

Sedarias was the name Kaylin heard most often, when Mandoran referred to the members of his cohort who still resided in the Hallionne Alsanis. Her opinion was either valuable or dangerous—but it was never dismissed out of hand.

"And this is dangerous to Teela because?"

"Because some of her allies will be directly—and badly—impacted should the cohort decide to reclaim what is technically theirs. If Sedarias remained in the green, she could finesse the situation; Sedarias was not Lord of the High Court. If Sedarias is coming to Elantra—"

"She'll become a Lord." If she passed the Test. "And she'll

attempt to secure her place as head of her family." The family that had abandoned her.

"Yes. Teela is currently the cohort's only toehold in the High Court; she is a Lord, she is the head of her line, and she carries one of the three weapons that were proof against Dragons. She's already felt some of that pressure, and the—"

"Tain."

Tain shut up. Kaylin could almost hear his jaws snap.

He didn't give up. He retrenched. This time, however, he spoke to Teela. "What you will need, if they set foot outside the Hallionne, are allies at Court. You did not require those allies in that fashion before. I have never had a desire to be a Lord of the Court. It wasn't worth the risk, given my own origins. It is worth that risk to me now." He folded his arms.

Kaylin caught Mandoran by the sleeve before he could vacate his chair and sneak out of the room. *You brought him here,* she mouthed. *You can suffer with the rest of us.*

Kaylin stared at the grim and silent Hawks. She was used to bickering and minor disagreements; she'd come to believe it came with the tabard. But this was different, and everyone in the breakfast room knew it. Someone had to interrupt them. One glance at Annarion and Mandoran told her there was no help coming from that quarter.

She was enough of a coward that help was unlikely to come from her, either.

But there was a Dragon in the house, and that Dragon appeared, as if by magic, in the dining room doorway. Kaylin was almost positive that the magic was called by Helen. Bellusdeo cleared her throat; Teela and Tain were probably aware of her presence, but were still glaring at each other across a suffocatingly quiet table. Since Bellusdeo was a Dragon, clearing her throat made a *lot* of noise.

It was Teela who turned toward her first, but Tain was quick to follow.

"Good morning," Teela said, her eyes a martial blue that was only fractionally less dire than it had been when she was glaring at Tain. Although historically the Barrani and the Dragons had been enemies, Teela actually liked Bellusdeo.

The Dragon returned that affection. For Teela. She seemed to approve of Annarion, but Mandoran frequently caused her to exhale smoke. "Annarion and Lord Nightshade have only just stopped screaming at each other at the top of their Barrani lungs. I'd just as soon have a little bit of peace and quiet before things blow up again."

"Lord Nightshade has merely accepted that he cannot change Annarion's mind at this point. Do not think he has surrendered." Teela seldom hesitated, but did now. When she started to speak again, she spoke to Helen.

"Mandoran has informed you—"

"That your friends are coming to visit? Yes, dear." Helen could get away with calling Teela *dear*. Anyone else would have been picking up teeth. "And Kaylin has already offered you our hospitality at any time you wish to stay. I should, however, ask whether you would like to room with Tain."

Kaylin cringed.

Teela said no at the same time as Tain said yes.

Bellusdeo's grimace was exaggerated, but her eyes were gold.

"I would just as soon not involve him."

"I'm involved." Tain's voice was curt. He was angry.

Helen rushed in to prevent silence from once again shrouding the table. "I will, of course, have rooms for you. You are allowed across my threshold without Kaylin's express, explicit permission. She considers you—"

"Family. Yes. I know."

"In the mortal sense, not the immortal one." Kaylin knew

mortal families that would have fit right in with the Barrani families of Teela's acquaintance, but failed to point this out.

"In the Kaylin sense," Teela said.

"That is the only one with which I am concerned," Helen replied. "You are welcome here."

Bellusdeo took a seat at the table on the other side of Mandoran. The smile she gave him was almost feline. "How many other guests will I be sharing a roof with?"

Teela's answering grin was humorless. "Ten new guests, unless I can convince Annarion to change his bloody mind."

"You are not going to convince me to change my mind," Annarion said, finally joining a conversation that both he and Mandoran had managed to steer clear of.

Teela turned to stare at him, and to Kaylin's surprise, it was Annarion who looked away. Teela had clearly chosen to reply to the statement in the privacy of their name bond.

It was, strangely enough, Mandoran who broke the silence. "Annarion was the youngest," he said, looking at the table. "Nightshade was the eldest. Not the firstborn, but the eldest survivor of the war. He went to the Tower, and he returned." He flinched. "I'm telling her. It's not like she can't find out."

"Find out what?"

"Annarion had a sister. She was the middle surviving child. When it came her time, she went to the Tower to take the Test of Name." He inhaled. Paused. Kaylin thought he was done.

He was. Teela, however, took up the slack his silence left. "She was the daughter of an ambitious family. Those who fail the Test, with one possible exception, have never returned. Annarion assumed—as we all did at the time—that she had died. He grieved privately; it is not the way of my people to otherwise discuss the failure of their own kin. I therefore know very little about her. If the rest of my cohort has become something other, something larger, than Barrani, they are nonetheless Barrani in thought. Had she died, nothing would change."

This time, Annarion bowed his head. And Kaylin understood, in that moment, that Annarion *knew*. He knew the fate of those who failed that test.

Teela, seeing her expression, said, "Yes. Now he knows. Those who fail do not simply die; they remain where they fell. They will remain there until the creature at the base of the High Halls is destroyed."

Her words almost a whisper, Kaylin said, "He intends to free the trapped."

"The damned, yes. He intends to destroy the Shadow at the base of the Tower. He intends to free the dead. To be fair, he intends to free his sister."

"...So, the reason—the real reason—he was so angry at Nightshade..." Kaylin lapsed into uncomfortable silence.

"No. You are not Barrani. The reason he is angry with his brother has been stated truthfully, and often. His brother chose to reject duty and honor by abandoning his bloodline."

"He was *made* outcaste, Teela. He didn't choose it."

Teela just shook her head and made that *you'll understand when you're older* face that Kaylin hated. "Annarion does like you, and I understand why." She held up a hand. "I never had any qualms about leaving him in your hands. Or rather, I never worried about what you might do to, or with, him. All of my worry went in the other direction. Annarion is not a fool. Or rather, he understands why the Test exists. He understands that were the Shadow beneath the High Halls to escape, it would be a disaster that would make the previous attack on the High Halls pale to insignificance."

"But?"

"But, yes. My cohort was sent to the green. It was sent to *be* transformed. The experiment was not successful in the eyes of the High Court of the time—but it is being argued now that it was a success."

"By your cohort?"

"Yes. No one likes to feel that they are a failure," Teela added, with a rueful smile. "Shadow does not hold the same terror for Annarion or Mandoran that it does for you or the rest of my kin."

"They think they can destroy that Shadow."

"They think they have a chance."

"And if they don't succeed? If, somehow, that Shadow can subvert them?" She turned to Annarion who was still studying his plate as if it fascinated him. "If the Shadow takes *your* name, you can do things—you can *all* do things—that no other Barrani can. The Shadow's released at least one person we know of into the High Court." She did not mention who, and no one asked. "But if it has you and your cohort as its agents…"

Teela nodded, grim now. "Exactly."

Kaylin was technically a Lord of the High Court because she'd inadvertently taken the Test of Name—a test that she couldn't really fail, except by dying, as she hadn't *had* a name at the time. She'd seen what lay at the base of the Tower. It was a Shadow, and in its folds, it held the names of those who had failed. It held the substance of who they had been in life. Kaylin didn't exactly believe in ghosts, but didn't have a better word to describe it.

It had shaken her.

It had enraged her.

It had, as so many, many things did, brought her face-to-face with her own insignificance, and her helplessness. There was nothing she could do to disperse that particular Shadow, and nothing she could do to free the trapped.

The creature at the base of the High Halls was the *reason* the High Halls had been erected in the middle of what was otherwise a Dragon-ruled empire. But death wasn't the worst of it, for the Barrani. He could *also* control those he chose to allow to leave the Tower, because he had their names. He knew them.

For years, for centuries, probably for millennia, the Barrani had been feeding their children—or themselves—to that Shadow. And Kaylin even understood why. What the Shadow could not take, what the Shadow could not mislead or distract, it could not alter. Those Barrani had a base immunity to the effects of Shadow.

That base immunity was necessary. She knew what would happen to the city, *her* city, if the creature was no longer imprisoned. The Dragons might be safe. No one else.

After a long pause, in which Kaylin's drink practically congealed in her hands, she said, "So...they're all coming here."

"Yes. Sedarias now feels that some exploratory testing is required." Teela's eyes were marginally less blue; Bellusdeo's presence had shifted some of the tension out of the lines of her face.

More silence.

"We are aware of the danger—to others—if one of the cohort is subverted or controlled. Annarion was calling out to the Shadows without ever being aware that he was doing so. If he could be made to do so deliberately, the Shadow beneath the High Halls wouldn't need to be unleashed.

"*If* this happens, the rest of the cohort could exert influence and possibly counter the control with controls of our own."

"But to do that some of the cohort would have to remain at a distance."

Teela nodded. She lifted a long-fingered, pale hand to her brow and massaged her right temple. "At the moment, the argument has devolved into who those people will be, and how much distance is distant enough. For obvious reasons, my friends will stay here if you permit it."

Now, the disadvantage of having a Dragon join the conversation was made clear. Kaylin fidgeted but chose to speak. "While Bellusdeo is living here, the Emperor keeps a close watch on Helen. There's no way he's not going to know if a cohort of Western Barrani descend on my house."

"That is the other concern."

"She could just move out for the duration," Mandoran suggested. "*I'm* seriously considering it." He winced. "I can safely live elsewhere. And if Tain's going to be staying here, I could stay in his old place."

"Dear," Helen began.

"Don't 'dear' me. My entire life in the past week and a half has been nothing but argument, screaming argument, icy silence, and general condescension."

"I laughed at your bad joke yesterday," Kaylin pointed out.

"Fair enough. I'd shelve that under general condescension myself, but I'm not mortal and don't always understand how you think. I'm not that fond of the Dragon," he continued. "But I'd just as soon not fight an angry Emperor for no reason whatsoever." For Mandoran, this was progress. It implied that there were actual reasons *not* to fight Dragons. When he'd first arrived that would have been unthinkable.

Bellusdeo exhaled a stream of smoke. Her eyes were now orange, but Kaylin suspected that was due to the mention of the Emperor, and not Mandoran's commentary. "I am not moving out."

"I've had some time to get used to you," Mandoran continued, dropping the third person 'Dragon.' "You've had some time to get used to me. Annarion—well, he's Annarion. He practically considers you a friend. Not everyone is going to see you the same way."

Kaylin now understood why Teela was massaging her temple. "You haven't been defending Bellusdeo to your cohort, have you?"

"Don't make me lose whatever appetite I have. Of course not." Food appeared in front of Mandoran. He touched none of it. Kaylin, however, started eating, purely by instinct.

"He doesn't consider it defending her," Teela added. She gave the food in front of her the side-eye. There were many things Teela's childhood had lacked, but food wasn't one of them. She could ignore it. "The truth, however, is that we like Bellusdeo."

"Speak for yourself."

"Fine. I like Bellusdeo and Mandoran tolerates her. I understand what the wars cost her. She in turn understands what the wars cost me. Neither of us chose the wars. Neither of us were consulted by those who did." Teela shrugged. "You saw what Mandoran was like when he first arrived."

"You think the others will be like him?"

"No. Most of them have better manners. But the substance will be similar. They understand what we see in her. They also understand that the feeling is personal, emotional. They are likely to form their own opinions, but the forming might be, ah, fractious."

Helen did not appear to be concerned. Since it would be Helen who would keep the consequences of 'fractious' to a minimum, Kaylin didn't share Teela's anxiety. Well, she did, but not about that.

"None of your cohort went to the Tower in the High Halls."

"No."

"None," Mandoran added, "except Teela. But she did it later. And before you think she's being selfless or anything, she's not. Not entirely. She had problems readjusting to life in the Court, and she spent a lot of what remained of her so-called childhood under observation. She was tested constantly; the High Court knew what had happened to the others, and they were waiting to see that power manifest in Teela.

"She wasn't exactly a *pariah*, but she was only accepted because her father was a very powerful man. Only those who were certain to survive crossing him made demands of her. You've always said the Barrani are arrogant."

"When they're breathing, yes."

"Well, there were a lot of people who felt certain they'd survive. Time moves slowly for Immortals. But it does move. Teela hasn't been considered an abomination or a subhuman liability for centuries."

"...And if the cohort arrives in force..."

"She's too stubborn to abandon us, and we're too stubborn to push her out."

Since they knew each other's True Names, Kaylin doubted that was even possible, but said nothing.

"You are not being fair," Helen told him. She often spoke to Mandoran as if he were not quite out of childhood. "That is a natural part of her concern, of course, but you are not presenting it well." To Kaylin, in the face of Teela's silence, she said, "Teela is considering the political costs because she intends to preserve her cohort."

"I think we're capable of preserving ourselves."

"Yes. So, too, is Lord Nightshade. Teela, however, does not desire that you all be made outcaste. As outcastes, you would naturally be denied the Tower—and the High Halls. As outcastes, no Barrani would be required to lift a finger should outsiders, such as the Dragon Court, be called upon to end your existence. If, over the next few centuries, you prove yourselves to be considerable powers, you will be, as Nightshade is, grudgingly accepted. But the cost of waging that war could be profound.

"And of course, if you are made outcaste, there's a possibility that Teela will join you. It is not a guarantee. If she was willing to publicly disavow you, she would, given her history in the Court, be excluded from your fate."

Kaylin had a few thoughts then. Some of them could even be said in public—as long as public involved the Hawks, which was where she had learned most of the ruder words. "Someone has already made the motion."

Mandoran's smile, as he lifted his head, was bitter. "How did you guess?"

"Relatives of Annarion's?"

"And the already outcaste Nightshade, yes."

"When?"

Mandoran shrugged. "Does it matter?" He made a face at Teela. "She was going to find out anyway." Teela clearly made her reply in the silence of their name bond; Mandoran couldn't be bothered. "She's a *Lord* of the High Court, Teela. She has access to the Consort. She's *seen* the Lake of Life. She's considered the Consort's emergency replacement. If she wanted to, she could find this out by taking a walk in the Consort's garden!"

Teela relented. "Yes, *if* she wanted. How much of Kaylin's desire strikes you as political? It wouldn't occur to her to ask. She's accepted at Court because she is so firmly outside of the power structure she does nothing to shake it. Start down this road, and she won't even last the few measly decades allotted her.

"The rest of us *have* forever. We *can* wait. Kaylin has forty or fifty *years*." Teela stood, her eyes a shade that wasn't quite blue but was definitely as far from green as it could get. "I'm not asking for any of you to put your lives on hold indefinitely. I'm *asking* that you *wait*. A handful of decades isn't going to change your lives."

Mandoran glared at Teela. Clearly he'd heard it all before.

"You understand," Kaylin began, but Teela lifted a hand.

"I understand everything in exhaustive detail. I have had enough notice to form a skeletal defense against the worst of the politics."

"Sedarias thinks you'd be more successful getting information than Teela has been," Mandoran told Kaylin. "Because of your position as emergency mother to the Barrani."

There was a flash of blinding light that made the dining room vanish because Kaylin hadn't had time to close her eyes.

"Corporal," Helen said, in a more steely voice.

Teela immediately said, "My apologies, Helen. The spell was not materially harmful."

"No, I understand that. I know Barrani don't require sleep, but in my long experience, they require some moments of privacy and peace. Come. I have rooms waiting for you."

Teela's shoulder's sagged. "Affection," she told Kaylin's house, "is a curse and a terrible, terrible weakness."

"So thought the people who built me," Helen replied serenely. "I do not believe they were correct."

"No?"

"There are reasons I am less than fully functional. I chose to destroy some parts of myself to preserve the parts I value. It was painful, and there are lingering regrets on the bad days. On the good days, I am grateful that I was sentient enough to be able to make that choice. Come," she said again.

Teela quietly followed the Avatar of Kaylin's house.

"And eat, Kaylin," Helen's disembodied voice added.

CHAPTER 2

Teela, who had come prepared for work, left immediately. Tain, also properly attired, went with her. Kaylin, who had stumbled from sleep into several arguments, wasn't ready. She headed to her room to start a day that already felt too damn long.

Something political was happening in the High Court, and some of—if not all of—the cohort felt that Kaylin had actual political power there. Of course, one of them was Mandoran, a man not known for his wisdom or caution. She dressed quickly and competently, no longer being half-asleep, and headed out the door, Bellusdeo in tow.

"You're thinking," the gold Dragon, in her distinctly human form, said. "I approve."

"Probably because you can't actually hear most of it. Don't eat that," she added, to the familiar who was gnawing at the stick in her hair. She was lucky that most of the stick was invisible, because it looked distinctly like a puppy chew toy when examined.

The orange in the Dragon's eyes faded to a more prominent gold. "It's not Teela you need to worry about. Or," she added, "me. Although I admit I don't find it as offensive most of the time. I have some respect for Annarion. I daydream about breathing fire on Mandoran. And I actually like Teela. I'm not concerned about the cohort and its arrival. Helen will keep me safe. Helen," she added, her lips twitching up at the corners, "will keep them safe if they happen to anger me."

"I'd bet on you, if that happened."

"With your own money?"

"You're getting the hang of this."

"And you're not answering the question." But Bellusdeo's eyes were a warm gold. "You remind me of one of my sisters."

"Given what the Arkon has said about them, I'm not sure that's a good thing."

"We were children, then. And children are often both beloved and difficult. But it's not me you should worry about."

"It's the Emperor."

"It is," Bellusdeo agreed, "the Emperor. At the moment, he and his Court are heavily preoccupied. He trusts your intent, but also credits your uncanny ability to find disaster. I believe he used the equivalent draconic word for 'epic.' He will not, of course, demand that you turn over your guests— or that you turn them away. He is cognizant of his own laws, and will not create new ones simply for his own immediate convenience." She hesitated.

Kaylin understood why. With no intent whatsoever, Annarion had caught the attention of Shadows in the fiefs—and they had crossed the Ablayne to find him. In and of itself that wouldn't have been a problem; Shadows were the reason the Towers in the fiefs existed. But he had also been somehow loud enough to wake things ancient and slumbering, and they had not been subject to the Tower's will.

When she finally spoke, her words surprised Kaylin. "I am concerned about the cohort's arrival."

"We're all concerned—"

"As in, I am uncertain that they will survive their travel here."

Kaylin's mouth opened, but no words came out. Of all of the possible future disasters she had expected or considered, this wasn't one.

"I believe it is one of the handful of things Teela fears. Mandoran and Annarion do not, but they are young. Stay out of it. I mean it. I might survive entanglement in Barrani politics—I have before—but you're not a Dragon. I'm sure it's the biggest reason that Teela doesn't want the cohort here. You stick your nose into everything, and these matters are not remotely safe for any of us."

"I live here."

"It might have escaped your notice, but so do I, and I fully intend to avoid the cohort as much as possible. And if you keep arguing, you're going to be late."

Clint and Tanner were on the door, which wasn't strange. Tanner looked alert and Clint looked worried, which was. Neither appeared to be interested in the how-late-will-Kaylin-be betting pool, which was not a good sign. Kaylin slowed as she approached the stairs. "There's bad news," she told Bellusdeo.

The Dragon didn't argue. "Do you think it's personal bad news, or is there some difficulty in the Halls?"

"Not sure. I don't think it's me. I haven't been late in days, I'm not working on a sensitive case and I also haven't pissed Margot off, so Marcus isn't wading through the mountains of paperwork she constantly requires."

"You could just climb the stairs and enter the Halls. It's probably faster than speculating, and likely to give you more accurate information."

"That's what I'm afraid of." Kaylin drew breath, heading resolutely toward the doors Clint and Tanner were guarding.

"You look," Bellusdeo said, out of the corner of her mouth, "as if you're heading to an execution. Probably your own."

"It's Tanner."

"What about Tanner?"

"He expects real trouble."

"And Clint?"

"He...expects trouble from or for me." Kaylin had done nothing wrong—that she knew of—and she was certain Teela hadn't brought her personal troubles to the Halls of Law.

Was it Moran? Although she was technically still employed as a sergeant, she had been winding down the duties she performed for the Halls and had been training her replacement. Or rather, had been interviewing and browbeating the possible applicants. Her excuse for this—besides her obvious desire to remain in the infirmary—was that the infirmary needed someone who was fully capable of glaring down a Leontine when the Leontine was in an almost murderously foul mood.

To give her credit, Moran was perfectly capable of that.

But most people, Kaylin included, wouldn't be. Bellusdeo had suggested that Kaylin be considered for the position, pointing out that Kaylin's ability to heal would be well suited to the job. Moran's eyes had nearly fallen out of their sockets. "Absolutely not. The Hawks would walk all over her." Kaylin attempted to protest, but in truth, she was a *private*, and when Marcus went all fang-faced, she had to control the visceral urge to dive under the nearest desk.

Moran had faced him down. And to be fair to Moran and her interview process, Kaylin couldn't think of many people who could, Hawk or no. Bellusdeo could, but she was not seconded to the service. Serving the Halls implied serving the Emperor. And she hadn't so much warmed to him as cooled enough that his title did not send her into red-eyed Dragon resentment.

"You're thinking with your mouth open," Tanner observed, while Kaylin tried to choose smart words.

She shrugged and gave up. "What's happening inside?"

The two guards exchanged a glance. "It doesn't concern you directly," Clint said. Of course it was Clint.

"It's not Moran, is it?"

"No—but even I've come to pity the possible candidates for replacement."

"I don't think she wants to leave."

"Betting?"

Kaylin considered it. "No."

"And now I know I'm actually dreaming."

"She'll go. The thing that made her a good sergeant won't let her stay in the Halls. I just hope she beats the Aerian Caste Court into decent shape. It might be the first time in Aerian history that we have someone in high places on *our* side. But if it's not Moran, what's happened?"

"There's been...a bit of a problem."

"Tanner."

"Fine. There's been a lot of a problem."

Kaylin wanted to shriek.

"We're not allowed to discuss it," Clint added. "But you'll want to step carefully the moment you pass Caitlin's desk." He hesitated, his eyes a shade of blue that meant worry, fear. "It's the Barrani. Ours."

Kaylin was silent as she sped through the Halls. Bellusdeo kept easy pace with her, but her eyes had shaded to Dragon orange. Her facial expression hadn't changed at all. She didn't consider the Barrani a threat.

But she was worried.

The Barrani Hawks were a small force in and of themselves. Their partners were other Barrani, except on very rare occasion, and usually when a Barrani and a human were partnered, it was Kaylin and Teela. The Barrani could be sent in to break up a drug ring and be expected to both succeed and survive. Humans had a much higher mortality rate.

They had lost one member of the Barrani force during the difficulties with the Aerian Caste Court; one of the Barrani guards had carried an offer from a member of the High Court to one of the human prisoners. That he hadn't murdered the prisoner was in his favor, and Kaylin, in the end, felt that booting him off the force was too harsh. But Teela considered it necessary. There'd been an argument or two about it, and it hadn't been perfectly civil, either.

Even the West Room, with its magical silence, couldn't entirely absorb Leontine cursing. As far as Kaylin was concerned, the Hawk hadn't broken any laws, and hadn't disgraced his oaths. He had, however, introduced new problems for the High Halls.

In the end, Teela called Kaylin softhearted, and Marcus called her softheaded. So, they were down another Barrani. They had already lost Barrani Hawks on the night the Barrani ancestors, for want of a better word, had attacked the High Halls. Kaylin had mourned—everyone had—at a distance. The Barrani considered public grief a besetting weakness, to use Caitlin's words, and no one wanted to offend them. Not when they were so very blue-eyed and grim.

"You're worried about Teela," Kaylin said to the gold Dragon, as they jogged down the hall.

"You aren't?"

"I am, but Teela will rip my throat out if she sees it."

"Teela is not Leontine."

"Fine. She'll snap my neck. Better?"

"Marginally. There are days when I do not understand why the Emperor attempts to force all of his racially diverse population into one office. People *are* different." She stopped, shook her head, and added, "And I'm being unfair."

"You don't usually worry about that."

"No, but if you're correct, it's better than worrying about Teela."

Teela was not at her desk, which wasn't unusual. Given the absence of Teela, Tain wasn't at his, either.

But Caitlin was sallow. Not white, because that wasn't a color she often adopted, but a kind of pale yellow that implied nausea. Since she was human, her eyes were their usual brown, but they seem to have adopted new creases. She did smile when she caught sight of Private Neya and her Dragon friend—the only civilian, for want of a better word, allowed to accompany Kaylin on actual police work.

"Bellusdeo," Caitlin said. She didn't rise, and she didn't address her by stuffy title. "I should warn you—"

"Red-eyed, long-fanged Leontine?"

This added welcome color to Caitlin's cheeks. "That isn't the way I would have worded it. But at the moment, I'd suggest Kaylin note the duty roster."

"Was it changed?"

"No, dear."

"Then I know where I'm supposed to be."

"I think she's implying—heavily—that you would like to be there instead of here. Or possibly that the office would appreciate if *I* were there, instead of here."

"I'm sorry," Caitlin said, sounding genuinely apologetic, "but there have been…communication difficulties this morning." Kaylin stiffened, and seeing this, Caitlin added, "On Moran's strict orders, the infirmary is, at the moment, off limits. She will allow you through the door if you are bleeding or suffering from a broken limb, and made clear that toes and fingers don't count."

"There was a fight?"

Caitlin did not reply.

Marcus did, in a fashion. His low growl filled the office, which was otherwise unnaturally silent. Silence was never good, here. Kaylin glanced at Bellusdeo, whose eyes remained a remarkable gold as she inclined her chin in Kaylin's direction.

Kaylin then went to stand at attention in front of the sergeant's desk. Hardwoods, she decided, were good. They didn't scratch as easily, and it was clear from the surface of the desk that Marcus had been working at making a few gouges.

"You are to meet your partner and head—immediately— to the East Warren."

Kaylin, who had expected the word "Elani" to crawl out from between the folds of a growl, blinked. The East Warrens, as the area was colloquially called, was a Hawk beat; its boundary ended at the Ablayne, and the enterprising fool who chose to cross it ended up in one of the fiefs. Kaylin's geography was sketchy at best; she mostly knew what she'd walked across. She hadn't walked into that fief.

Bellusdeo, however, had a strong interest in the fiefs—or, more accurately, the Towers that stood at their centers. "The East Warrens?" Her eyes had lost their gold, but at least that made sense; Marcus's eyes were red. His facial fur, however, hadn't jumped up two inches; it had settled. He looked sleek, his upper fangs more exposed than they usually were, his claws extended.

He wanted to tell Bellusdeo to get lost, except with ruder words. And he wanted to tell Kaylin to go home. She felt some sympathy for this, because *she* wanted to tell Bellusdeo to go home. The East Warrens were not Elani street in any way; they were vastly more dangerous. It was not a beat given the groundhawks of the mortal variety. The Aerians could fly patrol over the streets, but at a safe enough height crossbows wouldn't be an issue.

No, it was a Barrani beat.

Marcus, for whom low growling had replaced all sound of

breath, waited, daring Kaylin to argue. She wasn't stupid. In his current mood, she'd agree that black was the new pink if that's what he demanded, and consider herself lucky. Enraged Leontine seemed far more dangerous than a strolling walk through some of the city's poorer streets. A Dragon would certainly make that patrol safer.

Until the Emperor heard about it.

"May I ask," Bellusdeo began.

"No."

"—if this has something to do with the fief of Candallar?"

Marcus said nothing. He growled, but didn't bother with words. Unfortunately, he was facing a Dragon—a Dragon who hadn't been forced to swear an oath of allegiance to the Emperor, whose laws the Hawks served. And any attempt to rip out her throat or tear off her arm—or leg—was going to be unsuccessful, in the best case. In the worst case—and given Marcus's mood, worst was a distinct possibility—the office would be reduced to charred wreckage. Charred, broken wreckage.

And that was above her pay grade.

Bellusdeo, however, folded her arms and looked down at the sergeant, her eyes narrowed. They stared at each other for three long, half-held breaths. It was, to Kaylin's surprise, Marcus who looked away first—but by the time he did, his eyes had shaded to a much safer orange.

"Yes."

"And does the fief of Candallar have something to do with the current mood of the office?"

"I don't discuss rostering issues with anyone who doesn't outrank me."

Bellusdeo's smile was gem-like: hard enough to cut, but bright anyway. Kaylin wanted to leave to find out what had happened, but knew better. She waited. Marcus finally dismissed her, although he didn't bother to look in her direction. Bellusdeo, however, did not follow.

"What happened?" Kaylin asked, keeping her voice as low as she could. Marcus's hearing was good, but he was unlikely to hear her when she was in Hanson's office. Hanson was the choke-point for the Hawklord's time; he was like, and unlike, Caitlin. This morning, the dissimilarities were stronger.

"It is not a going to be a good day," he told Kaylin. "The Hawklord hasn't demanded your attendance—which is about as much luck as you're likely to have in the near future. If I were you, I'd remember that you're a *private*. Whatever is happening, it is not your problem."

"Did I mention that Teela and Tain are coming to live with me?"

"Fine. It is your problem. Your problems, however, are not *my* problem."

"East Warrens is a *Barrani* beat."

"You don't say."

"Bellusdeo is coming with me, wherever I happen to be assigned."

Hanson grimaced; she could practically hear the lines around his mouth crack. "Emperor's problem," he finally said. But he knew that if something happened to Bellusdeo, it would be everyone's problem. And in this case "everyone's" problem was a matter for the Hawklord. Which, of course, would become Hanson's problem. "There was an altercation this morning between two of the Barrani Hawks."

"Go on."

"In general, Corporal Danelle handles difficulties between the Barrani Hawks. She is not the only corporal among their number, but her word carries weight with the Barrani for entirely extralegal reasons. The altercation occurred before her arrival; it was considered severe enough that she booked the West Room in which to resolve the difficulties."

Kaylin nodded. In and of itself, this was business as usual, although Barrani altercations were on the wrong side of "intense."

"The altercation was between Corporals Tagraine and Canatel."

She frowned. They were partners. While altercations between Barrani could be intense, in general they had greater respect for—or at least care for—their beat partners. "What set them off?"

"The office was largely empty when the altercation occurred. Barrani don't need sleep; they usually arrive early. Today, they arrived early. Teela did not." He raised a brow, as if expecting that Teela's tardiness—for a Barrani—was somehow Kaylin's fault. "She entered the office as the altercation was in progress, broke it up and booked the West Room."

Kaylin had heard nothing that would justify removal of Barrani Hawks from the duty roster. "She couldn't stop the altercation." It wasn't a question.

Hanson bowed his head for a long minute. When he raised it again, he looked exhausted. "It appears that the altercation between Tagraine and Canatel was a fabrication. The purpose of the altercation was to separate the rest of the office from the Barrani."

She froze then. The only good reason to do that was the laws of exemption: if only Barrani were involved, the Imperial Laws took a back seat to the caste court laws. A Barrani confrontation in the normal office could not be guaranteed not to cause extraracial collateral damage—and that would void the laws of exemption entirely. The implications of that...were not good.

She thought of the morning's events, the morning's arguments, the fact that the cohort were coming to stay with

Helen, and Tain's comment—cut off angrily by Teela—that Teela had already been under "pressure." The Barrani definition of pressure.

"Something happened to Teela."

"Something," Hanson said, exhaling, "almost happened to Teela. She survived. One of the two would-be assassins did not."

"Tagraine and Canatel?"

Hanson nodded.

"The survivor is in the infirmary that we're not allowed to visit by order of Moran, unless we want to join him."

He nodded again. "The High Court has been on the mirror network, demanding an explanation. The East Warrens may, or may not, have been involved with the altercation in some subtle way. Therefore the Barrani are off that beat." He exhaled. "They are off their beats until some of the issues are resolved."

"Meaning investigations are ongoing." It was a catch phrase used in place of *hells if I know.*

"Meaning exactly that."

"How, exactly, did the High Court even know?"

"Apparently they were informed."

"By who?"

"Oddly enough, no one in the office even thought of asking that question. I'm sure if someone had, we'd have that information in our hands by now and everything would be resolved." The sarcasm in Hanson's voice should have been lethal; it was embarrassing instead.

"The Emperor's going to reduce me to ash if anything happens in the warrens."

"Figure out a way to survive a lot of fire then," Hanson replied. It was the warrens; *if* was not precisely the right word. It was simply the hopeful one.

★ ★ ★

"The warrens are okay," Kaylin told Bellusdeo on the way to said warrens. Severn said nothing. "They're nowhere near as bad as the fiefs. They're more crowded than the rest of the city, and more run-down. But: no Ferals."

"I have no fear of Ferals," Bellusdeo replied. "And before you warn me of all the other dangers, please remember I'm a Dragon. A prickly Dragon."

"If it helps, this is considered a Barrani beat."

"Because no one is stupid enough to think a few underfed thugs present a danger to the Barrani, of course." Her chilly tone was a warning. She considered Dragons to be stronger than Barrani, and any implication to the contrary was not going to be well received. "Do yourself a rather large favor and worry about your own survival."

She wasn't worried about Bellusdeo; she was worried about the Emperor. She couldn't point this out if she didn't want to add to the hostility between the two Dragons. Since the Emperor had come to dinner at Kaylin's house, there'd been something close to peace between them—but it was a peace between previously warring nations. It was fragile.

"Besides, I think your assignment in the warrens was a deliberate choice."

"Oh?"

"I go where you go, with Imperial permission."

"You think they're expecting *real* trouble? No wonder Marcus was in a mood."

"Oh, I think your sergeant's mood had a lot to do with the Barrani unrest. He's a sergeant. He expects everyone under him to operate under the same rules." Bellusdeo smiled fondly. "It's almost nostalgic."

"You had to deal with sergeants?"

"Or their equivalents, yes. But never from beneath them." She shook herself. "He is fond of you, of course, which is why you come in for more of his public displeasure than the average new recruit. He can't afford to show favoritism. It bleeds solidarity from the ranks. If he's fond of you—and he is, no one could miss that—and he treats you the way he does, it means no one is safe." She wrinkled her nose. "I take it this is also where the tanneries are."

Kaylin did not detest the warren. She didn't feel the need to make excuses for the people who lived here; life had already done that. But she knew theft from the inside out. Knew that she'd been good enough not to get caught often. She needed to eat, same as anyone, and if there was no way to do that legitimately, she'd made other choices. She wasn't proud of them, but she wasn't humiliated by them, either.

She understood that once you started, crime became another tool, another way to survive. That you could want a better life, dream of it, of being a better *person*, and it didn't matter. Dreams didn't fill a stomach. But the warrens were on *this* side of the Ablayne. They were subject to the Emperor's Law. The worst excess of human behaviors was curbed here. It wasn't like the fiefs.

She knew that the tabard she wore put a wall between her and the warren's residents. But at least it was the East Warrens, not the south.

"Power," Bellusdeo said, "is always interesting. It is not an absolute, with few exceptions."

"Exceptions?"

"The Eternal Emperor would be one of them. But he is considered out of reach. His position is not visibly contested in any way. People gather. It's what people do."

"Dragons don't."

"No. But Dragons have hoards, and hoards can make a Dragon dangerously unstable if they are not prepared for it. We do not make friends the way mortals do."

"Or the way Barrani do?"

"Or the way Barrani do, no. We have not found there is strength in numbers, except perhaps in the case of war. And even then, it is questionable. I ruled. In any gathering of mortals, at any station of life, there is always a question of power. Or perhaps hierarchy. Even in the fiefs, where one could arguably say there is little true power, people struggle for position. People kill for it, one way or the other."

"That doesn't make humanity sound all that appealing."

The Dragon smiled. "If that was all that humanity contained, perhaps it would be unappealing. The power games of most mortals makes no material difference to my life. But no, power itself is inert. People want it for different reasons. In the warrens—as in your fiefs—they want power because it is tied to survival. But so, too, family, kin, clan. To belong to a group is to gain a negotiable safety from it. It is why gangs clash. It is why reprisals exist.

"I would imagine the warrens are no different from the fiefs. Tell me, have you lost many Hawks to the warrens?"

Kaylin glanced at Severn. It was Severn who answered. "Yes. Not, however, since Barrani joined the force. Aerian patrols were also successful in preserving lives, but they were not considered as effective at deterring crime."

"And the Barrani themselves are trusted not to add to the crime?"

"They have been," Severn replied. "Teela, however, has been crucial to their performance."

"And someone tried to kill her this morning."

CHAPTER 3

Each beat had its own route. Even Elani. Those routes, however, were considered by most beat Hawks to be general guidelines, and deviation from the suggested norm was not career-threatening. Flexibility was a necessity in the life of a beat Hawk, something that the higher-ups did understand, except when it came to quartermasters and uniforms.

Kaylin knew the warrens because she had come here with Teela and Tain before she had been given a rank and a uniform of her own.

Being *with* Barrani, and not hiding *from* them, had been a novel experience. She understood why people in the warrens vanished from visible windows or door frames as the two Hawks walked by. She also understood that the very young, very stupid, or very ambitious could—and occasionally did—attempt to take Hawks down.

It was the reason this was considered a Barrani beat. If the gangs felt they were equal to two officers with tabards, the equation changed markedly when the people who were wearing the tabards were Immortal. The gangs here had lived their lives in the maze of buildings and compromises that were the warrens. They could be forgiven for assuming the law was irrelevant, because in most obvious ways in their limited experience, it was.

It had been both irrelevant and a daydream in the fiefs of Kaylin's youth, and at least these streets didn't have Ferals literally devouring the unwary.

But...was that really any better? She wanted to slap herself for even thinking it. Clearly she'd been too comfortable, too safe, for too long. The Ferals were death. You had a hope of negotiating with anything else.

"You're thinking, again."

"Ferals," Kaylin told the Dragon. "We were more terrified of Ferals than almost anything else." Small and squawky snorted dismissively. Bellusdeo didn't bother, but it was clear she felt the same.

"That wasn't a terrified face."

"It's just...they weren't personal. They weren't plotting against us. They wanted one thing: to eat us. We wanted one thing: to avoid them. The cost for failure was high, but...it wasn't *personal*. Does that make sense?"

"Yes. Why are you thinking of that here?"

"Because the East Warrens are the closest the city comes to the fiefs I grew up in."

Bellusdeo frowned. "I would like a word with your Emperor."

"Have several. But before you do, are you implying that your city didn't have warrens?"

Bellusdeo was silent for several steps. "No. I couldn't realistically imply that. Some of my best soldiers, however, probably came out of my version of your warrens." She smiled and added, "We're being followed."

"Oh, probably."

"Will they attack us?"

"They might. They're used to seeing Barrani in these tabards; the Barrani have been doing this beat for a long time, now. Seeing normal mortals—"

Bellusdeo coughed.

"They can't see the color of your eyes from here, and you don't look Barrani at a distance. Even if they could, I doubt over half would realize what the eye color meant. For obvious reasons, there aren't a lot of Dragons randomly wandering the streets. If they do attack, though, going full-on Dragon would probably be the fastest way to end the fight."

"I thought that was illegal."

"You've always gotten away with it before."

"Kaylin."

She stopped talking at the sound of Severn's voice. She didn't, however, stop walking. She didn't even glance in his direction. She knew where he was, knew how far away, knew how ready he was for a fight. "Where?"

"The old town hall."

She glanced down the street toward the tallest building in the warren. It stood at the edge of this particular beat, but it had, some indeterminate length of time ago, been a rallying point in a besieged city. It was called the town hall because historical rumor suggested it had been built for that purpose. Whether it had seen any use in that capacity was an entirely different question.

Her small dragon, however, drew himself into the seated posture that implied he was ready for a fight. Or a bellow of outrage. Since she hadn't done anything to warrant the latter, she tensed, but didn't break her slow, steady stride.

Not until a familiar voice said, "This is *not* the place for you."

Bellusdeo came to an immediate stop. Golden eyes reddened significantly into the orange that was anger, worry or fear—and Bellusdeo was not afraid of the owner of that voice. "What," she said, in her icy, regal queen tone, "are *you* doing here?"

Mandoran, however, failed to materialize.

The small dragon squawked and then lifted a wing to cover Kaylin's eyes. The wing was translucent, of course, but looking through it often revealed hidden things. Or worse. Mandoran wasn't so much standing in the street as drifting above it.

"What are you doing here?" Kaylin demanded, repeating the gold Dragon's words. Because Bellusdeo had stopped walking, she had come to a stop as well, the rhythm of patrol abruptly broken.

"Teela found out that you'd been sent to the East Warrens on patrol."

"Yes. And?"

Mandoran made a face. "She doesn't want you in the East Warrens. But it's not actually you she's worried about."

Mandoran, Kaylin decided, was an *idiot*. Had she been in possession of his True Name, she'd be shouting at the top of her lungs in his figurative ears. His wince made clear that someone in his cohort—likely Teela—had had the same thought.

Sadly, Bellusdeo wasn't as oblivious as Mandoran. "She couldn't possibly be worried about *me*."

"Maggaron's been sulking for weeks now because he's not allowed to accompany you—and you know how he hates being left out of a fight."

Bellusdeo's brows rose, briefly, in Kaylin's direction—but to do that, she had to break her glare. "Ask Teela how political this is."

Mandoran, unlike most of the Barrani she had known before the cohort, was *terrible* at lying. He didn't try. "She says you're likely to survive, and the miscreant she's worried about—the soon-to-be possible miscreant—would take heat for any attack against you in the High Court. Problem is, he's not part of the High Court, and hasn't been for some time."

"You have an outcaste living in the warrens?" At Mandoran's expression, Bellusdeo added, "It wouldn't be the first time it's happened."

"This would not be my idea of a safe hiding place." Mandoran's grimace was heavy with disgust; it was also brief. He turned to Kaylin. "Teela wants you out of the warrens."

"Marcus doesn't. And you can tell her I said so."

"I won't repeat what she just said."

"Why not? I've heard it all before."

"Yes, but the Dragon probably hasn't, and you know the Emperor's just going to blame you if she starts using that kind of language." For a moment, his expression looked normal but his color was entirely off. His hair seemed almost white, his skin, blue. And his eyes were not Barrani colored at all.

The small dragon squawked, and Mandoran cursed. He turned toward the old town hall. Kaylin tracked the direction of his gaze with little effort.

She froze.

Standing at the peak of the decrepit tower roof was a Barrani.

Unlike Mandoran's, his coloring was more or less the norm for Barrani: his hair was black, his skin ivory. At this distance, his eyes couldn't clearly be seen, but Kaylin would have bet her own money that they were Barrani blue. She hadn't managed to contain her surprise enough to look away, and although she couldn't see the color of his eyes, she saw the subtle shift in their shape.

He was invisible, and had expected to remain so. She had seen him. Math had never been Kaylin's strong suit, but even she could handle one plus one.

"Time to move. *Move.*"

Severn was armed, but had not yet unwound his weapon chain; not even in the fiefs did he fully arm himself unless it was night. She headed into the nearest narrow alley to break the line of sight, and everyone except Mandoran followed.

She practically spit his name in a whisper that would have been a hiss had his name had any sibilants.

"He can't see me."

"Don't be so certain of that."

"Even if I were visible, I wouldn't be too worried. It's the Dragon he's going to be aiming for."

"He can try," the Dragon snapped. It obviously annoyed her to have to run and hide from Barrani. Then again, it often annoyed her to have to run, period. She was a Dragon.

"Are all Dragons like this?" Mandoran asked, as if he did have Kaylin's True Name, and had heard the thought.

"Not the time for this," Kaylin snapped back. "What is he doing?"

"Moving."

"Coming down?"

"Yes. In case you're worried, he's not using the stairs."

"Given the rest of the exterior, I doubt the stairs would support his weight."

Mandoran swore.

"What's happening?"

"He can, apparently, see me."

Bellusdeo snorted smoke.

"I'm going to head back home now, while Teela is only enraged. She can't leave the office if she wants to retain the tabard—but she's considering it anyway." True to his word, Mandoran faded from sight. Kaylin didn't see him leave, but knew the moment he was no longer present.

"I'm going to strangle Mandoran," Bellusdeo said, in a soft voice. "The minute we get home. I'm going to throttle the life out of him."

"Fire would be faster," Kaylin observed. She had retreated— they had all retreated—to the middle of the alley; there were walls to either side, and the windows they possessed weren't large enough to cause tactical problems.

"Exactly."

Severn had finished unwinding the chain, although this was not the place to make full use of it; the alley was too narrow. All of the alleys in the warrens were. "He's coming."

Kaylin nodded, her expression shifting. The familiar kept one wing across both of her eyes. She shook her head. "Go to Bellusdeo," she told the translucent, winged creature. "Now."

"I don't need his protection—"

"No, *I* do. If anything happens to *me*, I'll recover. Unless I'm dead. If anything happens to *you*, I'll only wish I was dead. Probably forever." She grimaced.

Severn said, "Magic?"

She nodded. Her skin was beginning to tingle. Tingling was not painful, but in general, it didn't stop there. Kaylin's allergy to magic—if *allergy* was the wrong word, it was the one she used anyway—made certain types of magic actively painful. It was why she hated doorwards and other modern security features. Invisibility—and there were whole libraries about how it worked, all jealously guarded by mages—was not a small magic. It wasn't considered nearly as insignificant as a doorward.

The small dragon resolutely remained on her shoulder. "He's not ditching the invisibility," she said, glaring at her familiar. If he wouldn't leave her shoulder, she'd have to move. The familiar was the only certain protection that either of them had against a large influx of magic, but his protection didn't work at a distance.

The familiar squawked. It was a surprisingly quiet sound, given that he was sitting so close to her unprotected ear.

"Severn."

He shook his head without looking back. He carried both blades; the chain was slack between them, traveling around his back. He shifted position. The links of chain made no sound as he did so.

★ ★ ★

The possible assailant did not pause to summon guards of any kind. Kaylin heard exactly zero footsteps; if he was moving—and the growing ache of her skin heavily implied that he was—he was moving silently. As silently as Severn would were their situations reversed.

Bellusdeo muttered something Kaylin didn't catch. That should have been a clue. The Dragon did not mutter. But she felt the sharp sting of new magic in the silence that followed.

"I never enjoyed magical studies," Bellusdeo said. She didn't bother to lower her voice; she might have raised it a notch. She walked past Kaylin, but remained—barely—in the periphery of the familiar's possible protection.

The ostensibly invisible Barrani who had the ability to fall well, if not fly, rounded the corner. He came to a stop, framed by the corners of the two buildings that formed the alley's walls. His hair was a long drape of black that framed his face and fell out of sight down his back. His eyes were, as Kaylin expected they would be, blue.

Kaylin moved to stand beside the gold Dragon, rather than behind her.

Severn, who was closer to the alley's mouth than either of them, did not move at all.

"So," the Barrani said, "it is true. There *is* a Dragon among the Hawks."

Kaylin knew the moment the Barrani chose to drop his invisibility; the familiar lowered his wing. But the motion caught the Barrani's eyes, and they rounded. When his glance returned to Bellusdeo, they instantly narrowed again. "He is yours?" he demanded, of the Dragon.

The familiar squawked.

The man blinked. Barrani were famous for their composure under duress, and he seemed to recall this as he once again focused on Bellusdeo. "Magic was used to great effect in the wars against your kind."

"Oh, indeed. But magic wasn't required against yours."

He stiffened. Bellusdeo was already pretty stiff. Kaylin, familiar notwithstanding, was irrelevant. Severn was apparently irrelevant, too. The Barrani had not once looked in his direction.

Not once...

Yes, Severn said. *I am, while I remain still, effectively invisible. It doesn't last.*

It just lets you get the drop on your enemies.

Yes. If necessary.

It's not necessary yet.

No. I'm uncertain who will break the law here first: Bellusdeo or the outcaste.

Kaylin was silent for another long beat, even on the inside of her own head. *What do you mean, "outcaste"?*

You don't recognize him?

How could I? I've never seen him before. If he's a fugitive, he hasn't been captured in Records, at least not in the last five years. She'd made a furtive study of the Records that involved Barrani, Barrani crime, and the law. There hadn't actually been that many available to an official mascot. *Severn, who is he?*

When he is addressed at all, I imagine he is called Candallar.

She frowned. *Candallar? That's one of the fiefs.* And stopped. And looked. She'd asked, of course, before she'd come out on patrol. She'd had suspicions. But suspicions, apparently, weren't visceral enough.

She knew what a fieflord could do in his own fief. If Severn was right, he wasn't in his fief now. He was separate from the power that made him fieflord. Then again, so was Nightshade when he visited, and she would never consider his power insignificant.

She reached out and touched Bellusdeo's regulation sleeve. "I think we should have this conversation somewhere else."

"Oh?" the Dragon replied—without looking away from the Barrani. "Where did you have in mind?"

"Someplace less instantly flammable." Before Bellusdeo could answer, Kaylin stepped forward, and then in front of her. Bellusdeo was taller, but not by as much as Teela or Tain. The tabard of the Hawk was front and center, and it grounded Kaylin. She understood it was nothing to hide behind—not safely—but it had never been about hiding, to Kaylin.

"Private Kaylin Neya," she said, to the man Severn had named fieflord. The familiar squawked. "And this is my familiar." His eyes did widen again, and it took them longer to revert to their less surprised shape. "You aren't a citizen of Elantra."

"In as much as citizens of any power are required to swear allegiance to the Eternal Emperor?"

"Yes."

"It may come as a surprise to you, officer, but yes. Yes, I am."

Bellusdeo snorted. There was smoke in it, which wafted across the back of Kaylin's neck without charring anything.

Candallar's gaze was pure Barrani condescension. "You presuppose I am not a member of the Barrani Court, or possibly the Barrani race. The supposition is correct: I am not. But my vow of allegiance to the Emperor—forced on me many years ago, I might add—has never been broken. I believe that I would still be considered a citizen of Elantra. The discretion would, of course, be the Emperor's. And given politics, it would be difficult were he to accept me as a citizen of his empire when my own people do not acknowledge my existence at all, except perhaps as a blood sport." His smile was slender, cold, and very sharp.

Bellusdeo snorted again. This time, Kaylin heard irritation, not threat, in the sound. She moved.

"The Dragon, however," the Barrani said, "is not technically a citizen of Elantra."

Kaylin was aware that she'd started this line of reasoning.
Marcus had often said she was too clever for her own good,
and too lacking in wisdom for anyone else's. "Neither are most
mortals, if citizenship is defined by a literal oath of allegiance.
Most of us can't talk from birth, and even if we could, the
Emperor wouldn't consider an infant's oath binding." She remembered just how much she hated politics. It shouldn't have
been hard to forget.

"I'm an officer of the Emperor's Law, and according to an
officer of that law, the Dragon is a citizen." She folded her
arms. The familiar squawked.

"And the…familiar…as you call it, is now standard issue
for an officer of the law?"

"The familiar is considered acceptable to the Emperor."

"You've asked in person?"

"Yes, as it happens."

Don't let him goad you, Severn said, an urgency to the words.

She didn't argue, because he was right. She was annoyed.
She'd let annoyance speak.

"I see." He smiled. "I mean no disrespect to the tabard, officer, and none to the Emperor to whom I swore my oath."

"Why are you here?"

"I occasionally come across the Ablayne—or the wall—to
meet with old friends. Surely that is not considered criminal."

"Not in and of itself, no. Would those friends by chance
be Hawks?"

"I have a great respect for Imperial Law."

"Why are you even here?"

"As I said—"

"I heard what you said." She was absolutely certain that
his presence and the altercation that had grounded all Barrani Hawks were connected. He could have worn a sandwich

board the size of Margot's stupid sign declaring himself part of a conspiracy, and it wouldn't have been more obvious.

To make it worse, the Barrani blue of his eyes had faded into blue-green, which was as casual a color as Barrani ever adopted when dealing with strangers. They darkened again as Bellusdeo snorted. Clearly, if a mortal Hawk was insignificant, a Dragon was not.

"I will take my leave, officer, unless you wish to abuse your power by attempting to—illegally—arrest me."

For one long minute she entertained fantasies of doing exactly that. But if he resisted, it would be the Dragon who would bear the brunt of the fight. The Dragon and the buildings in the warrens, which, although run-down, still housed a lot of people.

And it wasn't as if it wouldn't be obvious who he'd come to meet, or who he'd been meeting. The duty roster was the Hawk version of public knowledge. She gave him a curt nod, and headed out of the alley, making certain not to turn her back on him.

He stopped her—with a word. Given Bellusdeo's presence, he kept his distance. "Wait."

Kaylin didn't answer.

"You had another companion before I arrived."

She thought of Severn, said nothing. Severn, however, said, *He's not asking about me. Mortal, remember.* He still hadn't moved, and the fieflord did not appear to have noticed him.

"You must be mistaken," Kaylin said sweetly. "Without Imperial permission, Hawks don't patrol with random people."

His gaze narrowed instantly at the tone of her voice. "I warn you," he began.

Bellusdeo exhaled a small stream of fire. It was focused on the road some three feet to his side. She said nothing, and did nothing else. Her eyes were red orange. His were now dark blue.

"Don't bother with the sword," Kaylin told him, her voice conversational and much more cheerful. "Unless it's one of The Three, it's going to do more damage to the weapon than it will to the Dragon—but it'll probably make her angrier. And before you say anything else, I've seen two of the three, and I'm pretty sure I know who owns the third one."

She could practically hear Severn smacking his forehead, and shut her mouth.

"Private Neya," Candallar said. He surprised her; he swept her a bow. "Give my regards to your master."

She frowned and then remembered the mark—the flower—that adorned her cheek.

Yes, a familiar voice said. *He understands what it means. If he harms you—at all—I will destroy him.*

The word "master" really rankled. She opened her mouth. Shut it. "I seldom have occasion to meet the Emperor in person, but if I do, I'll pass it along."

"What in the hells was all that about?" Kaylin demanded an hour later, when Severn extricated himself from the warrens. She'd wanted to wait—she knew that you didn't patrol solo, and Severn would be solo. Severn, however, pointed out that he'd spent the greater part of his Halls of Law career as a Wolf, and that was the definition of solo unless really big crap was about to go down.

He also pointed out that she had Bellusdeo.

"You know as much as I do."

"You knew he was a fieflord."

His shrug was pure fief. "I've spent a few years dealing with fugitive Barrani. Fugitive Barrani, unlike fugitive mortals, are frequently exceptionally political when they have the personal power and influence. Candallar has some power. He isn't Nightshade; Nightshade's closest ties are at the heart of the High Court."

"The Consort?"

"She is not considered political."

"But she's—"

"She's powerful. She might be the only Barrani who has a great deal of personal power coupled with the will to be neutral. No one will openly slight her, but...her brother is High Lord and there is no one he values more. Insulting or slighting the Consort is more dangerous than insulting or slighting the High Lord when it comes to the High Lord's very political response. The High Lord fails to acknowledge Nightshade. He has never forbidden his sister's acknowledgement."

Kaylin nodded, preoccupied. "This beat was Tagraine and Canatel's."

"...Yes."

Technically, they weren't done with their patrolling duties. But given Mandoran and Teela, Kaylin thought the appearance of the fieflord of Candallar was newsworthy enough she'd be forgiven for abandoning them this one time. Had she been patrolling Elani, she would have dropped by any of a number of places to borrow their mirror and report in; most of the citizens of the East Warrens were too poor to own mirrors—and those who weren't were likely to respond to such a request with violence.

Kaylin wanted to pass the information on to someone who was paid to deal with politics, but she was still disgruntled as they headed for home. Or rather, the Halls of Law. "You're sure we couldn't just arrest the bastard?"

"On what grounds?"

"Suspicion of conspiracy?"

"Conspiracy to do what? At best, we'll have the caste court dropping on our collective heads via the Hawklord. This is Barrani politics. The Hawks don't touch it for a reason."

"But—"

"Even if it involves Annarion, Mandoran or Teela, it's still

Barrani politics. They're never going to drag the Halls into a Barrani political war. Until and unless we can show that Candallar is illegally affecting non-Barrani, we have no grounds for either arrest or suspicion."

Bellusdeo had said very little for half of the walk back to the halls. She did, however, add, "Do you really want a fieflord strolling through the Halls of Law? Severn is right, of course; we're not going to be able to hold him. He clearly understands the full weight of Imperial Law, and he knows what the Hawks' constraints are. Which marks him as somewhat unusual."

"Why?"

"Because he actually believes those constraints are genuine. Even were he to agree to accompany us to the office, he believes that the rules that govern you would protect him. Is he right?"

Kaylin kicked a stone. "Probably."

"How many Barrani do you know who would believe that?"

"Almost all of them."

"Until recently, she only knew Hawks," Severn reminded the Dragon.

"Yes, well."

"And the Barrani Hawks believe in the law," Kaylin added.

"The Barrani Hawks *uphold* the law. I would not, however, be surprised to hear that they consider it a game—much like the card games you play on breaks. Yes, they accept the various rules, but they're looking for ways to game the system to win. Breaking the rules forfeits the game."

"No one dedicates their lives to playing cards." Kaylin frowned, considering the petty crimes divisions. "...Almost no one."

"No, probably not. But I wouldn't put it past Mandoran."

"What are the odds we've done business with Candallar before?" Kaylin suddenly demanded. Of Severn.

He raised a brow.

"We know that Nightshade's been contacted—or at the very least had his contact returned—by someone in the Halls. Is it that unlikely that Candallar is similar?"

It was Bellusdeo who answered. "To the Barrani, if I understand Teela correctly, both Nightshade and Candallar would be considered—*are* considered—necessary evils. They hold the Towers. The Towers keep Ravellon and its Shadows from spilling out into the rest of the world and destroying it." There was a moment of bitter silence. "In my world, Towers such as those did not exist. Had they, I would not be here."

The reminder of the enormity of the Dragon's loss kind of killed the rest of the conversation, and it didn't resume again until they'd reached the Halls of Law.

CHAPTER 4

Caitlin seemed relieved when Kaylin entered the office and stopped at the choke-point of her desk. "I'm glad to see you're safe," she said. She didn't bother to pitch her words in a whisper, which was the only way Kaylin knew she was not happy with Marcus's decision to send them to the East Warrens.

"I'm not sure we're done yet," Kaylin replied. "But we're fine. Nothing, aside from the legally questionable use of invisibility—*not* on our part—happened. But we've got some news to report in. Is Teela in?"

"Teela is in the infirmary."

"...Where Moran said no one who was not half dying was allowed to be."

"She is not, as you put it, half dying, dear. But she is not, strictly speaking, very happy at the moment. I haven't seen her this upset since—" Caitlin stopped, reddening slightly. "And that's neither here nor there, and I shouldn't be gossiping. If you've got things to report, you should report them. Don't mind me."

Marcus was already in a foul mood. Kaylin approached his desk and was left standing at attention while he regained control of his seemingly permanent growl. He couldn't, however, keep Bellusdeo standing at attention, not that she actually bothered. She wasn't part of the office hierarchy, wasn't beholden to it, and had been given permission by the Emperor to disrupt that hierarchy as she saw fit.

For some reason, this didn't bother Kaylin. Possibly it was because Bellusdeo was a Dragon. Possibly it was because she didn't particularly consider life to *be* fair. Dragon female trumped almost everything, as far as the Emperor was concerned.

But no, a little voice said, that wasn't true. The empire trumped everything. Bellusdeo was considered important to the *race*, but that race didn't really care about the empire, except in the abstract. It was the Emperor's hoard. You disturbed it at your ultimate peril.

It was Bellusdeo who cut through rank and file behavior to tell Marcus that they had met the fieflord of Candallar in the East Warrens.

Marcus's eyes couldn't get any redder without spilling into the Leontine Frenzy color. Bellusdeo failed to mention either Mandoran or Teela. She spoke respectfully, but spoke as if to an equal. In the end, Marcus mirrored Hanson. He had a direct line to the Hawklord, but hadn't chosen to use it, which meant that this wasn't considered an emergency.

"There was no difficulty with the fieflord?"

"If you mean did he attempt to harm me, no."

"Did he attempt to harm the officers?"

"No. Had he, what was left of him would be in the holding cells."

"The Hawks would not—"

"Yes, I realize their hands are tied. But I'm not a Hawk, Sergeant Kassan. I'm a displaced person. A Dragon."

Some of the red bled out of Marcus's eyes then. "It was easier," he said, "in the old country."

"For you, too?"

"Yes. We could rip out the throats of our enemies—and our enemies seldom pretended to be our friends before we did."

"I'll suggest it to the Emperor," Bellusdeo replied, with a sunny smile.

Marcus growled.

"I'll suggest it on my own behalf; I shall utterly fail to mention your comment. You see, we also—in the old country—could rip out the throats of our enemies. Or their wings."

Kaylin coughed. "I lived in a place where you could—if you had the power—kill your enemies with zero consequences. It was an awful place, and I don't recommend it. The Emperor created the laws for a *reason*, and I think the reasons are good."

"You would, though," Bellusdeo said. "You've thrown your life into them, and no one wants to waste their life."

Dragons.

Hanson's reply came about fifteen minutes later. Or rather, the reply to the message Marcus had sent to Hanson did. The respondent in the mirror, however, was the Hawklord. Marcus didn't seem to be surprised. He did seem disgusted. "You're wanted upstairs," he told Kaylin.

Given the part the fiefs had played in Kaylin's childhood, she wasn't surprised, either; the surprise would have been no response, or a rote one.

"He wants the Dragon as well," Marcus added.

"The Dragon," Bellusdeo said, unfazed, "wouldn't miss it for the world." At Marcus's lowered browline, she added, "He has no right of command where I'm concerned, no. But I'm not so petty that I would deprive myself of something interesting simply to spite him."

Marcus said nothing. Loudly.

★ ★ ★

When they hit the middle of the tower steps on their way to obey the Hawklord's command, Kaylin said, "Could you *maybe* try not to antagonize him?"

Severn was silent, and almost invisible; it was a neat trick. Kaylin wondered if he'd learned it while training with the Wolves. Or if he'd always had it. He'd survived the fiefs for a lot longer than she had, after all—and had it not been for Severn, she was uneasily certain she wouldn't have survived at all.

"Your sergeant makes no effort not to antagonize me." Bellusdeo snorted. "He dislikes the Dragon Court."

"You're not part of the court."

"Fine. He dislikes Dragons."

"Because it was the Dragon Court that pretty much decided I should be put down. As in executed. I was thirteen." Bellusdeo stopped speaking, although she continued to walk. Kaylin, aware that she was being petty, said, "I'm sure I've mentioned this before. He's got a long memory when you threaten his kits."

"And he considers you one of them."

"Well, his first wife does. You want a terrifying Leontine— it's her. He's never going to forgive the Dragon Court. But you're not them, and he'll eventually accept you. Just—he's got a long memory."

At that, Bellusdeo chuckled. "Nowhere near as long as the memories of my kin. It rankles, but I must also remind myself: I am not ruler here. This is not my country."

The Hawklord had done Kaylin the kindness of opening the doors, which otherwise operated by wards. He was standing to one side of an inactive mirror; Kaylin could see herself—and Bellusdeo, and a silent Severn—as they approached.

It was no surprise to Kaylin that the Aerian's eyes were a

martial blue. He tendered Bellusdeo a very correct bow—
which in Aerians involved wing motions and stiffness in the
right order—and rose. "My apologies," he said. "Sergeant
Kassan sent Kaylin on patrol in the East Warrens. It has been
struck from her duty list for the time being."

"For the time being, meaning, if I am to accompany her?"
The Hawklord said nothing.

"I believe," Bellusdeo said, because it wasn't her job or her
dreamed-of promotion on the line, "that the *reason* Sergeant
Kassan chose to send the private and the corporal to the East
Warrens at this time was *because* I have been given blanket Imperial permission to accompany her. He expected difficulty of
a type that the Barrani Hawks, and only the Barrani Hawks,
could easily handle."

"There were other teams he could have chosen."

"Yes. But none of those teams happen to have a Dragon
as a shadow."

The Hawklord was not Leontine. "Yes, a remarkable coincidence, since I am confident that no one under my command would knowingly put you at risk in an encounter that
might involve strange or dangerous magics." His tone was
bland. "Having made that coincidental decision, he has been
informed that it will not be made again. We are all, I am certain, much happier." He turned to Kaylin then. Although
he'd offered Bellusdeo the very respectful bow of an inferior
to a superior, he had no intention of allowing the Dragon to
commandeer the discussion. He had made a decision. It was
not hers to argue.

"You claim to have made contact with the fieflord of Candallar."

Kaylin nodded.

"You are certain." His glance moved to Severn.

"Yes." Severn answered the question, but offered nothing
else. He did not, however, bristle.

"Was he in the warrens to meet with my Hawks?"

"He was to meet, he said, with friends. In my opinion, yes; without corroborating evidence—"

The Hawklord held up a hand, which stopped Severn. "You have heard that there was difficulty this morning."

"Yes."

"You've heard, no doubt, that a political storm is brewing in the Barrani High Court."

"Actually," Kaylin said, "we hadn't. Until this morning."

"Candallar may well be part of that. What is the word in the office?"

"About?"

"This morning's incident."

"That Moran will make certain we belong in critical care if we show up in the infirmary for any other reason than that we already need it, sir."

The Hawklord almost winced. "Sergeant dar Carafel is never going to leave the infirmary at the current rate of emergency."

Kaylin, who still felt that Moran's entire race had treated her horribly, couldn't see this as a bad thing—for either the Hawks or Moran. Clearly the Hawklord had a different opinion, and she managed to keep her own to herself. Or at least to keep the *words* that would express it that way. "Teela is in the infirmary."

"I was not informed of her presence there," was the bland reply. It implied that he wished to remain ignorant. Ignorance, after all, had its uses. "At ease, Private."

Given his eyes, ease was impossible, but she did relax her stance.

"What is happening?"

"I'm not Barrani, sir."

He turned, then, to Bellusdeo. "Lord Bellusdeo, I am aware that you are not Barrani, but you have experience with both politics and assassination attempts. In your opinion, what has caused this…conflict among my Barrani Hawks?"

Bellusdeo's eyes had shaded into a more natural gold. Orange deepened the color, but she was not struggling to contain Dragon rage. "You are aware," she said, "of Teela's companions."

He nodded.

"I believe the political difficulties involve them."

Kaylin wanted to kick her. She also wanted to continue to breathe. She said nothing, but, because she was Kaylin, was not entirely silent about it.

"And the fieflord?"

After a much longer pause, Bellusdeo replied. "I admit that I do not understand your fiefs or their lords. I understand their function; I understand why they are considered a distasteful necessity. I do not, however, understand why the lords of the Towers themselves are left to almost random chance. Were this my city, we would have chosen those Lords ourselves, and we would have had strict criteria by which to do so."

Judging by expression, the Hawklord agreed. He was not, however, he Emperor. "I am not a scholar. My understanding of Shadow and its nature is pragmatic, but it is not deep. If you wish to discuss the nature of the Towers, it is to the Dragon Court you must look. But in my superficial and meagre understanding, the Towers have a sentience of their own. It is said that the Towers choose. Private Neya and Corporal Handred were present when the Tower of Tiamaris adopted its newest Lord; perhaps they will shed some light on the subject." But not now, his tone implied. "Corporal Danelle was not forthcoming when questioned."

"The assassin in question—"

"The *incident* in question involved the corporal, yes. She is not, I am told, in the infirmary to finish the job she started,

or is said to have started. The Barrani in question is technically alive."

"Technically, sir?"

"I expect we will receive a writ of exemption at any moment that will excuse his attempt to assassinate one of my
Hawks. I have been told that the mirror network has been
somewhat compromised, and not all of our messages are currently arriving. And no, Private, you are not considered an
expert in the mirror networks; we have put in an official request for the oversight of an Imperial Mage."

"That'll take three days, sir."

"It is a pity that the Imperial Mages are so heavily over-
burdened with official business that we are required to wait, yes."

"You expect a writ of exemption?" Bellusdeo said. It was
on the tip of Kaylin's tongue, but she bit it. She could practically taste blood.

"I expect a writ and a demand for remand of custody, yes."

Kaylin had expected a writ of exemption. She had not considered what most frequently happened when such writs were
exercised: the criminal ended up as a conveniently packaged
corpse on or near the steps of the Halls of Law. She paled.
"So...we have three days to figure out what the hells is going
on?"

"Given it involves Barrani, politics and a fieflord, I would
guess that three days will not be nearly enough time. Three
days is also not an exact measure. There is some possibility
that the Imperial Order of Mages will, in fact, consider the demands of the Halls of Law a serious emergency, and rearrange
their pressing schedules to accommodate us."

Kaylin snorted.

"You will not be patrolling the warrens again."

"Sir. Does that mean we're back to Elani?"

"The duty roster is otherwise in the hands of the sergeant.
I expect the difficulties with the Barrani to be resolved before

the writ arrives. Did Candallar give any indication of what he wants from his involvement in this murky affair?"

"No, sir."

The Hawklord's eyes narrowed.

"He did, however, point out that while he's outcaste—he *is* outcaste—he still retains citizenship in the Empire. His oath of loyalty *to* the Eternal Emperor has never been retracted or disavowed. And he probably understands the Imperial Laws at least as well as I do."

"Interesting. Is there a reason this was relevant to your discussion with him?"

"She was threatening to arrest him and drag him back to the holding cells," Bellusdeo replied. "He pointed out that this would be an unlawful detainment."

"Very interesting. He is correct in this case. I assume no such attempt was made?"

"No, sir."

"Good. Dismissed."

Teela was, according to Caitlin, still in the infirmary. Tain, however, had drifted back to his desk, where he sat stiffly, blue-eyed and grim. Grim wasn't necessary; Kaylin had seen Barrani with eyes of midnight laughing. But not often.

"Is Teela still in the infirmary?" she demanded.

"You're expected to head out to Elani." Which meant yes.

Kaylin folded her arms. Tain was seated; she could look down at him. It was Bellusdeo who spoke. "Teela's enemies in the High Court are better prepared than you expected."

"Characterizing them as Teela's enemies is not, or was not, accurate. Sedarias is cunning, ambitious, and political in a way the High Court understands. She is not of the High Court; none of the cohort are. But were she, she would become a power to reckon with. Perhaps not in your lifetime, but perhaps at the end of it—and that would be meteoric in Barrani terms. But if their opposition is prepared to orchestrate an attack in the Halls of Law—where there are other races as possible collateral damage—it's not a good sign. This won't be the only assassination attempt; it's merely the first."

"You think they'll attack Teela again?" Kaylin's hands were fists.

"Teela is better prepared than the cohort. If the cohort arrives intact, it will be a small miracle. Or a large one. If they weren't staying with Helen, I'd ask you to stay out of it."

"You think she'd stay out of it if they weren't staying with her?" Bellusdeo asked.

"I think the chances that we could keep the worst of it from her would be much higher, yes."

"Oh, and assassination attempts in the *Halls of Law* would completely go over my head." Kaylin folded her arms. She had never liked being treated as if she were stupid. And Teela was *important*.

"No one expected that." Tain hesitated, which was unusual for Tain.

"Including Teela," Bellusdeo then said, finishing the thought. "Who must be something of a political force herself if she can both retain her power at court and serve as a Hawk." Kaylin knew Teela was a Lord of the High Court— but even that knowledge had been gained in the last year or two. She thought of Teela as a Hawk, and as a friend; sometimes as an older sister.

Tain did not reply.

The Dragon cleared her throat. "I believe I will visit Moran. I'm a Dragon, and I served as her bodyguard during the worst of the friction with the Aerian Caste Court. She will have a much harder time shutting her door in my face." Her smile had long teeth in it. "I have Imperial permission to be in the

Halls of Law. Moran is not my commanding officer. She can neither threaten nor command me."

Kaylin wasn't certain she wouldn't bet on the Aerian, but said nothing.

Tain remained at his desk. Severn remained at Tain's desk. Both suggested, with varying degrees of subtlety, that Kaylin remain there as well. Kaylin didn't have time to argue, because when a Dragon made a decision—or when Bellusdeo did, at any rate—she acted on it immediately. The private had to scurry to keep up. If she followed in Bellusdeo's wake, she'd be allowed in.

The old infirmary was still being rebuilt. In the weeks that had passed since a bomb had reduced it to splinters of wood, stone and glass, new floors and new walls had been installed, as if by magic. It wasn't magic, of course; not yet. Magic would come later, when Moran had approved of the base rooms.

The conference room which had been the largest space available for emergency operations had been reclaimed by the Halls, but the infirmary itself had taken up temporary residence in a smaller set of rooms that were seldom used and more functional than a room that was essentially created to house a huge table and a bunch of chairs. They were less easily accessible, in part because they had been used as general storage. Kaylin didn't ask what had happened to whatever was being stored here; that was the quartermaster's problem.

The door was closed. The door was warded. Bellusdeo lifted golden brows in Kaylin's direction, but touched the ward herself. Kaylin wasn't entirely surprised when the door opened. She wasn't surprised when a bristling Aerian with high, spotted wings stood almost in the frame. Nor was she surprised when the bristling wings folded as the Aerian caught sight of the Dragon. Slightly envious, but not surprised.

Moran's eyes were Barrani blue. Her expression took a turn for the worse when she looked past Bellusdeo to see Kaylin.

"The private is my escort," Bellusdeo said, in a perfectly friendly, perfectly bland tone.

"There is nothing here that requires the private's attention, and a great deal that does not."

Kaylin opened her mouth. Closed it. It was smarter to let the Dragon do the talking because Moran couldn't do anything to the Dragon. Small and squawky, almost forgotten, lifted his head and batted Kaylin's cheek with the top of it. He looked bored.

Teela appeared in the door frame behind Moran. "Why are you here?" she asked.

"It was here," Bellusdeo replied, although Kaylin was pretty sure the question wasn't aimed at the Dragon, "or the East Warrens." Kaylin couldn't see Bellusdeo's expression, but the bland, cheerful, *neutral* reply was like a red flag.

Severn had probably made the smarter choice. Tain's desk was safer. But Kaylin had really wanted to see Teela for herself. She'd wanted to be certain that Teela was whole.

It was the sergeant, not yet retired, who said, "The East Warrens. Marcus sent Kaylin to the East Warrens." Clearly she had not been informed, and while the duty roster was not her responsibility, she knew it was a Barrani beat. Her glare traveled down the hall, as if she were considering offering Marcus a few choice words herself.

"I was, of course, with her."

Moran folded her arms. "Come in," she told the Dragon brusquely. She ignored Kaylin entirely and Kaylin followed like a shadow.

"You met Candallar. In the warrens." Teela was now lounging on a chair so bare it should have been uncomfortable. To her left, in one of three beds in the small room, a Barrani

Hawk slept. Since Barrani didn't need sleep, he was probably unconscious. Or wishing he were.

It was Canatel. He was, like Teela, a corporal. He'd been part of the Hawks for as long as Kaylin could remember, which really only meant about eight years. In Barrani terms, that was a blink of the eye.

"This is well above your pay grade, kitling. It is not for you."

"How many people are descending on my home in the near future?"

"If I have any say in it?" Teela exhaled and stood, losing the studied nonchalance of chair lounging. "You're certain it was the fieflord?"

"I've never met him. Severn was certain."

More Leontine followed, but it was soft. Clearly Teela trusted *Severn's* opinion.

"Why is Candallar involved?" Kaylin asked, as Bellusdeo said, "Candallar is outcaste, yes?"

Teela only answered the Dragon's question. "Yes."

"Does he happen to be related to any of the cohort? Because I've got one furious fieflord visiting my home at least three times a week, and I think I could do without another one."

"You would rather he visit your home than encounter him elsewhere. Candallar noted your mark?"

"Nightshade's mark? Yes."

"Good."

Kaylin thought she'd take the nearest seat, she was so shocked. "Good? You still hate him for putting the mark there!"

"Yes. But it will serve as a warning to Candallar, if a warning is required. He is not Nightshade."

"Nightshade is more powerful?"

"He was, before he was removed from the High Court. There is a reason he possesses one of The Three."

And a reason, Kaylin thought, wanting to smack herself, that Teela possessed one as well. Three swords created to fight *Dragons*. They were called The Three; the capital letters were practically pronounced. Had she never really considered that they weren't just handed out randomly?

"Candallar is younger?"

"We are *all* ancient compared to you. Candallar is younger. He was of the High Court. He took, and passed, the Test of Name."

"Why was he turfed out?"

Teela pinched the bridge of her nose. Bellusdeo suggested Kaylin speak in Barrani, or High Barrani. "Which part of 'above your pay grade' isn't clear? I can repeat it in all of the languages you know, and three you don't. I am certain that Bellusdeo could repeat it in her native tongue—"

"That's illegal without permission—"

"And suffer few ill consequences."

"East Warrens was Canatel's beat. His and Tagraine's. Candallar was there—invisibly, by the way—to meet them."

"He said so?"

"He said he was visiting friends."

"Of course he did." Teela cast one backward glance at the unconscious man on the cot. It was not a look of loathing; it was not a look of anger.

"What happened?" Kaylin asked.

"Tagraine and Canatel had an argument. They came to blows in the office. I invited the Barrani to the West Room to discuss, among other things, self-control. In retrospect, this was unwise." Her smile was grim, but genuine. "It was clever," she added, as if to explain her expression. "Only Barrani were present, as they must have known would be the case. I did not get far into my ill-tempered lecture before Tagraine attempted to kill me. With a dagger," she added.

What was Teela not saying?

"Canatel attempted to stop Tain from interfering. Canatel was injured. Tagraine died." Both her voice and face were devoid of expression.

This was not exactly the story Kaylin had heard. She knew better than to trust gossip for accuracy, but... "Canatel didn't try to kill you? He didn't help?"

"He attempted to come to the aid of his partner." Teela's glare was ice and steel.

Bellusdeo cleared her throat. "Candallar."

"That's not the direction I expected the politics to travel. I have limited access to fieflords. In theory, so does the rest of the Court—but the rest of the Court does not serve as Hawks, with the legal boundaries necessitated by that office. I was... unprepared for that avenue of pressure. Did you attempt to engage him?"

"She threatened to arrest him, if that helps," Bellusdeo offered.

Teela covered her forehead with her left hand. "Of course she did."

"He seemed surprisingly conscious of Imperial Law," the Dragon continued, "and entirely unintimidated by it. He did not ask Kaylin for either information or concession; I believe he was distracted."

"By the presence of a Dragon?"

"By the confirmation of the presence of a Dragon within the Halls of Law."

That was not the same thing, and Teela knew it.

"On the other hand, if his contacts were Hawks, it is not entirely surprising he would have that information. Nor are the Hawks the only way that information might reach him; the Hawks themselves might speak with members of the High Court, and the High Court is, of course, very aware of my existence."

"You are much more likely to survive involvement in my

life than Kaylin is," Teela said. "But the arcane bomb that would have ended your life was thrown well away from both the Halls and the High Court."

"I would not be certain that my involvement in your affairs would be the cause of another assassination attempt. Nor," she added, as Teela opened her mouth, "could the Emperor be. How much of a concern is Candallar?"

"He's a concern. Whatever pressure he put on Tagraine—and I won't know until Canatel wakes—he's just a lever."

"Do you have any idea who might be pushing that lever?"

"Some vague suspicion. I know Canatel's family. Candallar was made outcaste for purely political reasons; he did not attempt to harm the Consort. Nor did he engage in illegal activities involving other races—at least not until he was forced to flee and found himself at home in the fiefs."

"And he wants?"

"I would guess he wants to be repatriated. He wants to be forgiven."

"But—"

Both the Dragon and the corporal turned toward Kaylin. "But?" Teela asked.

"But it's the High Lord who decides, isn't it?"

"In theory, yes. In practice? No. I do not believe the High Lord is behind Candallar's movements."

"You say that like you have some idea who is."

"No, kitling, I don't. I have some idea of who isn't."

"Why would they do this?"

"Tagraine? Canatel?"

Kaylin nodded. At heart, this was the only question she needed answered. The politics and malice of Barrani who were not Hawks was like rain or heat; it existed outside of the Halls.

"I can't speak for Tagraine. I can't speak for Canatel—he cannot speak for himself at the moment. And I should not tell you even this much. But Canatel has a sister. She is older, and she *is* a Lord. She is, however, a very, very minor lord whom most feel survived the Test of Name because the sheer terror of it drove her to mindless—but ultimately pragmatic—flight. She is surrounded by Lords of greater age and far greater power, be it economic, political, or as is generally the case, both. Had she never taken the Test, she would not now be in danger."

Kaylin raised a brow, and Teela exhaled. "They would have to find her. Many of the Barrani who are of the High Court do not make their homes in the city."

"And the ones who aren't do?" This made no sense to Kaylin.

"It is frequently where the landless poor among the mortals dwell."

"Teela, if rumor has *any* truth to it, Canatel tried to kill you."

Teela said nothing; her eyes were a shade of gray blue.

Bellusdeo exhaled smoke with a bit of actual heat in it. "Kaylin," she said, to make clear that her target of annoyance was not Teela, "you can be forgiven your ignorance; it is remedial. It can be alleviated. Teela, however, has enough to deal with. Corporal, Sergeant, my apologies for intruding while you are so clearly busy. We will take our leave now, as Kaylin is expected to begin her interrupted patrol on Elani."

Teela actually chuckled. "I feel almost sorry for Margot today."

CHAPTER 5

"What am I missing?" Kaylin demanded, when they were safely quit of the halls and halfway to Elani. The word "ignorance" still stung; there were better ways to point to lack of knowledge, but given Kaylin wasn't terribly diplomatic on the best of days, even thinking that was kind of hypocritical.

"Teela feels that the failure lies with her."

"What?"

Severn, Kaylin's actual partner, was silent and steady. Small and squawky actually left her shoulder to sit on his for half the march, glaring balefully at Kaylin as he did.

"I have not discussed this with Teela; I doubt she's discussed this with anyone. I am therefore guessing, based on some minor observation."

"Skip the part where you imply that I'm stupid."

"I did not imply that; I implied that you are not observant."

"Bellusdeo—"

"You focus on your job. You focus on your home. Where it is necessary, you will focus on other things as they effect the former or the latter. Beyond that, however, you still feel that the world is somehow other, or foreign." She exhaled at

Kaylin's expression, and added, "You know nothing about knitting."

Kaylin blinked.

"I do not expect that you will know anything about knitting. But when you are wearing a sweater of some intricacy, I will unconsciously assume that you know something of what went into its making. Let us say I know something about knitting. Don't make that face, I chose this example for a reason. I have seen the same sweater you have seen, but I have marked the intricacies of stitch and design. I know that the sweater could not be made by, well, you. But I understand that it could not be made by me without painstaking effort. I assume, at times, that you will also see what I see.

"You have been given such a sweater. Your concern is the cold, or laws of public decency. You don't care that it's oversized. You don't care that it might be inappropriately heavy given the weather. You understand that it is clothing, and some clothing is better than none. You don't appreciate the quality of the sweater itself. It seems almost irrelevant to its function. I occasionally forget this. When someone wears such a sweater, it is, like most expensive fashion, meant to be a statement. No, it *is* a statement. Most people who make such statements are pretentious—but not all, and regardless, even the pretentious understand what they think they are trying to say. You don't.

"Were knitting, however, integral to your job, you would. You would see the stitches, the wool used, the dyes used on that wool; you would know what size the needles were, and whether or not different sizes were required to knit the whole. You are not *stupid*. You are, however, too narrowly focused. Better?"

"I'm not sure."

"That's the best I've got." She glanced over Kaylin's head at Severn and the familiar.

"What Bellusdeo was trying to say before she started on

knitting," Severn then said, "was that Teela considers the attempt an act of desperation and fear. If she's insulted at all, she's insulted because Canatel—and Tagraine—didn't come to her *first*. They didn't ask for her help. They assumed that the people threatening them held all the cards. Barrani are, at heart, snobs.

"Teela *is* a Lord of the High Court. She has one of The Three. We all know this. But we also know Teela best when she's wearing the Hawk. If she weren't in service to the Halls of Law, none of the Barrani Hawks would know her. They'd know *of* her, the same way we know of the humans in the human caste court.

"When Teela's wearing the Hawk, she's just like them. Or you. Or me. She's a Hawk. The Barrani can't see someone who wears that Hawk as a power."

Kaylin opened her mouth and shut it again.

"When they first started out as Hawks on the force, they were probably allowed to do so because they were considered— by their own people—barely better than your average mortal.

"They haven't considered that their ability to *be* Hawks was guaranteed by Teela as Lord of the High Court. They've had at least a decade to see Teela in action on the ground. They can no longer hold her in awe. They can't think of her as an actual power *because* she does exactly what they do. She even obeys a Leontine. She is not called Lord when she's in the office. That had to be a deliberate choice on Teela's part—and I'm not certain she's happy with the results.

"The people who are threatening them, however, are powers, in Tagraine's and Canatel's minds. They didn't come to Teela first because they felt, viscerally, that she was just another Hawk. They didn't trust the protection she could have offered. That's why she's insulted. And I believe she holds herself responsible for their attempted assassination."

"Because she knew things were getting political," Kaylin said, after a more thoughtful pause, "and she wasn't prepared."

Severn nodded. "The Barrani Hawks have already been used."

"Against Moran, though."

"It doesn't matter. It's recent enough that she knew they could be used. She didn't shore up her own defenses—and part of those defenses would be providing protection for the Hawks. They were threatened *because* she was too caught up in the concerns of her cohort."

Kaylin thought that was hugely unfair.

"I'm not agreeing with her assessment," Severn continued. "My agreement won't matter to Teela one way or the other."

"I'd suggest you stay out of it," Bellusdeo told him quietly.

Severn glanced at Bellusdeo. "We need information."

"Teela's a Lord. Leave the information gathering to her."

"Teela is a Lord," he agreed. Severn could agree as if agreement were irrelevant. "But a Lord doesn't enter the warrens. A Lord doesn't—ever—meet with outcastes."

Bellusdeo's eyes had shaded to a gold orange. Kaylin intervened. "Teela's met with Nightshade before."

"Not under her own instigation. Her tabard and her choice of employ protects her in such situations. While the High Court does not consider the Halls of Law a suitable place for the Barrani nobility, they have *all* sworn oaths of service to the Eternal Emperor."

She remembered what Candallar had said, and nodded.

"Teela's interactions with Nightshade are considered, by the Barrani, to be a direct result of her tabard. Were she not a Hawk, she would not have met with him. Teela's enemies are Lords of the High Court."

Kaylin nodded, thinking. "The Barrani Hawks met with Candallar. They probably didn't meet him by accident. Either he was told to approach them, or they were told to approach him. Do you think they left the East Warrens and headed into his fief with an offer of some sort? Or do you think he already had an offer on the table and left the fief to meet them?"

"Either would work," he replied, in his neutral tone. "If the Hawks crossed the Ablayne, there are bound to be witnesses."

"They're from the warrens. They're not going to talk to us."

"They're not going to talk to Hawks, no."

"Corporal," Bellusdeo said, in a sergeant's tone of voice. "Teela is no doubt waiting for Canatel to regain consciousness to *ask him*."

"He has a vested interest in giving her the answer she will find most acceptable," Severn countered.

"It's none of our business."

"It's not," Severn agreed. "Until the cohort descends from the West March. We've got six weeks, if they travel overland the way we did." And he clearly intended to use those six weeks to their full advantage. "Although I believe Mandoran is attempting to talk them out of it."

"No one listens to Mandoran," Kaylin pointed out.

He chuckled. "That's certainly how Mandoran feels. But Helen is concerned. She cannot—and would not—refuse to house them; she's your home and you wouldn't."

Kaylin opened her mouth.

Severn spoke before she could. "She's a *building*, Kaylin. She's sentient. She has will. She's made choices that were physically almost ruinous for her in order to maintain some sense of her own autonomy. You think she did that to buy her freedom."

"She did."

"Yes."

"And no," Bellusdeo cut in. Severn fell silent, allowing Bellusdeo to carry the rest of the conversation. "She bought a *measure* of freedom. She injured herself so that she had a measure of choice. But her choices are, and have always been, confined.

She *is* a building. She was created to be a building. Her sentience was bound into her nature. It is not that different from you—or me, or Teela. There are things we might want to do that our actual existence does not allow. You cannot live forever, no matter how cautious you might choose to be. Not," she added, "that you ever choose to be cautious.

"Helen is a building. She is your home."

"I'll tell her she can say no."

"She knows the likely outcome of that—and it is an outcome that affects you directly. You want them under your roof because you trust Helen to minimize the danger, both to them, and from them. But Helen, I think, is less certain about that ability, precisely because of the choices she made in the distant past.

"But they will not stay in Tiamaris, and it is a disaster to even think of placing them in Nightshade—and those are the only two Towers that might, just might, be able to do what Helen is afraid she cannot." She exhaled steam.

Something in her tone of voice caught Kaylin's attention, and she stopped walking in order to catch Bellusdeo's. It took the Dragon half a block to notice, but she did reverse course. "The Emperor does not yet know about the cohort and their imminent arrival. According to Annarion, I'll have six weeks in which to smooth over future difficulties.

"The politics of the High Court, when it comes to the internal hierarchy of Barrani lords, has been largely irrelevant to his concerns. An attempted assassination at the Halls of Law will not be."

Kaylin winced. "And you're living with me."

"Yes. The Emperor is confident of Helen's ability to protect me from the immediately lethal: arcane bombs, for one. I am uncertain that his confidence will remain intact with the addition of eight Barrani would-be Lords of the High Court.

In the worst case, I expect that I will be 'invited' to return to the palace." The orange of her eyes made clear just how welcome that would be.

It was not a surprise that the Hawks ended up at Evanton's shop. It wasn't intentional, but Evanton's shop was part of their beat, and Grethan had appeared at the window to wave as the Hawks patrolled.

"Is he in?" Kaylin asked Evanton's apprentice. Her familiar immediately leapt off her shoulder onto Grethan's, who—as always—seemed delighted to have him. Hope had always liked the Tha'alani apprentice.

"I think—I'm not certain—he's expecting you."

"Good or bad?"

"He's been absentminded, but not grouchy, if that helps. I think he's in the garden. I'll tell him you're here."

They gathered around the kitchen table in the cramped, small space. Kaylin understood that the cookies Evanton offered were a type of bribe, and truly didn't care. She also drank the tea he made. He wasn't having enough of a bad day that he was willing to drink any himself, which was probably a good sign. Then again, with Evanton, it was hard to tell.

"I have had the opportunity to speak with the elemental water this morning," he now said.

The cookies lost all taste. "And she told you to speak to us?"

"I am not sure that 'she' is the appropriate pronoun, but I will endeavor not to criticize."

Try harder, Kaylin thought. "What did the water have to say?"

"I would consider it mostly irrelevant to you in different circumstances." He was not in a terrible mood, but was obviously feeling testy. Kaylin, however, understood this test, and she could pass it, if not with flying colors, at least with passable grades.

One bushy brow rose as he considered her. "Very good. Teela's confederates are—as I believe you must now know— leaving the green. The heart of the green is concerned."

Kaylin nodded, but had to bite back the obvious *how do you know this* that wanted to leap out of her mouth. He wouldn't answer and it would annoy him, which meant there was no possible gain.

"The water believes they will travel between Hallionne, making use of the portal paths to avoid unwanted attention. You are expecting visitors?"

Kaylin hesitated; Bellusdeo—who treated Evanton with far more respect than most mortals did—stepped on her foot. "Yes. What does the water want from me?"

"I do not believe the water intends to command you in any fashion," was the slightly defensive reply.

"Fine. What do *you* want?"

"I'd like you to stay out of trouble, if that's at all possible."

"Something I can *actually* do."

This pulled a smile from the older man. He looked worn, tired, and entirely more fragile than he had when she'd first met him. He didn't look any older, though. "I would like to make certain that Teela's friends are staying with you. Helen's intervention to date has been both fortuitous and necessary, especially with regard to Annarion. That young man has an unfortunate temper."

Kaylin blinked. "Annarion?"

"You cannot hear him."

"No. He's generally the quiet, reasonable one."

"A terrifying thought." Evanton exhaled. "His actions— over which he does have some control—are quiet and reasonable. But he is in pain, Kaylin, and when he leaves Helen—on the rare occasions he does—his anguish can be heard. It can practically be felt."

"And Mandoran?"

"Mandoran does not have that effect."

"You think the others will?"

"That is the question. The water does not hear as I hear. The heart of the green hears more. The Hallionne in which Teela's friends have made their home since your intervention, hears all. There has been much discussion, and much concern shared. I believe that at least two of the visitors would have voices as loud, as detrimental, as Annarion's were they to be left to their own devices. They do not need to break the law you have made it your life to uphold," he added. "No conscious choice is required.

"But they are not—as I am certain even you are aware— what they were. Some of them recognize and accept this fact; some do not. It is those who do not who are the biggest danger. And no, don't make that face. Annarion *is* a threat, with no intent, no desire to be one." His eyes narrowed. "Do not let them interfere with Helen," he said, which was not what she'd expected.

"They can't."

He said, after a long pause, "You rescued them, in a fashion. You believe that the Hallionne Alsanis sheltered them because that was the purpose for which the Hallionne were constructed. You believe that they were forced to change their nature to better slide between the bars of a very forgiving cage. You have correctly divined that the Hallionne, being sentient, have some access to living emotion; you have even correctly understood that the Hallionne are subject to isolation and loneliness.

"But you have failed to understand the subtleties."

"And you're going to explain my failure."

"Yes, now that you've asked."

It wasn't a question; Kaylin shrugged.

"Annarion's friends didn't just reform or reshape themselves. They created subtle changes in the Hallionne as well. Before you ask, no, I do not know the specifics. I am not Hallionne. I have access to the Hallionne in a fashion, because I am Keeper, but the language of the Hallionne is notoriously difficult to learn, let alone master. Were I Barrani, or High Barrani, I do not think it would be this difficult; I am not. Nor is Grethan.

"The Hallionne Alsanis was altered by the children who were themselves altered by the green. This will likely make their passage through the portal paths safer for them. It will make any presence in Hallionne other than their own more difficult. I do not think the changes they made were made immediately. I am less certain that they were made unintentionally. I am not," he added, at some twitch of Kaylin's expression, "blaming them; it serves no point. They were captives, they were children, and they desired freedom.

"It is possible, however, that their sense of what 'home' is or means is radically different from your own. They were captives for far, far longer than they were Barrani children. Helen can create living quarters for Annarion. She is therefore confident that she can create those same quarters for the rest of Teela's friends. She was, if I understand her history correctly, equivalent to the Towers that guard the borders of the fiefs, but the commands at her core were not the same.

"Discuss this with Teela. She will better understand the dangers." He looked at the cooling tea. "What did happen this morning?"

Kaylin explained. She left out names, with the exception of Teela's. Severn's expression made clear that he didn't think this was an appropriate discussion to have outside of the Halls, but he didn't actively try to shut her down.

Evanton looked vastly less pleased when she'd finished. "I am almost sorry I asked," he said, pushing himself up from his chair. "But politics are entirely political. Meaning they are not my problem."

"Neither is my home," Kaylin pointed out.

"If things go awry in your home, it could well become my problem, and I would like to avoid that. I am *old*, Kaylin. In the past decade I have seen more threats and upheavals than in the previous century, with one or two notable exceptions, neither of which can be blamed on you."

"None of them can be blamed on me!"

"Grethan!"

Evanton's apprentice appeared before the last loud syllable had died out. The familiar on his shoulder sighed and squawked before leaping off to land at his home base, Kaylin's shoulder.

Evanton headed out the door into the rickety hall that led to the Keeper's Garden. He turned in the door frame. "Understand," he said softly, "that the world and the Keeper will almost certainly continue to exist if there are no people in it. My job is not actually to choose sides. The elements are adversely affected by Shadow, but not in the same fashion as we are. My job, such as it is, is to stop the elements from destroying the world in their attempts to destroy each other. There are no Shadows in my garden. Do you understand?"

Kaylin nodded.

"I am the Keeper. My power, where it exists, exists because of that. I am, however, partial to people in general. The location of the garden does not change, and I would rather have the occasionally irritating company—"

"Most people call them customers, in this part of town."

"—than not. I understand what exists beneath the High Halls. Where I can, I will aid you, as I have always done. But the political—and yes, when we speak of politics with the Barrani it inevitably defaults to assassination or war—is not my arena."

"It's not mine, either."

"Not yet. It will be. I'm sorry."

"If I'm forced to enter that arena, will I have to be diplomatic?"

"Only if your commanding officers drop dead and someone who has never had to work anywhere near you is then put in charge."

The first thing Kaylin did when they returned to the office from their shortened Elani patrol was stop by the duty roster to see if the Barrani were once again being assigned their regular patrols. The second was to visit the infirmary. Teela was no longer there.

Moran, however, was, and the long day hadn't improved her temper any. The sergeant was glaring at a small mirror. If looks could kill, that mirror wouldn't be in pieces—it would be melted glass with little rivulets of silver in it.

"Go home."

"Moran—"

"I mean it."

"Has anyone else come to visit your Barrani patient?"

"No one has been permitted to visit, with the exception of Teela." Moran turned away from the mirror to face Kaylin directly. "Given how successful I was at getting you to ignore the politics of my *entirely personal* situation, I am not going to waste breath telling you to ignore hers. But kitling? I wouldn't have broken your arms or legs."

"Teela won't—"

"No, she probably won't. Being a Hawk has been a lark for the Barrani—or at least that's the impression they've always given. It's the reason that most of the nonpatrolling Hawks find it hard to work with them."

Kaylin nodded again.

"It is not a lark at the moment. Teela may take a leave of absence when things get truly tense."

Kaylin did not ask how assassination attempts *in the Halls* failed to qualify as truly tense. "At the Hawklord's request?"

"No. The Barrani wear the tabard. He would not ask them to leave the office; it would send the wrong signals."

Kaylin blinked.

"Having Barrani Hawks on the force give the Barrani an accessible public face. People are often terrified of the Barrani."

"People are sometimes terrified of the Hawks. But most of those are criminals."

"Most yes, but not all. Having Barrani on the street and wearing the Hawk makes them a little less frightening." She was silent for a beat. "But surely you already know this."

Did she?

She'd been a Hawk for seven years, unofficially. The Hawk had never terrified her the way Barrani in Nightshade had. It had never terrified her the way the howls of hunting Ferals did. It had never terrified her the way the cold did, the way hunger did. But the warrens were as close to the fiefs as anyplace inside the city could be—and if she'd been born there, and the warrens were her home?

Would she love the Hawk then? Would she be unafraid of it?

Fear of the Barrani made sense to Kaylin. Outside of the Law, they could kill most mortals on a whim. Barrani against Leontine was not as sure a thing.

"I don't know," she finally said. "There wasn't a lot of difference for us between Shadows and Barrani when I was a kid. And if I'm being honest, most mortals of my acquaintance I tried real hard to avoid as well. You don't understand what it's like. If I met me from back then—"

"Yes?"

"I wouldn't have given me a chance if I didn't want my throat slit."

Bellusdeo exhaled and moved to stand beside Kaylin. Moran's glare did not—had never, apparently—included the gold Dragon. "It's so hard to have productive discussions with you," she said, but fondly. "Most men—most Barrani, most Dragons—when forced into the space you are standing in now might deflect. They might, if pressed in an unavoidable way, justify. They might give excuses—ah, pardon, I believe they would call them explanations."

Kaylin shrugged. "Look, I'm not proud of what I once did."

"No."

"But I understand why I did it. If I were there *now*, if I lost everything *now*, I'd make different choices. But I didn't even see the possibilities, then. I saw death. When all you see is death, or probable death, you don't trust much."

"And the tabard?"

"I doubt I'd've trusted it, either."

"Even before you lived in Barren?"

"Even then. I believed that paradise existed across the Ablayne. But none of that paradise came into the fiefs, and the Hawks? They didn't, either. Can we drop this?"

"Yes. But I expect you to accept Teela's leave of absence." She hesitated.

Kaylin stared at her.

"Or her resignation, if it comes to that."

CHAPTER 6

"Kaylin," Helen repeated, in her most patient tone, "I cannot answer that question."

"You can."

"I cannot *ethically* answer that question."

"Yes, you can."

"Teela is a guest. Teela is not present. If she wishes to share that information with you, she will."

"She won't!"

"Then perhaps there is a reason for that."

"Yes—she thinks I can't do anything. She still thinks I'm helpless—"

"She does not think of you as helpless. She has told you so. It is hard for her to make that adjustment, but given your age when she first met you, you must be able to understand that."

"She treats me as if—"

"You *are* mortal. You are not Barrani. You are not a Dragon. You do not, objectively, have her power. Even were she not trained to the arcane, even were she entirely without magic or magical weapons, you would stand very little chance against her. Her enemies, at the moment, are not mortal." Helen frowned. "Or perhaps some of them are; I find the politics of your cities confusing at times."

"Welcome to my life." Kaylin looked down at her hands. They were fists. "Bellusdeo thinks Teela might resign." Kaylin spoke the last word as if it were suicide. Or worse, somehow.

"And Bellusdeo is speaking as a former ruler and an observer of Barrani, admittedly in a more martial context. She is not speaking with any certainty."

"No, she can't. But *you* could."

"No, Kaylin, I can't. Were I an entirely different building," she added, "you could force that information from me, and I would have no choice but to give it to you."

"...That's unfair."

"Yes, dear. But it is also fact. Teela is your friend."

"And you're my home!"

"Yes. But I do not think friendship is best served by using that home as a spy."

Kaylin flushed.

"You are tired and hungry. I think this is possibly one of the only times I've seen you refuse food." It was true. Kaylin could eat anything, at any time, because some of her instincts were still those of a starving, underfed street kid. You didn't turn your nose up at food when there was never any guarantee of another meal. "In the morning, or perhaps even after you've eaten, I think you will see things more clearly."

She is correct.

Kaylin bit back the urge to tell Lord Nightshade to do something anatomically impossible. And then glared at the Avatar of her house. Helen had fairly granular control of incoming communication; if Nightshade was speaking to her, it was because Helen let him. Yes, he was speaking to her because she knew his True Name—but Helen had proven that she could limit or curtail the connection.

Her house smiled gently.

You've heard.

I have been speaking with Annarion, yes. I am apprised of all of the complications.

She ate, because talking to Nightshade did not require her to open her mouth when it was full. She also drank spiced milk. Helen clearly thought Kaylin was in a *mood* because the milk was warm and apparently contained honey.

Tell me what you know about Candallar, Kaylin finally said.

Candallar is a fieflord.

Okay, let me amend that. Tell me what you know that I don't.

This elicited two responses; the first, a sharp annoyance; the second, amusement. *You frequently know things I would expect no mortal to know, while being ignorant of things that appear to be common knowledge. If you wish information, you will have to bear with me. Candallar is a fieflord. He is, as I am, outcaste. He had less choice in the designation, and less support within the High Court. He is younger than I, and his fall more recent. You will have noticed, no doubt, that the Consort does not treat me as outcaste.*

Kaylin nodded.

She is the only Lord of the High Court to have that option. Ah, no. Her brother could, if he desired—

If you're talking about the High Lord—as opposed to the Lord of the West March—if her brother wanted to, he could repatriate you. You could be part of the High Court again.

To do so would imply—strongly—that the customs of the High Court have no weight; that the decisions of the High Court have no consequences. Do not be angry; I am not.

But...he's the High Lord.

She could feel Nightshade's frustration, and was surprised to feel his exhaustion, as well. The only other time she had felt such exhaustion he'd been injured.

I am not injured. I am frustrated. He is High Lord, yes. But if An'Teela has not made this clear, his rule is contested, even now. There will be a series of tests, skirmishes if you will, for the remain-

der of your mortal life—no matter how long you live. His tone implied that he expected that to be a handful of years, if she were lucky. *Even to you, this must imply that his power is not absolute. He is not the Eternal Emperor, Kaylin.*

Frustration drove his pause; Kaylin was almost surprised when he continued. *When power is not absolute, when it is not guaranteed, alliances are made. They are alliances, often, of convenience, as a majority of alliances are. He is close to his Consort; she does not intrigue against him.*

She's the Consort!

Another full silence.

Nightshade?

I am...attempting to remember how appallingly little is taught to your Hawks. You will speak with An'Teela about this. Or Annarion. Or Mandoran. They will attempt to correct your appalling ignorance.

She is the Consort.

Yes. It grants her immunity until and unless another is found who can fulfill the role she has undertaken. To our knowledge, there is only one who might—but she is entirely unsuitable in every other way. Before you ask, it is you. You are aware that many families push their children into the Test of Name.

Kaylin nodded.

Are you further aware that many push their children into the more complicated and far more deadly tests required to become Consort?

Was she? She thought about it; the Consort had certainly spoken of the tests, the difficulty, the failures.

They do not do this primarily for the benefit to the race; they do it for political reasons. The Consort is the only position in the High Court that is nonnegotiable. But do not imagine that it is not, in the end, political; everything about the Barrani is. Only those who absent themselves from the Court are outside of the political sphere.

Like you.

She felt his bitter smile.

Like me, yes.

You think this will pass.

I believe that if the High Lord retains his seat in the next century, or perhaps two, I could be repatriated, or at least offered the opportunity to return to the High Court. It is what the Consort desires. But there are many who do not desire it, and a handful of those are of significant power.

If they don't want you, they don't want Annarion.

Indeed.

And for the same reason? Because he'll have a legitimate claim to the lands—or whatever—that you once held?

Claim and legitimacy are polite fictions, in the end. If we have the power, *we can embroider any claim and make it, as you say in Elantran, "stick." The facts of the matter give Annarion an open field; the base arguments against legitimate claim cannot be made, and were he to start a war, it would be less difficult to do so without open censure.*

So...claim of blood gives him early room to maneuver?

Yes. It is not, of course, legitimacy that is the real concern.

It's the regalia *and the centuries jailed in the green.*

An'Teela suffered prejudice because she survived—but she was never captive in the Hallionne. She returned from the green—the only child to do so. She is, to our eye, Barrani. She was tested, Kaylin. She was pushed. She was powerful, but had she not had that potential, she would never have been sent to the green.

Her father desired her to undergo the test of the Lake. She refused. Here a glimmer of amusement adorned his words. *She was unwilling to give him anything he desired of her. She had gone to the green under his command.*

And he had killed her mother there. Kaylin exhaled. *Your brother's still angry.*

She almost felt the fieflord's wince, and liked him better for it. But...in truth, his concern for, his devotion to, his only remaining brother was one of the few things about him she admired. She had never, ever expected to admire anything about the fieflord of Nightshade.

Annarion's anger is focused and traditional. He intends to take the Test of Name. I cannot stop him. Discussion will not move him. He is...almost unchanged with the passage of time. It is frustrating.

If you were reinstated, I think he could be reasoned with. I think if the High Lord offered you your name, your position, if you could reclaim your family line—which he thinks you should never have surrendered—we could keep him here.

And I have told him that this will, in all probability, happen, but not now. He understands that. But he understands, as well, the necessity of the Towers, of the fiefs. Do you honestly think that I could wage an intelligent war from Castle Nightshade, as you are wont to call it? Ah, I see that you do.

She was revising that opinion as they spoke. Some of her anger—at Helen, at Teela—had subsided, as it always did.

"That's because you've eaten something, at least," Helen said quietly. "I understand your concern. If you were not the type of person who feels such concerns, I am not certain I would be the right home for you. But Kaylin, there are always limits. Your concern, your worry, is *yours*," Helen continued, bringing the conversation back to where Kaylin had started it. "Love is not a reasonable excuse to ask me to invade a guest's privacy. I do not answer Teela's questions."

"She asks you about me?"

"On occasion, yes. Oh. I've surprised you."

"...And you don't answer her questions, either."

"I will answer questions that you would answer, if you heard them or remembered them. But everyone who is not Tha'alani has boundaries and a need for privacy. Young children—of any race—will ask questions without regard for privacy; everything is new to them. They have not yet learned the weight of responsibility and the weight of poor decisions. But you are not, as you so often tell most of your friends, a child. Your concern is admirable. But you cannot use concern to justify things that are less so."

Kaylin's shoulders sagged. "I'm sorry." She exhaled. *You're willing to wait because you know the Towers are necessary.*

Yes. And because I have no great desire to return to the High Court.

Does your brother know this?

Perhaps. We have exchanged very heated words in the past month. His loss of control is understandable; he is a child, still. The intervening time has not given him the experience required of the Barrani; it has given him experiences for which the Barrani were not created. Most of us cannot understand them. But I have made clear that finding a fieflord is not as simple as the Test of Name.

The Test of Name was *not* simple.

He does understand Ravellon's threat. He is willing, grudgingly, to allow that I am not entirely without honor or a sense of duty.

...Which means he really can't be talked out of it. I mean, from Annarion's perspective, what other options does he have? Kaylin exhaled. *Does this have anything to do with Candallar?*

It is likely. If you have met him at this time, it cannot be coincidence. Have you spoken to Teela about this?

I doubt very much she'll talk to me.

She is not the only Lord of the High Court to whom you have access. She is not even the most significant.

Candallar, Kaylin said, trying to pin the conversation down to the important point, even as it squirmed away.

I am not Candallar; I am not much in contact with him. I can be, of course; the Towers can communicate with each other. In a grave, grave emergency, they can work as one. There has never been such an emergency, he added. *My experience is therefore entirely theoretical. Be that as it may, I can bespeak Candallar without leaving my fief. But I cannot guess at his involvement until I understand more fully the movement within the High Court.*

Speak to the Consort, Kaylin. She will have questions for you. You will have questions for her.

And Candallar?

I will speak with Candallar—but I do not expect to glean the in-

formation you desire at the speed you desire it. You are much like my brother: everything is an emergency. Everything must be immediate. He is truly young: like a mortal he is afraid of lost time. But unlike a mortal, he has time.

Would Candallar be in contact with the High Court? I mean, with some of its elements?

Oh, undoubtedly. But he is not me. I could attend the ceremony in the green with impunity because the green chose me. I could attend because the Consort accepted me as a High Lord. And I could attend because I wield one of The Three.

Those are meant to kill Dragons.

Yes. But they can kill any other enemy just as well. I am not hunted as outcaste. This was not always the case. But we are Barrani, not Dragon; power is its own legitimacy.

And Candallar doesn't have it.

She could feel the shrug she couldn't see. *He has survived,* was the eventual, noncommittal answer.

Kaylin was awake far earlier than she wanted to be the next morning. She was tired, but not sleepy, the two words being slightly different, and thoughts of Candallar, Teela, the Hawks and the cohort immediately demanded attention. It was a day off, so she couldn't retreat to the Halls of Law—and the demands of work—to distract herself. She gave up on sleep, got dressed, rearranged the familiar and decided that turnabout was fair play. She therefore headed out of her own room, with its comfortable, creaking floors, into the hallway, and eventually deposited herself outside of Mandoran's room.

There, she knocked. Helen didn't stop her.

"I'm sleeping."

"Liar. Barrani don't need sleep."

"I'm sleeping anyway. It's better than angst." Mandoran's voice was not muffled although a closed door stood between Kaylin's ears and the Barrani.

"You talk in your sleep? I guess that shouldn't be surprising given how much you love the sound of your own voice."

Mandoran laughed. "If you promise not to nag me about Teela or Annarion, I'll get out of bed."

"Are you actually *in* bed?"

"Yes. You can join me, if you want, but I can't promise—"

"I'll pass."

He laughed again. "No Teela, no Annarion?"

"Done."

"What's the penalty for failure?"

"What?"

"What do I get when you fail?"

"Dinner."

"Helen will feed me anyway."

"Not if I ask her not to."

"Helen?" Mandoran said, raising his voice. "Will you starve me if Kaylin demands it?"

Helen failed to answer, and Mandoran chuckled.

"Don't disturb your brother," Helen then said.

"Nothing I could possibly do would make him any *worse*."

Kaylin, in the hallway, waited for another minute; the door opened. Mandoran was tugging his left arm into the empty sleeve of a jacket. He did not otherwise look rumpled. Or unshaven. Or sleep deprived. She opened her mouth.

"We have a deal. No Annarion. No Teela."

"Fine. Can I ask about Tain?"

"Boring old nursemaid."

"He is not!"

"Is too." Mandoran held up a hand. "Have you ever had to live with him?"

"Not yet."

"Well, you'll soon see what I mean. I'm beginning to understand the phrase *misery loves company*." He grinned.

"Barrani don't have that one?"

"No. But it's oddly useful. If someone makes us miserable, we generally feel justified in attempting to end their lives."

"Annarion makes you miserable all the time, according to you."

His grin deepened. "Exactly. So. Misery and company. And—no Annarion, remember? Annarion's situation is far, far simpler than—" His Elantran segued into expressive Leontine. "Apparently," he said, "I'm not allowed to talk to you about this."

"According to who?" She guessed Teela.

"Sedarias." Apparently, she guessed wrong.

"Sedarias is the one with the complicated situation?"

"Not the only one. Look, I told you I was an orphan, right?"

"You lied."

"Very good! I admit I despaired—" He stopped again. "Someone told you."

"Yes."

"Then I take it back. You spent your formative years—not my phrase, don't make that face—in the fiefs."

"Yes."

"You must have lied, and you must have at least been decent enough at it to survive."

"I was never good at lying."

"What did you do instead?"

Kaylin shrugged. "Groveled in abject fear."

"I would think lying would be easier." He flicked something invisible off his sleeve. "Clearly you've never been lazy enough. Food?"

Kaylin made a face. "Helen?"

"Yes, dear," the disembodied house replied.

"At what point does someone *stop* being a guest?"

"I imagine the moment you ask them to leave."

Mandoran laughed at Kaylin's expressive, but silent, response. "Fine. I guess we're feeding him."

His good mood did not last through an early breakfast. It didn't last through the start of breakfast. While he enjoyed teasing Kaylin—his words, as she had ruder ones to describe it—he couldn't entirely forget the predicament his cohort were in.

"What did you want to know about the great boring nurse-maid?"

"Nothing. I did want to know about Tain."

"I've pretty much described everything you need to know. I cannot *believe* you're inviting him to stay with the rest of us. I can't believe he'd even consider it. He's not particularly fond of us." Mandoran's grin reappeared. "He's a protective, jealous bastard. Well, not bastard, not exactly—but he's not from a great line."

"Unlike the rest of you?"

"Unlike Teela. He hadn't met the rest of us when he started associating with her. Were it not for my name—for all of our names—and the history associated with those names, he would have assumed that I was his social equal. That's not good," he added, in case this wasn't clear.

There were days when she liked Mandoran; he was accessible in a way the Barrani generally weren't. And then there were days like these. Mandoran didn't appear to notice the difference.

"Look, don't get defensive. He's stodgy and boring because he's too damn cautious. We might as well be the unawakened, waiting helplessly in the arms of our parents for the gift of our name." He hesitated, and then his shoulders drooped toward the tabletop. "He's been good for Teela. She doesn't have his name—he's never offered, and she's not stupid enough to ask—but she might as well."

"He's her partner."

"The only person who thinks being a Hawk is more significant than being a Lord of the High Court is you."

Kaylin folded her arms and tilted her chair up on the back legs. It was either that or leap across the table to strangle him. "He's her partner."

"Fine, fine. The point is, he's not one of us."

"Technically, neither is Teela if it comes to that."

"Teela *is*. She's not as changed as we are. She doesn't have trouble passing as normal—well, not now."

"But she did."

"Duh."

"I think I prefer it when you speak High Barrani."

"You probably prefer it when I don't speak—but you did ask."

"About Tain."

"Tain's been her ally for much longer than he's been a Hawk. They didn't just meet when they joined. Every Barrani Hawk in the Halls was vetted, one way or another, by Teela first."

"And none of them are Lords of the Court."

"Nope. But there's no other Lord of the Court who would join the Hawks. If Teela weren't Teela, she'd've suffered for it. But she's never stayed strictly within the Court's circumscribed social rules, and in the end, it would have been too much trouble to make her pay for straying outside of them. Her father was powerful, and her father is dead. So are most of the Lords who chose to ally themselves with him, in the beginning. But not all.

"The Barrani who haven't taken the Test of Name—and passed it—are mostly invisible in the High Halls. They're not considered significant. They can be servants—and we do have those—or guards; they can be soldiers, if war demands soldiery. But they can't be anything else. If they have ambition or pretension, they take the Test. Tain didn't."

"So he's considered insignificant."

"Yes. She's hoping to change his mind," he added. "She's never considered him insignificant, and I think she's afraid she'll lose him." He winced. Kaylin couldn't hear Teela, and was very grateful for that fact at this particular moment.

She didn't know Tain as well as she knew Teela, but she knew him well enough by now. "He won't listen."

"That's what I told her. Does she believe me? No, of course not. She might believe you."

"I'm not stupid enough to try."

Bellusdeo found Kaylin in the breakfast room three hours later. The Dragon, like Kaylin, preferred Kaylin's work days to her days off, and probably for similar reasons. "What did Mandoran do this time?" she asked, drawing Kaylin's attention from whatever it was she'd been looking at. Her hands, probably. Or the table. Helen had long since caused the plates to vanish, although technically cleaning up was Kaylin's job.

"Nothing."

"You're worried."

Kaylin nodded. "I was thinking of paying a visit to the High Halls."

Bellusdeo wrinkled her nose. "Take Severn with you."

"It's not Hawk business. Not officially."

"Almost everything you do is Hawk business. You intend to visit the Consort?"

"If she'll see me. I have a hundred questions, and I think I have to whittle them down to the important ones."

"And those are?"

"The ones I can ask without giving offense to anyone."

"In which case, you might as well stay home." But the

Dragon was smiling fondly. "I don't suppose you could invite her to visit you here?"

"I could—but I highly doubt she could accept. This isn't exactly a safe space—" Helen cleared her throat, and Kaylin flushed. "*Getting* to Helen isn't exactly safe for the Consort."

"Who would destroy her?" Bellusdeo asked. "Dragons might have, once, but the Dragons that would have are dead or asleep. And the Dragon that rules now would fight to the death to preserve her because she is, in part, of his hoard."

Kaylin flinched. "I'll thank you to never *ever* say that where the Barrani—any of them—can hear you." She pushed herself off her chair in order to pace the length of the large room. "I hate politics."

"Then you hate the living—of every race. Politics exist wherever the living congregate. What you call politics in the comfort of your own home are the things you feel are above you, beyond you. The Emperor is political. The High Lord is political. The Hawk Lord is political. What you fail to understand is that even within your office, politics happen. You call it something else—but at base, it is not that different. The reach of the powerful is greater, therefore the effects of their gambits are both more visible and less easily affected."

"Office politics don't get people killed."

"No, with the possible exception of Teela."

"That wasn't office politics—that was High Court politics."

"But office politics can get people dismissed. And Hawks—like any other living beings—need food and shelter."

"How do you know this?"

"I listen. I talk, but mostly, I listen. I look for the rules of the game being played, because any game requires a winner. And I don't play. There is nothing, here, for me to win, and very little to lose."

"But not nothing."

Bellusdeo exhaled. "I would almost suggest you move out

for a month or two, if I thought you could. But Helen would not be happy, and I have no wish to hurt her. Teela personally chose the Barrani Hawks. One of them attempted to assassinate her. If she is not foolish enough to trust Barrani, she desires what she once built with her cohort: trust."

Bellusdeo held up a hand as Kaylin opened her mouth. "The Barrani Hawks are not Lords of the High Court. They do not have power, and lack a Barrani measure of wealth. Teela's personal power has been enough, in the past, to protect them. She did not anticipate the necessity of demonstrations of that personal power to those who might consider becoming her opponents; she has been secure in her power for too long. Such necessary demonstrations will be neither peaceful nor entirely safe."

"For me."

"For you."

CHAPTER 7

Kaylin woke to the sound of shouting. Some of it was in Elantran. Some of it was in Dragon. The rest was more or less Barrani. The small dragon was pretty much trying to put his claws up her left nostril, and his squawks, while quieter than real Dragon roars, were much closer to her ears.

She rolled out of bed, noted that she had not grabbed the dagger she kept under her pillow, and considered this—more or less—progress.

"It wouldn't help," Helen said. "It is not morning by any standard definition. Would you care for light?"

Her house did not wake her up in the middle of the night unless there was an emergency call from the midwives. Midwives did not enrage or terrify either Barrani or Dragons.

"Where are they?" Kaylin asked, squinting as her eyes acclimatized themselves to bright light. She got dressed while the familiar circled her head, waiting for a place to land.

"I am currently trying to keep Mandoran and Annarion calm, with lamentably little success. I did call for Teela."

"How?"

"The mirror." Helen disliked and distrusted the mirror

network. The fact that she had used it made things much more dire.

"Bellusdeo is roaring."

"She isn't angry. She felt she needed to get the boys' attention—and native Dragon certainly did that."

Kaylin headed to the door, her floors creaking comfortably beneath bare feet. At the door, she slid those feet into boots. She wasn't certain what had happened, but if running or fighting were involved, bare feet wouldn't be helpful. "What caused this, anyway?"

"The cohort."

"The cohort's not even here yet!"

"No. But they are traveling by Hallionne and portal path, and...they seem to have encountered some difficulty."

Kaylin froze, hand on the doorknob. "Pardon?"

"I believe you did hear me."

"But—" She was cut off by Dragon roar. "Did that bit involve fire?"

"Yes, but it's contained. Bellusdeo is trying to stop the boys from doing anything catastrophically hasty—and she has my absolute blessing. I would advise you to hurry, on the other hand."

"Oh?"

"Teela is almost at the door."

Teela was. But so, to Kaylin's surprise, was Tain. Their eyes were midnight blue, their expressions grim. In the distance Bellusdeo roared, but this time it had intelligible words in it.

Teela made a beeline for the kitchen.

"The boys are downstairs," Helen explained. "I had to move them to the training rooms. Mandoran is not particularly happy with this."

"Is Bellusdeo with them?"

"Yes."

"What's going on?" Kaylin demanded—of Tain.

"You probably know as much as I do. There's been some trouble with the cohort in the West March. The impressions left by the cohort are chaotic and unclear."

"What do you mean?"

"I am not certain, at this point, that they can communicate with Teela and the boys. At all."

Kaylin cursed. In Leontine.

Barrani could run for longer than most mortals; they were taller than Kaylin and their legs had a greater reach. It took Kaylin five minutes to catch up to Tain, because the training rooms were down an intimidating spiral staircase that seemed to go on forever. Kaylin couldn't see the floor. She did, however, see a closed door on the wall side of the descent.

"They're here?" Tain demanded of thin air.

"Yes, dear," Helen replied.

What, a familiar voice demanded, *has happened?* It was Nightshade. Kaylin didn't even fight him as she answered. *I will be there soon. If Annarion reappears do not let him leave.*

I'm not his boss, and I'm not his jailer.

I was not speaking to you. It took her a moment to understand that he was speaking to Helen. That moment, however, was spent watching Tain's back as he opened a short, squat door. It was thick and old and scarred. She had been to rooms in Helen's basement before, but this one, more than any other, reminded her of holding cells, except for the light.

Bellusdeo and Maggaron stood in the room's center; the Dragon's eyes were orange red, and the Ascendant was armed. Not that weapons appeared to be necessary.

There was no sunlight, no window into the external world. There were no obvious sources of illumination, and even had there been, Kaylin might not have noticed. What she noticed were the moving, swirling splashes of color that seemed to spread across the walls and the ceiling as if they were alive. It reminded her of Shadow, although each color was too bold, too definitive, otherwise. There was a conversation going on that Kaylin couldn't hear, and this was its detritus.

Tain appeared to see what she saw, but color wasn't what he was looking for.

"Teela!"

To Helen, Kaylin said, in a much quieter voice, "Is this the room Teela entered?"

And Helen said, "Yes."

Teela was nowhere in sight.

"She is," was Helen's grim reply. "She's with the boys. Those flashes of color you thought of as argument? She's one of them."

Tain stepped into the room, Kaylin practically hugging his back. He hadn't drawn a weapon, but both of his hands were lifted. To Kaylin's eye, everything was a blur of color, and none of that color was Teela. Or Mandoran or Annarion either, if it came to that. "Are they even here?" Kaylin demanded of Helen.

"Yes." As she spoke, some of that color shifted, becoming less of a flat, moving splash against stone as it did. Kaylin was suddenly reminded of Annarion in Castle Nightshade and was glad that she hadn't bothered to eat much.

"Guys," she said, raising her voice to be heard. There wasn't much sound in the room if she stopped to think about it, but something about the kaleidoscope of color implied shrieking. "There is *no way* you are going to the *High Halls* like this! There's *no way* you could even *enter* a Hallionne in this shape or form!"

The slowest of the racing colors recombined; they came together in a way that resembled Annarion, had he been sculpted by someone who wanted to suggest his form artistically, rather than render it realistically. Even his eyes—which were very blue—did not look solid or whole.

"Your brother is coming to visit," she told him. "And I'd really appreciate it if you'd give Teela back—Tain is about to explode."

It took another five minutes before Annarion resembled his usual, breakfast-room self. Teela emerged more quickly, but her color was off. Kaylin would have been gray or green; Teela was simply pale. Her eyes were the same shade of midnight that Annarion's were. Mandoran did not coalesce.

Tain was at Teela's side the minute her feet were solid—and it was her feet that took shape last. In all, it was disturbing; it was not something that Kaylin had seen Teela do before, and she had a very strong desire never to see it again.

"Look, I appreciate that you guys had to learn how to talk to, and live in, a Hallionne. But Teela *didn't* and she is *not cut out for this.* You're guests here. I'm happy to have you. Mostly. But this has got to stop."

Mandoran lacked a mouth to reply.

"No, he doesn't, dear, but I don't think I'll repeat his answer."

Kaylin folded her arms. To Annarion she said, "Your brother will be here soon. Anything you can do to become more solid would probably be good."

"Oh *great*," Mandoran said, speaking for the first time. "Tell him we don't want visitors."

Kaylin's arms tightened. "If this is what you do when you're upset or worried, you're *never* going to become Lords of the High Court. I doubt they can actually kill you—but they can make you all outcaste if you push it."

Bellusdeo dropped a hand on Kaylin's left shoulder. Small and squawky curled his tail around her neck. He didn't lift a wing to bat her face, and he didn't press it over her eyes, either. If he could see Mandoran as he was, he didn't feel it was necessary for Kaylin to see him, too.

"If you're all outcaste, you'll never take that Test. You won't make it past the front doors."

"They can *try* to stop us." Mandoran's disembodied voice again. The splashes of flat color across the room's walls moved as he spoke. It was not comforting.

"Kaylin," Helen began.

"They *will* try. But you're not the people they'll put pressure on first. Maybe you've got no friends and no living family. Maybe you've got family, and they don't want to give your stuff back. But Teela *has* friends. She *has* allies. They'll start there first, because they don't have a choice. They've already started.

"Teela may be part of your cohort, but she's lived in the High Halls for centuries, on and off. She's the wedge in the door. She went to the green, and she returned. She fought Dragons. She did it well enough that she has one of the three damn swords.

"If they can kill her, they're free to shut you all out."

Tain cleared his throat. Teela locked her hands behind her back, which was unusual. She really did look terrible.

"This is the *only* place you can afford to do this—and it's hard on Helen. If you could *please* pull yourself together, we can have the rest of this discussion."

"What *rest*?" Mandoran demanded, not really budging. Or not really staying still; the colors were practically vibrating.

"Your cohort," Kaylin snapped back.

The rest of the colors bled from the walls back into the center of the room, as if they were liquid and someone had just pulled a plug. Mandoran stood three feet from Annarion, his arms folded in almost exactly the same way Kaylin's were. His expression was grim, his eyes narrowed slits. "...Fine," he said. "I'm listening."

It was Teela who turned to Kaylin. "We are not in contact with our...cohort, as you call them. Helen says the lack of communication is not by her choice; she doesn't interfere with us."

"I contain the unintentional noise," Helen added.

"You *can* stop communication between people who are bound by True Names," Kaylin pointed out, more for Teela's benefit than Helen's, since Helen already knew this.

"Yes. But again, I do not interfere with the cohort in that fashion. I interfere—on occasion—on your behalf. You are not entirely guarded, and I believe there is some information that you have deliberately chosen not to divulge. I merely maintain some privacy of thought while you are within my boundaries. Teela is capable of doing so on her own."

"I notice you haven't mentioned Mandoran or Annarion."

There was a small pause. "They are not, as you imagine, terribly private in their communications with their cohort. I don't think they're capable of it, but it is not necessary. For all intents and purposes, all of the cohort except Teela are like a much smaller Tha'alaan."

The Tha'alaan was not small. It was a living repository of the thoughts of an entire race, dating back—if *dating* was the right word—to its creation.

"So...the cohort sent one message and they're gone?"

"Yes."

"Are they still alive?"

Mandoran was looking slightly stretched. Annarion, however, was looking entirely like his usual self.

Again, it was Teela who answered. "Yes. If Nightshade died, you would know. We know they are still alive. But that's all we know." She let the silence stretch again before she said, "I've lived most of my life without contact with my cohort."

"But...you knew they were alive."

"I knew they were not dead. But I knew, as well, that they were beyond my reach. I could not hear them. They could not hear me. I assume this was the Hallionne's decision, but have never asked. I am not Tha'alani. I am Barrani. My life, my existence and my sanity are not predicated on my connection to the thoughts of others. There is a natural expectation of silence.

"Annarion and Mandoran don't have that. The centuries I spent in the natural silence of my interior thoughts, they spent in constant communication." She hesitated, glanced at Annarion and Mandoran, and then continued. "I am not sure they would have remained sane, otherwise. Terrano was the most...adventurous...of all of us. I haven't heard his thoughts since their return to us—but neither have they."

Terrano was the lone member of that long ago cohort who had had no desire to return to his kin. He had not reclaimed the name that had been his from just after his birth, and the names themselves were the binding that held the cohort together.

"Are you afraid that he came back for them?"

Mandoran snorted. "No. Look, he wanted—for us—what we wanted for ourselves. And we wanted, for him, what he wanted for himself. There's no way he would come back, attack them, and carry them off. There's a small chance that he approached them and attempted to convince them they'd be happier where he is now—but the rest of us would *know*."

"Fine. What *did* they see?"

Silence.

"Teela?" When Teela failed to answer, Kaylin turned to her House, figuratively speaking. "Helen." Her voice was flat; there was no wheedling in it. "What did the boys see?"

"They have been trying," Helen replied, "to describe it."

"They can't. You can."

"I can describe it to them, yes. It is not a matter of privacy, Kaylin. It is a matter of words, of experience. Something happened. The cohort have been learning from Mandoran and

Annarion. They have been practicing to live outside of the Hallionne. But they have had less practice and less contact with people like you. The closest analogue is Teela, but it is hard for them to think like Teela, because to do so, they have to experience only a narrow range of their existence.

"It is like trying to pour the contents of a pitcher into one glass. For you, it is natural; you understand how quickly water flows. You understand when to stop pouring. They are attempting to do what you naturally do when they can see neither the pitcher nor the glass."

Kaylin turned to Mandoran. She poked her familiar. Her familiar squawked and squawked again, like an angry bird.

"It is not that you would not see what happened were you there," Helen said, after a pause. "You would. But you would not see it as they saw it. You would not understand it as they might."

"If I try to stab Mandoran right now and you don't attempt to stop me, he's going to see it the way I see it."

"Yes."

It was Annarion who said, "No."

"Did someone try to stab them?"

It was Teela who said, "I think so, figuratively speaking." At Kaylin's expression, she added, "Just because you can see what someone else is seeing doesn't mean that it makes more sense. I haven't had the experiences the rest of my cohort has had. I *have* had more experience with the arcane arts that are confined to the reality I perceive. I believe, if you were to venture to the location in which they disappeared, you would find obvious—and large—traces of magical aftershocks.

"It is *possible* that those aftershocks exist for perfectly under-standable and harmless reasons—"

"But not bloody likely."

"Not in my opinion, no."

Kaylin opened her mouth. Before words came out, Helen said, "I believe Lord Nightshade has arrived."

Annarion said nothing. Mandoran, however, said a lot. In Leontine.

By this time, everyone was more or less "stable" as Helen called it, and she ushered them all into the parlor. Kaylin would have preferred the dining room, but Helen chose to ignore those preferences, probably because Nightshade was involved.

Moran was not in residence, which was the one silver lining of the evening. The last thing Moran needed was the political infighting of an entirely different caste court, given her current position.

Everyone else, however, was in the parlor. Mandoran had attempted to have Bellusdeo excluded, but Helen vetoed it, and Kaylin—who really didn't want to put the Dragon at risk— hadn't the heart to agree with Mandoran. Bellusdeo was more likely to survive extreme danger than Kaylin herself.

Nightshade appeared composed and almost casual. He also looked like he'd gotten sleep. While she knew the Barrani didn't require sleep, every other Barrani in the room, Tain included, looked like they needed about a week of it. She was certain she didn't look any better.

"Not really, dear," Helen said.

Severn was the only regular who wasn't in attendance.

Annarion's bow, when offered to his brother, was stiff and overly formal, which was not lost on Nightshade. Since the brothers had had almost two weeks of relative peace, Kaylin had hoped that this meant arguments were behind them. But no, of course not. The issues that had caused the argument hadn't been resolved.

The attempt, on Annarion's part, to resolve them had become the point of contention, widening the conflict to encompass everyone else.

Helen offered drinks to everyone present. Teela and Tain immediately accepted. They didn't ask for water. Kaylin, who already had a headache, decided that alcohol wasn't going to make it any better, but Mandoran followed the Barrani Hawks' lead. Annarion and Nightshade did not.

"Kaylin has told me some of what has occurred."

This wasn't entirely accurate, but Kaylin let it go. What mattered right at this particular moment was the cohort. All of it.

Annarion was silent. Teela, however, took the reins of the conversation, such as it was. She had always been a reckless driver—no one with any experience in the Hawks let her drive anything if they had to be a passenger—but she steered this particular conversation with ease. Probably because it was short and the Barrani were good at implying things without actually using the words.

"But they were not in the Hallionne?" Nightshade asked, when it was clear Teela had finished.

Mandoran answered. "No. They were in transit to Hallionne Orbaranne, on the portal paths."

Annarion did not glance at his brother, but it wasn't required. Kaylin suspected it was Annarion who was directing the conversation because Mandoran spoke High Barrani, and he spoke it politely and perfectly.

Nightshade considered them all. "Lord Bellusdeo," he finally said.

She was orange-eyed and regal as she nodded. Teela's eyes were blue; Tain's eyes were blue. They were seldom any other color in the presence of Nightshade.

"Lord Kaylin has been granted access to the Hallionne, should she be the agent of investigation. You however..."

"Have not."

"No."

"And would not likely be granted that access."

"No. The Hallionne are not duplicitous, in general; they would not offer you rest or shelter with the sole intent of destroying you once you were entirely within their power. At best, they would become a prison, should they be inclined to grant permission they were not built to grant. If, as I suspect, intervention is required, it would be inadvisable for you to travel west."

"And you, as outcaste, would be granted that permission?"

"I have offered blood to the Hallionne; I have paid the price of entry. Once accepted, the Hallionne will not reject me unless there is deliberate intervention."

"I do not understand how there could not be."

"No, you do not. The Dragon outcastes and the Barrani outcastes are not the same. Among your kin, you would have had both friends and enemies, as is the case with the Barrani. But the designation of outcaste has a physical meaning to your kin that it does not have to mine. The Barrani designation is political. It is oft deadly, but not, as you are aware, always.

"If the High Court considered me the danger that Dragon outcastes are considered, they might bespeak the Hallionne— but it is both time-consuming and dangerous to do so. They cannot merely mirror the Hallionne and change the guest list; they must travel in person. And the request is not delivered by the simple expedient of word."

"The Consort could do it," Kaylin said.

"Yes. But it is not without cost to her, and the High Lord seldom countenances such an action."

Kaylin hesitated again. It was marked by everyone in the room, but they were all on high alert. "Your brother's friends aren't outcaste."

"Not in the political sense, no. And they had permission to travel; they gained it during the war and it was not revoked."

"During the war."

"When they traveled to the West March at the behest of the High Court."

"...They're not the same as they were then."

"No. They carry, I am told, their names. But they are closer now to Dragon outcastes than Barrani outcastes have ever been. It is tacitly unacknowledged. The Hallionne Alsanis has restricted the flow of information about their time in his care, but he is in contact with the other Hallionne that form the road they will travel. Not until they leave Kariastos, if they travel that far, would they be required to travel across land—and Kariastos is well away from the shadowlands and ruins the Hallionne were built to guard against."

"Annarion and Mandoran did not travel the portal roads to reach Elantra."

"We'd spent enough time in the damn Hallionne," Mandoran said, dropping High Barrani in favor of the Elantran he usually preferred. "We thought it would be a nice change to travel outside of one. Mostly, it was boring. And sullen."

Annarion's expression was not nearly as neutral as Teela's as his brother continued to speak.

"The Hallionne are capable of limiting communication of any kind beyond their borders. You are aware that Helen... oversees our communication to a greater or lesser extent. Helen is not the equal of the Hallionne. If she has that functionality, it would be naive to think the Hallionne do not possess it as well."

Kaylin struggled with resentment; she didn't want Nightshade to talk about Helen as if Helen were a thing, an inanimate object.

Helen, however, did not appear to suffer the same resentment. Her gaze went to Kaylin, and one brow rose in curiosity. "He speaks of me," she said, "as if I were a building. And Kaylin, I am. It is the core of what I am." She turned once again to Nightshade. "I am not in contact with the Hallionne; I cannot say if his assumption is correct. But I believe it must be." To Nightshade, she said, "Do you believe that Kaylin will be required to visit the Hallionne?"

"I am uncertain at this point. But I do not believe it would be in the best interests of either Annarion or Mandoran to investigate in person."

"And Teela?" Kaylin asked.

"Teela has been a guest at the Hallionne after her return from the West March; she has been more, at the behest of the green. The Hallionne will not cage or attempt to destroy her. They know her and they accept her." He turned to Teela. "I have heard that there has been some difficulty in the Halls of Law."

She failed to glare at Kaylin, not that it would have made much difference to the color of her eyes. If Helen could limit communication within her boundaries, she had no control of what Nightshade could hear outside of them.

"If it is true that there is some unfortunate political unrest, this may be an appropriate time to investigate."

"I will take that into consideration," Teela replied. Her voice, like her expression, was a forbidding wall. Kaylin could well imagine what consideration meant, in this case.

Mandoran cursed in Leontine. Since no one had said anything out loud, Kaylin assumed it was at something that passed privately between the three who could speak without speaking.

"There is nothing you can do tonight," Helen said, and Kaylin revised that number to four. "Kaylin intends to visit the Consort in person."

"Oh?" Teela's word was cool. Chilly.

"Yes, dear. Her initial concern was Candallar. Kaylin is

sensitive to the idea of fieflords and their interactions within Elantra."

Teela exhaled. She did not, however, look any friendlier as she turned her glare on Nightshade. Nightshade countered with an elegant smile that was about as friendly as Teela's glare. Helen stepped between them with drinks.

"Candallar is not your problem," Teela said anyway.

"Did I encounter him while on patrol?"

"He didn't break any laws."

"Not on this side of the Ablayne, no. And frankly, I'd like to keep it that way."

Tain winced. Mandoran whistled.

"While I'm visiting the Consort, I can ask about the Hallionne."

"I consider that unwise," Teela replied.

"Probably. But she might have answers that we don't, and we're going to need them."

Mandoran coughed. "I think I'm supposed to say that the Hallionne and our friends are not your problem."

"If I'd never gone to the green, none of you would be here. You wouldn't be able to travel. The High Court politicians wouldn't be up in arms."

"I don't think there's anything wrong with asking the Consort, myself," Mandoran added.

"There is everything wrong with it at this time," Tain said. "It may have escaped your notice, but Kaylin is *mortal*."

Kaylin tried not to bristle. She failed. "I'm a Hawk." She folded her arms.

"A mortal Hawk."

"I was sent to the East Warrens. Not you."

"You wouldn't have been sent to the East Warrens if—" He stopped.

"Ifs don't matter. I was sent. I met Candallar. Candallar is a fieflord, and Candallar appears to be involved. And probably not in a good way, given what happened with the rest of the Barrani Hawks. I won't push into Teela's political problems—those are above my pay grade. They're probably above the Hawklord's pay grade. But I *will* talk to the Consort about Candallar."

"Why would you think she would have any information about Candallar?" As he asked, his gaze shifted to Nightshade.

To Kaylin's surprise, Nightshade inclined his head. It appeared to surprise some of the Barrani present as well, but did not surprise Annarion. "You are all familiar with Private Neya, surely. She will not pester—" he used the Elantran word "—the rest of the Barrani Hawks. I can give her very little relevant information about the current political substructures in the High Court, or she would pester me.

"She could ask the Lord of the West March, and may be forced to do just that if the situation with your friends deteriorates; he is familiar with Hallionne Orbaranne, and the Hallionne appears to be attached to him. But if his political strength is significant, his reach is compromised by his position; he does not dwell in the High Halls. Any threat of retribution made is made and taken with that understanding: time and distance are issues.

"She could, of course, ask An'Teela, but An'Teela will not answer. She might ask Lord Andellen, but he is almost a political outsider; his tenure as Lord of the High Court expires when Kaylin expires. He cannot build positions of true influence when he serves an outcaste.

"I believe that Kaylin is safe with the Consort; the Consort is safe with Kaylin, and not solely because she is mortal and relatively harmless. We speak that lie frequently, but the Consort does not believe it. Regardless, she will ask. Let her ask there. If she is with the Consort, no one will attack her;

if she is with the Consort, none but the most subtle will attempt to engage her at all."

"Such subtlety does exist at Court," Teela said.

"Yes."

"I will go with her."

Kaylin used Helen's begrudged mirror room to make what amounted to an appointment to speak with the Consort; the Consort was not Kaylin, and no one except perhaps possibly the High Lord, just "dropped in" for a visit. Because Barrani didn't need to sleep, the High Halls were never closed for business. Someone in official, or at least elegant, clothing responded to the mirror, activated it, and—with a narrowing of blue eyes, bid her wait.

He returned, his expression completely neutral, informed her that the Consort was willing to entertain her very "unusual" request, and told her when to arrive.

And then, hearing Annarion's raised voice in the background, Kaylin cringed and snuck back to her room and her interrupted sleep.

CHAPTER 8

"Look, you don't have to come. I'm not a four-year-old foundling caught sneaking cookies before meal time, and you are not my mother."

Teela wore Court dress, not Hawk tabard. Kaylin, technically a Lord of the High Court, was in work gear and did not intend to change. It was hard, however, to stand beside Teela in all of her elegant finery and not feel dirty, undereducated and powerless. The Hawk helped, but not much. On the other hand, her relationship with the quartermaster had never recovered from the only time she had dressed in Court-appropriate gear, and frankly, the quartermaster could make her daily life a lot more miserable than the High Court could.

Severn, likewise in tabard, accompanied her. The Hawklord had not only agreed to the meeting, but had insisted that Kaylin be paid for it—which meant it was official duty. This had drawbacks, of course. If it was official, everything was to be reported, and those reports—at least the ones Marcus didn't shred in frustration before signing—were headed for Records in one form or another.

Because Teela was not on duty for this particular meeting, Tain wasn't with them. Bellusdeo, who had Imperial permis sion to tag along on Kaylin's duties, excused herself. Technically, Bellusdeo *could* demand to be allowed to follow, but the cost of that would probably be drastically reduced Imperial permission in future.

Also, she didn't like the Barrani much. Thumbing her figurative nose at a gathering of their most powerful—and most ancient—did not strike her as wise. It was a small mercy.

If Kaylin was not part of Mandoran and Annarion's cohort, she was not absent knowledge of other True Names. Of those that she knew, only one had been taken, rather than given, and the owner of that name was generally not subtle about his dislike.

So of course, it was Ynpharion who interrupted a quiet carriage ride, Teela not being allowed to actually drive. *Tell Lord Teela that it is recommended that she avoid the great hall.*

Why?

Tell her. If I have to explain why, *you will be in the great hall before I am finished—if I am finished by then.*

"Ynpharion says that you are advised not to enter via the great hall."

"Does he?" Teela's response was cool. "Did you, by chance, ask for this advice?"

"I don't know why you insist on asking questions when you already know the answers."

"That is the very nature of tests. I know the answers, you don't."

"Fine. No I didn't."

"Sadly, that is the wrong answer." Ynpharion seemed to find this amusing.

"If we aren't entering through the great hall, how are we supposed to get to the Consort?"

"Through a less well-traveled entrance." Teela smiled. It

was not a very encouraging expression. "You're probably not going to like it much, unless your constitution in this regard has improved."

Kaylin didn't like it at all.

Teela exited the carriage at the incredibly impressive entrance, mounted the stairs and took a sharp turn at the leftmost giant statue. That statue had seen some recent damage; there were cracks in the stone base, and those cracks extended, like webbing, up the statue's height. Magic held the pieces in place for the moment, or at least Kaylin assumed it was magic, given the way her arms turned to goose bumps beneath her shirt.

She had taken off her bracer and left it on her desk; although it looked valuable, it couldn't be stolen. No matter where she dumped it—and sometimes, in a fit of frustration, she pitched it into the waters of the Ablayne—it returned to its keeper, who was standing beside her looking sympathetic.

The sensation of magic grew stronger as she followed Teela's brisk march—a march that suited the Hawk Kaylin wore, not the dress Teela had chosen. Barrani Court clothing had full skirts that allowed for running, kicking and weapon wielding. They probably only worked for Barrani.

The High Halls sported guards, but those guards were in theory unaligned; they served the High Lord. She could feel Ynpharion's frustrated contempt at her naivete and told him, *I said in theory.*

Since in his opinion the theory was at best questionable, his frustration didn't abate, but that was fine, because Kaylin recognized what Teela was leading toward. It was a portal. Portals that functioned as doorways made Kaylin literally sick, and she was doubly grateful that she had not reconsidered her choice of clothing.

"It's possible," Teela said, "that both you and the Corporal can enter the halls the normal way, if that's your preference."

"It's my preference, but we'll take the portal."

"You're certain?" Teela's reply defined the word *dubious*. It also implied that she would have no patience with Kaylin's postportal whining, if there happened to be any.

Kaylin nodded.

"You won't be much use to me in a fight after you've just gone through a portal."

"You don't think I'm much use to you in a fight, period." This pulled an almost reluctant smile from the Barrani Hawk. "And if I'm not useful, Severn will be."

Teela nodded. "Brace yourself," she added. "This is not like a normal portal."

As far as Kaylin was concerned, there were no normal portals. But Barrani structures used portals as defensive measures. The Hallionne all had portal entries. The Towers in the fiefs, with the single exception of Tara, Tiamaris's Tower, had portals. Helen would have had a portal entry if they didn't make Kaylin so profoundly nauseated.

And nausea, while bad, was not nearly as horrible as the possibility of losing a friend to internal Barrani politics. Barrani politics involved death as a matter of course; it was almost as if no game was worth playing if the stakes weren't high enough. Kaylin personally preferred her bets to be payable in cash.

This particular portal was small in shape and almost, but not quite, invisible. The delicate outline of a door frame—a Barrani door frame, which was more work-of-art than pragmatic—stood out in relief against a flat, pale piece of stone. The interior of that carved and chiseled doorway was the portal. Teela approached it quickly.

Severn waited on Kaylin, and Kaylin approached it as if it were a wall, because that's what it looked like. "I really hate this stuff."

"So does Teela," Severn said, without much sympathy. "I'd

offer to let you wait outside, but without you, we don't have an appointment."

"I know, I know. But if I'm going to do it anyway, aren't I allowed to complain?"

Severn shrugged, and Kaylin, taking that for his answer—it was a fief shrug—took a deep breath and walked into the wall.

The wall did not immediately become permeable; Kaylin cursed in mild Leontine as she whacked her nose against stone. While Teela wasn't known for her practical jokes—and why were they called practical anyway?—the wall did dissolve. But it dissolved as if it were loosely packed sand, and at that, really damn *cold* sand.

The familiar squawked loudly and bit her ear, but the sand that also surrounded that ear was cold enough she almost couldn't feel his teeth. The nausea that normally hit crept up more slowly than usual, because everything seemed to slow, except the cold.

The familiar's squawk grew louder, but his teeth didn't grow any sharper. Kaylin opened her eyes, which was not as bad an idea as she feared; she could see, and her eyes didn't immediately sting the way they would have had they been full of what she'd thought of as sand.

It wasn't sand.

To her eyes, it was almost worse. As if someone had taken visual, solid images and broken them into their component parts, reality swam in her field of view, blown this way and that by her actual movements. She couldn't see Teela, but that was fair; she couldn't see anything but random colors, gathering and resolving into partial shapes. There was no road here, no path to follow, no sense of forward that wasn't the direction she was pointing.

She almost jumped when a hand touched her back; had she not been constrained by the atmosphere she would have pivoted. As it was she stiffened, opened her mouth, sucked in particles and coughed.

But the hand was warm, and after a disoriented pause, she recognized it: it was Severn's. Her own, she could barely feel. She bent her head, closing her eyes again, and began to move forward, pushing everything aside as she did, although her feet ached and her knees almost locked.

Brace yourself, Teela had said. It was no bloody wonder she didn't use the damn portal on her usual visits.

Had she not been afraid of the ground, Kaylin might have crawled the rest of the way, however long that ended up being. She had done it before, in portal passage. Endurance was more important than dignity. The portals, which were in theory instant, were a type of unreality that caused everything in Kaylin to rebel. She was afraid she'd sink beneath whatever was under her feet, and end up buried here.

She was still thinking in Leontine when she emerged. It was sudden, startling; one minute she was pushing through an almost solid storm of intermittent physical color, and the next she was running, almost full tilt, into a wall.

She put her hands out so that her nose didn't take a second—and much harder—hit, and was shocked at how warm that wall was. Wood was never as cold as stone, but it felt almost alive beneath her frozen palms.

Teela was leaning, arms folded, against a closed door looking blue-eyed and rather bored. She raised one black brow as Kaylin coughed, loudly and repeatedly.

"What in the hells was that?"

"I told you it would be difficult."

"It was like walking—and breathing—in *sand*!"

Severn did not have the same forward momentum that had introduced Kaylin to the wall. He didn't even look cold; Kaylin's teeth were still chattering.

"Didn't you feel the cold?" she demanded.

Severn shook his head. "It had a different feel than Night-shade's portal."

"It would. The High Halls are not a Tower or a Hallionne. They are not like Helen is, or was. The portal itself is not created by the building."

"How was the portal created?"

"It's not covered in training classes," Teela replied. "And it is, at the moment, irrelevant."

"Did *you* make it?"

Teela opened the door. "We are going to be late." She left the room. The room was small, almost bare; the walls were wooden. Brass lamps hung three quarters of the way up those walls. That was it. There were no chairs, no tables, no side tables, no paintings or adornments. This was not a room in which any actual living was done.

She heard Teela bark—as if she were a sergeant—on the other side of the door and scurried to catch up. Small and squawky was spread across her shoulders as if he had just done an enormous amount of unappreciated work. The one-eyed glare he shot her implied that he resented it.

Four guards, wearing something that was the Barrani variant of a tabard, formed up around them—two in front and two in back. Teela, dressed for Court, looked every inch a Barrani High Lord. Kaylin didn't have Barrani hearing, but understood from the half-heard words that at least one of these guards had tactfully suggested that four was cutting it too close; he wanted to increase the number.

Teela was not impressed by this and the suggestion wasn't repeated. Nor did any of the other guards chime in with support. She commanded, brusquely, and they obeyed.

This was not the first time that Kaylin had been in Teela's personal rooms within the High Halls, but she felt less overwhelmed—in part because she wasn't wearing an awkward, expensive dress that made her feel a bit like a clown—and she paid slightly more attention.

She was accustomed to seeing Teela within Helen's boundaries. And before that, in her apartment, or in a tavern. She now had familiarity with Teela as a High Lord, and she was less uncomfortable with the concept than she had been. It's true she *wanted* Teela to be all Hawk, all the time, but she had come to accept that the fact that Teela had a life outside of the Halls didn't make her any less Teela.

Outside of the vestibule, for want of a better word, the walls were adorned with both hangings and paintings; there were small statues in stone alcoves between stone frames that otherwise housed wooden doors. One of those doors was warded; the others were not. There were carpet runners of a deep, deep green, with dark blue embroidery that seemed to seep up in a pattern. Edged in ivory and gold, they implied a forest at night. Or a forest of night.

"These are enchanted," Kaylin observed.

"They are. I apologize if it makes you uncomfortable. Almost anything of value within these rooms has rudimentary enchantments; some are passive, some active."

"And if I ask how they're active?"

Teela failed to reply.

Leaving Teela's personal chambers, once the outer doors had been reached, was a journey through forbidding, almost martial, stone. Where the entrance to the High Halls boasted light, magnificent statues, and pillars at least three times Kaylin's height, these halls spoke of blood and death and war for succession—any succession, any line. There were weapons, not hangings or paintings, as decorations; some had chipped blades or worn grips.

To Teela, they were irrelevant; it was the people in the

halls—dressed, Kaylin assumed, as servants—that were not. Although Teela didn't appear to actually see them, Kaylin wasn't fooled. No Barrani Hawk had eyes that blue when they weren't on high alert.

The guards formed an outer layer of protection, but Teela was at its heart. She had not chosen to wear the Dragonslaying sword, and Kaylin wondered, as the halls became slightly more crowded, if that had been smart. The weapon was almost a symbol of rank and power within the High Halls.

Kaylin wasn't terribly surprised when her arms began to ache. The High Halls, like the Imperial Palace, was meant to be relatively secure. Security meant magic. While Teela's gaze swept the Barrani in the halls, Kaylin's was focused on the walls, the floor, the small alcoves, and once, on the beams of a transitional ceiling. What Teela couldn't take down in personal combat would flatten Kaylin without difficulty; she was therefore free to practice magic recognition, such as it was.

Most magic just gave her hives. But some magic was more powerful, and to Kaylin's vision, the casting of the spell left a weave of telltale sigils in its wake. The sigils were unique to the caster; if there were three sigils, it meant that there were three different enchantments in place. Sometimes it meant three mages had worked in concert, but more often, it meant they worked in sequence. Sigils did not decay with the passage of time; they decayed with the passage of the magic itself.

Teela had once been a member of the Arcanum. Kaylin knew this, but did not know anything else, like, say, when. Or why. Or why she'd quit. Teela was sometimes like a closed book and sometimes like a bloody vault. The part of her history that involved the Arcanum was in the vault. As a result, Teela had the ability to see and recognize magic; she didn't have the ability to do so without preparation and time.

It was therefore Kaylin who said, "Stop!" in Elantran.

Teela stopped instantly. "Where?" she asked, in the same Elantran.

"Straight ahead. Maybe another ten feet." Kaylin poked the familiar. He chirped like a bird. An angry bird.

"You're frowning."

Kaylin nodded. "I can see one strong, sharp sigil. It's almost like it's been carved in the air itself—and it's not like a door ward. It doesn't seem to be embedded in anything."

"Do you recognize the sigil?"

"No, but that doesn't mean much. I can say without doubt that it's not one of Evarrim's spells."

"Lord Evarrim."

"Whatever."

"This," Teela replied, as she lifted her hands, "is why I prefer to leave you at home."

"If it helps, I don't use Dragon titles, either."

"Or table manners. Although, to be fair, yours have improved markedly in the past month. Manners, however, are particularly useful among my kin. They are tools of diplomacy when used correctly."

"According to Bellusdeo, so is war."

This pulled a chuckle out of Teela that Kaylin would have bet wasn't there. "It is to avoid deploying that tool that manners are frequently best used. Now be quiet and let me concentrate."

Severn unwound his weapon chain. If the Barrani guard found this offensive, it didn't show. Then again, both Kaylin and Severn were wearing Hawk colors, and the Barrani generally considered the Hawks barely worth notice. There *were* advantages to being invisible.

There were advantages to being multilingual as well. It meant Kaylin could understand the very quiet, very Leontine phrase that Teela used. "Can you break it?"

"Not safely—for you."

"Severn?"

"Probably." He didn't start the weapon chain spinning, and wouldn't until the guard formation changed. He looked to Teela for permission.

"What, in your opinion, does the spell do?" Teela asked.

Kaylin, however, missed the first iteration because her arms had begun to glow. Although the marks that adorned most of her skin were hidden by long sleeves, the cloth could only mute the light when it reached a certain level. "Nothing good." She swiveled her head in the familiar's direction. "Are you willing to risk him eating it?"

"There are other halls we can take, but they have different drawbacks, the biggest being the height of the ceiling."

People had passed through the sigil; it had not appeared to harm them. Kaylin pointed this out, but dubiously. Teela accepted it in the spirit with which it was offered. "The familiar?"

The small, translucent creature in question lifted a wing and folded it more or less across both of Kaylin's eyes. This time, it was Kaylin who gave in to Leontine, but hers was louder and more disgusted.

"What are you looking at?"

"I'm not completely certain but if I had to guess, I'd say it's a portal."

"A portal."

"The sigil seems to sit in the center of what might otherwise be a window—it's transparent, but it seems to sort of reflect light. Not well," she added. "But beyond that window, I can't see the hall at all. I can see something dark, and a flicker of light a few yards in that implies torches. I think there's stone or dirt floors; I can't see ceiling. Just darkness."

"When you say not certain, would you be willing to bet on it?"

"Definitely."

"With your own money?"

"Yes."

Teela was silent for another beat. "Let him eat it, if he can."

The familiar then withdrew his wing and launched himself off Kaylin's shoulder, leaving tiny claw marks in his wake. What Teela could see as a spell by casting a spell herself, he could see without apparent effort. He didn't look worried. Wings spread, he hovered directly in front of the sigil that Kaylin had first seen.

His roar at this size had never been terribly impressive, but he roared anyway, and followed it up with Dragon breath in miniature. A stream of sparkling silver smoke left his open mouth. Unlike actual Dragons, it wasn't smoke created by fire, and the cloud that formed in its wake didn't burn what it touched. It did, however, melt it.

"You know," Kaylin said, as she watched the familiar at work, "this would be a great way to erase magical evidence."

"I imagine that's just one reason why the Arcanum in concert would love to have familiars of their own," was Teela's dry response.

The sigil began to collapse, the solidity of its carved form running like the wax of a poorly made candle. It did not hit floor; it didn't hit anything. The air seemed to absorb it as they watched. Only when the familiar was done and had returned to Kaylin's shoulder did Teela signal to her guards.

"We're going to be late," she told them. They walked decisively down the hall, to no obvious ill effect. Teela followed.

The rest of the walk to the courtyard was uneventful. It was longer than it should have been because people who were apparently delighted to see Teela at Court stopped to exclaim, and there was no polite way to shut them up. They were all blue-eyed, on the other hand, and even Kaylin's inexpert knowledge of manners couldn't disguise the fact that their delight was dripping condescension—or worse.

Teela, however, answered graciously, as if their condescension was so trivial she could fail to notice it at all. Kaylin had never been confronted with so many exquisitely perfect and delighted people who nonetheless felt like they were going to war, and by the time they reached the interior forest that led, at last, to the Consort's chair she was exhausted. Teela was not.

Her guards were also accustomed to this type of interaction, but they were as blue-eyed as Teela, and to Kaylin's eye, much more obviously alert.

"Were *any* of those people your friends?" Kaylin asked, when there was a decent chance that no one, except the guards, could hear her.

"Don't be naive."

Kaylin accepted this without apparent annoyance—which took a lot of effort.

"If my actual friends were here, we would be in so very much more trouble." Her brief grin was edged; no doubt she'd said that in a way that Mandoran and Annarion could hear. She took a few more steps, and then slowed to a much more stately walk. "You consider the Hawks in the office to be friends?"

"Yes."

"That's where we differ. These men and women are my associates. We are, in one case, distantly related kin. But the distances we keep define us, not the similarities. Would they fight for me? Yes, if my interests and theirs coincided. You dislike Lord Evarrim, but he has intervened in ways that have been extremely beneficial to you in the past. We do not have to *like* each other in order to work together, when the goals are large enough to encompass our diverse interests.

"Where they are not..." She shrugged. "They suffer from the same thing Joey at the office does: curiosity. They are of course aware of the undercurrents that imply a possible shift of power in the near future, and would consider my presence at this time to be confirmation of rumors. And bold." She smiled again. "Mortals are more frequently bold when they are confident; my people are more cautious. They wish to ascertain whether my presence is indicative of bravado or certainty."

"And I'm chopped liver."

"Sadly, no."

"Why is that sad?"

"If it were not for your presence, we would not be speaking with the Consort. Since you are here with me—and since many of my people cannot conceive of a friendship or alliance with a mortal of your social insignificance—"

"Thanks, Teela."

"—the assumption is that I am manipulating you. They believe that it is my desire to speak with the Consort that has brought you here."

"But it's not."

"I did not argue that they were wise; merely curious."

"Why did you come, then?"

"I would rather they believe that you are mine, of course."

"But—"

"I am not known for my sweet temper or my pliancy. I am a woman who executed her own father. In the centuries between his crime and his punishment, I did not waver once. You are mortal. Your life span is insignificant. But my memory, and the lengths to which I will go, are not. My presence here reminds them of this, with every step I take. If you are harmed by any of the Lords here, I will destroy them. You are *kyuthe*, to me."

Kaylin glanced at Severn; his expression said, clearly, *you asked*.

"Now I ask that you be more circumspect. The Consort is not alone."

Kaylin couldn't see the Consort for the trees that girded either side of the decorative path, but the trees ended abruptly, and the circular meeting place came into view.

The Consort will see you. Approach slowly, if you wish to be politic; approach at your current speed if you wish to make a very public statement. It was Ynpharion. *She finds your immediate confusion amusing,* he added, in a tone that made it clear that he did not.

Having a head full of Barrani was not terribly comfortable, but before she could say as much—not that it was necessary, given the existence of his True Name—someone familiar stepped onto the path.

Andellen. Or rather, Lord Andellen while he was here. He swept a bow that was just one side of obsequious, but it was meant for Teela, and Teela accepted it with the same easy elegance she had accepted the far less humble approaches.

"Lord Andellen. I trust we find you well?"

"I have been busy for the past several weeks, but I am not unique in that." He then offered Kaylin and Severn a much shallower and briefer version of the same bow. It was still uncomfortable for Kaylin. Severn, however, returned it.

"I do not mean to encumber you, Lord Kaylin," he said, voice grave. "But should you require it, I will be here."

You did that on purpose.

If you refer to Lord Andellen's presence, I assure you that I am not in control of his actions. He elected to visit the High Halls today, and my schedule permitted his absence. Nightshade's interior voice was a balm when compared to Ynpharion's. This thought amused the fieflord. *I see you did choose to bring An'Teela with you.*

She chose to come, and before you say anything else, I am definitely not in control of Teela.

No. No one would assume that you were.

Teela took the lead, but subtly, and her guards shifted formation, allowing her to step forward. Which made sense. If an attack of any kind was going to occur, here was not the place it would happen. She approached the two thrones; to Kaylin's surprise both were occupied. Etiquette lessons did not involve the niceties of paying court of any kind among the Barrani. If Barrani etiquette formed the base of Imperial norms, the two weren't identical. Kaylin watched the people who seemed to be loosely milling in proximity to the thrones. She watched the way they stood, the way they conversed, the way they watched the other Lords, and the way they moved— or stood their ground.

She didn't recognize them. Lord Evarrim, whom she could recognize two city blocks away, was not present.

She wasn't shocked when the crowd more or less parted for Teela. She was, however, surprised. Teela approached the High Lord with no obvious signal from him. She then bowed, as perfectly—as obsequiously—as Andellen had bowed to her. But she held the bow until he bid her rise, and she rose slowly and gracefully, as if granting him respect that no etiquette could demand.

Kaylin watched the gathered Lords for reaction, because there was some. Most of it, however, did not involve words.

Teela approached the throne, but Kaylin lagged behind. She didn't hate the High Lord, but his position made her uncomfortable; she was far too aware of all of the skills she lacked, and even if she hadn't, she was still sworn to serve the Imperial Law with her life. Her accidental acquisition of both a name and a title didn't change that.

But the Hawks had called her a mascot, and while that was embarrassing, there was affection in it. She couldn't be that in this court. Yes, she was mortal, and yes, she was an oddity, a curiosity—but affection was no part of these Barrani Lords.

The familiar shifted position on Kaylin's shoulder, drawing himself to his full height, which wasn't terribly impressive. Or wouldn't have been had he not been alive. He nodded at the

High Lord. The High Lord raised one dark, perfect brow in the familiar's direction. Or in Kaylin's.

"You have come to visit my sister," he said, turning his attention to the familiar's perch.

Kaylin did bow, then. If her bow was awkward, that was a function of race. The Barrani would have been far more put out if she'd managed perfect anything. Thinking this, she vowed to practice until she *was* perfect, because the idea of thumbing her nose at the Barrani while doing nothing wrong that they could point out filled her with momentary glee. And that wasn't going to get anything done, and perfect would probably come through Diarmat, so she'd pay for it in up-front humiliation first.

Because she was thinking all of this, she actually waited to rise until she was given permission.

"It has been some time since you have visited us," the High Lord said.

It hadn't been that long, but Kaylin supposed that riding Dragon-back while everything beneath her that surrounded the High Halls was on fire didn't count as a visit.

"We find your company refreshing, and would be pleased should you visit us again." Kaylin sifted through these words and reached the uncertain conclusion that this was, in fact, a dismissal.

Of course it is. He knows why you're here, and he knows just how wise it is to keep the Consort waiting.

Kaylin thanked Ynpharion. Or thought she thanked him. She had been in gang wars that had caused her less anxiety. She almost backed into Teela, but Teela righted her with a subtle hand in the small of her back, and gave her a nudge in the direction of the Consort's throne.

The Consort smiled. Of the Barrani, hers were the only green eyes present—or at least the only ones Kaylin could easily see. She did not rise; instead she waited for Kaylin to approach her throne. The metrics of such an approach were fuzzy; the Consort was in theory subordinate to the High Lord.

She is not.

Fine. Kaylin offered the Consort the same deep bow she had offered the High Lord, and waited. The Consort had once left her kneeling for an entire meal—a Barrani meal, which involved a lot of empty chatter and several courses. Kaylin had endured, because she understood that this snub was punishment, and the alternative punishments were more permanent.

The Consort had, eventually, forgiven Kaylin for their extreme difference in opinions, but Kaylin, now aware that she could enrage the Consort, had never felt quite as comfortable in her presence.

"Rise, Lord Kaylin."

Kaylin rose.

The Consort then left her throne. She didn't hug Kaylin, as she had done in the past. To the High Lord, she said, "We will walk in my personal garden. I do not wish to be disturbed. If it is necessary, we will speak by the side of the Lake."

The High Lord inclined his head, and the Consort walked past the thrones until she reached a path that led away from the gathered Court. No one followed except Teela and Severn, not even Teela's guards. The Consort, however, had no bodyguards of her own. Kaylin frowned. The Consort almost never had personal guards except during actual war.

We are all *her guards. Without her, we have no future.* Whenever Ynpharion spoke of the Consort, he spoke with pride and reverence. Given that the Consort was the most approachable, the least stiffly hierarchical of the Barrani, Kaylin sometimes found the reverence hard to understand.

CHAPTER 9

When they were well away from the eyes of the gathered Court, the Consort turned to Teela. She didn't hug the Barrani Hawk, but her eyes shaded blue in an expression that spoke of worry-as-concern, and not anger or danger.

"You misunderstand," Teela said, before the Consort could speak. "Kaylin wished to speak with you, and I am here as *kyuthe*. She is not accustomed—and will probably never be accustomed—to the High Court and its undercurrents." She bowed. "I will not entangle you in the minor difficulties I face. They are not the worst that I have historically faced, and doubtless, they will not be the last. If I cannot stand, I will fall, and someone who can will take my place. That has always been our way.

"Kaylin is mortal; she doesn't understand this viscerally."

The Consort looked as if she would speak, but demurred. She then turned to Kaylin. "If you are not here for An'Teela's sake, why have you come?"

Kaylin indicated her tabard. "It's Hawk-related. I would say it's Hawk business, but I haven't found out why, yet."

The Consort chuckled. "Meaning you require a crime and have not yet found evidence of one?"

"Something like that."

"And you feel that she does not understand the Barrani." The Consort's smile was fond as she turned it on Teela.

"She is not attempting to invent a crime; she is genuinely certain one exists. Were she to be convinced that one did not exist, she would move on. It is not political on her part."

"Ah. Well. What crime am I to help you uncover then? I admit that I have been feeling somewhat—how do you say it? At loose ends? Yes. At loose ends, lately."

Teela said, to Kaylin, "She is bored. And you are never boring, in the end. Frustrating and sentimental and frequently oblivious, but never boring."

Kaylin tried not to resent this, and mostly succeeded. But she frowned. Which of course, everyone noticed, even Severn. "You're not feeling bored."

"*Bored* was not the word I used, and if you dislike it, you must take up the word choice with your *kyuthe*."

"You *are* worried." This almost entirely derailed Kaylin's attempt to put together a politic sentence that involved Candallar.

"I am always worried about something, Lord Kaylin. It comes with the responsibility of my position. It is also not considered terribly wise to make such a statement so baldly."

"Sorry."

"Distract me."

"I wanted to ask you about Candallar."

"Candallar? You speak of the outcaste fieflord of that name?"

"He's the only one I know of."

"Why do you ask about him?"

"Because I met him in person in the city I patrol."

The Consort's eyes darkened into the familiar shade of Barrani blue. "When?"

"Two days ago."

"Where?"

"It doesn't matter. I was on patrol, and he was there. He was, I believe, invisible—which is questionably legal—and he meant to meet the Barrani who otherwise patrol that area."

"Meeting with Barrani is not illegal by Imperial standards, surely?" The emphasis on *Imperial* was not flattering.

"No, of course not. But he's a fieflord, and the fieflords, with the exception of Tiamaris, don't generally come to the city for legal reasons. The people from the city who visit their fiefs don't generally visit out of the goodness of their hearts, either." Kaylin rigidly avoided looking at Teela. At all.

But the Consort didn't. "An'Teela?"

"It is your decision, Lady."

"Why do you believe I have information of relevance?"

Because you know Nightshade and you even like him was not actually a good answer. *Because Nightshade told me I should talk to you* was an even worse one, on reflection. "I don't," she finally said, speaking in Barrani. "But you are the person closest to the High Court I can talk to. You do not play politics the way that the rest of the Lords do because until there's another Consort candidate, political games are irrelevant. You see everything from above, but you can afford to remain neutral."

"Do you think I have much choice?" The Consort waited until the silence stretched thin enough for breath to break it. "I am the mother of the race. I have power. I can, in theory, refuse to offer names to my enemies. I can refuse to wake the children that are already rare enough in number. I can, in theory, do worse.

"But Kaylin, all of this was considered before the Lake was created. There are tests we must pass. The initial tests are difficult, but they are in keeping with any other test for any other training we receive as simple Barrani Lords. The Test of Name is less forgiving." The Consort bowed her head. Lifted it. "There are tests that come later, when the first are passed, that are far, far more difficult. The politically powerful often send their daughters to the Lake as supplicants. Very few are the daughters who pass the initial tests who have returned.

"In order to be mother to our race, we cannot engage in the politics which are lifeblood to many of our kin. The ambitions of our parents aside, we cannot be beholden to anyone. If the line is more important to us than the race, we will never be given the duty and the task of guarding and guiding those names."

"But I didn't *take* any of those tests!"

"No."

"And I—" Kaylin stopped. Her familiar had bitten her ear hard enough, she was certain, to draw blood.

"I have spoken at some length with Lord Andellen, purely socially. Did you know that he remains almost awed by the work you have undertaken with your mortal midwives? It garners you no acclaim—from my understanding, midwives are deplorably underappreciated by your kind. It affords you no monetary gain. It certainly does not benefit you personally. Why, then, do you do it?"

"Because I'm Chosen."

"Oh?"

"The *only* good thing that came with these marks was the ability to heal. People died because I have these marks. They were horribly murdered, and they were kids. If I can save the lives of babies, if I can save the lives of their mothers, it's like—it's not that it brings the dead back. But..." She shrugged, uncomfortable now.

"You do not do it because the marks compel you."

"No."

"You are aware that you are not the only bearer of these marks in our long history?"

Kaylin nodded.

"You are aware that their power is not sentient in any obvious fashion? That the use to which the power is put is, in theory, in large part in the hands of its bearers?"

Kaylin nodded again, but less certainly. She didn't really know what the power was or how to use it, beyond the act of healing itself. But…the words sometimes lifted *themselves* off her arms. And that implied purpose or awareness, to Kaylin.

"Could you condemn a baby to death for political reasons?"

"Of course not!"

"Of course." The Consort's smile was slender but genuine; there was a dangerous affection in it.

"The Lake tests for that? I mean, can it?"

"In a fashion, yes. More than that I cannot say. The neutrality of the mother is not absolute in matters of Court politics; we are Barrani, after all. But there is a sharp divide between that Court and our duties. It is not as difficult for me as it was for my mother; many of the people who conspired against her and her sons were people she had personally awakened. But it was not their treachery that placed the greater burden upon her."

"It was the voices of the lost." The voices of the damned, really, trapped beneath the High Halls because they did not have the strength of will—or the callousness—to escape the horror they found there.

"Yes, Kaylin. You have seen them. You have heard them. Everyone here now, everyone who *can* hear, has. I hear them," she added softly. "And the Lake weeps at the sound."

Kaylin bowed her head for a moment, a gesture of instinctive respect for the lost. But when she lifted it, she said, "Neutral doesn't mean unobservant."

The Consort's smile deepened. "No. It is unusual for someone to come to me seeking political advice, however." Unusual as a description didn't cut it, according to Ynpharion who was just one side of enraged. The wrong side, as it happened.

"There's no one else. Teela won't talk to me at all."

"Perhaps there are reasons for that. And perhaps that is why she accompanied you today."

"I doubt it."

"Then explain why you want information about Candallar." The Consort was watching Teela, although in theory the question had been aimed at Kaylin.

Kaylin sucked in air. *It's Hawk business* as a reply wasn't going to get her anything, and she knew it. "Fine. You know that Mandoran and Annarion are living with me, right?"

"I'd suggest you continue to speak in High Barrani," Teela said quietly.

"I am aware, yes. I believe most of the Court is aware of their current placement." The words and tone were neutral.

"I like them both," Kaylin continued, trying—and failing—to keep defensiveness out of her voice. "Mandoran, I'm told, is what you'd consider childish. Annarion isn't."

The Consort nodded, her expression hooded.

Kaylin teetered for one long minute, trying to choose the words for her next sentence, and finding that there were far too many of them demanding her attention. Or demanding the Consort's. She wanted to know about Candallar. It had been the reason she had requested the meeting—a meeting that had been granted with almost alarming speed.

But last night had upended priorities, as emergencies often did. And if Annarion and Mandoran weren't like Teela anymore, Teela was still one of them. She was just better at hiding panic because she'd had centuries of practice.

"You're aware that the rest of their friends have decided to come to Elantra." It wasn't a question.

The Consort nodded.

"They left the West March. They were traveling the portal paths—don't ask me why, I think it's suicidal. But something happened to them on the way there, and now we have no contact with them."

The Consort's eyes had not shifted back to green, and given the way the rest of her expression changed, they weren't going to today, either.

"We think they were attacked."

"Were they attacked by the Hallionne?"

"We don't have that information."

"The Hallionne are not political."

"They were created *for* war."

"Not entirely. Hallionne Alsanis protected Teela's friends. In as much as they were allowed to be, they were his only company. But in order to escape the cage he made for them, they altered themselves—or so Alsanis believes."

"You've spoken with Alsanis."

"Does it surprise you?"

Did it? Kaylin examined the question. "You spoke with him after we returned from the green."

She nodded. "I will not ask you how Annarion and Mandoran fare. They have not come to the High Halls, and they have not been formally introduced to me. Even were they to desire such an introduction, it is likely it would be denied. I could actively campaign to meet with them, but the High Halls are not the Hallionne. If Annarion and Mandoran are a danger—if they are an *unintentional* danger—I cannot in good conscience take that risk." She waited.

And Kaylin heard herself say, "You could come meet them at my place."

"That is very thoughtful of you," the Consort said, affecting a surprise Kaylin was suddenly certain she did not feel.

Ynpharion was both elated and furious. Elated because Kaylin had managed against all odds to do exactly as the Consort wished her to do, but could not—for political reasons—demand or even ask, and furious because Kaylin had failed to understand the very obvious request until the last minute.

"I know you're pretty busy," Kaylin began.

An'Teela is correct. Speak in High Barrani.

"So you might not be able to make it anytime soon," she continued, irritated enough to ignore what was just possibly good advice. "But you'd be welcome to just show up at any time."

The Consort laughed. Her laughter was almost the essence of delight, and her eyes practically glowed green. She did hug Kaylin, then, and Kaylin didn't even hesitate to return that hug.

"Ynpharion is much more typical of my kin than either Lord Nightshade or my brother."

"I don't suppose you know how to rid someone of the knowledge of a True Name?"

"Outside of perhaps death, no. And even if I did, I would not share." In a more serious tone, she added, "He is my one conduit to you, and he understands why you are important. He is not, perhaps, overjoyed—but joy is not a characteristic of my people; it is considered too youthful, and therefore, too easily destroyed." She stepped back. "We are not so informal as An'Teela might be, for she is *kyuthe* to you, and I am not.

"But if you would be willing to entertain in perhaps three days, I will visit."

Kaylin said yes, without thinking.

The thought part came later, in a carriage that was almost chilly with Teela's silence.

Since Teela and Kaylin did not share knowledge of a True Name, Kaylin wasn't privy to Teela's thoughts—not that it was actually necessary.

"You did not get the information you sought," Teela said pointedly. "You allowed yourself to be sidetracked."

"I allowed myself to be sidetracked," Kaylin countered, "because it's probably impossible for her to say much that isn't heard or reported on. I can guarantee that that won't happen if she's with Helen."

"That is almost a good excuse."

"Almost? No, wait, I've got this. Almost doesn't cut it."

Teela exhaled. She glared at the familiar, who squawked and shrugged. "I realize you are not responsible for her, but honestly, could you not do *something*?"

Squawk.

"Look—being shouted at is probably better than being third-personed. And I did what *she* wanted."

"I have no doubt of that; she was not particularly subtle. In fact, she was possibly the exact opposite of subtle. But she *is* a power, Kaylin, and she is Consort to the High Lord. The concerns raised at Court about my cohort are valid; they are real concerns."

"Someone's trying to use those concerns in an entirely invalid way."

"And?" Teela wore her most water-is-wet expression. "Everything is a tool."

"I'd like the Hawks to go back to a semblance of normal."

"Ah. That."

"I'm sure Candallar was meeting with Barrani Hawks."

"Yes." The water-is-wet look receded. "I would like you to stay out of my business."

"No dice. You're living in my home."

"And so are Mandoran and Annarion." Teela tilted her head back against the seat, exposing the line of her perfect throat. She even closed her eyes. "Candallar has not been outcaste for as long as Nightshade. I am uncertain whether or not he is working in concert with members of the High Court in the faint hope of being somehow reinstated; I assume that is the case—but I do not know. Nightshade has never made that attempt. And given the circumstances, I think it far more likely that Nightshade would be granted his title; he would, of course, have to fight for his lands and his ancestral home."

"They're not really his anymore."

"Oh?"

"Well, they've kind of been home to other people for a lot of centuries. People have probably been born there."

"And died there. I believe the death count outnumbers the birth count, but it is often the case that births are secluded, private, and frequently hidden affairs. There is too much risk, when the families play for power. It matters little. Were he somehow to receive the High Lord's approval, were he to become the returning son, those lands would in theory return to him."

"And the people against this are powerful enough that it's not a possibility?"

"Anything is possible where there is will and drive, but the cost might be prohibitive. Annarion understands this," she added softly. "I think, in the end, it is not a price you would be willing to pay. From your perspective, his claim predates the Empire. In your world, were you the long lost scion of Kings, and the throne still extant, you would have to slaughter untold thousands to return to it—you would not be able to take it back without an army to clear the way.

"And you would not have the stomach for that."

"Would you?"

"Yes. Were it of import to me, yes." She opened one eye and added, "If you don't like the answer, don't ask the question when the answer is obvious. While I have nothing particular against lying, I see no reason to do so merely as a sop to your sentiments." She closed the eye and continued. "Do you think Annarion is not aware of the cost of his return? He is the line—or was; his claim is almost impeccable."

"Almost?"

"He was lost to the ceremony in the green. Kitling, I know

you like them both. I am fond of them myself. But when he loses his temper—or when he's distracted—he loses his *form*. He loses cohesion. Helen has done work with him; she has worked with both of what she calls 'the boys.' Annarion is easily upset, easily offended; we all were, when we were his age. Except Sedarias. Sedarias, however, is perfectly capable of nursing a grudge while waiting for an adequate moment to act on it."

"So...she's like you."

Teela did smile then; it was feline. "She is somewhat like me, yes. Or rather, it was of Sedarias that I thought in my long isolation." The smile dimmed. "I want them back," she said, voice low, eyes closed. "I want them by my side. But I understand the danger, Kaylin. The Consort doesn't—but she will. She will fully understand it when she visits. You confuse trust and affection; you believe that people you both like and trust will, by the nature of your attachment, share your views.

"It is a mistake. The cohort will not harm her, or so I believe; only Terrano was willing to do so. I trust the Consort, I hold her in high regard, but I also believe it likely that she will agree with those who now work to prevent their entry into the High Court. She will not do so for the same reasons—no one who has power or claim has any desire to shed it, after all—but the reasons won't change the facts."

"I'm not so sure about that," Kaylin replied.

"Of course you aren't."

"No, I mean it. You can't hear what she hears, day in and day out. I could hardly bear it for the hour that I could. She hears the wails and the cries of the damned—it's a literal version of hell. I think she has hope, somewhere, that if the cohort are so very changed, they might be able to do what no one has dared to do."

"Don't say it."

"Fine." But she could think it, and did. They might be able to free the damned. "She might be willing to take the risk."

"And if they fail? Do you understand what happens if they fail?"

"They're trapped."

Teela's laugh was bitter and joyless, a stark contrast to the Consort's. "No. If it were that alone, it would signify little, except to friends and possibly family. Imagine that they are one with the Shadow. Imagine that they are twined with it. They don't *have* to stay solid. They don't have to remain in the bowels of the cavern that jails that Shadow. They can leave, as they left before. They can do irreparable damage to the High Halls, and to Elantra. It would be worse, in many ways, than the attack of the ancestors upon the Halls, and that was very costly for the Hawks."

Teela knew how to shut her up. Kaylin never wanted a police action that had such a high body account again. Ever.

"Were you Consort, would you take that risk?"

Kaylin considered it. She didn't like any of the answers she could come up with.

"The Consort's anger with you over your last disagreement—which was very, very short-lived for one of my kin—was due to the fact that you were willing to take a risk that she could not, and would never have, countenanced. She could not prevent you. She *could* prevent this."

"But it worked out."

"Yes, and I am certain that that is the only reason her anger has abated. I believe that this is a greater risk to my people. In the case of the Devourer, the risk was universal, shared, absolute."

"You think I shouldn't have invited her?"

"I think you would have, regardless. I would just like evi-

dence that you had thought about all of the consequences before you opened your mouth."

"Oh."

By the time the carriage had reached the Halls of Law,
Kaylin had had more than enough time to think; thinking
had devolved into fretting, which had sunk further into self-
recrimination. Severn was so silent, he might not have been
there at all. But he'd been that way in the Court as well. The
Consort seldom addressed him directly, as if he were a simple
bodyguard or even servant, neither of which Kaylin had the
money or the status to acquire.

Teela dropped them off at the front gates. The Barrani
Hawks were still not on the active roster, and she was not
therefore expected to be in at a given time. Her clothing was
meant for the High Halls, and while she *could* perform her
duties dressed like a queen, the rest of the Hawks would find
it uncomfortable. Either that, or they'd be gawking.

"I didn't think," Kaylin said, almost before her foot hit
actual street. She glanced up at the Halls of Law, and at the
door guards.

"You're worried about Bellusdeo," Severn observed.

"I'm not worried *about* her. The Consort would never try
to harm her. I'm worried about what's going to be said *to me*
if I don't somehow clear the visit first."

"But you're not going to clear it."

She shook her head. "My home isn't a political place, all
visitors aside. If I have to ask permission to have guests in my
own home, it won't feel like it's mine at all. Plus, it'll just piss
Bellusdeo off. Especially if they say no."

"And by *they* you mean the Dragon Court."

"Diarmat's going to flip a table. Or worse."

"And the Emperor?"

That was the crux of it. "He won't say no. He just won't say it really, really loudly. If Bellusdeo's around when he's doing it, she'll say something."

Severn's grimace made clear that he understood what "something" entailed.

"They've just started almost speaking like civil adults. I'd just as soon not break that immediately."

Severn lead the way through Clint and Tanner before he continued. "And Annarion?"

"What if Teela's right?"

"Look at it this way. If Teela's right—and I consider the chance high—it's information that would come out regardless. This way, they'll have warning."

This didn't make Kaylin feel any more cheerful. "If the High Court can pretend the cohort doesn't exist, the cohort are safe. But what if the High Court decides that they're all to be made outcaste? Before the cohort made the decision to join Annarion, we could all pretend that they were normal Barrani.

"Now? Not so much. And if the not so much holds true, the High Court has to make a decision."

"And this is part of Teela's business."

"Yeah. The part she asked us to stay out of."

"Not us."

Kaylin glared at her partner. "But...Candallar's probably involved in it as well. And there's the not insignificant fact that Teela *is* a Lord of the High Court and someone tried to kill her."

"She considers that both normal and acceptable."

"I'm not so sure." Kaylin could clearly recall Teela's expression in the infirmary. "Oh, about the assassination attempt? Sure. But not the method. She's angry. If the High Lord attempted to kill her—without making her outcaste—she'd consider it normal and acceptable. She's a power. He's a power.

"But the Hawks? They're not. For one reason or another, they didn't take the Test of Name. They followed her when she came to join the Hawks, as far as I can tell. They're *not* powers. It's like they decided not to join the game when they decided not to face the Test. And they're being dragged into it as well."

"And you think Candallar has something to do with it."

"You don't?"

He shrugged. "What you are to Teela, I'm not. When she tells me to stay out of her business, I listen."

"But—it interfered with the *Hawks*. It's Hawk business."

He was politic enough not to bother answering. Even the Hawks stayed out of Barrani business if the Barrani happened to be Hawks.

After filing her report, Kaylin made a detour to the infirmary, and was not surprised—or not *very* surprised—to see Teela sitting by the bedside of the man who had tried to kill her. She would have looked like thunder, if thunder happened in the middle of a very icy blizzard.

Moran gave her the side-eye as she entered the room. "If you were any other Hawk," she said, her voice pitched low enough that it wouldn't disturb the patient, but not low enough that it wouldn't be picked up by Teela, "I'd tell you to mind your own business. I have, however, lived with you, and what you define as your own business is almost criminally broad."

"Teela will be moving in with me for a while."

"Then she either accepts that you're going to be involved, or she is extraordinarily optimistic for a Barrani." Moran did, however, catch her by the arm as she attempted to move past her to evade the rest of the lecture. "I've half a mind to ask Helen if I can come for a visit."

"You just left."

"And I regret my timing. I won't tell you not to do what

you feel is right. But I really want you to consider the ramifications."

"So I'll change my mind?"

Moran snorted. "So you'll have some warning and be a little bit better prepared. That's the trick to being a power. It's also why anyone sane and reasonable doesn't really want to become one." She released Kaylin's arm. "If this kills you or harms you…"

"I'm not going to feel any worse than you would have felt," Teela said sharply.

"And I know how I would have felt," Moran replied. "I think she's probably in less danger right now—but I wouldn't bet on it, given Mandoran and Annarion."

"She invited the Consort to dinner. The Consort accepted."

"I *really* wouldn't bet on it."

CHAPTER 10

Kaylin did not understand the point of dinner guests. Or rather, of having guests over for dinner. She understood the concept of eating. She understood the concept of eating with friends. Clearly a meal that one was serving, and to which one invited friends, was somehow *entirely different*.

Bellusdeo, who disliked the fussiness of what was now considered good table manners, was inclined to agree, but without the frustration. Her eyes had shaded orange, but only slightly, when she had been informed of the Consort's pending visit.

"No," she said, before Kaylin could suggest it, "I think it highly unwise to have the Emperor and the Consort together at the same dinner table. I would like to meet your Consort, and I admit it might be amusing to watch the two of them in the same room—but in this case, amusement would likely be fleeting, and consequences would not."

Annarion, on the other hand, was practically hyperventilating. Mandoran, the more laid back of the two—well, technically, *the* most laid back Barrani she had ever met— was also blue-eyed and tense. Since they occupied the dining room, which was kind of Helen's equivalent to the mess hall in the office, Kaylin pulled up a chair.

Nightshade had once again been allowed to speak to Kaylin through the shared bond of his name. When Helen was not feeling charitable, he couldn't—not when Kaylin was at home. Clearly, Helen was feeling charitable. Either that or she thought Nightshade would say something she wanted Kaylin to hear. Regardless of Helen's motivations, Kaylin wasn't terribly surprised to hear Nightshade, loud and clear.

The fieflord was not Ynpharion, but he found Kaylin's entirely casual invitation almost as dumbfounding as the disapproving Barrani Lord did.

She is akin to an Empress, he said, in a chilly internal tone. *To the Barrani, inviting the Consort to dinner is only slightly less political than inviting the* High Lord.

It's not political.

It is. You did not have political intentions. Your intentions, however, do not matter. I am slightly surprised that the Lady agreed to your request. And not entirely pleased, Kaylin thought. She disagreed. Politics was all about intention.

No, it is not. You are thinking like a Hawk.

Because I am one.

Very well. Politics of the nature with which you are familiar are about preventing crimes, or rather, preventing their consequences in regard to oneself. Think of yourself as a corpse. To you, it doesn't matter if you died because you caught a disease, got hit by a carriage, or had your throat slit. In the case of the latter, it is probably a much kinder death than the illness. As a Hawk, the only death that matters is the latter.

But you are not a Hawk here. The outcome is the important factor because it is the only one which will be seen. In the case of my example, that is the death. In the case of the Consort, it is her condescension. Her presence. You have extended an invitation. This is not unusual, although in your case, given your race, it would be considered presumptuous.

Of course it would.

She has, however, accepted. *In the best case, she will be considered overindulgent and willfully sentimental—you would be seen as a favored pet.*

She'd been on the books as official mascot before she was old enough to join the Hawks as an actual officer of the law. She could live with that, and had.

In the worst case, you will be seen as a threat. The Consort's dignity is above visiting an insignificant mortal who is not even a member of the Caste Court. If she is willing to publicly accept this loss of dignity, it must be because you hold power over her.

Or maybe we're friends?

The powerful do not have friends.

Kaylin's teeth were going to be smooth nubs, she was grinding them so heavily. She didn't, however, want to have an argument with Nightshade about friendship. Or anything, really.

I am not arguing, he predictably said. *But you have entered into a political arena. What matters is not what* you *believe, here; it is what will* be *seen* and *believed by others. And I concur with Bellusdeo. If the Emperor is to visit again—*

He is.

—it would be best for all *involved if that visit did not overlap with the Consort's. The Consort is not your enemy, but she has enemies. She has fewer enemies than any others who would hold rank in the High Court, but fewer in the case of the Barrani does not imply safety.*

But no Barrani would hurt her.

Not directly, no. Nor would they kill her if they had that option; it is not in the best interests of the race, and not in the interests of those whose families are not secure. But to control her? Yes.

Kaylin frowned, thinking. *What would they want from her? She won't refuse to name their children—I don't think she can.*

No. But it is the belief of my kin that the Consort chooses the name. Always. For some, interfering with, and heavily influencing, that choice would be considered in the best interests of the family. And that, she could do.

I don't think it works that way.

No. And for the record, neither do I. But the mysteries of the Lake are shrouded and uncertain to my kin; only the Consort knows and understands them. She is also the Lady, wife to the High Lord, and her political power and influence is strong. She might decline to use them as most of my kin would, but it is not because she lacks the tools.

Why do you think she wants to come here?

It is secure, for one. But I believe that she wishes to meet and evaluate Teela's kin, and at the moment, they are not precisely welcome in the High Halls. They could go. I could not, however, supervise a visit there. Andellen could. But he considers it highly unwise.

So do you.

Ah. You'd noticed that? His voice was dry as kindling. *It is not too late to rethink the invitation you have extended. Were I you, I would do so.*

I think Annarion would be upset.

Nightshade said nothing.

The Barrani Hawks were back on duty the following day, minus the one who remained in the infirmary under Moran's care. Teela and Tain were sent to the warrens. Kaylin was almost certain that the request had been made by Teela, which was technically against the rules—but the people who handled the paperwork were Hawks, and they knew when technicalities had to be ignored.

There had been no word from the Imperial Mages; investigation of the security of the mirror network was clearly not their first priority, but that did give the Hawklord an excuse to curtail acceptance of external mirror messages. It was an obvious attempt to delay acceptance of Barrani Caste Court notification. Kaylin did not believe there had been a breach of the mirror network, and she was pretty certain the Hawklord didn't, either.

Severn and Kaylin were back on Elani. If the office was

quiet—and it was—it wasn't the fear-laden variety. It was the breath-held variety, and Kaylin was just as happy to patrol as remain there. She'd never been good at figuring out when to break an awkward silence, and even when she had managed to make this intuitive leap, was pretty bad at breaking it in a way that wasn't as awkward.

Annarion, after overcoming his initial shock, had doubled down on practicing with Helen with the news of the Consort's visit; he was grim, silent, and absent at breakfast. Mandoran was present but looked hungover, which in theory didn't happen to Barrani. He gave Kaylin a baleful glare, followed immediately by a wince.

"When's Teela coming to stay?"

"Soon."

"Meaning you don't know."

"Meaning I don't know exactly, no. In case you missed it, she's not my responsibility. And she really hates it when people fuss over her." After a brief pause, Kaylin then asked, "Have you gotten any more out of her?"

"About the assassination attempt?"

"That, yes."

"Nothing. I think she's afraid I'll tell you."

"It's Hawk business."

"And when you're the Hawklord, I'm sure she'll open up and become forthcoming. Until reality fractures, it's not happening. Don't look at me like that. Thanks to you, I'm living with Mr. Obsessive." His grimace deepened as he pushed himself up from the table. "And when I say *living*, I use that word because there's no suitable bad one."

Mandoran stayed home when Bellusdeo and Kaylin left for the office. He had clearly regretted the necessity, but Annarion insisted on company in his misery.

Kaylin was surprised at how used to Bellusdeo's company she'd become. She was apparently enough of a fixture on the

Elani beat that Kaylin had gratefully resumed that most of the merchants and regular customers now failed to notice her.

Her familiar was perched alertly on her left shoulder, and occasionally he chittered like a bird. This grabbed more attention than when he sprawled like a lifeless scarf, but if she was being fair, not a lot more. She had become completely accustomed to having Hope around, and wondered if *he* could be made the Hawk's official mascot, since the position hadn't been filled when Kaylin had graduated from it.

Someone, however, had pointed out that something that looked like a Dragon, even if glass and in miniature, was never going to be made an official mascot. To anyone who didn't know Kaylin's familiar, the visual would be thumbing the Hawks' collective nose in the Emperor's direction, and given that the Hawks in theory served the Emperor, that would be bad.

"Evanton?" Severn asked.

Kaylin shook her head. "And no Margot, either. I'd like a normal, boring day if it's all the same to you."

"That's a pity."

"Oh?"

"I think I see Grethan in the window."

Kaylin liked Grethan. Given their first encounter, she would have bet that would be impossible. But he worked hard, he obeyed Evanton, and he seemed to be helpful. It didn't hurt that Kaylin's familiar seemed to really like him as well; he immediately pushed himself off Kaylin and landed on the apprentice.

Grethan's forehead antennae were weaving in and around the familiar's face as Grethan spoke. Kaylin waited until their greetings had more or less finished, and then cleared her throat.

The apprentice blushed. "He's waiting for you in the kitchen."

"Any idea what he wants?"

"No, sorry. If it helps, he's not in a bad mood today." He hesitated and then added, "He's been in a bad mood all week— if you could maybe not irritate him, I'd really, *really* appreciate it."

Evanton was, as Grethan indicated, sitting in the kitchen in front of a pot of steaming tea, none of which he usually drank.

"Is this going to take a while?" she asked as she slid into a chair and looked for the cookie tin.

"Why do you ask?"

"You made tea."

"It happens on occasion when I'm entertaining guests."

"You were expecting someone else?"

"I was expecting you, of course."

"I'm on duty," she told him.

"Corporal?"

Severn smiled and shook his head; he could drink tea, but seldom did while on duty. Kaylin, however, looked at the counter, on which the cookie tin rested. Evanton nodded and she rose to fetch it.

"I have heard disturbing rumors," he said, while she was prying the slightly warped lid off.

"About?"

"The West March."

Kaylin cringed. Because she could eat at any time, she took a cookie before she returned to the table, leaving the open tin on the counter. At a raised eyebrow, she rose and put the lid back, as Evanton wasn't terribly fond of mice, and apparently had some anyway.

"Yes," she said, deflating, "there have been some problems."

Bellusdeo treated Evanton with respect; in Kaylin's experience, Evanton was the only obvious recipient of Bellusdeo's deference. The Dragon's eyes were orange. "You seldom mention rumors that are irrelevant. What do you feel it is important for us to know?"

Evanton smiled, which deepened the lines around the corners of his mouth and eyes. "I call them rumors for a reason. In this case, the information conveyed to me was done so indirectly. There is some danger involving the Hallionne."

Silence. Bellusdeo passed the conversation back to Kaylin with a glance.

"Did your rumors detail which Hallionne?"

"Ah, no. It appears to be a collective problem. I am not," he added, "Barrani, and I have not traveled by the Hallionne paths for a very, very long time. Before you ask, my prior experience is irrelevant, and regardless, I am not in a position to travel now."

Kaylin's frown grew extra lines. "Have you talked to Teela?"

"It so happens that she dropped by to pay her respects, yes. And by respect, I do not mean slouch at the table and eat all the cookies."

Kaylin straightened up.

"Better. She wanted to speak about Mandoran."

"Specifically Mandoran?"

"The garden was not pleased to see him the first time he visited, if you recall. She wished me to speak specifically with the wild elements to ascertain exactly why."

"The elements don't work that way."

"No. Very good, by the way." He waited.

"She can't possibly expect *me* to talk to the elements?"

"I assure you she doesn't."

"...You want me to talk to them."

"I would appreciate any attempt you might make to talk to the water. Teela did not seem particularly interested in that solution. But you appear to have an affinity for it. The water is the primary source of my rumors, and the water is...very concerned."

"Did the water explain what her difficulty with Mandoran was?"

Evanton exhaled. "No, not precisely. The water does speak in a fashion that the other elements do not—no doubt due to the influence of the Tha'alaan. But the words the water offered were opaque. The element understands their meaning. I do not; Teela did not appear to understand them, either.

"But the water's replies to An'Teela's questions—through me as intermediary—were broader than Mandoran. There is concern about people who are similar to Mandoran, at least if I understood what was said." He did not look at all certain. "In your parlance," he added, "and with deference to Bellusdeo, there is a possibility of the involvement of Shadow." He held up a hand as Bellusdeo opened her mouth. "It is not a certainty, and I do not guarantee certainty without some conversation with the water itself."

"Did I mention I'm on duty?"

"I would, of course, as a merchant who pays taxes, expect you to do this on your own time."

Of course.

Bellusdeo was not happy to wait, but understood Kaylin's reasons. Barely. The Dragon was aware, however, that even the mention of Shadow sent her into panic mode, and she was willing to walk out the duration of an Elani beat that had become irrelevant to her.

The rest of the Elani patrol passed without incident. Kaylin returned to the Halls, filed a brief report which went into the "not an emergency and can be shredded" pile on Marcus's desk, and then paced the office floors. She was now afraid of two things.

One: the Consort would agree with the Lords who wanted Teela's cohort to be made outcaste, and two: the Emperor would lose his scales when she attempted to cancel *his* dinner.

The former would mean that she would once again be in conflict with the Consort, and she wasn't certain that she would be forgiven as easily or as quickly a second time. The latter meant that she would be in conflict with the Emperor, because she would have to explain *why* she was canceling the informal dinner. She had never explicitly said much about either Annarion or Mandoran.

While it was true that the attack on the High Halls at the heart of the upscale part of the city was technically their fault, they hadn't called the ancestors on purpose. They wouldn't have been aware they were calling them at all had it not been for Helen, and they remained indoors—or at least Annarion did—in a desperate attempt to learn to be *silent*.

Mandoran found it easier; Kaylin wasn't certain why. Mandoran was therefore allowed out of doors, because Helen didn't consider him to be a danger. Either that or she just wanted peace and quiet; Mandoran was chatty. And whiny.

But the Emperor's hoard was the empire, and the heart of the empire was his city. He was unlikely to calmly accept that the loss of so many lives had been accidental, and seen that way, Kaylin wouldn't entirely blame him. But she was a Hawk, and intent did matter.

Helen was waiting at the door when Kaylin arrived home.

"What happened?"

"You have an appointment at the palace."

"Since when?"

"Since this afternoon. I believe both you and Bellusdeo are expected to attend Lord Diarmat."

"Since when?"

"As I said—"

"We've been given indefinite leave from those lessons!"

"You were given leave from them during the Aerian crisis,

yes. And during Lord Diarmat's recovery. He believes, however, that he has recovered enough to recommence."

"But—"

"Word has reached the Imperial Court of your invitation
to the Consort. In and of itself, this would not constitute an
emergency. Word, however, has also made clear that the Consort has accepted."

Kaylin wilted. "I'm supposed to go talk to Evanton after
dinner."

"Evanton, I'm afraid, will have to wait."

"I think it's about the cohort. And the Hallionne. He wants
me to talk to the elemental water, because he thinks she knows
something."

Helen sighed. "I'll leave it up to you, dear. I know it might
make things easier for the boys—and for Teela, who is very,
very worried. But I also know that ignoring Lord Diarmat
means that your interactions with him in future will be even
more difficult."

Kaylin snorted. "I don't think that's possible."

"Oh, it's possible," Bellusdeo said. "Why are you just standing there? We're going to be late."

Kaylin had about a hundred good arguments for why she
wasn't going at all—but the thought of being late to a lesson
taught by Diarmat was enough to swamp them all with a kind
of visceral dread.

"Your carriage is almost at the door," Helen announced.
"It should be here momentarily."

Of course there was a carriage, feet being inappropriate for
a Lord of the Dragon Court. Then again, wings were better
than feet, and they were technically illegal without Imperial
permission. Bellusdeo did not ask anyone for permission. The
Dragon was wearing her feline grin as she made her way to
the front door, where Helen waited.

Kaylin was surprised when she therefore spoke in her serious voice.

"I'm worried about the boys, too."

"Mandoran will have conniptions if he knows you're calling them that."

"Mandoran has conniptions when he's breathing. He'll live." Bellusdeo exhaled a thin stream of smoke. "I admit that I've been curious about the Consort for a while, and as your last informal dinner was surprisingly enjoyable, I think I'd enjoy this one."

"Did you tell Diarmat?"

Bellusdeo raised a brow in Kaylin's direction. "Since I don't consider a dinner an emergency, no. I generally attempt to curtail all communication with Diarmat."

"Would you mind very much if I strangled Emmerian?"

The second brow joined the first. "Why Emmerian?"

"If you weren't the source, he probably was."

"I wouldn't mind terribly if you tried—he doesn't seem to have our racial temper, and it's not likely to get you killed. It is, however, likely to be humiliating for you, and I have to live with you." She exhaled again, without apparently having bothered to inhale first. "This is tied in to Candallar, yes?"

"I think so. One of the Hawks *did* try to kill Teela. She's officially saying Canatel's involvement was all a misunderstanding, by the way."

"Yes, attempts at murder are often misunderstandings. Unless it involves armies, in which case it's diplomacy. I understand why she lied, though."

"Maybe it's not a lie."

"Maybe I'm not a Dragon." The familiar squawked and the Dragon sighed. "Teela is a Lord. She's a ruler on a very small scale. The Barrani who joined the Hawks probably did so at her command. Implicit in that command is the power to protect, and in this case, she considers the failure her own. She does not feel betrayed."

"Would you?"

"I'm a Dragon, Kaylin."

"So…that's a yes? Or a no?"

"Yes, I would feel betrayed. But Dragons in the Aeries resolved these so-called misunderstandings immediately; they did not wait, lie, and attempt to discern the source of the difficulty; they did not stoop to politics. Either I would have died, or the attacker would have died; I would not be concerned with his life. Teela is. She's surprising to me, in many ways. I understand why Annarion and Mandoran are different— they're young." Before Kaylin could correct her, she lifted a hand. "If they are ancient, they are ancient in the same way I am. We are all displaced, Kaylin. We are all people who no longer have a home."

"You've got Helen."

"Helen is yours. None of us would have Helen if Helen had not chosen you, and she would have chosen none of us had we applied—is that the correct word?—for lodging."

"You can't know that—"

"She is correct," Helen said.

"But—"

"What Bellusdeo, Annarion or Mandoran want from a home is not what you wanted. What they want, I *could* give, but it's not what *I* want. I do not judge them unworthy," she added, correctly divining Kaylin's objection. "I like them all a great deal. But liking and living with are not the same. What I wanted to *be*, you wanted. That is why I chose you."

Bellusdeo nodded, unruffled. "You had no home for most of your living memory. Not until you crossed the Ablayne, and even then, you were out of place: you were far too young to be a Hawk, and too young to be living on your own."

"I lived on my own," Kaylin said, trying not to feel indignant.

"You had your own apartment, yes—one which Caitlin found for you. But everyone you knew had keys."

"Not *everyone*."

"The point is: you were also an outsider. And you wanted to come *inside*, which I believe is considered perfectly normal for humans. Barrani might, when very young, have some of that same desire—but they understand, if they survive, that inside is often far more deadly. And Dragons? We don't share well. It takes concentrated effort, and a type of self-control that is lamentably rare among my kin. We don't *require* company.

"If you want, I'll head Diarmat off, and you can go to Evanton's."

"The Emperor will have my head."

"Oh?" This was distinctly chillier. Kaylin almost kicked herself. She had not expected to like the Emperor—and in truth, he seemed a bit above something as petty as like or dislike—but she hadn't expected to feel any sympathy for him. Ever. Yet she did. She understood that in his own fashion he was trying his level best, where Bellusdeo was concerned, and she didn't want to become the reason that Bellusdeo continued her dogged anger at him.

"I didn't know this was going to turn political."

"No one with any familiarity with you—even a passing one—would expect that you had political motivations. No one, however, believes that the Consort does not. Teela will be moving in—I think she's halfway done. There was some argument with Tain which we all pretended not to hear. Helen's attempt to referee the argument—*referee* is the word, yes? No?"

"I don't think *referee* is the word you want."

"I can't think of a better one."

"Mediate?"

"Fine. Mediate. Helen's attempt at mediation was to tell

them both that it was entirely up to you." Bellusdeo snickered. "I thought you'd appreciate that. You're certain you don't want to go to Evanton's?"

Lord Diarmat reminded Kaylin of the very worst of her teachers at the Halls of Law. No, that wasn't true. It made her *nostalgic* for the very worst of those teachers. He was waiting for them in the large room that Kaylin thought of as the war room, his arms folded, a thin stream of smoke coming out of his nostrils. His eyes were dangerously orange. His color seemed off, but he was a Dragon and Kaylin had very little knowledge of Dragons that didn't come from Bellusdeo. She knew enough about this one, on the other hand, not to offer open concern. He was glaring.

"We're not late," Bellusdeo said, her voice the same shade of cool she used whenever she spoke of the Emperor, her tone as critical as Diarmat's when he was speaking to, or at, Kaylin. "And honestly, your color is terrible. We are not babes in arms; I believe that we could muddle through without dragging you from your warming stones."

This did nothing good for the shade of Diarmat's eyes.

"You are not a hatchling; you are fully politically cognizant. You are not, however, in charge of Private Neya. I am here to assess her ability to entertain the *ruling consort* of the Barrani High Court without embarrassment to either the Barrani or the Emperor."

"I highly doubt the Consort is so unfamiliar with *Lord* Kaylin that she expects to be treated as if she were a Dragon Lord."

Diarmat looked about as unamused as he could, short of breathing fire. Bellusdeo looked condescending. Kaylin probably looked ill.

"The correct form of address for the Consort?" His tone was pointed.

"Consort."

Bellusdeo winced.

"Sit down, Private. Let me explain what could be at stake for you and your putative career. As a private, you do not extend invitations to the High Lord or his Lady without permission from the Dragon Court."

"I didn't invite her as a private."

"And if you are not a private of the Halls of Law, you may feel free to do as you please. Until then, your behavior reflects on the glory of the Eternal Emperor." And not to the better, his tone implied. Given his eye color, Kaylin was grudgingly surprised that he left it at implication. "Lord Bellusdeo's presence within your domicile necessitates surveillance. The Barrani will likely accept this as a matter of course. We cannot, however, stop the Consort and check her thoroughly.

"We would like to have a representative of the Court present at your home."

"You do. Bellusdeo *lives* there."

"She is not a member of the Dragon Court."

"She's a Dragon Lord as far as the Halls are concerned."

"It is irrelevant what the rank and file at the Halls tell themselves. We are aware that she currently lives with you, but she has not undertaken the responsibilities of the Dragon Court in anything but a cursory way."

"Lannagaros has kindly offered to oversee the meal," Bellusdeo said. She didn't look like she'd breathe fire; she looked like she'd breathe ice.

"Has he?"

"Yes. If you would care to ask him, I am certain Lord Kaylin and I would be willing to wait. We might study the report you seem to have at hand; it looks infuriatingly like the layers of bureaucracy—that is the word, yes?" she added, to Kaylin, who tried not to cringe and failed to reply. "The bureaucracy in which your Court is mired. It is hard to imagine that you actually fought in the Draco-Barrani wars, given your adoption of so many of their peculiarities; I am uncertain how different their victory would have looked."

Kaylin did not take a step back, but that took serious effort. Had she realized Bellusdeo would be so openly antagonistic, she would have tried to leave her at home.

Lord Diarmat, however, did not breathe fire. Instead he handed the report—and Bellusdeo had not exaggerated—to the Dragon. "I will speak with the *Arkon*. Please feel free to peruse the report."

"Will there be a test?" she asked sweetly.

"Oh, most assuredly." He walked out. He actually opened the door first, which Kaylin wouldn't have bet on. Only when she could no longer hear his footsteps did she turn to Bellusdeo, whose eyes were a simmering orange. "Was that *really* necessary?"

"His part or my part?"

"Your part. Diarmat isn't capable of behaving any differently; I think it would kill him."

"It might kill him yet," was the dire reply.

"And he's going to march to the library, interrupt the Arkon, and discover that you lied."

"You know what I've said about betting?"

"That it's a waste of time and you don't understand its appeal?"

"I would like to rescind that. What would you care to bet?"

"You talked to the Arkon?"

"As it happens, I did not consult with Lannagaros, no."

"So you expect he's going to lie?"

"Not at all. I expect he's going to confirm that he would be delighted to join us for dinner. As it seems to be Diarmat's insistence that we have a minder for the visit, and the Arkon is the most senior member of the Court, there's not a lot Diarmat can say."

"I'm sure he'll surprise you—I think he can say a lot." She

grimaced and looked at the report which Bellusdeo had not even opened. "Let me see that."

"You can't honestly imagine it will have useful information?"

"Not that I want to defend Diarmat, but actually, I imagine it has a lot of what he considers useful or necessary information. And to be fair to him? Some of it probably is."

"You're actually going to read it." Bellusdeo was nonplused.

"The Imperial spies are probably a lot more forthcoming than the Barrani themselves. If the Emperor is concerned about political upheaval as a result of this dinner, it's probably going to have information on how or why that upheaval might occur. Yes, I'm going to read it. It'll probably tell me more about the High Court than the Consort or Teela would." She warmed up to that thought. "Diarmat was severely injured fighting to *protect* the High Halls, and I'm certain his personal preferences would be to see the Barrani as a giant heap of collective ash. He's going to look down on me no matter what I do, I can't change that.

"But this might be useful. Do you think he'll let me keep it?"

"Kitling," Bellusdeo said, her eyes as gold as they had been since entering a room that also contained Lord Diarmat, "Sometimes you really surprise me. In a good way. Yes, I'm certain he'll let you keep it. If you ask, he might be slightly mollified."

"Could you *try* to stop antagonizing him on my behalf?"

"I'm doing it on my own behalf."

"Then could you try to antagonize him when I'm not here? He's had it in for me since the first day we met—and I'm his only safe target."

"Which is contemptible; it is hardly deserving of consideration."

Kaylin generally agreed with this. "I don't think he's trying to be contemptible. I think he's worried." Before Bellusdeo could speak, she rushed on. "Look—I'm the last person *I* would send into diplomatic waters. I'm only sent to the expensive parts of town when there's been magical interference, or worse, and I'm sent with senior Hawks who do all the talking. I'm trying to learn how to behave—"

"I see nothing wrong with your behavior."

"—like a Hawk. I'm trying to think before I speak. But I often fail, and I don't want that to reflect poorly on the Halls of Law. He's not wrong about me and diplomacy."

"Why is it that you're expected to conform to everyone else, and not the other way around?"

"Because I'm mortal, and I'm a private?"

"That was rhetorical. From everything you've said, the Consort knows what you're like, and she accepted the invitation. She's hardly going to start a diplomatic dustup if you fail to behave like any other Barrani Lord."

"Oh—and that's another thing. Could you *please* stop calling me 'Lord Kaylin?'"

CHAPTER 11

Lord Diarmat was not gone long. Kaylin had made it through four pages of High Barrani when the door opened; she almost dropped the report. But she wasn't doing anything wrong, even by draconian standards, and managed to maintain her grip on what was essentially a large book.

"It appears," Lord Diarmat said, to Bellusdeo, not Kaylin, "that the Arkon is, indeed, planning to attend." The words sounded more like an accusation than a confirmation.

"We have therefore satisfied the Imperial condition. A member of the Dragon Court will be in attendance, and he will oversee *Lord* Kaylin's meeting with the Consort. Is there anything else?"

"Forms of address."

"Lord Kaylin has an appointment of some import this evening. If you could keep this short and to the point, I'm sure it would be appreciated."

The familiar sighed loudly in Kaylin's left ear. This was enough of a warning that she could lift her free hand—the one not gripping a sheaf of bound papers—to cover that ear. He squawked. Loudly.

Both of the Dragons turned to look at him. As he was

pretty much sitting right beside Kaylin's face, that meant they were staring at her. But they weren't glaring.

Squawk. Squawk.

"Can you understand him?" Kaylin asked Diarmat, forgetting entirely the correct form of address.

Diarmat's expression made clear that he noticed. Then again, he noticed everything. "I can. I do not understand all of what he says. Do you understand any of it?"

"Not well." As his expression shifted, she surrendered. "Not at all, not when he's this size. I understand him when he's bigger. Or when he's...not in this shape."

"I will not hold you responsible for his actions or his comments, but I suggest you train him."

This caused predictable outrage on the part of her left shoulder ornament, but it lightened Bellusdeo's orange eyes a bit.

Diarmat did not ignore this, however. He bowed to the familiar. "My apologies. It is your size. I forget myself."

Bellusdeo gasped in theatrical shock, which soured Diarmat's grim expression further. But for a moment, Kaylin felt as if she were at her breakfast table, and both Mandoran and Bellusdeo were champing at the bit in frustration and boredom. Diarmat did not keep score the way Mandoran did; he didn't make a game of it. But she thought he made a game of nothing in his life—nothing was play, to him. Everything was serious.

"I see you have already begun to review the material the Court has gathered for you."

She nodded. "I know it won't mean much, but thank you for this."

"I expect you to memorize its contents before the Consort arrives at your domicile."

Kaylin nodded. "I have every intention," she said, in High

Barrani, "of doing exactly that. What else do you think I should know?"

His eyes did round, then, although he brought the brief hint of actual surprise back into line in a heartbeat. "The correct form of address."

"Kaylin is a Lord of the High Court; surely her position there takes precedence."

Diarmat ignored Bellusdeo. Kaylin was very, very fond of the gold Dragon, but understood that ignoring her—for anyone—wasn't smart. "The Consort," she said quickly, and in the same High Barrani, "seems to favor informality from me. I can address her as you would address her in the same circumstance, but she would immediately assume that I was doing it because I'd been ordered to do it. And your orders would then supersede her comfort."

He raised one brow this time. "Very good. I would otherwise assume that your lack of respect was merely ignorance, not choice."

Kaylin swallowed, because she *was* ignorant: she simply didn't know. She resented being judged for her ignorance; she always had. But she wasn't thirteen anymore. She couldn't assume that he was saying she was stupid. At thirteen, she couldn't separate the two.

And if she was a Hawk, she had to do better. She glanced once at Bellusdeo, who shrugged, her eyes orange. "I would appreciate it," she said—trying to sound as if "appreciate" did not equal "would rather walk over hot coals in bare feet"—"if you would teach me the difference. I know how to address the Imperial Court, and I know how to address the Lords of Law; I know how to respond to sergeants and I know how to respond to members of the human Caste Court." Luckily, he didn't call her on the last one, although it wasn't technically a lie. Her natural distaste for men of power made her instinctive reaction twofold: one, to hide, and two, to treat them as if they weren't as special as they thought power made them.

"I've spoken with the Consort on many occasions. I have only once caused great offense, and no amount of respect for her position would have changed that."

"Do you regret it?"

"I really regret that she was angry at me," Kaylin replied, falling into Elantran as she considered the question. As Bellusdeo cleared her throat, she immediately switched to High Barrani again. "But there is no choice I could have made that would have altered that anger. We fundamentally disagreed about a course of action. I could—and can—understand her point of view; I do not condemn the choice she would have made. But I could not make it."

"And do you not feel that perhaps you are walking into the same trap, now?"

Did she? Kaylin started to say no, and stopped. Swallowed. "If I am, it will amount to the same difficulty," she replied, choosing her words with care. "She will be angry with me because we fundamentally disagree about the choices we feel compelled to make. I can assure you that whether I call her Consort, Lady, or nothing at all will not be what gives offense."

He exhaled smoke. "The Arkon will be present."

Kaylin nodded; he had already said as much, and looked about as pleased with the Arkon as he was with Kaylin.

"I ask you—I do not command it—that you not take advantage of his sentimentality and overindulgence."

She blinked. He was glaring at Bellusdeo. Still glaring, he began to answer Kaylin's earlier question. Apparently there were High Barrani words the Hawks had not been taught, probably because the rank and file were never, ever going to meet the High Lord and the Lady. Or possibly because the teachers—mortals all—didn't know.

He came up with a long word, or a series of words, that Kaylin had literally never heard, not even when she was *at* the High Court.

Oh, do try that, Ynpharion said, interrupting her concentration.

I'm kind of busy right now. With a Dragon. Do you think you could come back and be condescending later?

I could, he agreed. Ynpharion could always be condescending. *But the Consort wishes me to relay information to you.* Of course. There was no way that Ynpharion would ever voluntarily contact her just to chat. *Lord Candallar has left his fief; he intends to meet with mortals.*

How do you know this?

I merely repeat what I am told. If you wish to force the information from me, feel free to try, but should it be information that the Consort does not wish me to share, she will ensure that I remain silent.

Kaylin wondered what the effect on Ynpharion would be.

I would, of course, attempt to support the Consort. And yes, Lord Kaylin, should the attempt be made in earnest, it is likely to damage me greatly, if not destroy me. The choice, of course, is yours.

The annoying thing about Ynpharion was that he would respect her *more* if she didn't care at all about his health or well-being. It was what he expected of the powerful. It was what she *should* have been as far as he was concerned, if she had his name. But she also knew that the Consort would be disappointed in her, that the Consort made her own moves knowing full well that in the event that Ynpharion was a loathsome toad—

Thank you.

—Kaylin wouldn't think he deserved torture or death just because he failed to answer a question. She'd've been dead about a hundred times over if there was any justice in that.

Does she have any idea of when Candallar left?

He has just left.

Kaylin almost shrieked with frustration, and unfortunately, if Diarmat was stiff as a stone slab, he was very, very observant. His eyes were always orange when Kaylin was in his presence, but this didn't offend her; she doubted they were any different in anyone else's.

"Private Neya? You have something to add?"

"…There's some chance that the terms you are using predate the wars. They would be considered archaic in the modern High Court." This was not exactly what Ynpharion had said, but Kaylin could easily infer it from his sneering tone. "If I were to use the term, one of two things would happen. Either the Consort would know that I was being coached by outsiders—and quite probably Dragons, if we're frank—or she would assume that I was being sarcastic; that I was using an elevated, archaic term as a criticism of her current stature."

For the first time in her life that she could recall, Lord Diarmat looked baffled. Stiffly, although he spoke that way most of the time, he said, "It is a title that indicates great respect."

"It possibly indicated great respect centuries ago," she said, almost apologetically.

"And Barrani Lords now consider signifiers of grave respect to be…sarcastic? Insulting?"

"Barrani Lords can, if they desire it, consider *anything* insulting. Had the Consort desired it, she could consider my invitation to dinner to be insulting. Insults with the Barrani are a game, a sport."

He stared at her, and then glanced at Bellusdeo, who shrugged.

"I do not have extensive experience with Barrani Lords. Teela, while a Lord of the High Court, is a category unto herself. I understand games, however." The last implied heavily that Diarmat didn't. She exhaled smoke.

"In future, any such invitations are to be made only after consultation with the Dragon Court."

Bellusdeo's eyes darkened.

Kaylin wanted to put a head-shaped dent into the nearest piece of wood, that being a very pristine tabletop. The familiar, however, had had enough. He squawked up a storm, and both Dragons fell silent.

"Very well. I, too, have things to which I must attend. I will expect you next week."

"To report?"

He clearly wanted to say yes, but instead said, "The Arkon will tender a full report to the Eternal Emperor."

Bellusdeo and Kaylin took a detour to the Royal library after the much shorter-than-expected lesson. Kaylin said nothing; she'd expected the detour. She was no longer thinking of Evanton and the elemental water; instead, she was thinking of the East Warrens, of Candallar and of the mortals he might be meeting on this side of the Ablayne. Mortals did venture into the fiefs to cause misery that was entirely illegal in the city proper. And that was perhaps unfair. But Nightshade's visitors went to him, not the other way around.

This implied that whoever was meeting with Candallar did not wish to enter the fiefs. And possibly could not afford to be seen doing so. It also implied that the mortal was the person with the actual power.

The library door was open; clearly, the Arkon had also expected the social detour. He was even waiting by the desk that the librarians otherwise occupied when the public part of the library—less direly guarded, but no less jealously—was open.

His eyes were orange, his arms were folded, and the look he gave Bellusdeo was uncharacteristically harsh.

"I'm sorry, Lannagaros," Bellusdeo said, although she seemed a bit surprised.

"I am perfectly willing to lie—"

"'Lie' is a harsh word."

"It is the correct word in this particular case. I am willing, however, to intercede in a less than entirely honest fashion with any other member of the Dragon Court, the Emperor included. Do not expect that I will do so when speaking with Lord Diarmat."

"You did." She folded her arms, her lips lifting at the corners. Her eyes were now gold.

"I did, yes. I will never do so again."

"Might I ask why the aversion with that particular Dragon?"

"You may." He glanced at Kaylin. "The amount of trouble you can accidentally wander into is astonishing—and I have centuries of observed hotheaded stupidity against which to compare it. I would appreciate it if you left Bellusdeo out."

"I, however, would not. And Lannagaros? She lives with me." Bellusdeo's smile was feline, but with more exposed teeth.

"You live with her. And yes, I am old enough that I will not ask the impossible. Kaylin is transparent; if she attempted to be covert, I am certain the result would be failure."

"But possibly entertaining?"

"Possibly." His tone said *never*. "Lord Diarmat is, in some ways, like Kaylin."

Both Kaylin and Bellusdeo sputtered. The familiar squawked, obviously highly amused.

"In what way are they alike?" the golden Dragon demanded.

"They have an appalling lack of finesse when it comes to complex matters. Neither of them are particularly skilled at prevarication. If Kaylin's superiors deem it wise to leave her out of missions which require diplomacy, so, too, do Lord Diarmat's. In Lord Diarmat's case, however, his inefficiency is entirely his own desire. He considers prevarication, even with cause, to diminish the actual value of truth, as if there exists a single thing that could be called truth.

"He is highly honorable. He expects that we will be the

same. And while we are not, of course, his equal in this regard, we respect him."

"We?"

"The rest of the Dragon Court, excluding perhaps yourself."

"He is a humorless, judgmental, condescending—"

"Yes, he is that, as well. But he is not without value to the Court or to the Emperor. I understand why the two of you do not get along. I accept that. But I will not and cannot treat him or think of him as you do, and I find it painful to be caught out in a lie when confronted by him."

This seemed to almost shock Bellusdeo.

"I am older and wiser than I was when we both lived in the Aerie. I think, in my youth, I was much more like Diarmat."

"You were not."

"I was. But I was more indulgent than Diarmat. I was not less condescending. You were hatchlings—you and your sisters. What I expected from infants was not what I expected from adults. Lord Diarmat considers you a peer, not a child.

"And having said that, Lord Bellusdeo, I did as you indirectly asked. I will attend Kaylin's dinner with the Consort. I assume you will likewise be in attendance."

"I should say no, and leave you stranded in that room."

The Arkon's eyes had shifted, slowly, to their usual gold when in Bellusdeo's presence. "But you won't. And I would not find it a horror, regardless. I understand what the war cost both of our people, and I hope never to encounter that loss again. She was a child during the last war, but the Consorts have always been somewhat different than the rest of their kin." He bowed to her. "I am sorry to disappoint you."

Bellusdeo exhaled. "You have not disappointed me," she said, her voice much quieter than usual.

"Diarmat would die in your defense."

"Yes, but it wouldn't be in *my* defense. It would be in defense of what I represent, and in the end, that has little to do with who I actually am."

The Arkon acknowledged the truth of this with a nod. "But you have hardly given him a chance to know you at your best. I believe the private is the only person who has truly seen it. The private and your Ascendant."

"No, Maggaron's seen me at my absolute worst."

"He has *also* seen you at your worst, yes. But that is entirely because you trust him. I believe your dinner was three days hence? I will be there."

"Is the Emperor going to drop by as well?"

"No, most certainly not. Lord Diarmat is willing to countenance my presence; the Emperor's presence in the face of one of the Barrani rulers would be considered a security problem."

And they definitely did not want that. Kaylin could imagine it now. It took her mind, briefly, off the question of Candallar, of Teela, and of her cohort. Why did everything always have to be so complicated?

The palace mirror that Kaylin knew she could safely use happened to be in Lord Sanabalis's public rooms, or at least the rooms in which he met visitors to the palace. Bellusdeo was less sanguine about Lord Sanabalis than the Arkon, but when Kaylin explained the need for the mirror, agreed to a second detour.

Lord Sanabalis had apparently gotten wind of this—somehow—and happened to be in the rooms. His eyes were mostly gold, but his expression was also mostly suspicious. "Private Neya. Lord Bellusdeo." He bowed to the Dragon. "How may I help you?"

"You can let us use your mirror. I need to get ahold of someone thirty minutes ago."

"The mirror will not allow that in its current state."

"Very funny."

Sanabalis went to the large cupboard that housed the mirror; it was not on display on the desk. "The mirror network within the palace is secure."

"Is it safe?" she asked, remembering other occasions when the answer to that was a distinctive, definitive no.

"Yes. Or it has been. If it malfunctions only when you choose to make use of it, well..."

Bellusdeo chuckled. "I agree, we ask you to take a risk, Lord Sanabalis."

"It is a risk that will be overlooked given the general fuss being made about other risks." The emphasis on the last two words were aimed directly at Kaylin. She didn't mind; she just needed the mirror.

"Helen?"

"Kaylin," her house replied. As the image in the mirror coalesced, she was looking at a very bare, empty room. It was the room in which Helen allowed mirror connections; she still refused to trust them anywhere else. "Is something wrong?" The Avatar of the house remained out of the picture; it was like talking to air.

But Kaylin was used to this. Helen's *voice* could be in any room of the house simultaneously; her Avatar could not. Or not easily. Kaylin was fuzzy on the actual magic involved, and considered it house personal business. Probably because she was lazy.

"I need to speak to Teela. If Teela's not there, I need to speak to Tain. If neither of them is there, I need to speak to Mandoran."

"Teela is, I believe, in transit. Let me just ask the boys." Both of the boys, as she called them, could contact Teela the way Kaylin herself could contact Nightshade or Ynpharion. Teela didn't have to *answer*, but she'd be aware.

"Mandoran wishes to know why you want her—he says," Helen added, almost apologetically, "that she's 'in a mood.'"

Ugh. "Tell him I'm sorry, but the mood's probably going to get uglier before it gets better. I've received word that Candallar is leaving—or has left—his fief, and he's apparently heading toward a meeting with a mortal, or possibly mortals."

"Mandoran wants to know what you expect Teela to do about it."

"Did Teela ask that, or is he just being a coward?"

"I believe the latter, dear. Oh, never mind. Annarion just told her."

"And?"

"Annarion says she says she will intercept. She has Tain. If—I'm terribly sorry, dear, but I am just repeating what I was told—she sees you there, she will break your left leg."

"She really *is* in a mood."

"Mandoran feels vindicated, dear." Of course he did. "Annarion apologizes for his interference—but given Teela's reaction, he feels that it was nonetheless necessary. Will you be coming home?"

"Yes—I want to make one quick stop before I do."

"I don't think Teela was joking, dear."

"She said 'if she sees me,' right?"

Bellusdeo leaned into the mirror. "I will bring her home. She will not go anywhere near the East Warrens, which is where I assume Teela is heading. And if the boys know, *don't* repeat it until we're home. We may be late," she continued, glancing at Kaylin's mutinous expression, "but if we're late it will be because we have stopped by Evanton's. The Keeper requested Kaylin's intervention with the wild water."

"Oh?"

"It's about the Hallionne."

"Oh. I suppose you would like me not to mention this to the boys?"

"I don't particularly care if you do—you're the one who's going to have to deal with their reaction. But tell them if *they* attempt to leave in pursuit of either Teela or Kaylin, I will personally melt the hair off their Barrani heads."

Helen's Avatar opened her mouth.

"I will. You can protect them when we're all at home, but you can't if we're not—and if they leave the house, they won't have you to back them up." The entire sentence was offered in Elantran.

Helen smiled. "I will pass the message on. Mandoran is going to be annoyed."

"Mandoran is always annoyed." Bellusdeo lifted a hand and cut the mirror connection.

"The Emperor would be annoyed," Lord Sanabalis told her. He had waited until the only witness to the comment was Kaylin herself.

"And that will be his problem."

Kaylin winced. Sanabalis's eyes were a pale shade of orange. He turned to Kaylin and offered her a slight nod. "It's been a while since our last lesson, hasn't it? I'm sure you've been practicing in my absence."

"I...uh, I've been really busy."

"So I've heard."

"The Arkon's coming to dinner with us."

"That had escaped my attention. I'm sure the Emperor will be relieved."

Bellusdeo snorted smoke. "Come on," she said, grabbing Kaylin by the arm. "If I don't get out of the palace, I'll burn a wall down—and then hate myself for my lack of self-control in the morning. And in the morning, I'll be in our house, not here."

"...Where the rest of us will have to deal with it."

"Exactly."

"Leaving now." Kaylin turned, bowed deeply to Sanabalis—

and properly, judging by the way his brows rose in surprise—
and allowed herself to be bodily dragged from his rooms.

"There is no point fretting," Bellusdeo said sharply as she
settled herself into the carriage.

"Why can't we walk?"

"It will take longer and I need to cool down before I see
anything else that annoys me."

"Diarmat?"

"Everything. The constant reminders of my uselessness."

"No one said—" Kaylin stopped herself. She understood
how Bellusdeo felt because it was clear that Diarmat considered her exactly that. She was not, in his opinion, a member of the Dragon Court, because the vows necessary to join
it would never in a million years be uttered by Bellusdeo.

"Exactly. You're certain the Keeper is expecting you?"

"As in, to show up right now? Probably not. He won't
throw me out, and he won't throw you out, either. He probably won't offer me any cookies."

"He'll probably offer you something, given the noise your
stomach is making."

Evanton did not answer the door, but that was no longer
surprising. Grethan did. Grethan, however, was dressed in
a fine blue robe that was similar to the robe Evanton wore
while *in* the garden. His eyes were the Tha'alani color of relief—not quite gold, but not quite calm, either.

Kaylin stared at him; the familiar fled, as always, to the
apprentice's shoulders. "Is everything okay?"

Grethan shook his head. The Tha'alani were not among
nature's liars, and Grethan, cut off from their group mind
for the majority of his life, had nonetheless not fared much
better. Under Evanton's tutelage, he'd given up trying. The
Tha'alani didn't hide.

They didn't need to hide.

"Something's upset the elemental water. It's—"

"It's not storming around the garden, is it?" She thought of the first time Mandoran had entered the Keeper's domain and shuddered.

"N-no. The water is talking to Evanton, but...it's kind of agitated. We're kind of hoping to avoid a flood."

She remembered the flooding in the rest of the building, as well, and glanced back at Bellusdeo.

"Do not even think it. Anything you can survive, I can survive." Bellusdeo had a killer glare, which was leveled, all orange-eyed, at Kaylin.

"I was just thinking you don't particularly like swimming or almost drowning. And your clothing might get wrecked."

"I'm not the one who has to answer to the quartermaster, you are."

"Fine. But don't blame anything on me, okay?"

Bellusdeo chuckled. "If I wanted to do that, I'd have to stand in line. A very long line."

Grethan led them down the rickety, narrow hall that pretty much forced visitors to walk single file.

"Why are you wearing that robe, anyway?"

"Evanton thought it might calm the water."

"Pardon?"

"The color. And the gesture of respect."

Kaylin shook her head.

"I'm not the Keeper—he is. And it didn't make much sense to me, either, but I didn't figure there was any harm in trying." The familiar on his shoulder squawked—at Kaylin.

"Fair enough. Look—are we going to get soaked?"

"Not unless something's changed in the last five minutes."

"Time doesn't pass the same way in the garden."

"It does if Evanton's really determined—but yes, it takes

effort, and yes, it makes him grouchy. He says it gives him a headache."

"I don't envy you."

"At least he's not a Leontine who threatens to rip my throat out to keep me in line."

"Or fire her," Bellusdeo added. "He's done that a few times as well."

If the hall had been wider, Kaylin would have pushed past Grethan and into the garden just to escape the conversation she was sandwiched between. As it was, she counted. She'd been told that counting to ten was a way of cooling off. She was still skeptical, but apparently it only worked if you managed to reach a certain number.

Grethan could talk and open doors at the same time, and as the door opened, the room seemed to lurch out from around its frame to envelope the visitors.

Or rather, the water did. Like a hand made of liquid, enormous fingers reached out to wrap themselves around the Dragon and the Hawk. They seemed to ignore Grethan, but he was almost part of the garden, rather than a visitor. Or interloper. The water was cold.

"Remember," Kaylin said, as they were drawn into the room, "it's not my fault."

The water pulled them in.

Kaylin took a deep breath as the shock of liquid hit her. She didn't speak—she didn't want a mouthful of water or more—but she could hear the sound of water, and all that the water contained. She could, as she did when she was in the grasp of the elemental water, hear the voice of the *Tha'alaan*.

Kaylin? asked the Castelord of the Tha'alani, one of her favorite people in the world. *What's happened? What's wrong? Nothing?*

Amusement and worry collided in Ybelline's internal voice. *You are with the water.*

In the Keeper's Garden yes—ugh.

...The water appears to be...agitated.

Yes, but she's not mad at me. I think. There are no rocks here, and she's not trying to drown us.

Us?

Bellusdeo's here, too.

Kaylin, you need to open your eyes.

My eyes are—oh. Oh.

They were not in the Keeper's Garden. Kaylin turned in a panic, the movement slowed by water's weight, but her eyes found Bellusdeo, made less substantial when viewed through the water's odd light.

Her eyes also found wooden floors, stone walls, arches that, carved, nonetheless resembled trees. She saw lights on the floor beneath her feet that seemed to emanate at regular intervals from the wood in which they shone. She thought she recognized those lights, because she had seen variations of them before.

In the Hallionne. On the way to the West March.

"Where are we?" Bellusdeo asked, her voice attenuated but identifiable.

"I'm not—I'm not sure. The Keeper's Garden can be anything."

"I doubt the Keeper would decide that it had to be this—not unless he were entertaining Barrani lords of some note."

Kaylin felt the water thin, and reached for it instinctively.

I am sorry, Kaylin, the water told her. *This is as close to where you must be as I can bring you.*

Bellusdeo shouldn't be here! She's a Dragon! *She can't stay here—take her back, please, please, please—take her back!*

I cannot. I have permission only to do this much. But Kaylin— there is danger—

Ybelline!

Silence.

The water released them suddenly, withdrawing so completely not even their clothing retained a trace of dampness.

CHAPTER 12

"You're panicking," Bellusdeo observed, in a tone of voice more suited to mild criticism of bad posture. "I take it that means you have some idea of where we are?" She straightened her skirts, frowning. "If I had known that we were to travel, I would have dressed appropriately."

"I didn't intend to travel."

"Also: 'It's not my fault'?"

"Should I repeat it?"

"You should never repeat it again. Honestly, how can you waste breath—when breath might be in strong demand—on something like that? Would you like your last words to be 'it's not my fault'?" Bellusdeo's eyes were on the orange side. Given that they were not in the Keeper's Garden, this could have been a sign of natural caution, but Kaylin doubted it.

"...No."

"It also implies that you believe I'm likely to blame you for the actions of others—elementals, in this particular case—and I find that almost accusatory. I would go on in greater detail, but it's only likely to annoy me. So. Where are we, exactly?"

"I think we're in one of the Hallionne?"

Bellusdeo's eyes went full orange, and Kaylin didn't blame her.

"It wasn't—the Hallionne are like Helen, but stranger."

"Helen is a unique case."

"I think *all* of the Hallionne are unique. I mean, they're all one of a kind. I wouldn't be surprised if the Towers in the fiefs are, as well." Kaylin exhaled. "But, ummm."

"They were fortresses during the wars."

"...Yes."

"Impenetrable, deadly fortresses."

"I tried to ask the water to take you back—"

"Oh?"

"You're a—a..." She couldn't make herself say the word out loud, which was stupid. It wasn't like the Hallionne wouldn't notice.

"We're not at war, now."

"No," a new voice said. "Our people are not at war. And if you are willing to remain within my borders, you will come to no harm."

Kaylin turned to see the Avatar of the Hallionne. It was, as she had half expected, Orbaranne. But this Orbaranne was not the Avatar she had seen the last time she'd stepped foot in her domain. That Avatar had looked like a frightened young woman.

This one looked like an ageless, terrifying monarch. Her words reminded Kaylin that the Barrani themselves often chose to remain outside of the Hallionne's doors in all but cases of emergency. Even in an emergency, Kaylin suspected that many of the Barrani would be uncomfortable. They had no desire to have their minds read, even if the reader was an apolitical building.

"Of course," the Hallionne said. "They are a people who depend upon the secrets they keep from others—and no secret is safe from the Hallionne." She tilted her head to the side as she studied Bellusdeo.

"I live with Helen," Bellusdeo pointed out.

"Yes, I can see that." Orbaranne's Avatar frowned. "Helen is unusual, as you stated. She was not built as we were built, and not for the same purpose—but she has perhaps gone further than we would, or could, in pursuit of independence. Should you attempt to harm other guests, we will be forced to act—but not until then. I welcome you both." She hesitated.

"Blood?" Kaylin asked, remembering the demands of her own first entry into one of the Hallionne.

"It is not essential."

"Then why do you make it a condition of entry?"

"I do not. The Barrani demand it as a token of surety." She had not looked away from the golden Dragon, although it wasn't necessary. Nothing happened within the Hallionne that escaped the Hallionne's notice.

"I have nothing to offer as surety," Bellusdeo said.

"No. Nor would I demand it. I am gratified, however, to accept you as a guest. You are my first—my very first—Dragon." Hesitation again. "Not all Hallionne will view this as a privilege, but all will accept you if you travel with Lord Kaylin."

"Oh?"

"The Consort has asked it of us."

Kaylin's jaw would have hit the floor had it not been attached to her face. "She asked you to accept *Dragon guests*?"

"No, Lord Kaylin. She asked us to accept you and those who travel with you. I do not believe she intended your companion to be a Dragon. I believe she spoke of your familiar."

Kaylin reached up to her shoulder. The familiar was not there.

"We can, as your Helen does, stretch rules. We cannot break them."

"But—"

"And the Consort is precious to us, as you have perhaps noticed before."

"When? When did she ask this?"

"Yesterday. Ah." The Avatar's expression shifted and softened, lending a hint of youthful vulnerability to her intimidating perfection. "He is here. Pardon me. If you follow the lights, you will reach the grand hall, and we will meet you there." She vanished in the blink of a very slow eye.

"I hope," Kaylin said, as she turned toward the floor with the brightest lighting, "that she remembers to warn her visitor that he has a Dragon in his domain."

"Who are you expecting?"

"From her expression, I'd guess it's the Lord of the West March." Kaylin reddened. She was not, as it happened, wearing the ring that he had given her—the most obvious public symbol of his claim of chosen kinship. It was safe at home. Of course it was.

It is not required. I believe I would recognize you without it. But why do you leave it at home? It is not so plain or so poorly made that it would be an embarrassment to be seen wearing it, surely? Even among your mortal kin, who would not recognize its significance.

She had forgotten—she always forgot—what his voice was like. It was not Nightshade's, and it was certainly not Ynpharion's; it was warmer, somehow more open than either.

It is meant for those of my kin who might otherwise fail to understand your significance. It leaves them without the pathetic excuse of ignorance, should they decide to harm you. You have heard that there has been an...incident.

I'd heard something, yes. She exhaled. Out loud, she said, "The Consort told me the cohort were traveling along the portal paths."

Cohort?

"You are speaking to someone who is not me, I assume," Bellusdeo said.

"Yes, sorry."

"The Hallionne?"

"No. The Lord of the West March."

Bellusdeo smiled. "I really did resent being left behind, you know."

"When I was sent out here the first time?"

The Dragon nodded. "I feel almost grateful to the Keeper for the opportunity."

"The Emperor is going to kill me."

"I imagine he won't be pleased, no," Bellusdeo said. Her eyes were almost gold. "But he is a Dragon, not a mortal. I would be more concerned about your sergeant, in this case."

"Sergeant?"

"The Dragon Court understands both the function and necessity of the Keeper. The Emperor is therefore unlikely to blame you for anything that occurred. Your sergeant, however, might see it differently when you take a sudden leave of absence without permission." At Kaylin's expression, she snickered. "I have to admit, I've grown almost fond of him. I did not care for him when we first met."

"He doesn't care for the Dragon Court."

"Yet he devotes his life to defending and upholding the Emperor's Law."

"The laws are mostly good. And we owe allegiance to the laws, not the Emperor directly."

"They are not different."

"They are."

"In the worst case, the Emperor could merely change the law, and you would be honor bound to defend it."

"It's still different," Kaylin insisted.

"It is indeed different," Orbaranne said. Kaylin looked around for the source of the voice, but stopped herself; she should be used to it by now. After all, Helen's voice was frequently completely disembodied. "But these lands are not Imperial lands, and the laws are different here. The Emperor does not rule them. The Lord of the West March does."

"But..."

"Yes?"

"The High Court is in the heart of the Empire."

"Yes."

"And the High Lord is therefore expected to respect Imperial Law. He's part of the Empire."

"Yes."

"And the High Lord is the man the Lord of the West March serves."

"Indeed. But Lord Kaylin, the fiefs are also in the heart of the Empire. And the fieflords are not considered citizens."

"How do you know that?"

"I know it because you know it, and you once took shelter here. No," Orbaranne said, her voice softening. "You did far more than take shelter. Were it not for you, I would not be here now. The Hallionne Orbaranne would be gone. Come. The Lord of the West March is impatient."

Given Kaylin's prior experience of the Lord of the West March, she doubted that the impatience was his.

Indeed, kyuthe, *it is not. I have not visited Orbaranne much since you left, and this is not a social call. She is lonely,* he added, his internal voice soft as well. *Although you did much to alleviate that in your time.*

I don't get it. Isn't she with you?

Yes and no. She is in all places, as the Hallionne naturally are, but she wishes to simply be in one. Tell me, did you truthfully bring a Dragon?

Not on purpose, and no I didn't. Remembering what Bellusdeo had said about the phrase *it's not my fault,* Kaylin refrained from using it. *The water sent us here.*

His inner voice stilled completely. After a pause that felt long and significant, he said, *I have asked the Hallionne to shorten your walk significantly.*

Kaylin knew that the buildings could rearrange themselves to suit their guests, and guessed that Orbaranne would probably turn herself into a pretzel for the Lord of the West March's convenience. She therefore expected that the halls would shorten or even disappear.

She was very, very disheartened to see the portal that shimmered into existence three yards ahead of them. She managed a very politic "Ugh, portal," which probably hid nothing given the internal Leontine phrases she was picking between.

"It is safe," Orbaranne said. "And the Lord believes it necessary, now." Her voice was heavier, less polished with silent enthusiasm. "It will harm neither you nor Bellusdeo."

"Oh, I'm not worried," Bellusdeo said to the empty air. "I don't have a problem with portals. Kaylin, however, finds them very, very difficult."

"Oh?"

"They make her nauseous. Nauseated? I'm uncertain which is the correct word."

"It doesn't matter," was Kaylin's grimmer than necessary reply. "Let's just get this over with."

There were certain phrases Kaylin had learned never to use, chief among them: *How bad can it be?* She was ready to add *let's just get this over with* to the list of forbidden sentences. She was braced, had been braced, for the dizziness caused by swarming lights, the instability of visible floor, and the sudden shift in temperature between one step and the next. She was prepared for a great, long tunnel, with an end that could be seen but could not be reached, because while other people apparently stepped into portals as if they were open doorways, that did not happen for Kaylin.

But this time, it was worse. Magical theory held that portals were created by stitching two patches of reality together with binding magic, as if each segment of the real world were just a chunk of cloth that could be manipulated that way. This was almost exactly the explanation that Kaylin had been given in the magical education classes she'd received after her application to become a real Hawk, not just an official mascot, had been accepted.

Mascot. Ugh.

Sanabalis, in his personal lessons, had been more expansive, but as far as Kaylin could tell, his answer was essentially the same thing—just more easily interrupted with questions. She didn't have to *pass* his lessons to be a Hawk. But she'd never really understood what that "magic" was. Not until she'd entered the portal paths that existed between the Hallionne. Unlike these portals, or the horrible one that led into Castle Nightshade, the paths were exactly that: paths. But they crossed through a very strange dimension in which geography was fluid: it could be a forest. It could be a desert. It could be shimmering, ugly landscape that was just one step away from the Shadow that devoured the living who dared to enter Ravellon, the heart of the fiefs.

This space was not those paths. It was, in theory, very like the portal that led to Nightshade's interior domain.

Or it should have been. But to either side she could see what she could only describe as the ghosts of trees—majestic, tall, haunting and ultimately...lost. She could see spires, shimmering as if stone had brilliant color, in the distance beyond and above those trees. She could hear the faint, attenuated echo of birdsong—birds that were as insubstantial as these trees.

The ground beneath her feet rumbled, as if in time to her unsteady steps. She couldn't see Bellusdeo. She reached out to the Lord of the West March and heard...nothing. Nothing but birds.

Portals had tunnels that one could follow; there was a beginning and an end, no matter how wobbly they became. This was therefore unlike those paths. The trees weren't solid enough to be real landscape, but as she looked at them, she realized they weren't lining a path. It was as if she was lost in the dream of a long ago forest.

She did not want to be lost here. She took a step forward, and again, the ground rumbled, swaying beneath her feet. The motion transferred itself up her body and into her head; she clenched her jaw, took two more steps, and stopped. She gave up on walking on two feet. Placing her hands on the ground, she swore—but this was not the first time she would emerge from a portal she had traversed on her hands and knees.

And at least the ground here wouldn't wear out her clothing. She regretted eating lunch. Or eating anything, ever.

Not that way. Not that way, Kaylin.

Had the voice not been distinctly feminine, Kaylin would have assumed that it was the Lord of the West March. Maybe it was the Hallionne Orbaranne. But no, that seemed wrong. Something about the voice was familiar, and she lifted her head, turning to see where the voice had come from.

No. Close your eyes. You shouldn't be here. You have to leave.

"Who is this? Who's speaking?"

We will make our own way out. Or—

"This is a *portal*. It's meant to take me from one part of Orbaranne to another part. It's a shortcut." She spit the last word out with venomous sarcasm worthy of a Dragon.

It is not, Chosen.

Chosen.

It is not a path that we can follow. To even approach it is costly, and I cannot remain stable for long. But you are going the wrong way. Close your eyes. Close them, and your world will reassert itself. Move forward, Chosen. It would kill Teela to lose you.

She opened her eyes. "Sedarias? Wait! Sedarias—we're here because of you! What happened? Where are you?"

But there was silence. Kaylin waited for an answer on her hands and knees, but the voice did not come again. And after what felt like an hour, she closed her eyes and began to move forward, pushing against the viscous air.

Sedarias had not lied. Kaylin managed to crawl her way across the shifting nothing, and that nothing suddenly resolved itself into wood that was cool but not cold beneath her hands. Her palms were wet; her arms were shaking.

"Kaylin," Bellusdeo said, her voice accented with worry.

"Give me a second," Kaylin replied, struggling to maintain her grip on whatever it was she'd put in her stomach hours ago. She took several deep breaths, filling her lungs in an attempt to drive back the taste of salt and water that almost flooded her mouth.

"This is why you don't like portals."

"No—this is worse." She took deep, even breaths while she waited for the nausea to pass.

"Lord Kaylin."

Great. What she really wanted was to throw up on the feet of the Lord of the West March. At least she assumed they were his feet. She didn't lift her head to find out. As if he could hear that thought—and damn the True Name, he probably could—he crouched down.

"I'm not good with portals or certain types of magic," she told him. "Just give me a couple more minutes. We have a problem."

"More of a problem?" Bellusdeo asked.

"Yes. I think Teela's friends are trapped in the portal space."

Fifteen minutes later, Kaylin was seated at an otherwise unoccupied dining table. It was far too large for four people—the fourth being the Avatar of Orbaranne—but much more modest in size than any table that had appeared before the delegation from the High Court. Food had been laid out, but not even the lessons of early years of near starvation could compel Kaylin to eat any of it.

The warmth of concern on the Lord of the West March's face had been obliterated by an entirely different type of concern. "You are certain?"

"I'd bet my own money on it."

He raised a brow.

"Yes, I'm certain."

"All of them?"

"At least one of them. I almost got lost between the opening of the portal and the dining hall."

"Pardon?" he asked, as Bellusdeo said, "How did you manage *that*?" The Barrani Lord and the Dragon eyed each other warily.

"The usual way. I entered the portal." She exhaled, still feeling shaky. "Portals, for me, have almost never been like stepping through a door. I think that's the way they work for most people. I don't know if it's the marks of the Chosen, or if I'm just naturally incompatible. When I step through a portal, in the best case, I step into a long tunnel. Often a long, ugly tunnel with a very unstable floor. At the end of the tunnel, however long and punishing it is, there's the other side of the portal, and the exit. I just have to get there." Sometimes by crawling.

"And this time?" the Hallionne asked. Both Bellusdeo and the Lord of the West March looked at her, but she failed to notice. Or failed to react.

"I don't know how to describe it. But you can see what I'm thinking of, can't you?"

"It is very disjointed."

"So are portals." Kaylin exhaled. "I think we're here to find Teela's friends, and I'm almost certain that the person who spoke to me—"

"Someone spoke to you?"

"Yes. When I was trying to find the way out. They told me I was going in the wrong direction."

She turned toward Orbaranne, who was likewise standing. "What happened?"

"I am uncertain. How did you arrive?"

"I'm not talking about us. I'm talking about Teela's companions. Were they headed here?"

There was a marked hesitation before Orbaranne said, "Yes." Her eyes widened. "You did not learn of the incident from the Consort."

"...No. We learned about it from Annarion and Mandoran."

The Lord of the West March tensed. "How did you come to learn about this from them?"

"They live with me." Her gaze narrowed.

"Your pardon again, Lord Kaylin. You have been remarkably silent since your departure. This is the first time I have heard your thoughts so clearly since you returned to Elantra."

"But the name. The True Name..."

"Yes. But I do not hold your name; you hold mine. It is fine," he added, to the Avatar. "I surrendered the name willingly, and all she has ever done with it is preserve my life."

"My house doesn't let a lot through her protections." But Helen was willing, on occasion, to let Nightshade in, both literally and figuratively. Kaylin wondered why, then, and she didn't like the immediately obvious answer, because there was no way anyone intelligent would trust *Nightshade* over this man.

The Consort bids me remind you, Ynpharion suddenly said, *that the Lord of the West March is a power. You believe, because he would never have raised his standard against his brother's, that he is decent and honorable. And measured against the rest of his kin, that is even possibly true.* These last words were said with so much distaste it was a wonder he bothered at all. *But he* is *a power. Very little occurs within the West March without his knowledge.*

But not nothing, Kaylin shot back.

No. She is not saying that her brother is responsible for the mishap. She is, however, saying that she believes it is possible he could be.

Can't she just ask him?

Yes.

And?

She would have to do it through the regular channels. She has been attempting to contact him since word of the possible disappearance was carried to her. He has failed to reply.

Maybe he's too busy because he considers it an emergency?

There are very few emergencies that would cause him to deliberately ignore his sister. Or so she believes.

You believe it, too.

Yes, perhaps. My life would be immeasurably more comfortable if you were not in it, but the Lady would find your death or disappearance unexpectedly upsetting. Therefore, treat your life as if it has value.

Kaylin really disliked Ynpharion.

"Your house?"

"Yes. Her name is Helen. She's not a Hallionne; for one she's much smaller. But she's as close to Hallionne as any building I've ever lived in."

"Are you perhaps living in a *fortelesse?*"

Kaylin shot a glance at Bellusdeo, who shrugged. It was a High Barrani word, given inflection and pronunciation, but Kaylin had never heard it before.

"I would say yes," Orbaranne interjected. "But if so, the nature of the building is unusual."

Kaylin decided that discussion of Helen's faults, flaws or strengths was not on the table. Talking about Helen this way made her feel slightly disloyal.

"I see." The Lord of the West March began to pace. Fair enough; it was what Kaylin unconsciously did when she was thinking. But Kaylin was a private, not a ruler. "How did you arrive? Or rather, what was your perception of events?"

"We went to the Keeper's Garden, at the direct request of the Keeper himself."

His eyes darkened a shade, but they were already blue. "Does he regularly make such requests?"

"Not regularly, no. Only when he has information he wants to share."

"And he had information about this cohort."

"No."

"I begin to see why some of my kin find conversation with mortals so vexing."

Given that the Barrani form of verbal directness involved weapons or armies, Kaylin thought this a tad unfair. "He said that the elemental water was upset. I don't know how much you know about the Keeper's Garden—"

"I understand what it houses."

"The elemental water was…upset. Evanton—the Keeper—thought that the water would talk to me in a way that would help him make sense of her upset."

"And?"

"She did talk to me, sort of."

"It told you to come to the West March."

"Not exactly, no. She brought us here. She grabbed us and brought us here. The Consort has been in communication with the Hallionne—I think perhaps with all of them—and asked them to house me and my companion."

Barrani brows rose slowly and deliberately. "I am certain my sister did not ask the Hallionne to house a Dragon."

"Not exactly in those words, no. But she said companion, and Hallionne Orbaranne felt that Bellusdeo—oh, sorry. Bellusdeo, this is the Lord of the West March. And this is Lord Bellusdeo, of the Imperial Dragon Court."

Bellusdeo bowed. It was a stunning, graceful motion that made her appear almost Barrani. If Diarmat could see this, he'd either be gratified at the success of his lessons, or enraged that she chose not to make such perfect gestures when she was clearly capable of it.

On the other hand, if Diarmat could see this, Kaylin would be a pile of smoldering ash for her absolute failure to start with the proper introductions, so perhaps it was for the best.

The Lord of the West March tendered a bow as elegant and graceful as Bellusdeo's, which the gold Dragon appeared to take as her due. If he was ruffled by this, it didn't show.

"Anyway, Bellusdeo accompanied me to the Keeper's Garden. She was with me when the elemental water, uh, intervened."

"And at great cost, to the water," he said softly. "It has been a long, long time since we have seen such a direct intervention, and it is never done for something as simple as war."

War did not seem that simple to Kaylin, unless by simple, he meant stupid. She kept this firmly to herself. Or tried. "This has happened before?"

"Yes. But Lord Kaylin, it was done at the command of a sorcerer. It was not done by the volition of water alone."

"Believe that we didn't ask the water to dump us here."

His smile was slight, and it vanished as he glanced at the Dragon. "I do. The Hallionne has her concerns, but in this particular case, they are unnecessary. My concern, however, is not. Why did the elemental water bring you here?"

"Can we back up a bit?"

"Pardon?"

She switched to High Barrani. "Do you understand how the water brought us here?"

"Ah. Yes, and no. I have little personal experience with summoned water. As most of my kin, I am adept with fire, and with earth. Water is more elusive. My sister, however, is adept at speaking with the water when it proves necessary. And no, Lord Kaylin, I do not believe my sister responsible for your arrival. Had she been, she would also be here."

"There was no water, where we arrived."

"There was. There is no water there now, unfortunately." The Lord of the West March and the Hallionne shared a glance.

"...Is there any large body of water here?"

"There is no body of water with which you could commune, if that is your desire. Should you repair to the Hallionne near the heart of the green, there is the fountain. Or if you wish to visit my home, you might also make the attempt."

The Consort is getting annoyed, Ynpharion said.

At me? Or at her brother?

Very reluctantly—or so it felt to Kaylin—Ynpharion said, *at her brother.*

Does she—does she think he *had something to do with whatever happened to the cohort?*

I do not know.

Just ask her!

Lord Kaylin, what she tolerates from you, a mortal with terrible manners even for your kind, she will not tolerate from a Barrani Lord who serves her. She has not said that she does, and if she has not said it, she does not mean for me to convey that opinion.

You can't tell?

She holds my *name. I do not hold hers.*

But—Nightshade can tell what I'm thinking, and I hold his name.

That is because you lack will and strength. Truly, if the outcaste desired it, he could wrest control from you with very little effort. And that is true, as well, of the Lord of the West March. I understand the inhibitions placed upon the Lord of the West March; there would be consequences should he do so. I fail to understand what prevents the outcaste from regaining control of his name. Regardless, I cannot answer your question because I cannot repeat it.

The Lord of the West March turned to the Hallionne Orbaranne. "If it will not trouble you overmuch, we will perhaps entertain our guests in the hall here."

"Good," Kaylin said, deciding. "Perhaps you can tell us what happened to the people who made their way to Orbaranne."

He met her gaze and held it in uncomfortable silence.

CHAPTER 13

Kaylin sat at the table upon which food had magically appeared. Her appetite had not returned, and would not return for some time, but at least the sight and scent of food didn't make her nausea any worse. Bellusdeo looked at the food as well, as if assessing the likelihood that it contained poison. There was no fear in her expression; her eyes were orange, but that suddenly seemed a sensible color. At least they weren't the blood red of fury that implied someone was about to die.

Kaylin had no illusions. If Bellusdeo went full-on Dragon here, it was Bellusdeo who'd die. And Bellusdeo, no fool, probably understood this better than she did. But this Bellusdeo, Kaylin had almost never seen. She was Imperial. Regal. She looked almost disturbingly Barrani; no hair out of place, no motion that was not graceful or deliberate. She took the seat that was held out for her—by the Hallionne, not the Lord of the West March; she fiddled with the various bits and pieces of junk that came before formal dinner—napkins, cutlery, weird plates.

Kaylin felt almost embarrassed. This style of social manners had not been part of Bellusdeo's kingdom when she ruled it; she still considered it far too Barrani to be adopted by Dragons. But…she clearly, in spite of that, had learned, and learned perfectly. Kaylin once again felt like she was coming to the dinner table after she'd just run down a criminal suspect across two warrens.

"Hallionne Orbaranne, could you please tell us what you think happened? We know that Sedarias and the rest of her friends set out from the Hallionne Alsanis by the portal paths. They wished to arrive in Elantra quickly, and felt that the weeks of overground passage would cause too much of a delay."

"The portal paths are not taken except in cases of emergency," the Hallionne replied, "as I believe you know from your past experience." Her voice was neutral, the way stone was neutral. Kaylin hadn't expected that, and was surprised at how it stung.

"Could we take the portal paths now?"

Silence.

"Did the Hallionne not just say that they were not to be taken except in cases of emergency?" The Lord of the West March said.

"It's an emergency," Kaylin replied, in just as stony a tone as the Hallionne had used. "And I need to speak with Alsanis."

"You might, at the Hallionne Orbaranne's discretion, speak to him from here."

"It won't be the same, and you know it. They left the Hallionne Alsanis, and when they left they were safe. If they chose to take the portal paths, they did so from Alsanis. He's aware of them in ways that nothing else is." She tried very hard not to fold her arms defensively, and only barely succeeded. She was very, very troubled by the Consort's advice. "And I have a pressing emergency."

"Oh?"

"Your sister, the Consort, has graciously accepted an invitation to dine at my home in three days. If we can't use the portal paths—"

"There is no way that you will arrive in Elantra in three days. I suggest you avail yourself of the mirrors here to inform the Consort that you will have to reschedule her dinner."

"Fine. I'll also need to talk to Helen."

"Your home."

"Yes. She's probably going to be worried."

That was, of course, an understatement, if a hopeful one. Helen did answer the mirror call. She was standing in her one safe room, and her eyes were obsidian. Literally. She had also ditched the more maternal lines and wrinkles that implied gentle smiles from the corners of her eyes and mouth; her hair was pulled back from her face in a very, very martial way.

Her voice, however, was mostly normal. "Grethan carried word from the Keeper," Helen said, after Kaylin had blurted out both an apology and a précis of their current location. "I should possibly inform you that the Imperial Court is also aware of what happened."

Kaylin couldn't help it. Her shoulders sagged. "Has the Emperor called?"

"No. Lord Emmerian, however, visited in person. I would suggest that you make contact with him. Or possibly the Arkon."

"They won't accept a mirror call from this source," Bellusdeo unexpectedly said.

"I will endeavor to pass a message on, then. You are well?" she asked the Dragon.

"Yes. I have been treated as a guest, not a prisoner of war."

"I don't believe the Barrani took Dragons as prisoners," Helen pointed out.

An unfortunate silence followed her words. Kaylin rushed to fill it. "I need to let the Consort know—"

"I do believe the High Halls will accept the message that the Imperial Palace will not. I should add that your familiar was somewhat agitated, and he is en route to you now. He asks that you not do anything foolish before he arrives."

She looked past Kaylin to the Avatar of Orbaranne, then. "Kaylin," she said, to the Hallionne, "is my Lord. She is my *chosen* Lord." As if one building that was immobile could threaten another building that was immobile.

Orbaranne, however, nodded as if she had expected no less. "Lord Kaylin saved my life," she replied, voice grave. "I owe her a debt of honor."

"And that is not a debt you owe to Annarion and Mandoran's brethren."

"No, Helen. The two are with you, then?"

"They are, indeed, under my protection. As is the Dragon who is currently your guest."

"Helen—"

Helen, however, was not done. She spoke in a language that Kaylin did not know, but nonetheless felt she should. And Orbaranne responded in kind. The floor shook, rumbling as if the earth beneath it was about to break open.

The Lord of the West March looked surprised. Helen did not. Bellusdeo might have been carved of stone for all the expression she was willing to surrender.

"Kaylin," Helen said. "Find the water. Find it while it can still speak. I will leave you now to speak with the Consort, if she is available."

She is, Ynpharion said. His interior voice, usually so loaded with condescension and disgust it was a wonder it could be used to convey anything else, was utterly neutral.

The mirror's image didn't shatter; it swirled like liquid leaving a basin, taking the images with it in elongating streaks of color that no longer suggested Helen or the interior of the one room in which she allowed the mirror network access.

Bereft of color, the silver surface reflected the people in the room before it: the Lord of the West March, the Avatar of the Hallionne, Bellusdeo and Kaylin herself. Before Kaylin could speak, that silver faded, and with it the interior lights of the great hall. Instead, a shadowed darkness seemed to envelope the mirror itself, and it was slow to return even the outline of an image.

Kaylin almost stopped breathing as her eyes adjusted. This was *not* the Consort's room. Nor was it the cavern that was home in some fashion to the Lake of Life over which the Consort stood guardian, and to which she was servant.

The hair on Kaylin's neck suddenly stood on end. So did the hair on her arms, which were covered, as they always were when she was on any sort of duty. This was not shock, although she certainly felt shock; it was entirely other. When asked, Kaylin said she had an allergy to magic. It wasn't precise, but it was close enough. On most days.

This was not most days.

She was silent as the marks on her arms began to glow. The glow was faint, but she knew that everyone in the room had noticed, save perhaps the Lord of the West March, who was staring at the mirror as if nothing else existed.

"Sister," he said, his voice itself a kind of hush.

"Lirienne," she replied. She could not be seen. Her voice could be heard. But hers was not the only voice Kaylin could hear, and she lifted both hands to her ears almost instinctively as the hall filled with the sounds of the damned.

The Consort was at the base of the High Halls—the reason the High Halls existed. "Can you hear them, brother?"

The Lord of the West March did not reply. Kaylin glanced at his profile; he was white, his jaw clenched. His hands had become fists by his side, but his expression was otherwise almost neutral. Almost. His eyes were midnight.

What is she doing there? Kaylin demanded of Ynpharion.

I am not at her side, Lord Kaylin. His voice, like the Lord of the West March's expression, was neutral, devoid of the usual contempt, which was oddly creepy. This thought, on the other hand, annoyed him enough that his usual personality spilled out. *Unlike a simple mortal, I respect and value the orders that I have been given. Nor do I need to be where she is now standing to see what she sees.*

How in the hells did you let her go down there by herself? Kaylin wasn't shouting, but had she opened her mouth, she would have been.

She is my lord, he replied, all ice. *When she commands, I obey. She did not wish company.*

Did you even know *that she was going down there?*

She is safe there. She has passed the Test of Name. What exists within the bowels of that place no longer has the ability to harm her.

And yet, the screaming, the weeping, the verbal pleas— those hurt. Kaylin knew it, because they hurt her. And she was not the guardian of the names—the guardian of Barrani *life.* Ynpharion was wrong.

She is not alone, he finally, and grudgingly, said.

But Kaylin could almost see that, now. There was very little light in this darkness, but not none. And the man she saw made her freeze in place for one long breath.

Do not even imagine, Ynpharion said, before she could gather up anything that resembled a coherent thought, *that I have any control over the High Lord himself.*

The High Lord was there, his profile as tense as his brother's, half a continent away. What the Consort heard, the High Lord heard; that was the price of rulership. But the High Lord had almost failed the test. No, Kaylin thought, he *had* failed it. What had saved him—the only thing that had saved them all—was his name; it had been incomplete, unfinished, the weight of it too much for the previous Consort to bear.

If Kaylin had problems with the Consort being in this cavern, it was *nothing* compared to the issue she now had. She wanted to scream into the mirror. And because she did not know the High Lord's name, because she did not hold it, she had no other choice.

"What are you doing there?" she demanded, shouldering his silent brother out of the way without conscious thought.

It was the Consort who answered, her voice cool with warning. "It is not the first time I have traversed this long, long hall. Nor, I fear, will it be the last." She did not appear in the mirror; it was as if she was holding a portable one in her hand, and had it turned out and away.

"But—your brother—"

"No one, not a single Barrani, be they Lords of the High Court of long-standing, would ever consider telling the *High Lord* what he can, or cannot, do. He is not what he was—and you, of all people, should understand this."

"Why are you there, then?"

"Consider it a patrol, Lord Kaylin."

That was garbage. It was stinking garbage. Kaylin opened her mouth and shut it again, hard enough that the snap of her teeth made her jaw ache. "I…apologize…for interrupting you," she said, in slightly stilted High Barrani. "I would not have—" what was the word? "—been so presumptuous, but I had extended an invitation to dine in my home, and I do not believe I am able to meet with you on the agreed upon date."

"And why would that be? I must confess I looked forward to that dinner with some anticipation. It is not every day, after all, that I come face-to-face with Dragons outside of the Imperial Palace."

"The Dragon is also unable to attend."

Silence.

"She currently finds herself in the same situation I do."

More silence. Kaylin could feel the sudden absence of

Ynpharion, and whispered a mental *coward* at his retreating presence.

"And that situation?" The Consort's High Barrani had developed an almost martial edge.

"We both appear to be guests of the Hallionne Orbaranne at the moment." Kaylin resented having to say this out loud, since the Consort bloody well knew where Kaylin was. But... that was politics all over: a bunch of powerful people saying, diplomatically, what everyone at the table already knew. And then acting surprised. It seemed like a huge waste of time, and it didn't seem to serve any functional purpose.

"Lord Bellusdeo...is a guest in the Hallionne."

"Yes. She arrived with me. I apologize for not attempting to get the necessary permissions from the two courts; it was considered an emergency by the elemental water. The water did not confer with us; nor did she ask our permission. According to the Keeper, she was...agitated. He was right. She was agitated enough to pick us up in the Keeper's Garden and drop us here."

Another silence, this one less extended. "And the nature of that emergency?"

Kaylin wanted to *scream*. "It appears that compatriots of two of my personal guests chose to travel from the Hallionne Alsanis to the Hallionne Orbaranne. Something occurred while they were in transit, and they have been lost."

Silence. So much silence, all of it weighted, all of it harsh.

"Lirienne," the Consort said, and there was a definite edge in the name, "is this true?"

"I myself have only just been informed of the rumor," he replied, his voice much softer and smoother than the Consort's. "And I have not yet been able to ascertain the truth of it."

"And you will do so?"

"I—"

"As the Consort requests," the High Lord said. "If her voice is not yet enough, brother, let me add mine. I will not command you; the West March is, of course, yours, and I have seldom interfered in its politics; it has not historically been wise." And Kaylin knew that he referred, subtly, to a previous High Lord and his interference with the *regalia*, in the heart of the green.

That interference had almost destroyed twelve Barrani children; they had survived through the intervention of Hallionne Alsanis. From any other man, this comment might have seemed or felt self-deprecating, but not even Kaylin was that naive. She could hear the fire and the ice that gave those words shape, and she knew they were not offered to the younger brother; they were aimed.

The Lord of the West March bowed his head. "You have not spoken at length with the Hallionne Alsanis, brother. I have. Where we rejoiced in the salvation of the eleven, we also understood that they were no longer completely as we are. We were, however, content to allow them to remain as guests; Alsanis himself insisted on it. His attachment to them has grown with the passage of time. We did not expect that they would attempt to leave so soon. The Hallionne is not cognizant of all of their abilities."

"Annarion and Mandoran came with me when I went back," Kaylin pointed out. Bellusdeo nudged her. Coming from a Dragon, it was a gentle, subtle gesture—but Kaylin wasn't a Dragon; her ribs would probably be bruised.

"Yes, Lord Kaylin. And shortly after their arrival, the High Halls came under attack—and the attackers were ancient, dangerous. Were it not for the Dragons, the Halls might have fallen there." Lirienne's voice was dry, almost uninflected. But there was subtle accusation in the words, and it was aimed at people she now considered friends.

"Annarion and Mandoran didn't attack the High Halls!"

"No; had they, we would not be having this conversation.

But Alsanis felt that it was possible—perhaps probable—that their very presence woke the ancestors."

Since this was more or less fact, Kaylin bit back further words until she once again had control over what fell out of her mouth. "The Emperor's hoard is the empire."

"Indeed."

"He has not demanded their destruction; he has not made them criminal. They live in my house—"

"Your house is not a normal mortal dwelling; it is not even a normal Barrani dwelling."

"Lirienne," the Consort said, indicating that his conversation with Kaylin could wait. "I wish no harm to come to them. They were ill used once, or they would not now be as they are; they were abandoned by their kin. Were it not for the Chosen, their names would be lost to us forever."

"They intended to travel to Elantra. To the High Halls."

"Yes," the Consort replied. The High Lord glanced at her, but did not speak.

"They intend to take the tower's Test. They intend to—"

"Stand where we are now standing. Yes."

"You knew this."

"What other reason would they have for returning? I did not know, but I suspected."

"The risk is too great."

"To what? If you speak of the politics, of the small wars that are starting even as we speak, that is the nature of power and inheritance among our kin. They will either die, or they will triumph; that has long been the way of our people." She fell silent. Kaylin thought she was done, but after a pause which neither of her brothers broke, she continued. "That has never been *our* way. We three did not choose to fight those wars, did not choose to target each other. You have been Lord of the West March, and you have been—at a distance—the strongest of supporters the High Lord has among our people.

"You understand our burden."

"I understand it."

"We have come to remind ourselves," she continued. "We understand your fear; believe that we feel it. But Lirienne, I know what Annarion did during the attack on the High Halls. I know what he and his companions survived. They were meant to be our strength in our war against the Dragons—and perhaps that was folly or hubris on the part of the previous High Lord."

No perhaps about it, in Kaylin's opinion, which she kept to herself.

"But perhaps it was not that war they were meant to fight."

The Lord of the West March bowed his head. Head bowed, he said, "We will lose four allies should you decide to pursue this. Two of those chosen were—would have been—the heads of their line."

"Four, now," the High Lord said. "Two could take their houses, and it would not harm us; indeed, it might benefit us to have those houses embroiled in such conflicts."

"Do you think that they stand a chance in such a conflict? They have long been outside of the political sphere, and their ability to raise small armies beneath their own banners will be small, if it exists at all. They will, of course, be publicly accepted by their families—but I would be highly surprised if above half survive that acceptance. Highly."

Kaylin's expression was an open book; generally, people who were polite declined to read it. The situation, however, was grave enough that those manners were set aside.

"It is political," the Consort said softly. "The lines are ruled, and have been ruled, by those who were in line when the eleven were shut into the Hallionne. Teela survived. Had her father and elder brother likewise survived, they would rule. But regardless, should the eleven choose to return to their families, they would be welcomed."

"With poison?"

It was the High Lord who chuckled. "You are far, far too blunt, Lord Kaylin. What you say here may be said; the Consort considers you of great value to the High Court. But do not speak those words aloud in the presence of the assembled Court; such an accusation would be considered the gravest of insults."

"Even if it's true."

"Indeed; very often it is the truths we hide that have the capacity to destroy us should they see light. Lord Kaylin, you have experience now with Annarion and Mandoran. Annarion wishes to take back his family lands, and to do so, he must face the Tower. He must face…this."

"It's why—it's why the rest of his friends left the green. If he's going to face that test, they want to do it together."

"Lord of the West March." The High Lord turned his attention to his brother. "You are correct. We have spoken little with Alsanis. But our sister has. We would, however, appreciate the return of Lord Kaylin. While it is unusual for so junior a Lord to extend such an informal invitation to our sister, it is the first opportunity we have had to observe two of the children in a less heated, political context.

"Unfortunately, that opportunity appears to have been lost. Even if she chose to risk the portal paths, I do not believe Lord Kaylin would return to the city in time."

"Perhaps the elemental water could be compelled to deliver her."

"No," the Consort said, before Kaylin could speak. "We will wait. Take no unnecessary risks, Lord Kaylin. Although you are mortal and barely considered by the powerful to be part of the High Court, you have now engaged in the politics at its heart. Be wary.

"And now, we must part. The mirror that I am currently using is reaching the end of its life. I am grateful that you chose to call at this particular moment. Lirienne, be well."

The image shattered. Silver reflection, however, did not return to the mirror's surface. Instead, the mirror faded, slowly and completely, from sight.

The Hallionne and the Lord of the West March exchanged a long, silent glance.

Bellusdeo pulled Kaylin back, as if that glance was somehow dangerous. "*Now* the Emperor is going to be unhappy," she said, her eyes almost gold.

"Because?"

"Barrani politics were ever deadly to the Barrani. But at war, they could be magnificent in their own right."

"You didn't fight in those wars."

"No. In the end, I fought in a greater war. And lost."

"You're still alive."

"Yes." She smiled. "Wait until they are finished conversing, and then let us go in search of the water."

The conversation, such as it was, continued for long enough that Kaylin gave up on the waiting and started in on the eating.

"You are not afraid of poison?"

"It's a Hallionne. The food is produced by Orbaranne. If Orbaranne wanted to kill us, we'd be dead already."

"You're just hungry."

"Evanton didn't even offer cookies."

Bellusdeo snorted. With smoke. She took a chair at the table upon which food had appeared, but did so stiffly and almost regally. Kaylin felt a bit guilty. But mostly, she felt hungry. Around food, she said, "The Hallionne won't hurt anyone she's accepted as a guest."

"You like the Hallionne."

"I don't know them well enough to *like* them," Kaylin countered. "But...I feel mostly safe in them. When they're not under siege. I don't think the Hallionne can be ordered to kill their guests, even by the lords of the lands in which they stand."

"You are certain?"

"I couldn't order Helen to kill any of our guests."

"Tiamaris could order Tara to do so."

Kaylin shrugged, but thought about this. It was easier to think on a full stomach, anyway. "Yes. He could. But the Towers in the fiefs aren't the same as the Hallionne. I think that Helen *could* have been ordered to kill her guests at one point—but I think she broke whatever it was that controlled that."

"Could you order her not to kill?"

"I don't know. That's a good question. I think I could ask, and I think she would listen. She's not a weapon."

"No. More of a shield, I would think."

They ate in silence until the Lord of the West March joined them at the table. Then they ate in an entirely different kind of silence.

"Lord Kaylin," he finally said.

She looked up, chewed quickly, and swallowed. "Yes?"

"You have passed the tower's Test. You are part of the High Court."

Ugh. "Yes."

"You have sheltered Annarion and Mandoran, as you call them."

"What do you mean, as I call them?"

"Their names are longer, in our Court—or would be, if they emerge from that test themselves. You have seen them; according to my sister, you have fought by their side. Tell me, as the one who helped them emerge from their long captivity, do you feel they will succeed?"

She blinked. "Yes?"

His smile was crooked. "That is not, perhaps, the confident assertion I was seeking."

"I don't know what they'll see. They sometimes see things

I can't. My house can see what they see," she added quickly, "and my familiar can see it as well. But I don't see what they do. Teela can only see what they see if—" She stopped.

He allowed this. "And you think this without risk?"

Did she? She fell silent, and began to push food around in patterns on her plate. She understood what he was asking, and she was suddenly aware that she'd already been far too honest; she'd thought about the question, not the person asking it, and not the political environment that surrounded that person. She inhaled and put her cutlery aside. "Did you have something to do with their disappearance?"

Bellusdeo coughed.

"Is that what my sister thinks?"

"I don't know—ask your sister. I'm not her, and I can't answer for her."

How unusually perceptive of you.

Shut up, Ynpharion.

"Did you have something to do with their disappearance?"

"How could I?"

"That's not a no."

"Is it not? I might remind you that I am Lord of the West March, and you are currently situated almost in the heart of my domain. You are, of course, a servant of the Imperial Law, but Lord Kaylin, you are not *in* the Empire at the moment. Here, you are not a Hawk. Not a groundhawk. You are Lord Kaylin, but more shabbily clothed." It was a warning. Even if she had been extremely dense, she could feel the subtle threat through the bond of his name. She had never felt it there before.

"I owe you—and indirectly, An'Teela—my life. But that debt does not cover the safety of, the existence of, my people."

"The Lords who might be disenfranchised are not part of the safety of your people; at best, they're support for your rule."

"For the High Lord's rule, yes."

"But if I understand that mirroring, the High Lord is willing to take the risk."

"Perhaps it is because he does not understand that risk. Tell me that you honestly believe there is no risk."

She couldn't. Instead, she said, "Tell me that you honestly had nothing to do with whatever did happen to the cohort. I mean, to Sedarias and the rest of her companions."

"Sedarias, is it?"

"Lord of the West March," Bellusdeo said quietly, "that is what she has been called by her two friends. Lord Kaylin is unaware of any other title. No insult was intended."

"And none taken. But I am curious. Of all of the nine who left the Hallionne Alsanis, why was it Sedarias that she named?"

That one, Kaylin felt she could safely answer. "Because it was Sedarias I met in the portal."

CHAPTER 14

Given his expression, the word "safe" was obviously an over-estimation. "You saw Sedarias?"

"I mostly heard her." Before he could ask, she said, "I know what they look like. I know their voices—I brought them out of the green. It was Sedarias."

Bellusdeo's orange eyes were pointed in Kaylin's direction. If they'd been a weapon, they'd be resting against her cheek. Or just below its surface. Kaylin wondered if Dragon names worked exactly the same way Barrani names did. Then again, Bellusdeo wasn't subtle; having the name wouldn't give her any more information than the orange-eyed glare was doing already.

"Lord of the West March—"

"No. I did not directly influence the destination of Sedarias and her friends."

The Avatar of Orbaranne joined them, although she did not take a seat; at the moment, Kaylin privately thought if she bent, she was likely to break. Her eyes had become stone, although not the obsidian that Helen's could default to if she wasn't paying attention.

★ ★ ★

"You spoke with Sedarias and you detected no taint in her?"

He really *had* spoken with Alsanis. "No. I don't think they're in a good place, though." Kaylin was done with dinner, and rose. "Thanks for feeding us. We'd like to examine the portal pathways now."

"They did not approach by the path," Orbaranne said. "I watched for them."

"I don't think we have any hope of finding them if we don't at least start there, because they started on the path. Something either drove them off it, or the path changed unexpectedly." Kaylin had experience with that, and it still gave her nightmares.

She began to walk, confident that the Avatar's awareness—if not her physical form—would follow. Bellusdeo caught up immediately, falling in step easily given the differing lengths of their strides. The marks on Kaylin's arm continued their dullish glow, but they weren't painful, and she could mostly ignore them.

"I do not think that is wise," Orbaranne observed. "I believe that the marks awaken for a reason."

"When it's an emergency, it's impossible to ignore them—I feel like my skin is on fire."

"Lord Kaylin."

She blinked. The Lord of the West March lengthened his stride to catch up to them, although he kept Kaylin between himself and Bellusdeo.

"They did, as you surmise, set out from Alsanis on the portal path. Given prior difficulties, the pathways are somewhat delicate, but they have served us since your return to your city. There was some, ah, discussion about the wisdom of allowing them to use those paths en masse."

"Discussion?"

"The Hallionne Alsanis was against it."

Kaylin swore. In Leontine. Given the expression on the Lord of the West March's face, he understood every word. This, she thought, was why she was never going to be a diplomat. That and the ulcer she'd get trying to be polite and proper according to every single cultural norm. It was hard to be polite when certainty of failure was so high.

"When you say *against* it, do you mean he tried to stop them?"

"Ah, no. He attempted to reason with them; he pointed out the possible dangers that they might face—dangers that I, for example, would not. Some of them agreed with Alsanis. Others did not. I believe they held a…vote?" He used the Elantran word with marked hesitance.

"Meaning they all gave their opinion and the majority opinion won?"

"Yes."

"It's a vote. And clearly, the majority wanted to take the paths." She considered everything Mandoran and Annarion had said about Sedarias and privately decided it might be a majority of one.

"Vote." He spoke the word with less hesitance. "It is not, you must understand, our custom."

She didn't slow, but the Lord of the West March was taller and could easily match her stride. "How would you normally decide?"

"My lord would decide. In the absence of a lord, I would decide."

"But if your friends—"

"I am the Lord of the West March. My friends," and here he also adopted the Elantran word, "would wait upon my decision, were I asked to make one. They would accept any decision I made."

"But—the children brought here were friends. They weren't liege and lord. Or lieges and lord."

"It is not uncommon to have groups of the young clustered together."

"Well, how would you expect them to decide? They can't just appoint a 'lord' and obey them."

"Why not?"

Bellusdeo snickered. "Don't look at me," she said, over Kaylin's head. "I personally believe that nature abhors a vacuum, especially when it comes to command."

"Meaning?" Kaylin said.

"I generally find it more efficient to take command if there is no commander. I would have imagined the Barrani to be the same." She then said, "Don't give me that look. You're a Hawk. Your sergeant doesn't exactly gather you all together in one room and ask you to take a vote on his latest orders."

Much as she hated to admit it, this was true. "But that's only at work. And there's a reason we don't work every waking minute of every day—we'd probably kill each other or go insane."

"Given mortals and your criminal investigations, I'm not entirely sure how that would be different."

"I find the Hallionne impressive," Bellusdeo said, after a pause in which Kaylin heroically managed to say nothing. "Structures such as these were not home to many of our kin."

"Tiamaris."

"Yes, but he is young and his situation is unusal." She glanced, once again, at the Lord of the West March. "These were built for your kin by the Ancients."

He nodded. "The first of the Hallionne predate me, but not our kind."

Since Helen and the Hallionne were entirely unlike the buildings that most mortals called home, Kaylin said nothing. But she thought, as she walked, that if mortals lived in the Hallionne, or in Helen, things would be better. She could imagine an entire city built under the great roof of a similar building; there would be little conflict, no starvation, and no reason for laws.

Which would put her out of a job. Having a job was the silver lining, but privately she wondered if not needing the Halls of Law would be a far better alternative. If she were an Ancient, if she were a genuine god, wouldn't a city of that nature be desirable? A place where anyone, ever, could feel at home and safe?

"That is not, in the end, what the Ancients wanted," Orbaranne surprised her by saying. "And buildings such as I, or Helen, require the occupants to submit to the governing will of the Ancient's intentions and architecture. You think that we can create paradise."

"You can," Kaylin replied.

"No, Kaylin. We cannot. The Ancients themselves could not become the buildings they created, even had they desired to do so. Do you understand why?"

"No?"

Orbaranne chuckled. Her Avatar had remained in the dining hall, but Kaylin was used to conversing with essentially invisible Avatars. "Think carefully. What you desire in this moment is to open your figurative doors and encompass the homeless—people who are what you once were. And this desire is at the heart of the Hallionne. But it *is* the desire of a moment. When you arrived, you were confused and hungry. The hunger was the desire of *that* moment. When you are dressed down by your sergeant, you are frustrated and angry with yourself. You return to your home, but you do not shed that frustration or anger.

"All of these things are part of who you are. The anger. The hunger. The desire to help and protect. But they are very individual. There is some part of you that understands that there must be limits to their expression. Do you imagine that you could live for eternity with those limits? That your desires, your angers, your fears, would never exceed the boundaries that you choose to live within?" She waited for Kaylin's reply, but Kaylin found she had nothing to say.

"Imagine, then, that those desires, those angers, those hungers, those hopes, move worlds. Imagine that they create worlds—and destroy them. Imagine that the boundaries which you set—boundaries which are mortal and confined to a handful of decades if you are lucky—are so small that they are all but invisible. An Ancient could not become a building such as the Hallionne, because there are no boundaries for the Ancients. No boundaries that cannot be crossed, no boundaries that can be enforced.

"If, in your momentary anger, you could destroy the entirety of your city between one breath and the next, what home, what protection, could you offer? The Ancients could not destroy each other so easily—that took effort, will, planning. Even luck. But their creations perished in their attempts to harm each other. Do not wish to be a god. It is not an existence that will bring you anything but misery, in the end."

The Lord of the West March looked...surprised. And troubled. "Orbaranne," he began.

"No," she replied, before he could finish whatever he clearly meant to say. "I am fine. I chose this existence, and I understood what it entailed; in no other way could I have been recreated. Lord Kaylin does not. But I think it necessary that she understand as much of it as I can convey. Come, the stairs to the left."

"Stairs?" The Lord of the West March asked.

"Given the difficulty Lord Kaylin had with a simple portal to the great hall, we are taking a modified approach to the interior."

Kaylin was really, really grateful for it. Walking wasn't a problem in comparison.

★ ★ ★

She was not surprised to see that the stairs led down. Although she understood that the portal paths existed in an alternate dimension, she thought of them as strictly basement entities. A cavern, even a well-lit one, seemed appropriate. Her arms, however, continued their dull glow, and given the muted lighting in the cavern, they seemed to have brightened.

Bellusdeo noticed, of course. Her eyes were orange, but hinted at gold. She did not feel threatened by either the Lord of the West March or the Hallionne. Or perhaps she'd become accustomed enough to living with Helen that she could almost relax.

She did smile when the stairs reached the floor. "This," she said, "would make a magnificent aerie."

"It might," Orbaranne conceded. "But it is not open to sky."

"A pity. Could that be changed?"

"Yes—but the sky it would open to here would not be conducive to the flight of the very young."

Kaylin had been expecting forest, but said nothing. "When Alsanis counseled against the portal paths, did he—"

"He allowed them to leave. They are guests, now, not prisoners. He is fond of them; in the opinion of some of the Hallionne, too fond. Here," the voice of Orbaranne added. The Lord of the West March understood that "here" was a specific location; to Kaylin, it all looked like slightly uneven rock. To her surprise, he knelt.

Sensing that surprise, he said, "I am not my sister, but it makes the opening of the pathways less onerous if one of our kin aids the Hallionne."

"It is not necessary," Orbaranne said, in a different tone of voice.

"If it were necessary, Hallionne, I would not offer. Do not," he added, his voice warmer than his words, "argue against it. You know you will not win; it will merely waste time."

"You need to conserve your power," Orbaranne replied, clearly ignoring what Kaylin felt was probably accurate, if not good, advice. "It is not the first time—"

"My brother was not High Lord the last time an assassination attempt was made."

"If you intend to support your sister—"

"My brother is High Lord, and it is clear what his decision would be."

"He did not command you."

"No. He is my brother; he knows me well. Come," he said. He removed a dagger from a sheath that had been invisible to Kaylin's eye, and ran it across the mount of his left palm. Kaylin sucked in air.

I am not the Consort, he said, his interior voice inflected with an odd, wry humor. *She sings.*

It's better than bleeding.

She felt a wave of amusement, then. *Is that what you think? Tell me, Lord Kaylin, when she sang to the Hallionne, did it appear effortless to your eye? No. This? This is nothing.*

Orbaranne doesn't like it.

I am her guest; of course she disapproves. Asking one's guests to shed blood for you is not considered hospitality in any home of worth in any culture that I am aware of.

It's her choice, isn't it? I mean—this is essentially her body.

Yes, Lord Kaylin, it is. Do you think she is endless? You were here when things were at their most dire for her. Were it not for your intervention, there would be no Hallionne Orbaranne. We ask, we demand, we accept. But she is not a simple object, nor even a complex one; she is alive. Alive and encased, forever, in a small world of her own. I will not deprive her of purpose—but I will not demand more than I must.

Why is blood needed?

Ask the Ancients, Chosen. You have a far better chance of receiving an answer.

She thought, listening to him, that if he could free the Hallionne—if he could take her outside of herself without destroying her—he would do it.

"Yes," Orbaranne said, voice soft. "He has always heard my voice, and he has listened no matter what it contained. It is for that reason that I hate to see him bleed."

"I'd offer my blood—"

"Neither your blood nor the Dragon's would serve."

"And even would it," the Lord of the West March said, rising, "it would never be accepted."

"Oh?"

"The pathways you might open, in the end, are not the paths that were designed for our kin. I have often thought," he added, "that Dragons, at their core, would make excellent Hallionne; they do not seem to suffer loneliness or isolation the way that others do."

"Oh, we suffer it," Bellusdeo replied. "But it is often a choice: isolation or war."

"Ah. Then perhaps your kin and mine are not so different."

Kaylin wanted to know why blood was required, or if not required, useful. She didn't ask. Instead, she waited while the hairs on the back of her neck and arms began a slow, painful rise. As the discomfort grew, the rock in front of the Lord of the West March sprouted what looked like tentacles, which was very, very disturbing. It also appeared to be expected; neither Orbaranne nor Lirienne so much as blinked.

Those tentacles reached up, and up again, and when they were eight feet, ten feet, off the ground, they suddenly bunched and gathered, coiling as if they were springs. They leapt toward each other, stone fusing with stone, until, in the end, an arch stood in front of the three visitors.

Kaylin started toward the arch, moving slowly because she

could still see the shapes of tentacles, when Orbaranne shouted a sudden warning. "Lirienne!"

He did not look in the direction of her voice, because there was no direction. It surrounded them all. Bellusdeo lifted both of her hands in a deliberate sweep of motion; she spoke three words, all harsh, resounding draconian. Or at least that's what they sounded like, they were so damn loud.

A small barrier flared to life around her; it extended to cover both Kaylin and the Lord of the West March.

From the heart of the new arch, light flared; the stone that contained it began to melt. Kaylin had seen fire melt the stones in the expensive streets that surrounded the High Hall, and she locked her knees to prevent herself from leaping, automatically, out of the way. The shield that Bellusdeo had cast wouldn't follow her.

But as it happened, the melting stones shed no heat; they did not become molten. Kaylin wasn't certain if this was because they were in the Hallionne, or if this was like the effect her familiar sometimes had when he breathed. He could melt statues without heat, and remake the thick, almost liquid mess into something else entirely, which would have been more disturbing had he not spent most of his time on her shoulder, whining a lot.

"Bellusdeo, I think we should move back."

"I don't think it's safe to move at all. Hallionne?" the Dragon asked.

Orbaranne was silent. After the first anguished word, she had said nothing. Kaylin turned to look over her shoulder. The Avatar was not present.

But someone else was.

In the darkness of a cavern alleviated by magical light that seemed to have no real source, stood a familiar young man. He was Barrani in appearance; only his eyes made clear he wasn't Barrani in substance. They were a shade of obsidian;

there were no whites. Kaylin thought of the ancestors, then—the ones who had almost singlehandedly destroyed the High Halls while simultaneously facing the entirety of the Dragon Court. This man was not, however, an ancestor.

He was one of Teela's cohort, or he had been when he had first come to the West March.

He was the only one who had elected not to return from the green. He was also the only one who had attempted to either kidnap—or kill—the Consort.

"Terrano."

The Lord of the West March turned the moment the name left Kaylin's lips, his attention torn from the misshapen, falling archway.

Terrano offered a perfect, Barrani obeisance to the Lord of the West March, the movement fluid and controlled. "Lord of the West March." His eyes remained obsidian, flecked with speckled colors; they were almost opalescent, which made Kaylin queasy.

She remembered Terrano's attack in the forests of the West March. She remembered the Ferals that had come with him, and had appeared to obey his commands. And she understood all of Orbaranne's hesitation about the rest of the cohort. But the rest of the cohort had chosen to stay. The rest of the cohort were learning—in as much as it was possible—to be Barrani again. To be what they had once been before the decision of powerful men had sundered them from everything they had once held dear.

"You are Terrano of Allasarre," the Lord of the West March said.

"No. Not any more."

The Lord of the West March stiffened, but it was slight in comparison to Kaylin's physical reaction; had she not held

Lirienne's True Name, she would have missed it entirely. "Terrano—"

"Lord Kaylin." He bowed to her as well, and to her consternation, the bow was slightly deeper than the one he'd offered the Lord of the West March.

"Please don't call me that."

"It is what you are, in this place."

"Yes, but the only people who use that title use it for two reasons. The first: to mock me. And the second: as a warning to other Barrani."

His answering smile was pure, delighted urchin. "Then yes, I am using it correctly. I feel as if I have been gone from this place for many, many lifetimes. But I remember you." Since she'd been willing to kill him to preserve the Consort, this didn't make her feel any better.

"Why are you here?"

"I heard them. I...cannot hear them as I once did." He said this, his open expression turning pensive. She was surprised. He had seemed so jubilant at the prospect of freedom it had never occurred to her that he might miss what he'd left behind when he was finally unshackled.

But why wouldn't he?

She did not miss the fief of Nightshade. She would never miss it. She would never return there to live. But there were days—fewer and fewer as she aged—where she would have turned back the clock completely for just five minutes of her mother's warmth. The Barrani never exuded warmth, and frankly, were as likely to kill their parents as love them, if history were any guide. The cohort had therefore offered the rarity of absolute trust and acceptance. Who wouldn't miss that?

The Lord of the West March, however, was not thinking of love or sentiment. His voice as hard as Terrano's eyes, he said, "What have you done to Orbaranne?" And in the silence that followed the demand, Kaylin heard the sound of drawn sword.

★ ★ ★

Terrano did not draw a weapon in response, and the slightly confused glance he offered the Lord of the West March didn't seem to register that that Lord was now armed.

"Orbaranne?"

"The Hallionne."

Terrano turned to Kaylin, as if he expected her to be his personal interpreter. But the confusion in his expression seemed so genuine, she couldn't resent it. Much. "You are currently standing inside the Hallionne Orbaranne. You were, until very recently from our perspective, living in the Hallionne Alsanis with your siblings."

"Siblings?"

She shrugged. "At home, we call them the cohort."

"What do they call themselves?"

"Depends. I only hear Mandoran and Annarion, because they live with me."

"Cohort sounds almost military."

Kaylin shrugged. "Whenever I use the word 'family' or 'sibling,' they react the way you just did." Sensing Lirienne's growing agitation, she exhaled. "The Hallionne Orbaranne has not spoken a word since you arrived. What did you do?" The sword to her right rose, and she extended an arm to block it—not exactly the smartest move, given that her arm was mortal flesh.

"I did not—" He frowned. "I did not hear your Hallionne. I did hear Sedarias. She was angry," he added. "But then again—"

"Mandoran says she's always angry."

Terrano smiled.

"Annarion says she's only angry at Mandoran."

This widened, brightened, that smile. But his eyes remained the color of small pockets of shadow.

"Terrano—I don't know how you entered the Hallionne—but you have to leave."

"I'm looking for them."

"Yes, I believe you. But the *way* that you're looking is severely distressing the *Lord of the West March*."

He said, as if the statement had no meaning, "Is that a Dragon beside you?"

She did not reply in Leontine, but it was close. "...Yes."

"How can we possibly be in the Hallionne if a *Dragon* is here?"

"I promise I'll explain it," Kaylin said. "Please do not attempt to harm the Dragon, the Lord of the West March, or the Hallionne. If you didn't notice the Hallionne, you must have noticed that it was difficult to reach this space."

"It was," he agreed. "But there are many areas that are nigh impassible if one isn't clever." Clearly, Terrano considered himself clever, and was pleased to be so. "And this area, at least, was safe."

"It wasn't safe for Sedarias."

"She wasn't here. There's a..." Terrano struggled for words before finding them, as if he was struggling with a foreign language that he had studied years ago. "A storm? A storm outside. If we are standing inside the boundaries of a Hallionne, it appeared to be a..." He frowned again. "A cave? A shelter? I heard no Hallionne voice, and the cave itself was difficult to reach. But the storm made it highly desirable. I thought—if Sedarias were as smart as she thinks she is—she might have made her way here."

"She's not here. But Terrano—you need to go stand outside. I mean, outside of this space. I don't think it's good for the Hallionne—"

"No, no, wait. Just wait. I think I can figure out what went wrong. Wait."

If Kaylin had ever wondered what Lirienne's attachment to

what was, essentially, a god-like building was, she had her answer now, and it was not an entirely comfortable answer. She could understand why Orbaranne might, in the end, be fond of, or attached to, him; Orbaranne did not have the freedom to leave, to seek company, to make her life less lonely and less isolated. She required visitors; she required people to come to *her*. And to stay.

The Lord of the West March didn't suffer from the same restrictions. But if his visits to Orbaranne had once been an act of compassion, they were clearly more than that now.

The ground rumbled; the air flashed. Fire and ice passed through Kaylin like a series of very unpleasant blades.

Lirienne, she said, voice urgent. *Tell her—ask her—not to attempt to harm Terrano. Please.* Because she understood that Orbaranne was back, or that they were back within the confines of the Hallionne, and Terrano was still with them.

I cannot guarantee that. She has imperatives as Hallionne that she cannot ignore. If he is considered a threat—and I cannot see how he would not be—she will not have the choice.

If she tries to hurt him, he'll respond defensively—please!

I will try, Chosen. But think: this is what you want in the High Halls. This is what we will have at the very heart of the most important, the most dangerous, of our duties.

The others are not—they're not like him.

You hold my name, Kaylin; I do not hold yours. But even so, I advise you not to lie while speaking thus.

I'm not—

You do not even believe what you are telling me. Perhaps you are lying to yourself. I will return. While I bespeak the Hallionne, distract the intruder.

Before she could dredge up a reply, the Lord of the West March vanished.

CHAPTER 15

Terrano did not vanish. That was the good news. The shape of his eyes changed as he regarded Bellusdeo, which was the bad news.

"She's with me," Kaylin said. "She's with me with permission. The Hallionne accepts her as a guest." She moved to stand in front of the Dragon, without any confidence that it would stop him if he decided to attack. Gestures, however, mattered.

Terrano looked openly skeptical.

"You can ask the Hallionne yourself, if you want. But right now, Orbaranne probably considers *you* the primary threat."

She saw his expression ripple, which was an exact physical description. His eyes grew larger, changing the shape, the balance, of his facial features.

Please, please, please, she thought, at the absent Lord of the West March.

Distract him, that Lord replied.

There was only one way to do that. "Can you find Sedarias?" Kaylin asked. And then, because the constant small changes in his face reminded her of bad nightmares about dead people, added, "And can you *please* stop doing that thing with your face?"

Behind her, she heard a brief draconian snort.

"What thing with my face?"

"If I had a mirror you could actually see, I'd show you—but your face is constantly changing shape and size. Especially your eyes. And it is really, really disturbing." To her surprise, he did as she'd requested, looking almost embarrassed.

"It doesn't usually matter what I look like when I'm out there." He raised an arm and pointed in a random direction. "I don't talk to people like you much."

"We don't talk to people like you much, either. But it makes you look like a—a ghost. Or worse."

"Worse?"

"A Shadow."

This time, his limbs wavered, becoming opaque and elongating. Limbs were still better than face.

"Is that what you are, now?" she asked.

He seemed to consider this, his face creasing in an entirely normal, Barrani way. "I don't know," he finally replied. It was *so* not the reply she wanted. "To be honest, I don't really understand anymore what Shadow *is*."

"It's the thing that kills us or warps us when it comes in contact with us. You must understand it—didn't you send the forest Ferals to attack us?"

He frowned again. "The dogs, you mean?"

"They weren't what the rest of us call dogs."

"They weren't, no. They were Barrani, but they had the power necessary to transform themselves should they require it. I didn't choose the shape," he added.

"No, just the target."

"The Consort meant to destroy us."

"She *did not*." Bellusdeo's hand fell gently—for a Dragon, which meant bruises but not broken bones—on Kaylin's shoulder. It was a warning. Kaylin couldn't easily shrug it off, and didn't try. "She hoped to *save you*. She knew you were trapped."

"You can't possibly believe that."

"I believe it because *it's true*. None of you are prisoners. None of you are forced to stay with Alsanis. Not even you," she added. "All of you are free."

Terrano almost lost control of his face again, but managed to hold it—and his limbs—together. "Don't confuse what *you* wanted with what *she* wanted."

"She hasn't tried to harm you since."

"Hasn't she?" He shrugged. "If we're all free, where are my friends?"

"I have no idea. That's why I'm here."

"You."

"Chosen, remember?" she demanded, lifting her left arm and pulling back her sleeve. The marks were glowing brightly as they were exposed.

He spoke, then. She didn't understand a word he was saying, but felt that if she listened hard enough, she would. And because she'd had this feeling before, she thought Terrano might be reading the marks somehow, that he might be speaking True Words. None of the marks became physical words; none separated themselves from her skin.

"Look—if you could find them on your own, you would have found them by now, right?" She let her sleeve fall back into place as she lowered her arm.

"'By now' signifies nothing. Time is only a constraint for the lesser races."

"That is not true," Bellusdeo said, coming out from behind Kaylin. "Time *is* a factor in a state of emergency. We live forever, all things being equal. But all things are never equal. There are things that will kill us—in our mutual history, usually each other. It is possible that for the cohort, time is in short supply."

Terrano's eyes were black again. "You speak good High Barrani."

"In which case," Bellusdeo continued, ignoring the observation, "Lord Kaylin is best equipped to offer aid: she is a creature who is wed to time, her existence indivisible from it. What to either of our kin would be insignificant is not to her."

"Why are you even here?" Terrano demanded. And Kaylin remembered the reason the twelve children had been surrendered to the ceremony in the green: the Draco-Barrani war. The High Court had decided to imbue the twelve children with the power necessary to defeat their ancient enemies. Those enemies, of course, being the Dragons.

"She lives with us," Kaylin said quickly. "With Annarion and Mandoran. Mandoran doesn't really like her," she felt compelled to add, "but Annarion does, and so does Teela."

"Teela?" This was said with open scorn. "Teela *fought in the war*. There's no way—"

"She goes out drinking with Teela and Tain."

"...And they get along?"

"Yes. Or at least no one's reported them to the Halls of Law yet, and they all return home without wounds or burns." She folded her arms.

Terrano seemed outraged. "I leave them alone for a little while, and they forget *everything*."

"Sedarias forgets nothing."

"She's obviously forgotten how to *use the portal paths*."

"I see that you have more in common with Mandoran than the rest of your cohort," Bellusdeo said, voice cool.

The ground buckled beneath the Dragon's feet. Since the Dragon could more or less fly with a brief change of shape, this was only a minor inconvenience. For her. Kaylin, however, couldn't. She didn't want to leave Bellusdeo's side, because she was pretty certain that her presence was the one thing that kept Terrano from going all out.

"Not your presence alone, no," Hallionne Orbaranne said. This time, she appeared in the center of the room, her Avatar form girded with armor that seemed made of crystal, and weapons that seemed made of night sky. Her eyes, however, were much like Terrano's—black, opalescent.

Terrano met the unnatural eyes of the Hallionne with unnatural eyes of his own. He didn't draw blades; he didn't turn his physical arms into weapons. But Kaylin thought he could. "Orbaranne. Hallionne. I don't think he's a danger—"

"Do you not understand the danger he does pose? I cannot hear the whole of his thought. I can hear fractions of it, but his thought is a multitude of voices, and not all of them are clear to me."

Kaylin inhaled, remembering the forest Ferals. She exhaled, remembered the rest of the cohort. Especially the three that she knew. "Your eyes," she said, to Orbaranne, "are exactly the same as his."

Both Orbaranne and Terrano seemed surprised by this. Terrano was the only one who appeared to feel insulted.

"Is *that* how you see it?" he demanded. "You think our eyes *look the same?*"

Kaylin glanced at Bellusdeo; Bellusdeo shrugged. "I said it, didn't I?"

"And you?" he demanded of the Dragon, which surprised Kaylin.

"They look the same to me. They are not the same shape— the Hallionne seems to have much better control of her physical dimensions than you do—but they appear to be black, with flecks of moving color. I would not hazard a guess as to the physical composition."

Orbaranne, however, had lowered her swords. She was staring at Terrano as if she were truly seeing him for the first time, but her eyes were unblinking. Kaylin doubted she'd remembered something as trivial as eyelids when composing this particular Avatar.

"They are there," Orbaranne replied, distracted.

To Kaylin's surprise, she turned to Bellusdeo. She offered the Dragon a bow—which should have been impossible given the armor—before speaking again. "Your experience of Shadow is greater, in the end, than my own; I have knowledge, but Shadows are unique enough that that knowledge might not be relevant in all situations. What do you see?"

"As I told Terrano, I see what Lord Kaylin sees. When I ruled, I would have considered him a danger, but I would have considered you a danger as well."

The Hallionne had not looked away from Terrano. The swords she was carrying vanished as she began to speak. Her words shook the floor. They might have shaken the walls; Kaylin couldn't tell because her body was shaking, too. But Kaylin recognized the language that she couldn't understand when it was spoken—and it was spoken at a volume that made her instantly cover her ears. Only Dragons spoke this loudly naturally.

Bellusdeo had Dragon hearing; she didn't even flinch.

But Terrano's eyes widened. He waited while the Hallionne spoke; her words seemed to continue forever, as if the speaking of True Words nailed them into place, made them solid, real, as eternal as mountain edifices. Only when the words had become echoes, only when the Hallionne's lips had ceased their motion, did Terrano begin to speak.

It didn't surprise Kaylin that he spoke the same tongue, although he spoke it as if it were his native language.

The Hallionne listened; she listened as if fixed in place, as if she were of stone. But when Terrano was done, she lowered her chin, lowered her arms, and transformed her armor into a loose drape of flowing off-white robe. The cave around them melted more slowly than the armor had, and when shape was reasserted, the color was different. This would be because there was no longer a ceiling; as far as the eye could see, there was sky, a deep blue with a smidgen of cloud.

Where the portal arch had come into being, a round series of concentric circles remained, and there was a splash of brown red that spoke of dried blood.

Orbaranne turned to Kaylin, then. "Lirienne will be with us momentarily. I apologize for my anger and my suspicion."

"You're—"

"I was not, as you once suspected, Barrani before I made the choice to become the heart of the Hallionne. I was mortal, as you were. I was young, and new to this world, this place. Suspicion, among our kind, is not an absolute requirement of survival."

Kaylin shrugged, a fief shrug. "It doesn't hurt," she offered.

Orbaranne smiled, then. "Doesn't it?" And she turned, once again, to face Terrano.

The speech seemed to have drained something out of him; he looked much more solid, much more real, than he had moments—or hours?—ago.

He shrugged, miming Kaylin's gesture. But when he spoke, he spoke Barrani. "She asked," he said, glancing toward the grassy plane that had taken the place of stone. "I answered."

"The Lord of the West March couldn't answer the way you did. I don't think most of the Barrani—even the ancient Arcanists—could."

"No?"

"No."

Terrano looked away. "You learn a bit when you leave home."

"That's more than a bit."

"Are you *sure* you haven't spoken with Sedarias recently?"

At that, Kaylin chuckled. "Can he stay?" she asked the Hallionne.

"Yes. We were negotiating the terms of his occupancy." Before Kaylin could ask another question, Lirienne entered the circle, as if passing through a door to arrive by their sides.

Terrano once again offered the Lord of the West March a passable bow.

This time, the Lord of the West March returned it. His eyes were a shade of midnight blue that did not suit his expression, and he came to stand by the side of Orbaranne's Avatar as if he had no intention of ever leaving it again.

"Let us return to the portal pathways after we have had a chance to discuss all that has happened," Orbaranne said.

This time, when they repaired to the great hall, it took twenty minutes. Orbaranne apologized profusely for this, although no one complained. Especially not Kaylin. Terrano appeared to be interested in the Hallionne's interior, and he asked her questions every few steps. This was in keeping with his apparent age, but sadly, Kaylin didn't understand the questions—or the answers, if it came to that.

Neither the Hallionne nor Terrano were speaking True Words.

"It is not trivially done," the Hallionne replied, although Kaylin had had better sense than to speak out loud. "True Words are words of power, of intent, of consequence. We do not use them to say 'have a nice day.'"

"Are there ways to say that, in the language of the Ancients?"

Terrano and Orbaranne exchanged a glance. It was Terrano who answered. "Yes, but…it's not considered polite. It's— look, if the Ancients had said it, it would have been a *very* nice day. Instantly. Completely. They had no way of really asking questions; all words were statements of fact."

The dining table had shrunk by the time the group reached it. Bellusdeo had not spoken a word; nor had Lirienne. Terrano and Orbaranne, however, made up for the lack. Kaylin was from Elantra; she was accustomed to hearing languages she didn't know and therefore didn't understand. In the office, in theory, everyone spoke Elantran. And that was true as far as it went—but everyone also spoke their own tongues: Aerian, Barrani and Leontine. There had been spillover, of course, and all of the Hawks could curse in languages they couldn't otherwise speak.

She wondered if Lirienne understood Terrano. Decided against asking. Knew that Orbaranne had already heard.

She took a chair; Bellusdeo took the seat opposite her. The head of the table had been clearly reserved for the Lord of the West March; Terrano plopped himself gracelessly in the seat to Kaylin's right.

"We'll find them," Kaylin said quietly.

He said nothing. Loudly. When he finally spoke, it was grudging. "The Hallionne thought that I might be responsible for the disappearance of my kin."

"He is not," Orbaranne added, in case that was in doubt.

"Not even accidentally?" It was Bellusdeo who asked. Given that Terrano's eyes were no longer Barrani eyes, they didn't shade to the expected dark blue.

"They're more like me than you," Terrano answered. "Yes, I'm certain." He continued to stare.

"Blink," Kaylin told him.

"What?"

"Blink. *Try* to look less like a living statue and more like a person." She exhaled on a grimace as he obliged. Badly. "Never mind." To the Hallionne, she said, "We need to speak with the water."

"The elemental water has dispersed," Orbaranne replied. The words were stilted, the expression that accompanied them, troubled. "Water was never used as a conduit, a method of travel."

"It was," Kaylin said, thinking of boats. "It still is."

"No. Travel by boat is predicated on the existence of rivers or larger bodies of water—but there is no river between the Keeper's garden and the Hallionne. At least, not that I'm aware of. I have been troubled by your appearance."

"Because it should have been impossible?"

"In many, many ways, yes. The Keeper's garden exists to restrain the will of the wild elements. The elements are necessary for life—even my own. But when free to interact—"

"They try to kill each other, fail, and kill everything around them instead."

"Yes." She seemed relieved not to have to explain this. "It is possible that the Keeper is finally failing in his duty."

"I'm pretty damn sure the water wasn't responsible for the loss of the cohort." Kaylin folded her arms.

"You are sentimentally attached to the water, and that is inadvisable. Understand that the element itself, like any living creation, is not all of one thing or all of another. It is possible that the element could both destroy—or attempt to destroy—the cohort and simultaneously desire to preserve it. But...the voice of the water is silent, here. Your arrival required all of its substantial power."

"Has this happened before?"

"Never here, and not in other Hallionne, to my knowledge. The fire has been used as a conduit before—but only by ancient Dragons." She bowed her head. "You are not the only people to come to me with inquiries about the cohort." She had adopted Kaylin's name, but would: it was what they called themselves, now.

Terrano stiffened.

"Were the others Barrani?"

This time she did not answer. Kaylin understood; she turned to face the Lord of the West March. "Was it you?"

"I asked the Hallionne to monitor them. I also asked the

Hallionne to house them. Any evaluation of their abilities or their intent could not be carried out were they to remain outside of the Hallionne's boundary." Kaylin opened her mouth. The Lord of the West March, however, had not finished. "I wished to know," he continued, "if Orbaranne would recognize them. Once one has been accepted as a guest in a Hallionne, one will be accepted as a guest in future. The grant of blood—in most cases—is almost definitional."

"Outcastes?"

"The Hallionne do not recognize outcastes *as* outcaste unless exceptional circumstances arise. Once the Hallionne has accepted the responsibility of hospitality, it will always be extended. There is a reason Lord Severn could travel these pathways, even with the marked disapproval of the High Court. The...changes, the alterations, in the group you refer to as the cohort, are changes that would be impossible for any others of my kin."

Bellusdeo said, "I did not give blood."

"No. Nor will you be asked, but your circumstances are unusual."

"The water?" Kaylin asked.

Bellusdeo snorted smoke. "The Consort," the gold Dragon said, although the question had been asked of the Lord of the West March. To Orbaranne, she said, "Was the Water's decision to bring us here influenced by the Consort? "

Something wordless passed between the Hallionne and the Lord of the West March. It was the latter who replied. "Not in my estimation. My sister is not without power, but the power necessary to command the Water to do what was done—at great cost to the Water itself—is not power she possesses."

Or not power Lirienne was aware she possessed, at any rate.

No, kyuthe. It is not an ability she possesses. Even the potential for power of this kind would have been noted.

"She probably thought I'd arrive with the small Dragon, not you," Kaylin told the large Dragon.

"I believe it is immaterial. What she asked for, the Hallionne granted. I am with you, not the familiar. But that is not the question. How did she know to ask? If she does not, herself, have the ability to command the Water to do her bidding, how was she aware that you, at least, would be here at all?"

To Kaylin's surprise, Lirienne chuckled. Although his eyes remained blue, there was some hint of green in their shade. "Were it not for Lord Kaylin, they would not have emerged from the green as they did. Two of their number now dwell within Lord Kaylin's home. If my sister was aware that the cohort encountered unknown danger, she can be forgiven for expecting—or suspecting—that Lord Kaylin would immediately become involved."

Bellusdeo raised a brow. "And also for assuming that she would be accompanied by someone who had not yet ventured into the Hallionne?"

Silence. It was edged, sharp, suspicious.

Kaylin rushed to fill it, although Bellusdeo was right; neither of them would get answers from the Lord of the West March, and there were other things that were, in the end, more pressing. "Someone found the cohort on the portal paths." It wasn't a question.

"Demonstrably."

"What are the probabilities that their difficulties were caused by non-Barrani?"

The Lord of the West March did not answer.

Terrano, however, snorted. Loudly. He really did remind Kaylin of Mandoran; it made her wonder why Mandoran had stayed. On the other hand, the universe was probably safer for it.

"If not the Lord of the West March, and not the Consort,

then who?" Kaylin turned to Orbaranne's Avatar. "Did any other Barrani Lord come to you with a request or a query?"

Orbaranne looked to Lirienne, who shook his head. Unsurprisingly, the Hallionne failed to answer.

"It wasn't me," Terrano said.

"You're not a Barrani Lord."

Terrano shrugged. "Neither are my friends."

"No. But they're descending on my city—or they were—because they're going to take the Test of Name. If they pass, they'll be Lords of the High Court."

Terrano brightened at the thought. As he considered her words, his smile widened; in the end, he was laughing.

The Lord of the West March was not. "Lord Kaylin." He rose. "I ask that you speak with Terrano about the experiences of Annarion and Mandoran as they intersect with your city. I will retire for the evening."

"Everything has changed," Terrano said. Neither he nor Bellusdeo had eaten much. They retired to what Kaylin assumed was her room, given that Bellusdeo was in the Hallionne as an adjunct. Orbaranne, however, had allowed Terrano to enter as well, not a given in a Hallionne, whose duty was to keep guests safe, usually from each other. He flopped, chest down, across the nearest bed.

"You better not have your boots on," Kaylin told him.

"Why?"

"Dirt."

"You don't have to clean it."

"And it's rude."

"Rude."

"That's what I said."

Bellusdeo took a seat on the lounge chair by the wall, content to let Kaylin and Terrano maneuver for space. Only when they were done—for a value of done that had Terrano take off boots that Kaylin was almost certain were not actually real—did she speak.

"I want you to talk to Lord Nightshade about what happened in his Tower. Don't make that face," she added, which was technically hard to say in Barrani. She tried Elantran, and Terrano's face remained blank. Mandoran and Annarion had picked it up from Teela.

"Why him?" he asked.

"Because I have his name."

Terrano whistled. "I wouldn't have thought that was safe. I guess I underestimated you."

"He gave it to me."

"...Or severely overestimated him." Before she could speak, Terrano added, "Look we *all* knew each other's names. It's not about sharing names. It's about who you share them with."

"You knew him?"

"No. But we heard a *lot* about him from Annarion, who practically worshipped him."

Kaylin grimaced. "Not anymore. And believe that my house would be a much happier place if he did."

"They argue?"

"They argue in my house, yes."

"Why?"

"Because arguing in Nightshade's castle almost destroyed the High Halls." And before he could ask, she told him what had happened, or as much of it as she could clearly remember.

"Kitling," Bellusdeo said—a warning. Kaylin understood why. If the Emperor knew—if the Emperor understood— *why* the ancestors had attacked the High Halls, killing anyone that stood in their way...Annarion and Mandoran would be in trouble. The empire was his hoard. But there was no way that the Hallionne would speak with the Eternal Emperor. They were safe.

And Terrano needed to understand. He listened, his eyes

luminous although they were still obsidian. "They should have left with me," he finally said.

"Annarion didn't want to leave."

"Sedarias didn't want to leave. If she'd made a different choice, most of the others would have followed."

Kaylin hesitated.

But Bellusdeo said, "Sedarias, of all of your cohort, was probably the one least changed."

"All of us were changed."

"What you could—and can—do changed, yes. But Sedarias, from all accounts, *thinks* like a Barrani Lord. Even now."

Terrano buried his head in the crook of his arms. "What's the point?" he asked, his voice slightly muffled. "What's the *point* in thinking like that?"

"She is Barrani."

"What does that *even mean*? Her family abandoned her, same as ours. They were willing to throw us away because we might—*might*—become powerful. They thought they'd own us, if we did. And you know what?" He lifted his head. "We *did* become powerful. We are *way more* powerful than any of our parents. We're powerful enough—" He stopped. Kaylin didn't think he was finished, and waited. "Does she want to go home? Does she want to retake the lands that should have been hers?"

"I think," Bellusdeo said, her voice quiet and entirely free of emotion, "she wishes to reclaim the lands that should have collectively belonged to all of you."

"But *why*? We don't *need* them. They're no use to us, anymore. We don't need to sleep. We don't need to eat. We don't need to breathe—well, not the way you do. We don't need to hide under tall stone roofs. Or wooden ones. We don't need any of it!"

"Terrano," the Dragon said, when he once again fell silent, "why are you here?" It was the question Kaylin had asked, and the question the Lord of the West March most wanted answered, but the way she now asked it transformed the words. There was a softness to them, a different kind of assumption—it wasn't suspicion, though.

He didn't answer. Of course he didn't. She was a Dragon.

"I was born between two wars," she told him.

He looked up, then.

"We might be the same age. I was one of nine sisters in an aerie of grouchy Dragons. We were considered young for our age, and of course, fragile. We were fragile because—"

"You were female."

Her brows rose briefly before she nodded. "You know that much."

"Of course I do."

"Kaylin didn't."

He snorted. "Mortal. You can't expect any better."

The smidgen of sympathy Kaylin had almost started to feel vanished. But Bellusdeo merely nodded. "I was born on this world. But the aerie was lost to Shadow, and when we emerged—my sisters and I—we emerged to different stars, a different sky."

He lifted his head, placing his chin on his arms, arrested.

"I was not as you were. We were not sacrificed on the altar of war. But we were lost, regardless. We—none of us—were adults. We were as helpless as Lord Kaylin. And I lost my sisters, one by one, to the Shadows. I lost them, we lost each other, searching for our names. I lost some because, in finding names, their center could not hold. They could not maintain cohesion of one form or the other.

"Understand that Barrani make outcastes for political reasons, for personal gain. Dragons don't."

"Oh?"

"If we want political power, we kill our enemies."

"We do that, too," he said, quickly.

"We don't look for consensus. We don't attempt to gather armies. We try to kill our enemies. Or they try to kill us. I believe one of your historical High Lords called us barbarous savages, better than animals only because we were Immortal." She shrugged. "Our outcastes are therefore above politics, or beneath politics; opinions differ. Enemies are personal. Outcastes are like terrifying natural disasters. One might feel threatened by an earthquake, and one does what one can to survive it—but one cannot take revenge against the earth."

"I think it's been tried," Terrano said. His animosity had faded; he was looking at Bellusdeo as if he'd only just seen her and didn't quite understand what it was he was seeing.

"Had my sisters and I remained in the Aerie, we would have come into our power naturally. We start out as the feeblest of the children; effort must be taken to preserve us. It is not an effort that is made for the males, because it is not required. When we do come into our power, however, we have far less difficulty controlling its use. I am curious about your Sedarias."

"Not mine."

Bellusdeo's smile was brief, but genuine. "I confess I am fond of Annarion. I understand him. I understand his goals. I do not understand Mandoran." She exhaled a bit of smoke. "But were they Dragons, both would be outcaste."

Before Terrano's outrage could express itself in words— or worse—Bellusdeo continued. "To the Dragons, I believe I would be considered a borderline case; were I not female, were the Dragons not so few in number, safety would probably dictate my death."

"If they could kill you."

Her smile was deeper, and something in it implied serious fangs, although at the moment, she didn't have any. "Indeed. I would not lie down and expose my figurative throat; I feel that I have as much right to exist as they do. But I would, wouldn't I?"

He nodded. "Why are you telling me this?"

"Because the Barrani do not, and did not, do as the Dragons have done throughout our history. Barrani wake to one name. They live their lives, spend their existence, with that name. There are apparently those who attempt to divest themselves—deliberately—of their names. But absent that attempt, they are a single, indivisible whole.

"Dragons are not. They come into the world with a single name, but that single name is half of what they require. They have the capacity to hold a duality of names—but they are not considered Dragons if they cannot meld the duality into a single whole.

"Those who cannot are not considered dangerous. It is those who *can* that are."

"But...you all can."

"Yes, if we are adults, we can. But there are those who do not contain that duality. It is the foundation for their attempt to take more, to build more, to be more."

And Kaylin suddenly remembered the one time she had seen the outcaste Dragon's name. It had been far more complicated than any other True Word she had ever seen. It had reminded her, not of Barrani, but...of a world. A small world.

"You think we're like that."

"No. I was, I admit, concerned. I do not know the names of your kin; I do not know the names of my own. But they are alive because of those names."

"And I'm not."

Silence again. "I did not find my adult name on my own," Bellusdeo said. It sounded like a confession. "But it is mine, regardless.

"But you did not return to your name. I do not know what you are. Because the Barrani are political, they will accept your cohort *as* Barrani, at least in public speech and interaction. But they know—as you do—that that is now only a small part of what they are capable of being." She exhaled more smoke. "The world I grew up in, the world I ruled in its twilight, was destroyed by Shadow. And I see that Shadow in you."

He sat up.

"But I see it in your Hallionne, as well. And it is...possible... that my understanding of Shadow is too narrow."

Kaylin's jaw dropped.

"Do I have something on my face?"

"Uh, no."

"Gilbert was of Shadow to me. Everything about him proclaimed him Shadow. He himself didn't deny that he was from, and of, Ravellon. But—you were right about him." She exhaled puffs of flame. "Understand, kitling. I lost everything to Shadow. Shadow that mimicked life, Shadow that was clever, subtle. We all made mistakes—because we hoped, or because we took risks that we should not have taken. It made me very, very risk averse, the costs were so high. And it's possible—barely—that I destroyed people who might have been like Gilbert."

"And that bothers you?" Orbaranne asked, which surprised Kaylin. The Hallionne had been silent enough that she could forget she was in the room. Her Avatar materialized in such a way that she, Terrano and Teela formed the points of a triangle.

"No one wants to think of themselves as a murderer," Bellusdeo replied. "I could justify it. If I think about it now—and I do—I mostly *do* justify it. But there's a reason Kaylin Neya is a private and not a queen."

"My risks don't have the same cost."

Orbaranne said, "you are Chosen. Some of the risks you take might be very, very costly." The Avatar bowed her head, and when she raised it again, her eyes looked like normal human eyes. "But some of the risks you've taken have saved us before. I...would like to be able to take risks."

But she couldn't, Kaylin thought. Because she was what she was made to be; she was what she'd promised to be.

"Yes, Chosen. You see Shadow in my eyes, but I am not a scion of Shadow; it was not Shadow that created me. It might break me, in some future. But it is not what I am."

"Is it part of what you are?"

"Not in a way I understand. But...I see some of what you see because you see it. And Lord Bellusdeo, I...cannot think you are wrong."

CHAPTER 16

"I don't think it's a good idea for you to be here," Kaylin told Terrano, hands on her hips.

"I'm not thrilled about it, either. Everything feels heavy and confining. All of the sound is wrong. I feel like I'm trying to speak around a mouthful of water." Terrano's eyes were a surprising shade of Barrani blue. He looked pensive, his smile absent.

There was no water—no living water—in the Hallionne. There *was* water in the heart of the West March, and Lirienne had invited them, for a value of invitation that made the word equivalent to command, to his home.

Kaylin had suggested they take the portal paths. She wanted to investigate them, and she wanted to begin a practical search in earnest.

She received three instant refusals. The only person present who thought it was a reasonable idea was Terrano himself. Orbaranne had been willing to have Kaylin inspect the portal, and the foot of the pathway itself; she was unwilling to let Kaylin actually walk it. Bellusdeo considered it a terrible idea, given the continued absence of the cohort, and the

Lord of the West March looked at her with blue eyes above an impatient grimace.

So: no portal paths.

Terrano offered to meet them at the Hallionne Alsanis, as he had investigations of his own to conduct.

It was Bellusdeo who said, "Weren't you driven off the pathways? Isn't that why you disabled the Hallionne's protections?"

"I didn't *disable* them. I found a way past them."

"Which you implied you needed."

He was, of the cohort, most like Mandoran; if he hated Dragons, the hatred was impersonal and almost theoretical. "Is she always like this?" he asked Kaylin.

"No. Sometimes she's actually angry." Kaylin was surprised at the interaction between the two, and wondered if Bellusdeo privately missed Mandoran.

The four—Dragon, Hawk, Barrani ruler and uncertain— were stuffed inside a Barrani carriage which appeared to have magic wheels or something, because a road that should have jarred and bruised the carriage occupants felt smoother than expensively laid city streets.

The overland journey, on the other hand, was not short. Terrano lasted maybe two hours, judging by sun position, before he swung himself through the window and out onto the roof.

"He reminds me of Mandoran," Bellusdeo said. "Did he really try to kill you?"

"Not personally; he sent Ferals to do us all in, instead." She hesitated. "Well, not Ferals exactly."

"What were they?"

"I *think* they were Barrani. Some were. Or at least one was."

"He transformed them?" The Dragon's eyes were orange.

"I think—I think they might have transformed themselves. Look, it was confusing, chaotic and noisy. I don't actually know what happened. But Terrano was working with—" She stopped and stuck her head out the window. "Hey!"

"I can hear you perfectly well. You don't have to shout."

"You were working with Arcanists, right?"

"So?"

"Do you know how many were involved? I mean—was there more than one?"

"I didn't count."

"So, more than one. Or Barrani education is even worse than the education I received. Did you pay any attention to names?"

"If I couldn't even be bothered to count, why would I know names?"

"Because someone is responsible for the disappearance of your friends, and the sooner we discover who, the better."

Terrano shrugged. "I think it's more important to find them."

"That's because you don't live here. But they want to."

Terrano muttered something under his breath. Bellusdeo caught it; Kaylin didn't. Probably just as well.

Barrani carriage or no, by the time Kaylin stumbled out of the door she was sore and tired. Sitting still, or sitting as still as a moving cabin allowed, took a lot of energy; Terrano hadn't bothered. Although the Lord of the West March was in the carriage and obviously a witness to his antics, his boredom had grown, and he ended up trying to fly. This had caused two stops, because his first attempt would have broken bones had anyone else tried it. His second attempt was only a little better.

But his third attempt was very Mandoran-like. "Don't look at me like that. This is harder than it looks."

Since to Kaylin it looked impossible, she rolled her eyes. She tried to remember that Terrano had almost been responsible for the death of a Hallionne, that he had attacked the

Consort, and that he had no loyalty whatsoever to his own people. All of these things were true, but it was hard to put them in the right context when she watched him; his excitement made him seem almost like a foundling who has finally come to understand that he's safe.

But foundlings couldn't kill people. Except maybe each other.

As if she could hear the thought, Bellusdeo said, "There is a reason it is not unwise to fear them."

"But you like them!"

"Yes, I do. But I have the luxury of being a displaced person—something I never thought I'd say. I *can* like them. I can let that influence my decisions. I am not responsible for the well-being of everyone else. Were I the Consort—"

The Lord of the West March cleared his throat a touch too loudly.

Bellusdeo inclined her head. "I do not believe I would take the risk."

"Of?"

"Allowing them to take the Test of Name. It isn't about the resultant politics—I believe that is the Lord of the West March's concern—but about the resultant chaos. They don't have malicious intent. But Kaylin, Hawks died."

"Hawks died because of the ancestors!"

Bellusdeo said nothing. As was her wont, she said it loudly.

"So, if you were queen—or Empress—what would you do with them?"

"I would do what the Emperor is doing. I would wait and see." With an apologetic smile, she added, "I am not Barrani."

"I left Diarmat's report behind." It was probably a soggy mess, too.

"You have the Lord of the West March as a traveling companion. He knows more than the Imperial Court."

"He's not exactly objective. No offense," she added quickly.

None taken.

"But the Imperial Court will be. Less well informed, but more objective."

"Do you think so?"

"You said it yourself—they're not Barrani."

"Ah, you misunderstand. The Emperor's hoard is the empire. It is therefore in his interests that the Barrani rule be as peaceful as possible. Where the Barrani choose to intrigue with any subtlety, it is a matter for the Barrani Caste Court. The High Court, in this case. But where that intrigue cannot be ignored with a bit of effort, it will not be. The Barrani, I believe, understand this; it is not something that needs to be stated.

"The fact that the cohort disappeared while outside of the Empire was no doubt a strategic decision."

"Because it's irrelevant to the Emperor?"

"Yes." She looked across to the Lord of the West March. "I understand the cause for concern. Were you not prepared for this when they returned from the heart of the green?"

To Kaylin's surprise, he nodded. "But understand, we are none of us mortal; we did not anticipate the speed at which a possible crisis could blossom. Not all of the Barrani responsible for the previous events which occurred in the West March have been identified with any certainty. It has been convenient—perhaps too convenient—to lay blame at Terrano's feet. He was seen by many, heard by many, and he came with Shadows. Given the nature of the near disaster, we considered it unlikely that a similar attempt would be made.

"Men are oft ambitious when they fail to understand the consequences of that ambition. There was little doubt, in the end, of these particular consequences."

"So...you didn't expect Sedarias to move immediately."

"We did not expect Mandoran or Annarion to move; the decision was made so suddenly that we did not have time to

react. Time, however, has been taken since your departure."
He looked at her, his eyes predominantly blue. "Surely you do
not believe that the Consort has only recently taken an interest in them." He looked out the window at Terrano, who was
literally bouncing along the ground on the tips of his toes, his
Barrani hair streaming back from his face.

"He is a child," he said, when he pulled his gaze away.
"And had he returned, he would not have been so politically
contentious."

"Is it Annarion?"

The Lord of the West March almost glared at her. Almost.
Bellusdeo did snort loudly, which caused the Lord of the West
March to raise his brows.

"Sedarias," Bellusdeo then said.

"Annarion *is* contentious among the High Court. When
his brother became outcaste, it was, as you suspect, a political
maneuver. My sister did not agree with it then, and does not
agree with it now, but she was fond of Calarnenne. Calarnenne's line, his ancestral lands, were taken by a distant cousin.
We are not as numerous in our offspring as mortals of any
race, but it should not surprise you to know that there was
more than one cousin, and indeed, relatives far closer in blood.
Should Annarion take—and pass—the Test, he would have
some support for his initial attempt to reclaim what would be
his by right of our own laws.

"The lord who replaced Calarnenne was a close political
ally of the man who was High Lord at the time."

"Is he still alive?"

"Yes." The single word was curt.

"Does he have any relation, that you know of, to Candallar?"

"Candallar?" The Lord of the West March frowned, as if
searching memory for the name. "Ah. You mean the outcaste?"

"Yes. He's a fieflord."

"An interesting question. I cannot answer it with any certainty at the moment." Seeing Kaylin's expression, he said, "I am not a criminal, and you are not conducting an interrogation. I am the Lord of these lands, and you are making a request. Asking a boon or a favor. Given events, I will attempt to find an answer. But, as Lord Bellusdeo says, it is Sedarias who is the most contentious of the returnees."

"Who will she replace?"

The Lord of the West March smiled. It was not a pleasant expression. "An'Teela was a child during those wars; she is considered mature, now. I was not a child, but I was not ruler here; my brother was not High Lord, my sister not yet Consort. When Sedarias was sent into the green, her mother was Lord of her line. Her brother is An'Mellarionne now. He was her junior in age, and he was not considered, in their youth, her equal. He was not considered close.

"It is her brother she will unseat." He closed his eyes. "Her brother has lands that adjoin the West March; they are small. His holdings within the Empire are larger."

"He's an ally."

"He is, as you suspect, an ally of mine, and through me, of the High Lord."

"Has he visited his sister at all?"

Lirienne's eyes opened. He cast a glance toward the Dragon, who snorted and shrugged. "Understand that Mellarionne is not a child. As Teela, he has grown in stature, and in power, since Sedarias was sent to the green."

"That's a no," Bellusdeo said.

"But—"

"She's his sister?"

"Yes. She's family."

"If I recall correctly, you are an orphan. You have no siblings."

"So?" She tried to keep active hostility out of the word,

but it was difficult. She had never liked being talked down at, and she recognized it for what it was.

"You have an optimistic, even naive, view of family."

"If the Consort had been sent away at your father's orders, and she had returned, you would go to see her."

"If my sister had been sent away at the High Lord's orders, he would not have survived."

And she remembered Teela's father, and fell silent.

This amused Lirienne. *You are thinking of your Nightshade.*

She was.

Calarnenne was not son of the High Lord. He was not expected to rule our people. He built alliances, yes, but alliances require strategic opportunity on the part of one's allies. There was every chance that I would become High Lord in future. I had strategic opportunity. Had my father sent my sister to the green to die, he would have died. If not by my hand alone, by the combined might of my forces and my brother's.

But you would have visited her. You would have flown *to the West March from wherever you were—*

In the West March.

Fine. Your brother *would have flown to the West March from the High damn Halls the minute—the second—he had word that she was alive. I'm not naive. I'm not stupid.*

"You are not naive, and you are not stupid," he agreed—out loud. "But your experience with the Barrani is too narrow. We said—all three of us—that our family and our relationship was unusual for the Barrani. It was, and is."

"Nightshade spent *centuries* trying to find some way to reach his brother."

"Yes. And in the end, he succeeded. He found you. He is also outcaste and fieflord. Your experience with Barrani involves very, very few, and it is unwise to make assumptions about an entire race based on such a selective sample. And yes.

Were my sister to return to me alive—in any form—I would have been here.

"But your cohort are not my sisters or brothers. They are therefore potential rivals, potential enemies. They are certainly contentious. As they are not mine, I do not feel responsible for them, or for their survival. And Lord Kaylin? Very, very few of their families want them back; Calarnenne and Iberrienne are the exceptions. Honor at a remove of centuries is politically safe, and even wise. The dead can be created, recreated, their histories revised and transformed to suit the political needs of the moment. The living have never been so convenient."

"Did *any* of the surviving family visit?" Eddorian's brother had come, but not to visit; he had been one of the Barrani who had worked most closely with Terrano. And whatever had been done to him, or had been done to him *by* his self, had all but eaten his mind.

He was silent for one long beat. Almost reluctantly, he said, "Yes."

The West March was, in theory, in the middle of forested land. It was not, however, a small village by mortal standards. The forest path, which was not obvious, was nonetheless easily traveled. Kaylin knew the moment they had crossed a boundary invisible to her eyes, because she could see the shadows of the giant eagles the Barrani called the Dreams of Alsanis. Terrano didn't fear them; he remained on the carriage roof as they approached the bridge that separated the West March from the rest of the world. Lirienne did leave the carriage, then; the bridge was not fixed, and in fact, did not exist until he—or one of his kin—invoked it.

Kaylin would have disembarked as well, but she didn't trust Bellusdeo to remain in the cabin if she wasn't with her. For obvious reasons, she wanted the Dragon to be as invisible as possible while in the West March. Bellusdeo was not Teela; she didn't immediately fly into a cold rage if she thought someone was condescending enough to worry about her.

Lirienne returned to the carriage. "Can Terrano be persuaded to come down off the roof?"

By which he meant, could Kaylin persuade Terrano to get down. She grimaced, stuck her head out the nearest window, and asked. When Terrano apparently failed to hear her, she shouted, instead. Terrano, whining, did return to the inside of the carriage, although he sulked for the rest of the drive, which was thankfully short.

Kaylin was reminded that Lirienne was the Lord of the West March; a dozen armed and armored men stood at a kind of elegant attention as the carriage pulled up to the front of his dwelling. He asked that they remain in the carriage while he spoke—briefly—with his seneschal. Probably about the Dragon.

Definitely about the Dragon, among other things, Lirienne said. *I am certain you realize just how unusual a visitor she is. Or perhaps you do not, given your cohort and their place in your life.*

"The *reason* he was reluctant," Bellusdeo said, when they had been shown to their rooms by servants so frostily silent they appeared to made of ice, "was your reaction."

"There was nothing wrong with my reaction."

"He said, clearly, that most Barrani consider their direct siblings their most dangerous enemies. It's just possible that the visitor had no love of the sibling; the visitor might have been attempting to discern just how *much* of a threat their sibling posed."

Kaylin's arms were folded.

"I loved my sisters," the gold Dragon continued. "But I do not doubt that, had we all survived, we would have come into conflict. Serious conflict." It was the first time Bellusdeo had ever said that.

"You kind of did all survive," Kaylin pointed out.

"They are part of me, yes. They are part of *my name*. But they have no voice that I can hear. They cannot keep me company. They cannot fight armies at my side. They cannot argue with me, disagree, or suggest things I had not yet considered. I understand what happened; I understand why. I understand that were it not for their existence, I would not be alive; I even understand that I am more powerful and far more stable than I would otherwise be.

"But I miss them. I miss them especially in Elantra, where I have no role, no duty, no responsibility. And I nonetheless understand that we were *Dragons*. Sooner or later, one of us would have risen to lead the flight, and those who could not, or did not, fall into formation might not survive it."

Kaylin stared at her. "I don't understand Immortals."

"No," was the fond reply. "It's probably why we like you so much. Even the Lord of the West March seems fond of you."

"That's because I saved his life."

"And you assume that I'm fond of you because you saved mine?" Brows rose. "Kaylin...no Immortal likes to feel obligated to anyone else. It's a type of weakness. It implies that we are not strong enough, not powerful enough, to stand on our own. We're not fond of you because of that, we're fond of you *in spite* of it.

"I do, however, have a slightly different concern."

"Terrano?"

Bellusdeo smiled. "I forget, sometimes, that you're observant."

"Hawk." She hesitated, and then said, "When a crime has been committed. Terrano, of the eleven trapped in Alsanis, was the only one who could freely travel between the Hallionne and the outside world. But...he kind of reminds you of Mandoran."

Bellusdeo nodded.

"He reminds me of Mandoran, as well. If Annarion put his mind to it, I believe he *could* be political; he could make plans, and he would be focused enough, deliberate enough, to carry them out."

"But not Mandoran."

Kaylin nodded. "Not Mandoran. Mandoran does have the rest of the cohort sitting on him from a distance—but I think he'd need that cohort to keep him on the straight and narrow. The Barrani version of straight and narrow, at any rate."

"And you think Terrano couldn't have plotted what occurred the last time you were here."

"Not on his own, no."

"Sedarias?"

"I should have asked." Kaylin looked down at her hands. "My past is something I'm not proud of. I never wanted it to be revealed. If I could go back in time and talk to the girl I was then, I might have been able to—" She exhaled. "It doesn't matter. Sometimes my past makes me suspicious of everyone, because I know what people are capable of. I know it because of what I did.

"So I try not to question someone else's past. I try to see what they are *now* because...that's what I want, for myself. I haven't really grilled Annarion or Mandoran. I'm not even sure Helen would let me, because they're guests. But...they speak of Sedarias differently; she's one of the only names I hear spoken out loud. If I had to guess, I'd say that the plan, while carried out haphazardly by Terrano, probably started with her." She looked up. "What do you think?"

"I can't fault your reasoning."

"Mostly because it's the same as yours."

Bellusdeo smiled. "Exactly."

"For what it's worth, I don't think Sedarias would try to harm the Consort, or the High Court, now. I do believe that she's heading to the High Halls because Annarion can't be talked out of taking the Test of Name. And I do believe that she doesn't want to lose him. She's not stupid. She knows the risks. She might not be certain what that risk entails—but she knows that the success rate is not high. Regardless, I'd bet my own money she's not responsible for her own disappearance."

"You don't believe Terrano is?"

"I don't think Terrano can talk to the rest of the cohort the way they now talk to each other. Alsanis preserved Terrano's name, but...Terrano wouldn't take it back. What he wanted, at the time, was freedom. I mean, he wanted all of the cohort to be free. To be happy. To have choices—but his choice couldn't be theirs. He didn't want what they wanted."

"And you think that's changed?"

"...No. But I think he misses them. I mean, they were like one hive mind for centuries. I think that he kept an ear out, from wherever it was he ended up. And I believe that he came because he knew—or thought—they were in trouble. But if we ask *him* for political advice, it's going to be a mess. I'd be surprised if he remembered anyone's name. Except Iberrienne's."

"Why Iberrienne's? He was the one responsible for the worst of the attacks, wasn't he?"

"That's what I thought at the time. He was certainly the most visible. And Iberrienne was Eddorian's brother. One of the cohort. I'd imagine that what Eddorian knew about his brother, the whole cohort knew. It's just possible that's why Terrano approached him."

"Why didn't he approach Nightshade?"

"If I had to guess, he would have tried—but Nightshade lives in a Tower. They're not functionally the same as Hallionne; they might be worse. It would have been a risk to approach Nightshade, if it were possible at all; the Castle might have killed him or trapped him for a century or two. Iberrienne wasn't a fieflord. Or a Hallionne.

"Which is all beside the point. Terrano probably won't re-member most of the names. It's Sedarias we need."

"That's why we're here," Bellusdeo offered. "I'm just hop-ing the boys stay put."

"That's not why we're here. We're here because the water picked us up and dumped us in a Hallionne—without our consent, I might add." And without any explanations, because panic definitely didn't count.

"Are you afraid of Terrano?"

"I'm afraid that Mandoran's practice at walking through walls—which often has hilarious results—will seem boring and normal in comparison." Kaylin exhaled. "I don't think he'll deliberately harm us, but I'm not sure I'll care much while I'm dying." She glanced at the wardrobe by the far wall of the room in which they'd been deposited. The door, on the other hand, didn't seem to be locked.

And given that Bellusdeo was with them, it probably should have been. The Emperor was going to reduce Kaylin to ash—probably after he'd eaten half her limbs. She wanted Bellusdeo to stay *in* the room while she went in search of the fountain by which she'd once conversed with the water.

Bellusdeo folded her arms, which meant no—and Kaylin hadn't even asked the question yet. She started to. No, she *did*. But the sound of her voice was entirely drowned out by a roar that Kaylin would have thought came from the Dragon, if the Dragon's mouth hadn't been a shut, compressed line of denial.

Kaylin headed to the door instantly; she heard shouts and cries, but they were distant, almost attenuated, until she yanked the door open. Then they were a little more voluble. She drew a dagger, which probably wouldn't help her against anything that was causing the Barrani to panic, but Bellusdeo caught her arm.

The Dragon was smiling, and if the smile was rueful, it was genuine. "You won't need that," she said, "and given the Barrani state of mind at the moment, it might start something you don't want to start." She had to raise her voice to be heard, even though she was attached at the arm.

"What is it?" Kaylin had a sinking feeling that maybe, just maybe, the Dragon Court had arrived. But there was no way—even by direct flight—they would be here yet.

She headed down the hall toward the shouting.

Bellusdeo followed; the Dragon's eyes were a martial orange, which certainly didn't imply there was nothing to fear. Then again, as she approached a cluster of Barrani guards—swords drawn, shields raised—she tensed herself. If her eyes ever changed from their very normal brown, this would be the time to do it.

But...her marks were flat, invisible beneath the sleeves of her shirt. Whatever was attacking, it wasn't the kind of magic that kicked natural defenses into gear.

Take Bellusdeo back to your room, the Lord of the West March said. *Now.*

I think it's a little late for that. And also, Bellusdeo wouldn't go. Any argument they had would just attract attention. *What is it? What's causing the panic?*

These are fully trained and experienced guards. They are not panicking.

Another roar.

Several shouts. The men disappeared down the hall with barely a backward glance. That was probably today's miracle—although Kaylin privately felt well-trained guards would have noticed the *Dragon* in their midst.

She turned to Bellusdeo, who was still gripping her dagger arm. "Let go and I'll sheath it."

Bellusdeo complied. Her eyes, however, had shaded to an orange gold, which was as gold as they were likely to get. Kaylin looked at her suspiciously.

"You don't recognize his voice," the Dragon said.

"And you do?"

"Somewhat. He is not, however, attempting to converse at the moment. I think he is...afraid."

"Who?" Kaylin almost shrieked. She headed in the direction the guards had taken.

"I think you'll recognize him when you see him."

Kaylin could not strangle a Dragon, although she was seriously tempted to try.

Lirienne, what do you see?

I think it best that you come in person.

Even with the Dragon?

If you cannot talk sense into her, yes. Understand that it is not an issue for me should she die here, and there are not a few families who would take great pleasure in the attempt to accomplish that. His voice was dry.

They'd probably die first.

Yes, but they would consider the glory of their deaths to be a boon to their family lines; it would be an honorable death.

Do you have Terrano?

Yes. The answer was curt. *I am uncertain, however, that I will have him for long.*

What?

Hurry. Against my better judgment, I am attempting to preserve his life.

CHAPTER 17

Fear for Terrano eclipsed intelligent precautions, and Kaylin picked up the pace, sprinting down the hall. She had never been good with geography, and the building was like a maze to her inexperienced eye, but she had good ears, and she could follow the sound of Barrani voices as if they were money.

She tried, once, to tell Bellusdeo to go back to their room, and decided she'd rather face hostile, armed Barrani. Bellusdeo was a Dragon; she could take care of herself. And could probably take care of most of them, if it came to that. They were no longer in the safe space of the Hallionne, but that meant nothing was restraining Bellusdeo.

And even as she thought it, she felt uneasy. This was the heart of Barrani territory in the west. It had existed through three different wars. She slowed enough that Bellusdeo careened into her, which did nothing for the ability of either of them to remain on two feet.

Only the Dragon cursed. Kaylin got to her feet as a distant roar raised the stakes.

Kaylin.

I'm coming. I was hoping to leave the Dragon behind. She picked herself up and sprinted the rest of the way.

★ ★ ★

The Barrani were prepared for Dragons.

Unfortunately, a Dragon wasn't what they were facing, although the creature that towered above them in the courtyard certainly had the right form. He was the first silver dragon Kaylin had ever seen, and his wings—both of which were raised—were longer from end to end than even Bellusdeo's. His scales were not the same shape as any other dragon with whom Kaylin was familiar, but anyone could have been forgiven for making the assumption. His eyes, however, were all wrong; they were Hallionne eyes. Terrano eyes.

Familiar eyes.

Without thought, Kaylin pushed past the spears and shields of the second rank of Barrani guards; past the swords and shields of the first rank. Lirienne was not a human lord, or at least not a member of the human caste court. When he joined a fight, he led from the front.

And he was, as he had said, attempting to preserve Terrano. Terrano even looked as if he required the aid.

"Cut that out *right now*!" she shouted.

The silver, shimmering dragon's jaws snapped shut as his head swiveled toward her.

"What do you think you're *doing*?"

I...am saving you.

"You are *not* saving *me*! I'm not in danger here!"

"I think that's vastly overstating the case," the gold Dragon said. To Lirienne's credit, the nearest Barrani did not immediately reverse the direction of their weapons and attempt to skewer her. And given the color of their eyes, that wasn't a foregone conclusion. Kaylin tried—very hard—to remember how little her life was going to be worth if something happened to Bellusdeo. Yes, it wasn't her fault. No, she wasn't stupid enough to drag Bellusdeo to the West March intentionally. Regardless, she was the one who was going to be ash.

Even as she shouted, the shimmering serpent form began to dwindle.

"How did you even get here?" she demanded.

The dragon did not immediately answer her question; instead he became a much smaller, and much less solid-looking creature. Her familiar.

"If you're doing that so you don't have to answer, I'm not going to be impressed." She held out her arm. "If it's all right with you——" she said, in Elantran "——the guard can put up their weapons."

Hope flew to her shoulder and settled there. He squawked and bristled at Terrano, who was still cowering behind the Lord of the West March. He was the only person who was now cowering; at Lirienne's signal, the weapons were, as Kaylin had asked, put up. She noted that they'd waited for his command. Fair enough; in their position, she'd've done the same.

Squawk.

"I'm sorry," Kaylin said, to the Barrani at large. "Can someone tell me what, exactly, happened?"

The Barrani looked to their Lord, and Kaylin joined them. He bowed—to Kaylin.

He then bowed to Bellusdeo. "My apologies for disturbing your rest, Lord Bellusdeo," he said. "It has been far too long since one of your kind has accepted the hospitality of a Lord of the West March." He then dismissed the greater part of the men who had gathered in the face of this emergency. Greater part, however, did not mean all.

"Is your familiar now under your control?"

As much as he ever was. "Yes."

Terrano, however, now kept the Lord of the West March and Bellusdeo between himself and the small dragon. "He's not."

"He is."

"He's *not.*"

Kaylin exhaled. "Hey," she said, to her shoulder. "Whatever you're doing, *cut it out.* You're scaring him."

Squawk. Squawk. Squawk.

Kaylin exhaled. "Bellusdeo?"

"He feels that Terrano is an enormous threat to your safety. He apologizes for the landing; he apologizes for antagonizing your *kyuthe* and his men. He was focused entirely on preservation of your life."

"Does he *look* like he's attacking me?" she demanded.

Squawk. Squawk.

"He points out, in fairness, that it doesn't *look* like he's threatening Terrano, either. That is not, by the way, the name he used."

Great. "What was the name he used?"

"I don't recognize it. I'm sorry. It's clear to me that he meant to indicate Terrano, and it's equally clear that there is some derogatory connotation. More than that, I cannot decisively say."

Fine. "Whatever you're doing, stop it now."

Bellusdeo lifted a hand before the small dragon could reply. "He's going to insist that Terrano stop first."

Kaylin wanted to shriek in frustration. "Fine. Terrano, stop whatever the hells it is you're doing."

"I'm not *doing anything!*"

Kaylin exhaled slowly. She remembered Mandoran and Annarion, and she reminded herself that Terrano was not anchored to this particular life the way the other two were. Annarion had had no idea that he was calling out to the Shadows, either. And it had still been a disaster that had cost lives.

In a lower and more reasonable tone—she hoped—she said to the familiar, "Look, he's like Annarion and Mandoran."

Squawk.

"Fine, he's like them but worse. I can't see what he's doing. Neither can Lirienne or Bellusdeo." Lifting her head she said, to the Lord of the West March, "Is there anything like Ravellon in the West March?"

"No."

"Are there Shadows in the West March?"

"Lord Kaylin, there are Shadows everywhere. But there is no concentration of their power in a like fashion; Ravellon is unique."

Good. "I don't think he's doing anything on purpose. And I don't think terrifying him is going to make him stop. If it's all instinctive, it's going to make it *worse*."

Squawk squawk squawk.

"He does not entirely believe that it is instinctive. He is, however, willing to entertain the possibility, given prior experience."

"Terrano," Kaylin said quietly. "What do you *think* you're doing?"

"Trying not to die?"

She almost laughed. He unfolded slowly, his eyes darting to—and away—from her shoulders, where the familiar was now in residence. "Look, you've spent a lot of time—compared to Annarion and Mandoran—figuring out how *not* to live in the real world."

He bristled. "I live in the real world."

"Fine, if that's what you want to call it. It's not a world that the rest of us can live in."

"You're living in it now!"

Kaylin.

What?

I believe it is unwise to agitate him. I do not understand what your familiar fears—but it is clear that the fears are not entirely unfounded.

What are you going to do with him, then?

I? I am going to ask him to remain within Alsanis.

Like that's going to work!

I believe that he will accept the offer, given the appearance of your familiar.

It's not the first time they've met. She stopped. Thought a bit. "Terrano."

He looked at her. His eyes were like the familiar's eyes, but as she watched, he struggled to realign them with Barrani appearance. "The last time we saw you—my familiar and I— you *were* kind of trying to kill us all."

"You were going to kill us first!"

"I don't think my familiar cares what I was doing. He's more concerned about what you were doing, because he doesn't necessarily think there's much reason for you to have stopped."

Terrano looked annoyed. "We're no longer prisoners. We're not trapped in the Hallionne."

"The Consort had nothing to do with that, though, and you were willing to kill her."

He shrugged, uncomfortable.

"You were trying to undermine—or destroy, in the worst case—the Hallionne."

"We were trying to *rewrite* them. And we're not the only ones who made changes."

"I didn't make changes *to* the Hallionne."

"You made changes to their brothers."

"It wasn't the same thing!"

The Lord of the West March cleared his throat. Loudly.

"Look—we need to know what you were planning in as much detail as you can remember, because we're not at all certain that some of the people you were intriguing with aren't responsible for this mess."

"This mess?"

"The rest of your cohort going missing." To the familiar she said, "Can he stay in the Hallionne?"

Terrano said, "Yes."

She gave him the side-eye.

"I don't hate Alsanis," he continued. "And he didn't hate us. But he couldn't give us what we needed because of the way he'd been written. And frankly, I'll be safer in Alsanis than I will here." He glared at the familiar. The familiar glared back.

If it's all the same to you, Kaylin said to Lirienne, *I'd be a bit happier if Bellusdeo was a guest in the Hallionne, and she won't go if I don't.*

I am not certain that Alsanis will view it the same way. Historically, the Hallionne were our last resort against the Dragonflights.

But Orbaranne—

My sister appealed to her directly.

Can't she appeal to Alsanis the same way?

Alsanis and Orbaranne are not the same. Understand, Kaylin, he added, gentling his voice, *that the Hallionne were created to fulfill the same essential functions, but they are not identical beings. You are a Hawk, yes?*

Since this was obvious, she nodded.

Are you identical in temperament to your fellow Hawks? Are you physically identical? Are your goals—outside of your duties to the Halls of Law—the same?

No.

It is analogous to the situation with the Hallionne. Orbaranne is, where she can possibly be, amenable to my family. Alsanis might not be as amenable.

Why?

My father, and the constituent High Court of the time, sent the children to the regalia. They interfered with the customs of the green, and the effect has been felt for generations. The children survived, but Alsanis was isolated from that moment on. It is only since your intervention, Chosen, that he has been able to entertain and house guests—but after centuries of avoidance, people are still reluctant.

That wasn't your fault, though. And it wasn't the Consort's, either.

No. And he is aware that the Consort of that time was against exposing the young to the regalia. Nonetheless, it was done, and it is possible Alsanis will be...cool to our attempts to ask for a similar exception.

Kaylin spoke some heartfelt Leontine. Bellusdeo, perhaps feeling slightly uncomfortable in the stronghold of a people who had every reason to hate Dragons, and might have already supported attempts to assassinate her, said, "Your pronunciation is lacking."

Kaylin accepted this. Unfortunately, Bellusdeo then chose to demonstrate the correct pronunciation. She was right—hers was much better. It was also much louder, because she'd used a Dragon voice.

The familiar squawked loudly in her ear, which was still ringing from the Leontine which Kaylin now hoped the somewhat more remotely raised Barrani wouldn't actually understand.

Lirienne chuckled. *I would think the fact that she is a Dragon is of far more concern.*

Kaylin shrugged. *They're yours. They serve you. You wouldn't have brought us here if you thought you couldn't protect her.*

This surprised him. *I better understand my sister's concern, kyuthe. You are far, far too trusting.* He signaled. The last of the guards thinned in number until only one remained—a man with midnight blue eyes, but a pleasant expression. He bowed to both Kaylin and Bellusdeo.

"You wished to visit the fountain," the Lord of the West March said. "I have taken the liberty of instituting some precautions while you do so. I assume that after you have finished there, you would like to be escorted to the Hallionne Alsanis."

Kaylin nodded.

Terrano, utterly silent until that moment, said, "Can I just wait here and go with the two of you?"

Every intelligent instinct Kaylin possessed screamed *no*, very, very loudly. Before she could give voice to a politer, less visceral response, Bellusdeo said, "Yes."

Terrano gave her the side-eye. "Does she speak for you?"

"Frequently," the Hawk replied. To the Lord of the West March, she said, "Can we see the fountain now?"

The courtyard in which the fountain was housed was immaculate. And empty. Kaylin knew that the elemental water ran through it because it was the elemental water that controlled entrance into the heart of Lirienne's territory. As she neared the fountain's stone base, she told her familiar to go sit with Bellusdeo.

Squawk.

"I mean it. I'm not Barrani; I can't pay attention to more than two things at once."

Squawk.

"I trust Lirienne. I don't trust the rest of the Barrani I haven't laid eyes on yet. And frankly, Terrano's attitude toward Dragons is a touch on the hostile side."

"I like her better than your familiar," Terrano volunteered.

This was greeted with a hiss, rather than the usual overly loud squawks, but the familiar did push himself off Kaylin's shoulder. Bellusdeo accepted him without apparently noticing that he existed, which meant she didn't approve.

Kaylin, however, trusted the familiar; he'd already saved the Dragon's life once, in an attack that had destroyed Kaylin's first home in Elantra. She seated herself on the bench, lifted an arm, and reached out to let the falling water make contact with her palm. The water was clear and cool to the touch.

All of the marks of the Chosen flared to life on her arms; the hair on her neck stood on end. This was not a promising sign, and it wasn't entirely pleasant. Her skin was tingling, as if it had been slapped. The water, however, caused no pain. Kaylin closed her eyes and reached, in as much as she was able, for the Tha'alaan.

There was a moment of terrifying silence before the

thoughts of the Tha'alani group mind opened up to embrace Kaylin's more human isolation. Usually, this was comforting. Today, it was not.

Kaylin. Not the voice of the water. Kaylin recognized the caste leader, Ybelline. *Where are you?*

I'm in the West March.

A moment of confusion, a hint of other voices. *In the West March.*

Yes. Did you not hear it from the water?

We heard only that there was a grave danger and you had been sent to deal with it.

The water is overconfident.

A ripple of amusement. *The problem is in the West March?*

Apparently. It's not that simple. I hoped to reach the water, she added. *Can you—can you hear the water?*

I can—but her voice is very, very faint. We are not certain what was done, or how; it has caused confusion, and in some instances, panic.

The water dropped us in the middle of one of the Hallionne. We didn't exactly have time to pack.

We.

Yes, sorry. Lord Bellusdeo is with me. Kaylin tried to visualize the events of the past day; she was now worried. Usually Ybelline could touch those thoughts if Kaylin could hear her at all.

The water carried you to the West March?

Yes.

I would not have said that was possible without the intervention of a very gifted, very powerful elementalist. Are you certain—

We were in the Keeper's garden. We're now in the West March. I'm pretty certain that random elementalists or Arcanists didn't have much chance to interfere. And I'd bet my own money that Evanton had nothing to do with it, either. But—I can't hear the water. I can't ask why *there was an emergency here. Something did go wrong here, but...*

What went wrong?

Kaylin explained in the more awkward way: with words that she had to choose herself. Where once she had been terrified of the Tha'alani and their ability to ferret out hidden, dark secrets, now she was comfortable with it, even at home in it. Which is why, of course, it wasn't working properly.

For the water to make the choice it did requires a vast outlay of power—and will. The water is not, as you are aware, a single individual; it has a will that is divided, and the divisions are not always complementary. The part of the water that is the Tha'alaan was the part of the water that chose to move you. But it moved you instinctively, Kaylin. There is trouble, but…it can't clearly articulate what that trouble is.

Ybelline sounded troubled as well. Troubled and yet oddly relieved.

We thought the water was under attack by something new and terrifying. We do not have access to the Keeper's garden, and the rest of Elantra is…not friendly when it comes to my people; we were discussing our possible options. A runner has been sent to Grethan, in the Keeper's abode. Now, however, we understand that the weakening was at the will of the water, and not due to an outside attack.

I can't hear the water.

No. I am sorry. We can, but it is very, very weak. The water bids me tell you that she can hear you, and that you must…silence. The silence continued for a beat too long. *I am sorry,* the caste leader said again. *I am forced to contain the communication, to keep it separate from the Tha'alaan. We will…attempt to understand what she is trying to tell us; it is confusing. We can see what she sees—no, we can experience what she experienced—but we cannot…understand it. It is not an experience we, any of us, could have. But Kaylin? She is afraid.*

Fear was poison to the Tha'alani; it was the entirety of the reason they avoided contact with other races unless commanded to break into their thoughts by the Imperial service.

She felt Ybelline's presence, as reassuring as a hug offered in comfort, and she thought that fear itself, run rampant, writ large, was poison to *anyone*, not just the Tha'alani. But it was here, in the Tha'alaan, that she understood what its absence meant. She could be herself. She could reveal her thoughts. They could see her lack of confidence, her lack of intelligence, her lack of strength—and to them, that was *part of* life. It was not the whole of it. They accepted it so calmly, so peacefully, that Kaylin could accept it all as well. Everyone felt these things some of the time.

But one couldn't let those thoughts dominate all others; one couldn't make decisions based only on fear, large or small. She exhaled. *If I can, I'll try to contact the water again.*

If?

I have the only female Dragon we know about in the West March, an ancient stronghold of her enemies. I'd like to move to a different stronghold, just in case—but the water is active here, and I'm not certain it's active everywhere. Its presence in the Hallionne we arrived in was extinguished by our arrival.

And they needed to speak with the Consort. They needed to speak with the Consort someplace safe from eavesdropping. The Consort didn't trust her brother. Or perhaps she didn't trust someone close to her brother. Or perhaps she didn't trust Kaylin herself. The weave of suspicion, of the fear of deception, and of the actual deception itself seemed both fine and delicate—unless one were a fly.

But if you were a figurative fly, you couldn't ignore that web.

The thing is, she thought as she withdrew her hand, you couldn't live in it, either. If you were trapped in it, the only thing you could see was the web itself, and the web brought the fear of the spider until that was the whole of the world. But webs were in corners, in out of the way places; they weren't the whole world. And it would be easy to forget that.

It had been easy to forget it.

But…it was tricky. If the entire world wasn't treachery and deception, treachery and deception existed. How safely could one approach that web without being caught up in it again?

"You're thinking," Bellusdeo said.

Kaylin shrugged. "Brooding, mostly."

"Well, possibly now is not the best time. Your familiar is chewing on my hair and glaring at everything."

"That's not a glare—that's the way his face always looks. And, umm, sorry about your hair." Kaylin lifted an arm, retrieved her familiar, and turned to offer the Lord of the West March a very correct bow. This surprised him, so Diarmat's infernal lessons were clearly useful for *something*. "We would like, if possible, to visit Alsanis now."

He did not argue. He spoke a word to his attendant, and the attendant nodded, vanishing down one of the halls that led away from the fountain.

"Yes, we understand that," Kaylin said, with barely contained exasperation. "What we want to know is what your *other* allies wanted from the alliance."

"Well, the mortals probably wanted to live forever," Terrano replied.

"The mortals weren't your only allies. They weren't even the most significant of your allies. And they weren't the ones who were attempting to write the rest of us out of existence."

"It wouldn't have worked. I think." Terrano didn't seem all that upset about genocide as a concept, at least when it didn't involve the race he was born to.

"Did you never *talk to them?*"

"Yes."

"What did you offer them?"

He rolled his eyes. His response was High Barrani, but it was not a word Kaylin recognized. Or rather, not a series of words. The Lord of the West March, however, did, and he grew pale, which was not a terribly good look on the Barrani. His eyes devolved instantly from blue into a midnight blue that suggested black.

I take it that's bad?

No response. Kaylin understood that she could push for one, but didn't; it would cause them both unnecessary pain. And one of them, a lot of guilt.

"This was your idea?"

"Not really. We could have offered them ripe oranges for all the difference it made to the rest of us. Or gold. Actually, we did offer gold, if I recall."

"And where did the gold come from?"

"The mortal caste court—the human one. At least I think it did."

Kaylin could not remember wanting to strangle Mandoran this intensely, but maybe her memory was being kind. Had Terrano not been so confused and so…whatever he was, she would have seriously considered letting her familiar eat him. Or whatever it was he'd attempted to do the first time.

But if she wanted to see him as an enemy, she was failing. She thought if foundlings were given the power Terrano had been given, the world might be in just the same trouble: he didn't understand consequences. He didn't understand the world in which Kaylin and almost all of her friends actually lived.

"You don't happen to remember names?"

"You asked that one already. Humans don't *have* names, anyway."

"Well, neither do you, anymore."

"I don't need one."

"Neither do we!"

Bellusdeo cleared her throat, which sounded a little like she'd swallowed an earthquake.

Kaylin shoved her hands into her pockets and strode ahead.

★ ★ ★

Alsanis was not, like Orbaranne or the other Hallionne, a way station in the wilderness. He was situated in the heart of the Lord of the West March's territory. For centuries he had been an impassible prison, a symbol of the cost of ambition and hubris. Now, he was a Hallionne. But if what Lirienne said was true, old habits died hard; he had visitors, but they were few.

One of those visitors was, however, in the courtyard.

Kaylin recognized Lord Barian, the Warden of the West March. If she understood the position correctly, he was second only to Lirienne—but he was not a Lord of the High Court, which had caused some friction in his family. His eyes, when he turned to face her, were green; his smile seemed genuine.

"Lord Kaylin," Lord Barian said, offering her a low and deeply respectful bow.

"Lord Barian." She became instantly aware of the difference in their clothing, their deportment, and their appearance. Kaylin returned the bow, mindful of Diarmat's words, which now seemed to be replaying with annoying frequency in the inside of her head.

She rose and glanced around the courtyard, aware that it was the very edge of Hallionne Alsanis. "You've been visiting the Hallionne?"

He nodded, his expression serious; he glanced, once, at the Lord of the West March. It was not an entirely friendly glance, but Kaylin didn't have a deep understanding of the politics of the West March, except for those employed by Lord Barian's mother, who detested Kaylin, and whom Kaylin would be overjoyed to avoid on this unexpected visit. Contempt and condescension were things Kaylin understood quite well.

His glance once again flickered to—and away from—the Lord of the West March. "The Lord of the West March has, perhaps, acquainted you with the details?"

"I know only that Sedarias and her friends had decided to

visit us, and that they disappeared in transit. They chose to travel by the portal paths." She cleared her throat and started with the easiest introduction first. "This is Terrano. I'm not sure if you've been formally introduced."

His eyes widened. "You are one of the twelve."

Terrano nodded.

"You are the one who did not choose to remain."

He nodded again. He looked slightly nervous.

"Have you had word of your friends? Contact with them? The Hallionne Alsanis would be very interested."

"No. I heard them, but I was too far away to come to their aid, and I do not know where they are."

"Do you know if they are still alive?"

Terrano stiffened, but did not reply.

Lord Barian bowed immediately. "My apologies, Terrano. The Hallionne is concerned; it is much on his mind."

Kaylin cleared her throat and considered avoiding the introduction of the Dragon. Her familiar squawked, and she relented. "This," she said, when she had Lord Barian's attention, "is Lord Bellusdeo of the Imperial Dragon Court."

CHAPTER 18

Accustomed as she was to Barrani blue, Kaylin still found the instant transformation daunting. Lord Barian was not a Lord of the High Court, but Barrani across the world hated the Dragons. Mortal memories were fragile and imperfect. Barrani memories, like Dragon memories, were not. It made Kaylin wonder what she would have been like if her memories of life in the fiefs never dimmed with time.

She didn't really like the answer.

Kaylin almost blurted out a groveling apology, but held her tongue. She was not ashamed of Bellusdeo; the gold Dragon didn't deserve that.

Lord Barian's gaze went instantly to Lirienne's, held it for a few seconds, and then returned to the Dragon. Bellusdeo stood quietly, arms by her side, chin slightly lifted; her eyes were orange, but at this point orange was the new gold.

"Lord Bellusdeo," Kaylin continued, when no weapons had been drawn. "This is Lord Barian, the Warden of the West March. The responsibility of the Hallionne Alsanis has been his line's."

Bellusdeo offered Lord Barian an exquisite Barrani bow. It was lower and more exact than the bow she'd offered the

Lord of the West March. Kaylin wondered if Lirienne noticed. Wait, what was she thinking? He was a Barrani man of power. Of *course* he'd noticed.

Yes. It is interesting. She is not what I expected of a Dragon.

I don't think she meant to insult you.

No, kyuthe, *she did not. The bow she offers Lord Barian is exact and correct; it is also graceful, something for which the Dragons were not noted. The bow she offered me is the bow she might offer to the respected head of a familial line.*

Pardon?

She understands that you are kyuthe; *you are kin to me. Lord Barian, however, has made no such claim; you are not under his protection, and your death or injury will not be his to avenge.*

It wouldn't be yours, either.

He chuckled as she turned once again to face Lord Barian. She had a habit of turning toward the person speaking to her if he was in the room—and Lirienne was. Bellusdeo was giving her the pointed side-eye, as well. *Think, Kaylin,* she told herself. *You are in hostile territory. Every window could carry a person with a crossbow. Every shrub could conceal a person with a dagger. Or worse. Think. You've done this before.*

But when she'd done it before, there had been no making nice. There had been no bows, no courtesies. Just silence, fear, focus. The price of failure had been clear: injury or death, and probably not the fast painless kind, either.

No. But you are kyuthe *to the Lord of the West March, and it is his duty to avenge you. Even if he arranged for your death, someone would have to publicly pay the price of it; they would sacrifice their own lives—or the welfare of their family—in order to kill you.*

Hello, Ynpharion. Kaylin's head was a crowded place, these days.

The Consort feels you will be safe if you remain with her brother. She feels, however, that the Dragon is best housed in the Hallionne.

And Terrano?

She is not entirely certain what to make of him. Silence, and then, as if thought were whisper, *She is worried.*

He did try to kill her. Or capture her.

You do not believe he will do so again.

No. He won't. I think the only thing he cares about is the safety of his friends. Wait—she's not coming here, is she?

Silence.

It's too late—it'll take her weeks.

More silence. It was not replete with disapproval, and Kaylin realized, with surprise, that Ynpharion actually agreed with her. And was powerless to change anything.

I'm telling her brother.

No. Do not. There was a hint of plea in the words, which must have been costly. Kaylin accepted them. Ynpharion was never going to like her, but he was the bridge between Kaylin and the Consort, and he understood the Barrani Court—High or low—far better than Kaylin was ever likely to understand it.

She stopped talking to Ynpharion when her familiar bit her ear. She glared at him, but became aware of a widening circle of silence. Bellusdeo had raised a brow in her direction, but had done nothing else to catch her attention.

Lirienne was amused. *Lord Barian has asked you if you wish to request the hospitality of the Hallionne.*

Damn it. *When?*

Perhaps a minute ago.

Kaylin, red-faced, bowed to Lord Barian, mostly to hide her expression. She composed it as she rose. "My apologies, Lord Barian. We did not intend to travel to the West March, and we were not prepared for the journey; I am a little fatigued."

Lord Barian's smile was perfect, genial; his eyes, however, remained blue.

"If it is acceptable to the Hallionne, I request his hospitality for both myself and my companions."

"And your companions are?"

"Lord Bellusdeo of the Imperial Dragon Court, my familiar, and Terrano of…Terrano."

"Terrano may speak with the Hallionne on his own behalf; he has been guest here before."

Kaylin, however, did not retract the request. "I'm aware that Terrano is not considered a friend of the Barrani High Court at the moment. But he *is* a friend of Annarion and Mandoran's, and they currently live with me." Clearing her throat, she added, "I consider them family."

"You have claimed them as *kyuthen*?"

Kaylin nodded. "And Terrano is their brother."

"He would not be considered kin among his own people."

"I'm not even sure who 'his own people' are. Other than the people he lived with while in captivity in the Hallionne. But Annarion and Mandoran would make that claim themselves, if they were here. I'm pretty sure they'd die defending him. And they aren't here to make the request." She flushed as she realized she'd dropped into Elantran, and repeated the phrase in High Barrani, which took longer.

Terrano was staring at her. His eyes were natural in appearance, except for their color, which was brown. "I will ask the Hallionne about me," he told her. "Let me be responsible for my own mess."

"What mess?"

"You pointed out that I'm not what I was. I don't always recognize what I'm doing. No—I know what I'm doing, but I don't always see how it affects the rest of you. I don't want you to be responsible for my mistakes." At Kaylin's expression, he exhaled noisily. "Just let me speak for myself."

Lord Barian waited until he was certain Kaylin had nothing else to say, and then he turned toward the large arches that led away from the courtyard in which they were all standing. "Lord Kaylin, if you will make your request of the Hallionne, make it in peace. No harm will come to your companions until Alsanis makes his decision."

He led Kaylin toward the arches. Terrano followed. Bellusdeo and the Lord of the West March remained behind.

I know you hate Dragons, she told the man who had publicly claimed her as kin, *but please, please, please keep her safe.*

The arch led not to the interior of the Hallionne, but to a cloister of smaller arches that bounded an interior garden with a fountain as its centerpiece. Standing by that fountain was a man she did not recognize until he turned to greet her. His eyes were all of black.

"Hallionne Alsanis?" she asked.

His smile was both deep and warm. "Lord Kaylin." He bowed. "I did not expect to see you again so soon."

She relaxed in his presence and allowed herself to think of the events that had brought her here. It was easier by far than speaking about them, and she felt no need to pretend that he couldn't hear what she was thinking.

"You did not intend to bring a Dragon to the West March. I see. She is kin to you, as are Annarion and Mandoran." His expression was openly troubled as he turned to Terrano. "You understand the burden you place upon Lord Kaylin."

"I'm not placing a burden on her—I'm making the request for myself."

"That is not, sadly, the way it must work. I would accept you—and willingly—at any other time. But you tried to harm the Consort."

"She was going to—"

Kaylin clapped a hand over Terrano's mouth. "I'll accept responsibility for Terrano as well as the Dragon. The Dragon is not a threat to the Hallionne. She's not a threat to the West March or the Barrani."

"No. But she is not as Terrano is; she lives in the same space, and under the same constraints, as you do. Dragons are not much loved by the Hallionne. But we were not, as you believe, created as tools in the wars between the Dragons and the Barrani; we are older than that."

"Lirienne thought—"

"Yes. I understand his thought. And were she to arrive here without you as kin and sponsor, we would not accept her. It is not the way of the Hallionne to accept guests we intend to kill." He nodded to Kaylin, then. "If you will sponsor Terrano—"

"Terrano can speak for himself!" Terrano was almost shouting.

Kaylin glanced at the young almost-Barrani man, and noticed he'd lost control of his eyes again. She exhaled heavily. "He knows that. No one knows it better than he does. Look—I'd rather you stay in the Hallionne than in the Lord of the West March's residence. So would the Lord of the West March. You're not being practical."

"And you are?"

"Demonstrably. I'm staying as well. Look—what we want is to stay in the Hallionne. We've been given permission to do that." She forced herself to switch to High Barrani. "We can mark that as accomplished and worry about more important things. Or you can argue with Alsanis, but my prior experience in arguing with buildings doesn't imply you're going to win." She wished, fervently and briefly, that Annarion and Mandoran had come along with her; she thought they'd be able to influence Terrano in a way she couldn't. Hells, even Teela would have been helpful. Angry, but helpful.

Terrano did look as if he wanted to argue. Alsanis looked serene and immoveable. It was therefore a bit of a surprise when Terrano abruptly exhaled. He said something in Barrani which she didn't recognize and assumed was a curse word.

"It is," Alsanis said. "And no, Lord Kaylin, I am not about to teach it to you."

Terrano, however, calmed down. "Teach her what I just said?"

"Indeed."

"I'll teach you," he said to Kaylin.

"You have more like that?"

"A *lot* more. You don't?"

"I generally curse in other tongues."

He brightened. "Maybe I should become a linguist."

"Maybe," Alsanis said, more severely, "you should go and retrieve the rest of your companions." He gestured Terrano toward the cloister, and placed a hand on Kaylin's arm when she went to follow.

"He should not have returned," he said quietly. "He is not what he was."

"We don't understand what he was, never mind what he is now."

"You are beginning to. My apologies for subterfuge."

"You could have accepted him."

"Yes. It would have been difficult; I did not lie. He attempted to harm the Consort, and there is no greater crime, where the Barrani are involved. Not even matricide or patricide comes close. But I am accustomed to being shunned by the Barrani; I have had centuries of experience with it.

"Were he, however, to be held responsible for his own actions, he would not attempt to confine those actions. He is now aware that you will suffer for what he does, and I believe it will—how do you say it?—rein him in. I am no longer a cage for Terrano—for any of his cohort, as you call them—but it would be best for you, and for the rest of the Barrani in the West March, if he at least made the attempt to cohere and interact as if he were one of them.

"As for your Dragon, you need not worry. While she is a

guest in the Hallionne, she will come to no harm. I admit to curiosity, but she is not the first Dragon to have kept me company in my long existence, and if she is willing to stay, she does not appear to have the distrust most of her kind would have of my kind."

"She's practical."

"Oh?"

"It's you or the Barrani Court of the West March."

He smiled, then, a flicker of expression on an otherwise serene face. "Stay here a moment, Lord Kaylin. Ah, apologies, Kaylin."

"Where are you going?"

"I have something of a gift for you." He faded almost instantly from view.

Beware of Barrani gifts, Lord Nightshade said softly. She felt the edge of his curiosity. *You must learn caution, especially now.*

He's not Barrani, he's a Hallionne.

Yes. But remember, Kaylin: Annarion's friends—Nightshade did not care for the term "cohort"—*departed from Alsanis.*

Before Nightshade could continue, Alsanis returned. In his hands he carried a small, wooden box, into which had been carved both leaves and flowers. It was small enough to be a ring box.

"It is not a ring," the Hallionne said quietly. "And it may be of no significance to you at all in future. But if it is, you will know when to use it."

"What is it? Can I open this?"

"Try."

She did. The lid would not budge. "I don't get it."

He smiled. "No, Kaylin, you don't. It is a gift. What you call a home, some call a cage. Remember."

She slid the box into the small pack she wore across her hips.

"It is time to go back to your companions. Terrano is not malicious. Nor are his friends. Even the harm they did—the great harm—they did for the sake of each other. If the Hallionne are both Immortal and all powerful within our boundaries, those boundaries are fixed and immoveable. You have a power that we do not have: the freedom to choose. To judge. Judgment is oft misused, as any other weapon. Therefore, use both wisely."

Bellusdeo and Lord Barian appeared to be involved in lively conversation when Kaylin returned. Lively, even friendly, conversation. Although their eyes retained the racial hue that implied caution or danger, both the blue and the orange had lightened somewhat. Lirienne stood to the side in silence, but looked across the courtyard when Kaylin entered it.

What are they talking about?

The war, he replied. *Or rather, the shape of the lands before the final war. The placement of Aeries. The appearance of flights that have long since ceased to grace the skies. She remembers some few of their number and name—and of course, so does Barian.*

Weren't they trying to kill each other, back then?

Ah, yes. But as is oft the case with those who stood on the front lines of war, they have more in common with their individual enemies than they have with those who were not affected by war at all. The Dragonflights were worthy of fear and respect, but so, too, the Barrani units.

I thought Barian was younger.

None of us are young compared to you.

She looked pointedly at Terrano, who appeared to be trying to catch a butterfly. Loudly.

The Lord of the West March smiled, but even as Kaylin turned to catch a glimpse of actual warmth on his face, it drained away, and not slowly, either. She felt the moment amusement gave way to alarm. Before she could speak, the familiar did: loudly, and in her ear.

Both the Dragon and the Warden stopped speaking; they

turned toward the familiar and then away, to Terrano. And Kaylin realized then that her assumptions of immaturity were very, very wrong. Yes, he was chasing a butterfly.

And no, it wasn't playful.

"Go," she told the familiar, as she drew a dagger and started to move. "Alsanis!" There was no reply.

"We are not in his dominion, yet," Lirienne said. He had not drawn sword, but had brought both of his palms together in a strangely deliberate way that implied prayer without any of its actual reverence.

The familiar flew to Terrano. No, she thought, he flew to the butterfly. And now that she looked, she realized it had the appearance of a butterfly, but not its delicate, haphazard flight. Its colors were bright, the wings strangely glittery. And as she watched, she realized that the colors were not fixed; they were changing.

The familiar roared, its voice a kind of high screech given his size. Where the butterfly darted—with speed—from place to place, the familiar did not; his wings allowed him to hover as he inhaled. And inhaled. And inhaled.

"Terrano, watch out!" she shouted, and Terrano turned to see the familiar just as the small, translucent lizard exhaled.

No fool, Terrano leapt to the side, rolling along the ground, and uttering more unfamiliar Barrani as he did. Both Lirienne and Lord Barian appeared to be shocked by whatever it was he was saying. Bellusdeo didn't, but then again, she lived with Mandoran.

A stream of silver smoke left the familiar's open jaws, billowing as it expanded in a rush, like a kind of portable fog that could be wielded on command. It enveloped the courtyard, and Kaylin ran into it, unafraid. Bellusdeo did not move; Lord Barian attempted to withdraw. Lirienne, however, did not.

From his hands, sprouting suddenly, came a familiar globe; it covered him. It was permeable enough to allow Lord Barian entry. More than that, Kaylin didn't see, because the fog lifted itself from the ground it had first touched and rose.

"I'm not sure this is wise," Bellusdeo said, somewhere to Kaylin's left.

Terrano continued to curse.

"We don't want to hurt him!" Kaylin shouted. She could no longer see Hope.

"It will not hurt him," a familiar voice replied. Her familiar. "Unless he attempts to control it or fight it, it will not cause him harm."

The barrage of cursing stopped. "What are you doing?" Terrano demanded.

"I am attempting to contain the creature you were chasing," came the reasonable reply. "Did you recognize it?"

"Not exactly."

"You attempted to apprehend it."

"Yes." This was said with unraveling patience. "It wasn't exactly *subtle.*"

To Kaylin, until Terrano began to chase it around the courtyard, it had been entirely inconsequential. "It looked like a butterfly."

"Are you *blind*?" he shrieked. She could imagine his expression, which was just as well, because she couldn't actually see it.

"She is not," Bellusdeo replied. "To my eyes, and to the eyes of Lord Barian, it resembled a butterfly."

Kaylin could not see a butterfly. She couldn't see anyone. She couldn't hear Lord Barian or Lirienne, either.

Lirienne?

No answer. She wheeled, then, heading back in the direction she'd come from. "Hope! Drop the fog!"

"That is not the way it works," the familiar replied, "and I do not think it wise. The Lord of the West March attempts to protect himself, and his Warden."

She knew, then, where the butterfly was headed. "He's not answering me!"

"Kaylin—he's the *Lord of the West March*," Bellusdeo rumbled. And she did rumble. Kaylin stumbled, righting herself. Bellusdeo *could* speak perfect Dragon when in her human form. But Kaylin had a sinking feeling that wasn't what was happening here. "He is not helpless, he is not an orphan or a foundling, he is not mortal. He has had to *hold his title* against all who would wrest it from him, by either force of arms or magic. You are not responsible for him."

She felt the earth shake beneath her feet.

A plume of raw fire cut through the fog.

"I've got it!" Terrano shouted. She couldn't track the direction of his voice; it seemed to surround her. The fog rippled; the familiar squawked in outrage, presumably at the Dragon's fiery breath. "I *have it now*," Terrano repeated. The fog continued its odd climb, and Terrano cursed liberally. Kaylin was too worried to memorize the words.

"Kaylin, can you *do* something about him?"

"I don't think he thinks it's safe."

"He's making it *less safe* for some of us! I've got the damn thing—tell him to cut it out!"

Shouting *he doesn't listen to me* in front of Lirienne and Lord Barian didn't seem like a wise idea.

It is not, Lirienne said. *And we are both safe. He is yours?*

He stays with me. Yes, he's mine. I don't think he'd do anything that he thought would really upset me.

But?

Well, he's not me, and he's not mortal; he can keep up with Mandoran and Annarion, but he doesn't cause the issues they can—she stopped. Turned her thoughts to something else: Terrano's language.

This amused the Lord of the West March. *You are becoming wiser.*

Can you see?

I see fog. And Lord Barian. I admit that the fog is more pleasant. No harm has come to us. Although it pains me to concur with a Dragon, Lord Bellusdeo is correct. I am not your responsibility.

Can you see her?

No.

"Bellusdeo—"

"Yes, I understand." Her voice was a rumble of sound. Kaylin turned to her right, because unlike Terrano's voice, Bellusdeo's seemed to come from a concrete location. The fog drifted slowly away, and Lord Bellusdeo of the Dragon Court now stood in gleaming plate armor. Of course she did. Dragon clothing wasn't magical; it didn't change shape and form when its wearer did. It turned into expensive cloth scraps.

Both Lirienne and Barian froze as Bellusdeo crossed the courtyard to join Kaylin. The Dragon's eyes were a dark orange. She carried no weapon; Dragon armor didn't include swords. But they weren't really necessary for Dragons. She couldn't exactly bow well in the armor that she now wore, but ditching the armor—while it seldom seemed to cause Bellusdeo any embarrassment—wasn't an option at the moment.

"Lord of the West March. Lord Barian." She couldn't bow, and didn't make the attempt. "Terrano?"

They were staring at her, but there was, in their regard, both respect and something that might have been admiration. Kaylin did not understand the Barrani, and thought she never would. She had expected anger, fear, hostility.

Lirienne bowed to the Dragon. "We are unharmed," he said quietly. "You considered this a danger?"

The Dragon exhaled. "I do not know what you've been told about my life before my return to these lands, but most of it was spent fighting Shadow. And that small creature was very like the small Shadows sent ahead to scout communities that were not—yet—infested." She lifted her head. "Terrano?"

"Here," Terrano replied. His voice echoed, and Kaylin felt a sudden, sharp chill in the air.

Damn it, she thought.

Bellusdeo's eyes were almost red, because Dragon eyes were not quite the same as human eyes, and she caught sight of Terrano before Kaylin did. He didn't seem to notice her.

He was, unfortunately, not the Terrano of very recent memory; he was oddly, darkly beautiful, his limbs literally shining, as if they were composed of polished steel. Or silver. His eyes were completely black, and his clothing drifted off his shoulders and toward the ground in a moving swirl of color. A continually moving swirl.

His hands were cupped, as if around a sphere. "We're going to have to move inside," he said, entirely unaware of the way everyone was now staring at him. "I don't think I can hold it for long."

"What is she so angry about?" Terrano asked. He had drifted—and that was the right word for a movement that did not resemble walking at all—toward Kaylin, but stayed on the side of her that the familiar didn't occupy.

"She's not angry," Kaylin replied. She kept her voice low, but knew that Bellusdeo and the Barrani would catch every single word. "She's worried."

"Well, yeah. I'm not sure how this thing got in—"

"About you."

"I'm fine."

"Not about your health. About what you might do."

He stopped. "I'm not going to do anything. To any of you. I have no reason to try to hurt you."

"You did, once."

"And I explained that."

Kaylin believed him. Lirienne, however, was far more suspicious and remote. "You know you look like a silver statue with moving skirts for legs, right?"

His expression literally rippled with his confusion. "Do I?"

Bellusdeo snorted smoke. But her eyes retreated from the dangerous red into a more neutral orange. Not a pale orange, though. "Yes."

"Ugh. Look—I'm sorry. I can't really try to mess with my form while I'm containing this Shadow bit; I think I might lose it. It's...not really happy, and it's been trying to sting me continuously. And no, it only looks like a butterfly. It's got *teeth*."

"You realize that you look very, very similar to one of the more impressive Shadows?" the Dragon asked, her tone casual. Her eye color remained a steady orange.

"Not to *me*, I don't." He didn't particularly like Dragons, but could force himself to speak to one—or so his impression implied. "What exactly about me looks like Shadow?"

Both of the Dragon's brows rose. "Would you like to field this question?" she asked of Kaylin.

"...Not really."

Squawk.

Fine. "It's your form."

"The silver statue bit?"

"*Silver* isn't the word I'd use—unless silver is mostly black, but shiny anyway. No, it's the fact that you don't really *have* a fixed form as far as the rest of us can tell. You could probably just sprout a dozen arms—or heads, or whatever—if you felt like it."

"Yes? And?"

"Shadow does that, in case you hadn't noticed."

He continued to walk, as if concentrating, and as he did, his skin tone shifted from shiny, polished metal to something that looked far more natural. His arms, however, remained as they were: silver, reflective, hard. "*That's* how you tell the difference?"

"Yes. Normally." But she thought of Gilbert. And she thought, as well, of the Hallionne Bertolle's brothers, who thought of physical form the way rich people thought of clothing. Maybe he was now like those ancient brothers.

"It's not *Shadow*." Terrano was clearly annoyed. "We're tied to the forms of our birth by other things. But we mostly can't access our inherent power. Or we couldn't, before."

"And you can now." It wasn't a question.

"Yes."

"This is what you did to Ynpharion."

"I didn't *do* anything to Ynpharion that he didn't want done. Surely you must see the advantage in being able to control one's shape?" The doors that Terrano approached led directly into the Hallionne, and they were open, as if Alsanis was holding out his arms for the return of the prodigal. It was an odd thought, but Kaylin didn't think she was wrong.

"How do *you* see Shadow, then?" she asked.

"It's part of a web," he replied. "If you look hard, you can see it as it lies across the landscape. This?" he added, lifting his cupped hands, "is attached by a strand. It doesn't exactly have a will of its own. No, that's wrong. It has some initiative, some ability to adapt to its setting. But it doesn't have its own personality."

"I would think some of you have far more personality than is good for anyone," Bellusdeo said.

"Annarion doesn't."

"No. He's responsible. Mandoran, however, more than makes up for it."

Terrano chuckled. "Just wait until you meet everyone else." The amusement faded almost as quickly as it had appeared.

"We'll find them," Kaylin said.

"How can you, if I can't?"

"We wouldn't be here if the water hadn't thought we could do something."

"Meaning you have no idea."

The moment they cleared the threshold, the doors which had opened so invitingly rolled shut. They didn't slam, though.

"No," Alsanis said. His Avatar was waiting patiently. "I am Hallionne now, not prison, and my guests are free to leave should they so choose. That, however," he added, staring at Terrano's cupped hands, "is not a guest."

"Can I let it go now?" Terrano asked, as Kaylin said, "Is it safe?"

"It is safe."

"But—"

"It is too small and too insignificant to alter my structure in any meaningful fashion. Terrano and his kin were far more likely to cause difficulties—"

"And it took us centuries."

"Indeed. You were guests," he added quietly. "Available options to deal with you were not the same as the options open to me in regard to your captive. The thing you carry is causing you pain," he added, his expression one of concern. "Release it."

Terrano practically threw it from his hands.

It careened in the air as if it were drunk, wobbling in what might have been an arc of flight. But the wings that had seemed, in shape and size, butterfly wings were something different now. They were silvered, hard, dense; they seemed to make flight itself very difficult.

Terrano had said that the butterfly bit him. Kaylin wondered, idly, if it were vampiric in nature.

"No," Alsanis replied. "It did not absorb. It attempted to infect, to alter."

Bellusdeo turned the color of old cheese, which didn't suit the red of her eyes.

"It cannot effect Terrano in that way," the Hallionne continued. Very quickly. "But Terrano reversed the flow of that infection; the Shadow is now infested with...him." He turned, just as quickly, to the Lord of the West March. "No, he is not like the Shadow. Perhaps, were he the Lady, he might have some hope of becoming such a force—but it would be the work of millennia, and I do not think, in the end, he could achieve it."

"Who *wants* it?" Terrano demanded. "I hate being told what to do. I hate having to tell other people what to do. It's boring and frustrating. They don't understand half of what I say. Or more. There is *so much* to see. So much to try. So much *to be*."

"But you are here."

He exhaled. "They're here. No, they *were* here. I heard Sedarias." He grimaced. "You'd think, after a lifetime of hearing Sedarias, I'd be happier with the silence. Ask Mandoran," he added, not bothering to look in Kaylin's direction.

"She called you?"

"I think...she tried."

"And you came." The Hallionne's voice was warm.

Terrano said nothing for a long beat. Kaylin thought he would say nothing. She was wrong.

"I can't hear them," he finally whispered. "I can't hear them at all, anymore." Something in his voice spoke of loss, of grief, of the confusion it caused; it cut Kaylin, hearing it, because she knew how he felt. And wished that she didn't.

"No," Alsanis said, in the softest of voices. "You left your name here; you understood that it would be a cage. And Terrano, you were not wrong. The words are a cage. But cages have other names, and there are some creatures that cannot survive outside of them. Songbirds, for example."

Kaylin looked at Terrano's slumped shoulders. She realized

that he had been part of the cohort for almost all of his existence; that he had heard their voices, their thoughts, as if they were part of his own. Teela alone had been sundered from the Hallionne and her kin.

"He can't be what he wants with a name," Kaylin said, hazarding a guess.

"I do not know what he wants to be—but he cannot hear them or see what they see the way he once did. And you should understand this, Chosen."

She nodded, watching the flying creature as its shape continued to change. It was disturbing—but it was no more disturbing than watching the effects of Shadow's infestation. "Could you maybe stop that?" she said to Terrano.

"Stop what?"

"Stop trying to transform the Shadow."

"Is that what you think I'm trying to do?"

"I don't know what you're *trying* to do. It's what you're doing."

Bellusdeo, however, said, "What *are* you trying to achieve, exactly?"

"I'm trying to free it."

Freedom had never looked so unappealing. "What were you trying to do to Ynpharion?"

"Oh, that was different."

She could feel Ynpharion in the back of her thoughts; the Hallionne had clearly allowed those thoughts entry. *He promised freedom.* Ynpharion's presence was a ghost, a whisper. There was yearning in it, which surprised Kaylin. *You have always been free.*

Since freedom, for half her life, had included serious danger of starvation or freezing to death, Kaylin bridled. She didn't think about all of the other things that freedom had included in that childhood, because most of them had been the freedom to die.

"I'll stop now," Terrano added, with an undercurrent of smug that really did remind Kaylin of Mandoran. She had the sudden, visceral desire to take Terrano home to Helen, where the rest of the city would be safe from him, and where he could see some of his friends again.

But Alsanis said, "He is not, now, what they are, Lord Kaylin. He is not what they are trying so desperately to be, to remain. I do not think your Helen would have the ability you ascribe to her. But...he is correct. He is done."

She watched. The butterfly—badly drawn and not quite solid—was gone. In its place was something that looked like a sphere—with glittering spikes, most of which were silver. It had no eyes, no wings, nothing that suggested that it should be capable of flight. But fly it could; it drifted toward Terrano. He held out a palm, and it came to land, once again, in his hand.

Only once it nestled there did it reveal actual eyes. And teeth. Because it opened its mouth and screeched. The screech felt like it contained words, but Kaylin's hands were already covering her ears in an attempt to muffle the noise.

"What *is* it?" Bellusdeo asked. Her eyes were once again a darker orange. If she did not trust Terrano, she did not suspect his intent; she understood that Terrano was a walking, natural disaster. Those could easily kill the unwary, sometimes by the thousands, but there was no intent in earthquakes or hurricanes.

And regardless, earthquakes or hurricanes were unlikely to harm a Dragon.

Terrano frowned. It was a long, slow, fluid motion which changed more than the lines of his face. The screeching continued as he stared at it.

"What is it—"

"Be quiet. I can't hear it if you talk."

Since Kaylin could barely hear her own voice above the

high-pitched, unpleasant whine, she stared at him, but she did as he asked. The familiar whacked her face with one extended wing, and she sighed. Loudly.

Terrano frowned. At this rate, he was going to tell her to stop breathing. But she obeyed the familiar's unspoken command; she looked through his translucent wing.

What she saw in Terrano's hand was entirely different than what she saw when she relied on only her own eyes. For one, it wasn't the size of a fruit pit. It wasn't spiky. It remained an odd silver, but the silver was illuminated and glowing. No, worse, pulsing. The pulse was irregular, unlike a heartbeat. But that wasn't the worst thing about it. It was the size, the shape, of a man. No, an older child. The face, however, was diffuse, as were all elements about it except the thing Terrano had his hand around. It was as if Terrano had shoved his hand into a living person's chest, and cupped it around their heart, except the living person wasn't screaming in terror or pain.

"They are not in pain," Alsanis said. Kaylin noticed that the Hallionne didn't get told to shut up.

"Ah, no, Chosen. I understand the nuance of voice and pitch."

"Is this what you see?" she asked.

"I cannot see what you see. But I believe you are now seeing what I see, with small variations. It is…not what I expected. His heart is what you see without your familiar's aid, but you see it askew. It is his heart that was infested."

"What is he?"

"I do not know, Lord Kaylin. Ah, apologies. Kaylin."

You must learn to accept the title that comes with your position; it is one of the very few advantages you have, Ynpharion said.

Where I came from, an advantage was an invitation to robbery. Or worse.

It is not so different, here—but it signals, to the would-be thief, that there are consequences.

She would have answered, but at that moment, the stranger looked up to meet her eyes, through the veil of familiar's wing. She realized one of the disturbing things about him was that he had no eyelids.

The second disturbing thing was the eyes he did have: they looked like…bee eyes. Or bee hives. Like something was living *in* them that might emerge at any minute. She wondered, as she controlled a shudder, what he saw when he looked at her. As if in reply, the marks on her arms began to glow.

CHAPTER 19

He opened his mouth; he had no teeth. Where teeth might have been, he had fine, multicolored filaments; they moved in a wave that appeared to reflect light. She could see that the form and shape he now wore was diffuse, amorphous; that it suggested life—or rather, life as Kaylin knew it—without actually being it. She tried to concentrate on it anyway, because everything else screamed *wrong* to her. And he wasn't the one who had his hands in someone's chest, wrapped around their heart.

If it was even his heart.

"Chosen," he said. She could hear the word, could feel her body reverberate with the two syllables. The high-pitched, painful shriek was gone.

She opened her mouth to reply, but words deserted her; her mouth was too dry, her throat too constricted. She forced herself to breathe normally. Wondered what she was inhaling.

"There is danger, here." He looked away, to Terrano. "I am...free? I am free. If you release me, I will not harm you, and I will not return to Ravellon." The word he used was different; Kaylin could hear the clashing overlay of syllables, but it didn't change the heart of what he'd actually said.

Terrano hesitated.

"It is safe," Alsanis said quietly. "They will do no harm to me."

Terrano let go. As he did, Kaylin saw that his hand was bleeding. The person that he'd caught and held in its insect shape remained standing; he made no further attempt to flee. But he turned to the Avatar of the Hallionne, and lifted his hands in a complicated dance of motion that seemed deliberate, graceful.

It took a moment for Kaylin to realize that this was his version of a bow: a gesture of respect. What surprised her was Alsanis; he lifted his hands in a motion that, while far less fluid, appeared to be almost the same.

"It is a greeting," Alsanis said, glancing at Kaylin. "An old greeting. Words once had different meanings, different textures, and to speak them at all required power and will, focus and certainty; they were not unlike bright, beautiful cages. There are reasons why you cannot speak that ancient language. And no, Lord Kaylin, it does not come easily to even one such as I."

She wondered where he'd seen that greeting, where he'd learned it, what etiquette schools—and here, an image of angry Diarmat, not that there was any other kind, filled her mind—he had been forced to attend.

Alsanis laughed.

"I come from the east," the stranger said. "I was sent out to gather information. They will know that I am lost to them."

"Who sent you?" It was Kaylin who asked. Terrano was staring at the stranger, his forehead creased in a deepening frown, as if he couldn't quite bring his gaze into focus. There was no enmity in it, no hostility.

The stranger's eyes lit up. Literally. The facets that made the eyes look insect-like began to flash, to spark; he lifted his hands, and his fingers once again did a strange, deliberate dance through air. But what had she expected? That he somehow dislodge a name, an identifier, something that Kaylin, as a Hawk, might hope for when questioning the witness to a crime? He was a *Shadow*.

But he'd said he was free. Free, now.

"Alsanis, what the hells *is* Shadow?" It was a question she'd asked before, sometimes in desperation, sometimes in fear, but she'd never asked it like this.

There was no response. From out of the eyes of the stranger, bleeding into the air, came something that looked like multicolored smoke, if smoke were liquid. That smoke dribbled in all directions, spreading and meshing until it resembled something solid. Kaylin tried to think of it as a Records display, because those changed from mirror to mirror. She mostly succeeded, until she stopped having to try.

What she had expected to form was some envoy of Shadow; something that was a mishmash of body parts in the wrong places, and in the wrong quantities. Or a Dragon. A big black Dragon. Neither would have surprised her.

What she got instead sucked all the air out of her lungs—and everyone else's as well.

It was a Barrani man. He wore Court robes and a very slender tiara; his eyes were Barrani blue, his skin flawless, his posture elegant, his expression forbidding.

Lirienne shut down instantly. She could not hear his thoughts, could not feel any of his emotional reactions. Kaylin held his name, not the other way around. In theory, Kaylin could force her way in. But that would be costly for both of them.

More costly, by far, for you. It was Nightshade. His interior voice was ice. She was almost surprised to hear from him, given she was in the Hallionne; Helen seldom allowed his voice to penetrate her barriers.

You recognize him.

Yes. So does your kyuthe, *if I am not mistaken.*

He's Barrani.

Oh yes, Kaylin. He is Barrani, and a Lord of the High Court. If your Shadow is truly free, if it does not lie, there is a compromise in the structure of the High Court itself, and a failure in the tower.

Bellusdeo did not recognize the man, but recognized the significance regardless, and her eyes were already almost red. She turned instantly to the Lord of the West March. He did not appear to notice.

You are aware of the ways in which such a breach might occur.

She nodded, although Nightshade wasn't there to see it.

"He sent me," the Shadow said, his words almost superfluous.

Alsanis reacted first. His hands moved, all grace lost to urgency. But the stranger was looking, almost expectantly, at Kaylin.

She struggled to find her voice; it came out thin. "When did he send you?"

The concept of when clearly caused some difficulty, which wasn't entirely a surprise. But he said, "I traveled directly when word reached him of your arrival in this place."

There was cacophony in her head, then. Ynpharion spoke. Nightshade spoke. Lirienne was silent, but it didn't matter; the imperative, the concern, the anger, fell into her mind like a bad traffic accident on a busy, busy street. *Guys!* she shouted internally. *Can you please just shut the hells up for a minute?*

"My arrival? Our arrival? Or Terrano's arrival?" As she spoke, she pointed; she was aware that his sense of people as individuals might not be the same as hers, but his answer, if it could be extracted, was important.

"Yours, Chosen." He frowned. "Yours and the Dragon's."

She *needed* a measure of time, now. She needed a way to ask *how long ago was this* and have it be both understood and answered.

Alsanis spoke. She didn't understand the words. The stranger, however, frowned. Beside the image of the Barrani Lord, a second image began to form; at first Kaylin thought he was adding color and setting to the former; sky appeared, and beneath it, something that might have been grass or weeds.

Alsanis nodded, and Kaylin watched. Nothing changed, to her eye, except the color of the sky itself. She knew roughly when she'd left Elantra; she didn't know exactly when she'd arrived at the Hallionne Orbaranne. She knew that she'd lost time trying to walk through a portal, but not how much time. But to her the sky was a night sky, shading into morning.

Alsanis, however, saw more, or understood more. He frowned. "Lord Kaylin."

"Please translate," she said, in High Barrani.

He closed his eyes. Unlike the stranger, his eyes had lids. The silence was tense; seeds of fear and suspicion had taken root.

Kaylin. It was Severn. Severn who almost never approached her this way. Severn who held *her* name. She realized, hearing his voice—the actual weight of it, the pronounced word, that she wanted him here. This was an investigation. If her partner were by her side, she'd feel like a Hawk, and not a floundering incompetent in dangerous, diplomatic waters.

Next time you go to speak with Evanton, I'm going with you.

She almost smiled. *Have you been watching?*

She felt his nod. *Since you landed. I lost you briefly—that was bad.*

Where?

I'm going to guess it was when you heard Sedarias. Orbaranne didn't shut me out. His internal voice changed tone. For the worse. *We have a problem.*

We've got more than one. What's yours?

The Barrani High Court. No, some members of the Barrani High Court.

Kaylin stared at the image of the Barrani Lord.

Possibly. I wasn't there in person when a delegation was sent to the Emperor. And when I say delegation, I mean war band.

What?

According to the delegation, a Dragon has attacked the stronghold of the Lord of the West March.

Kaylin turned to stare at Lirienne.

Words are being exchanged; at the moment, no one is apparently ash. But the Halls of Law are a mess; the Lords of Law have been closeted away; the Imperial Mages are on alert. Technically, the West March is outside of the Emperor's domain.

So...someone is saying Bellusdeo *is attacking the West March.* Kaylin folded her arms.

She hasn't been mentioned by name. Just color. They're mobilizing a war band in the West March. They intend to either capture or kill her as an act of war.

Kaylin's Leontine was vehement, extended, and very, very rude. It caused the golden Dragon in question to raise both brows; clearly Mandoran had been teaching her.

The Emperor is...not pleased.

I've got the Lord of the West March here. And if he's somehow responsible for this...

Don't do anything stupid. But...if you're in the Hallionne with Bellusdeo, do not *leave it. Not by the doors.*

She thought of the portal paths, which had swallowed Sedarias and the rest of the cohort.

"Is there a problem?" Lord Barian asked.

"Yes." Kaylin folded her arms, trying to dig up High Barrani in place of her very inappropriate Leontine. *Look—can you tell them it was a misunderstanding? My familiar kind of winged his way out here in very large Dragon form. Maybe—maybe they're just confused.*

You don't believe that.

She didn't. She wanted to, though. She really, really wanted to.

Alsanis was watching her; the stranger was watching her. Bellusdeo was now watching the two Barrani lords; until Kaylin's loud outburst of Leontine, she had been watching the stranger.

"Lord Kaylin?" Lirienne said.

"Just one minute."

Ynpharion.

Lord Kaylin.

Oh, cut the crap. I mean it. Just cut it. What in the hells is going on over there? What is the Consort doing? No, she thought, that was unfair. *What is the High Lord doing? Bellusdeo is not attacking the West March in* any *way.*

The Lady is aware of that, was the cool reply.

And the High Lord isn't?

The politics of the High Court are not entirely in the control of one person, was the even more frigid response. *There have already been upheavals due to the simple existence of your friends. The Consort's planned visit to your domicile was an attempt to allay the fears that are the source of those upheavals.* There was a very faint—and extremely unfair—hint of criticism in his reply. *The Lady bids me tell you that the High Lord was not a member of the delegation sent to the Imperial Palace.*

But he didn't forbid it.

It is my suspicion—and the Lady has not confirmed it—that he did not know.

Leontine was becoming her new best language.

"While rudimentary exposure to foreign languages might, at another time, be informative, I believe this is not that time," the Lord of the West March said.

"Fine." The single word was Elantran. It was followed by more of the same, and Kaylin considered it a triumph that she did not sprinkle the whole with Leontine additions. "Apparently, a Barrani war band got together and entered the Imperial Palace."

Silence.

"They informed the Emperor that Lord Bellusdeo—no, sorry, a 'gold Dragon'—had attacked the West March. A war band is apparently being gathered in the West March *as we speak* with the intent to either capture or kill the hostile intruder."

Lord Barian and the Lord of the West March exchanged a glance that could have ignited large bonfires. Neither spoke.

Kaylin then turned to the Hallionne. "If we don't accept your hospitality—"

"I understand, Lord Kaylin." The Avatar turned to Lord Bellusdeo. "While you are guest within my boundaries, no harm will come to you."

Only, Kaylin thought bitterly, if she remained. And they couldn't remain here forever.

Ynpharion continued. *The Lady says the information arrived upon your arrival in the West March. It does not coincide with your arrival in the Hallionne Orbaranne.*

Well, that was something. On the one hand, Kaylin was glad, because had it gone the other way, it would have left only two obvious suspects: Lirienne and the Hallionne herself. On the other hand, suspects were littered everywhere in the West March, and narrowing it down was going to take a lot of work, work that her lack of experience with both the customs of the West March and its general terrain would make extremely difficult.

Add to that the reason they'd been sent here was to find Sedarias...

I do not believe that was the water's intent, Severn said. She reached for the words.

You spoke to Evanton.

Evanton sent Grethan to Helen; Helen used the mirror to contact me. I was, he added, with a hint of wryness, *already on the way to Evanton's.*

Which meant Evanton had no apprentice to snarl at.

The wryness deepened, becoming warmth. *Evanton's concern at the time was the outlay of power the water used. That, and the fact that water used it in the fashion it did. It is his opinion that, had you not been in the doorway, the water could not have transported you; the enclosure of the garden would have prevented it. But the water—and he finds it difficult to commune with it at all at the moment, although he has been trying—acted entirely on its own, without any offered warning.*

Ybelline said the same thing, but differently.

Evanton probably had better luck. The water didn't send you specifically to find the cohort.

But—

She sent you because there was something in the fabric of the physical world that was, that felt, entirely *wrong. She sent you because her own interactions with the world are limited by location. It's likely, in my opinion, that what the water sensed on the periphery of her awareness* is *the reason the cohort are gone, but the cohort disappearing is ancillary to the water.*

Ummm.

Yes?

The fire? The earth? The air? Do they not sense the same thing?

She felt his smile again; felt appreciation or approval travel through it. *Yes, but to a lesser extent. The water's interaction with the living has grown stronger because of the Tha'alani. But the earth, of the three remaining, was most disturbed.*

I don't suppose any of them offered any pointers, any advice?

Not precisely. I think they fear the Shadows. They did not use the word Ravellon; *Evanton is attempting to interpret what they did say. What will you do?*

We can't leave if the Barrani intend to kill Bellusdeo. I'm not at all sure they'd succeed, she added, *but the attempt will enrage the*

Emperor. And to be fair, will probably enrage Bellusdeo as well. I don't want the West March reduced to ash.

Or the Barrani?

I'm not sure I care what happens to the Barrani at this point. And I'm not even sure why you're asking. You can guess.

You want to leave by the portal paths.

I want to examine *the portal paths. Frankly, if the cohort could be somehow blown off them, I wouldn't give much for our chances. And,* she added morosely, *we've got Terrano. If he's anything at all like Mandoran and Annarion, he'll have Shadow swarming around him.* She stopped, then. *I think he already did. He just wasn't paying enough attention to* what *they were.*

Be careful. The Consort has left the High Halls.

*I told Ynpharion to tell her—*Leontine left her mouth. *I'm not sure we have the leisure to wait for her arrival.*

What choice do you have?

She didn't answer.

The stranger who was no longer enslaved did not evaporate or disappear. He remained standing in the Hallionne's hall. When Kaylin pushed the familiar's wing away from her eyes, she saw him as a diffuse, spiked ball. A floating one.

"His function," Alsanis said quietly, "is analogous to Records."

"Pardon?"

"He was considered a historian, a receptacle of information. He was sent to regions in which others might have difficulty surviving; it is why his form is inexact. It extends into the world in which you live, but it does not reside entirely in that world." He frowned. "Before the fall—those are his words—he...reported?...to—the word is *librarian*, I think. I am sorry. His mode of communication is almost archaic."

"Meaning?"

"It was archaic before I was born."

"Born? Or before you became the Hallionne?"

"The latter. He has served in Ravellon in a similar capacity. He has, until now, had no ability to breach the Tower barriers."

Bellusdeo seemed far more concerned with this statement than she had the information about the Barrani war band and their politics. "What changed?"

"He was carried out," Alsanis replied. His eyes had lost the appearance of living eyes as he spoke. "Someone entered Ravellon, bypassing the Tower defenses, and absorbed him as a passenger."

Kaylin's hands became fists. "Let me guess. The Tower that was breached was in Candallar."

Alsanis, however, did not reply immediately. He spoke to the Shadow, and eventually turned back to Kaylin. "The name has no meaning to him."

Kaylin turned to the spiky, floating ball. "I don't believe you."

"He does not understand."

"The Towers take the name of their lords."

"They do not," the stranger said. She could hear his voice, even if he in theory had no mouth with which to speak. The screeching had diminished, although she continued to hear a faint buzz. "They do not change. They are like this place. It is quiet here. It is not so quiet in Ravellon; a hundred thousand mouths speak in all places, all directions. I was sent to the border, the boundary, and I was told to accompany the one who would meet me there without absorbing his essential information."

Kaylin let that sink in for one long minute. "Fine. Tell me— show me—what you saw when you met the person there." She folded her arms and waited. Nothing happened. It was Terrano who interrupted; the tenor of his voice rose and fell, but the words were not words that Kaylin understood.

Clearly, the ball did.

The image of the Barrani noble did not fade. The clothing he wore, however, transformed as they watched, as did the ground beneath his feet. When the transformation was complete, the Lord of the High Court resembled one of Nightshade's thugs.

Kaylin understood that this disguise would be necessary if the Lord wanted to head into the fiefs without drawing attention to himself. What she needed to know, however, was not the how, but the where.

Instead of addressing the spiked ball, she turned to Terrano. "I need to see more of his surroundings. If he met the man on the borders of Ravellon, those borders are physical. I want to know what they looked like."

"If it was Shadow—"

"The Barrani lord didn't *stay* in the shadows, or Spike wouldn't be here."

"Spike?" Terrano interrupted.

"We have to call him something," Kaylin replied, adding a fief shrug. Spike did not seem to notice. Or mind.

"He does not mind," Alsanis said. "But I am uncertain that he understands the purpose of the word or your version of an identifier."

Kaylin, responsible for the digression, cleared her throat. "*Anyway.* He walked through the streets of the city; he walked through the streets of a fief."

Terrano spoke again, and this time, the ball surrendered a detailed map. It took Kaylin a moment to realize that's what it was; it was an amalgamation of the literal view of the street, with the wrong colors—too many, too spread out—and overlapping buildings. No, she thought, they weren't overlapping, not exactly; it was as if each building had been viewed a hundred times, over a decade or two, and the composite of each viewing had been laid over each other.

Candallar, Severn said.

"You think?"

Everyone glanced in Kaylin's direction; she flushed, realizing she had spoken out loud. Severn's presence was so much a given during investigations of any kind, she'd responded automatically.

I'll pass that information on immediately.

This time, she nodded; she was, for the moment, grateful that he had remained in Elantra.

That makes one of us.

That's the fief, Kaylin said, confining her words to the inside of her head, *but not the fieflord.*

Concur.

You know who he is?

I'd like to make certain before you speak with the Lord of the West March.

The Lord of the West March and I are going to be speaking about war bands, Dragons and politics.

She could almost see him cringe—and he rarely did that. *Avoid politics, if possible. If the Consort and the High Lord were unaware of the gathering of the war band, it's likely the Lord of the West March was unaware.*

Kaylin thought of the Consort's warning, passed to her through Ynpharion.

If he wanted you—or Bellusdeo—dead it would be almost trivial for him.

Not if he didn't want to add political complications for his brother, the High Lord. Not if he didn't want to piss off his sister. I don't know why, but the cohort's freedom is causing, or has caused, political difficulties for him, personally. She grimaced.

"Kitling," Bellusdeo said, "you even *think* loudly."

"Says the woman whose racial voice could deafen the entire Halls of Law—which is why it's not generally legal to *use* it."

Let me inform the Hawklord of our current information in regard to Candallar.

Tell Teela.

Teela is currently in residence in your home. She is keeping Annarion and Mandoran in check, but only barely. It's good they're here. If they weren't, she'd've joined the Consort.

She's worried.

Understatement.

Ugh.

Don't leave the Hallionne unless you have no choice.

Don't leave the city. I've got a Dragon and a familiar for backup. They're not you, but in a pinch, they'll do. And I need you there. If we manage to get out of the Hallionne and the West March, in more or less one piece, I'd like any welcoming party to be jailed or disrupted before we arrive. Oh—and can you mentioned Terrano to the boys?

Not if you don't want Teela to know.

Did she? *Terrano never, ever tried to hurt* her.

He did try to hurt you. Has Teela ever struck you as the forgiving type?

No—but he didn't *hurt me, and the only reason he's here is to help the rest of the cohort. I'm willing to trust him.*

I am not telling Teela that.

Darn. I was hoping you'd get the lecture out of her system before we get home.

Willing to die for you.

But there are fates worse than death?

Pretty much.

Bellusdeo was not angry. She was—to Kaylin's eye—both alert and amused. The former made perfect sense. The latter, not so much.

Although both Barrani lords were blue-eyed, they seemed to take their cues from the Dragon; they were as relaxed as their eye color indicated they could be. Terrano appeared to be clueless, but that might be unfair; he was keeping Spike company. The familiar was draped, once again, across Kaylin's shoulders. He looked, if anything, bored.

Alsanis opened the doors at the end of the great hall, and led the small delegation into the Hallionne's interior. There, he escorted them through arches that seemed too slender to actually bear the weight of ceiling for long, and into a small dining room. Or parlor. If the latter, it was a Barrani space; it opened to sky. It didn't open to the sky of the West March, however.

"I don't know why you're so annoyed," Bellusdeo said to Kaylin, as she took a wide comfortable chair.

"I don't know why you're not."

"Dragon. This is not my natural domain, and the Barrani here are, in theory, somewhat old school. We're all Immortal, and we all have long, long memories."

"Someone wants you dead."

"And this is news how? It won't be the first time an attempt has been made. Oddly, I find it refreshing."

Kaylin stared at her. On her shoulder, the familiar snorted.

"It isn't subtle. It's full-on, out in the open, hostility. It isn't my fault, and it isn't my responsibility. It is also, you must admit, somewhat clever; they had little time to craft a response to my arrival—and although forced to react with speed, they also did so with intelligence." She smiled, showing elongated teeth, a sign that she wasn't as sanguine as she sounded. "My own kin would just fly down and scorch the earth and everything that surrounded it."

"The Emperor—"

"My kin, not his." Tea appeared; it was the tea that Helen habitually made. Although the decor was nothing like the interior Helen had created—at least for the rooms Kaylin had free access to—Alsanis was attempting, as he could, to make them feel at home. Given the situation, she appreciated his attempt, but felt it was misguided.

"Look," she finally said, turning to Lirienne, "was this your idea?"

His smile, like Bellusdeo's, was martial but otherwise undisturbed. "Were it, do you think I would have escorted you to Alsanis? He is the only guarantee of Lord Bellusdeo's safety in the West March."

"That's not a no."

"If it will calm you at all, no. This was not my idea. And while I admire Lord Bellusdeo's point of view, I myself feel far less sanguine about it."

It was Nightshade who spoke next, not Ynpharion, as Kaylin had almost expected. *He will not be sanguine. To summon a war band is the act of a lord, not a liege; If this truly did not originate with the Lord of the West March, someone has attempted to usurp his authority.*

You wouldn't be as calm?

Ah, you mistake me. I would, of course, appear to be as calm. There is nothing to be gained by exposing either anger or pain; were there, we would do so. Bellusdeo is not, in my view, actually angry; she is resigned and even amused. Lirienne is angry.

And Lord Barian?

I am...less familiar with Lord Barian.

Kaylin glared at her shoulder. "You didn't have to show up as a giant Dragon, you know."

"It is perhaps a blessing," Bellusdeo said, before Kaylin could launch into a lecture.

"How?"

"He is your familiar. To those of power, in both the High Court and the West March, his status is understood. He took the form of an actual Dragon with his own unusual coloring, and if you recall, caused quite a stir. If politics with words alone are to be effective, there is now room to explain a possible 'misunderstanding.' Everyone involved can, if it is desired, save face."

"He wasn't *gold*."

"No. He wasn't a Dragon at all. And the downside, as you say in Elantra, is that the responsibility for the misunderstanding and possible war will rest entirely on the shoulders of his master." Bellusdeo laughed as Kaylin's jaw practically hit the table.

"There is merit to the Dragon's suggestion," Lord Barian said. He then looked to Lirienne, his expression making perfectly clear that the decision in its entirety belonged to the Lord of the West March.

"Pardon. My manners are somewhat lacking."

Nightshade was right: Lirienne was angry.

"I don't suppose this is the time to interrupt," Terrano said, interrupting anyway. Five sets of eyes immediately turned toward him.

Kaylin spoke first. "Unless you're about to tell me that I'm unexpectedly rich and everyone around me is safe and happy, no."

"Alsanis has guests."

"No," the Hallionne's Avatar said, "I do not."

"Fine. Alsanis has visitors."

"Please tell me it's not the war band."

Terrano frowned. "Why? I mean—I understand the concept of a lie, and I understand its uses. Sedarias made *very sure* that we all did," he added, with a grimace of distaste. "But I don't see much point in a lie that serves no actual purpose."

Bellusdeo shook her head. "You really *are* Mandoran's brother. It's a wonder to me personally, given what's said about Sedarias, that either of you survived her."

He winced. "She likes us, mostly. But, yes, there's a war band. Well, no, there's a delegation of three men, impressively armed and armored. If you want, I can go outside and see how many people are waiting behind them."

"That will not be necessary." Lirienne rose. So did Lord Barian. They exchanged a single glance; it was Barian who nodded, bowed and waited until Lirienne left the table. He then followed.

CHAPTER 20

"Yes, she does," Alsanis said, although no one had spoken.

Kaylin glanced at Terrano, who shrugged. "Don't look at me. I don't care if people hear what I'm thinking, so I just say it."

"When you remember," Alsanis added, in a slightly more aggrieved tone.

Terrano's shrug was a little less casual. "I haven't been speaking to others much, recently. Not with words." He then turned his focus on Bellusdeo. "Kaylin thinks out loud as well, so that only leaves you."

Bellusdeo exhaled, and as was often the case when she was frustrated, there was smoke in it. Alsanis, however, sharing some of that frustration, didn't mind. She turned to Kaylin. "I was thinking that you trust the Hallionne."

"They're kind of like Helen."

"To my eye, they are nothing like Helen."

"Well, she creates rooms on the fly, and she creates small pocket spaces in which she can kind of keep deadly things away from the rest of us. Oh, and she cooks."

Bellusdeo exhaled more smoke.

"And she cares about the comfort and safety of her occupants." Kaylin turned to face the Avatar of Alsanis. "You're going to get a good workout today."

Alsanis, however, did not reply. His eyes were once again obsidian, and as Terrano turned toward the Hallionne, his shifted into something opalescent. Bellusdeo rose. Kaylin did the same, but more clumsily.

Squawk. Squawk. Squawk.

Bellusdeo's armor—which really should have prevented her from sitting or bending in any way—shifted slightly. "Do you have any issues with draconic form? This hall is somewhat too confined for it, but the great hall is not."

"I do not believe Kaylin thinks that is wise."

The Dragon seemed nonplused. "I mean no disrespect," she said, which was usually followed by something disrespectful, "but *wisdom* and *Kaylin* are not generally put together in the same sentence. It would be similar to expecting wisdom from Terrano or Mandoran."

"Hey!"

Alsanis considered this, and to the chagrin of the not-quite-Barrani and the mortal, he nodded. "It has been a very long time since I have had a Dragon as a guest."

"I'm surprised you're allowed to speak of it at all."

"I am allowed," he replied gravely, "to speak of anything that does not make the guests feel threatened or endangered. And even then, there is nothing in the words that define my existence that would prevent it. Were there, the Hallionne would be used for political purposes. We were created in part to make safe the spaces in which rivals or enemies might gather. You do not fear the war band."

"Not really, no. Kaylin said that even on her first visit, half the Barrani chose to remain outside of the Hallionne's boundaries. I don't believe the war band will do anything but make noise at your doorstep; they must know they wouldn't survive an attempt made against me while I am here."

Alsanis bowed, but his eyes remained black, and his expression was troubled. He turned, then, to Terrano, although strictly speaking this wasn't necessary. "The doorstep, as you call it, might not be the main thrust of the attack."

Terrano said, "I'll go."

This time, no one stopped him.

"You don't happen to know where he's going?" Kaylin asked, after a minute had passed.

"Yes."

Bellusdeo snorted; she was amused. "I believe she intends for you to share that information."

"Ah. You will not be able to follow him; he has chosen to travel in haste." He then transferred his gaze to Spike. "He could."

Squawk.

"You are certain?"

Squawk squawk.

"Your familiar believes that I am incorrect; he believes he can facilitate your travel. I am uncertain, however, that this is wise."

"Did you see what happened to Terrano's friends?"

"No, Lord Kaylin."

"But they didn't try to return here."

"No."

Many things made no sense to Kaylin, but she focused on only one of them. The portal that had opened between one part of Orbaranne and her dining hall was part of Orbaranne, and it was there that Kaylin had heard Sedarias.

The Hallionne's eyes lost their lids, literally; they disappeared. His face, his facial structure, seemed to shudder; a ripple made it look far more liquid than flesh of any kind should.

"Alsanis?" Kaylin was the only person in the room who rushed to the Avatar's side. Without thought she reached out and placed both of her hands on his chest. The familiar did not seem to find this impressive.

"I am here," the Hallionne replied; the words did not come from the Avatar's mouth.

"What's happening?"

He replied, but there were too many unfamiliar words in the answer to make any sense of it.

"If Terrano is doing something bad, I'm going to strangle him."

"It would be difficult to strangle him," the Hallionne said, unperturbed. "I believe the purpose of strangulation is to restrict the flow of air. Regardless, he is not doing something bad. He is, however, doing something that guests do not usually do."

Hope bit Kaylin's ear. "We're going to join Terrano, if that's okay with you."

"Strangling your familiar would quite probably be even less successful than strangling Terrano."

Kaylin moved. Bellusdeo followed.

Around them, the halls of the Hallionne flowed, changing shape between the heavy steps of a running Hawk and an armored Dragon. Alsanis had widened the halls, granting silent permission for Bellusdeo to go full Dragon; for the moment, she chose to refrain.

What's happening outside? Kaylin asked Lirienne as she ran.

Three men in full armor have approached the Hallionne. There are another forty beyond the Hallionne's perimeter. The leader of the war band, he added, *is Lord Barian's mother.*

Kaylin let loose with a volley of Leontine.

The Warden, however, does not seem to have been aware of her plans.

You're certain?

Yes. He didn't elaborate. *This is not a good time for my sister to travel.*

Please don't think I have any control over what your sister does, or does not, do. She's far more likely to listen to you, if she can hear you.

You misunderstand.

Your sister has already left Elantra. I assume she intends to come to the West March.

He didn't ask her how she knew, and she didn't volunteer; she was fairly certain he could guess, and if he couldn't, Ynpharion would possibly be just a little less disgusted than he normally was.

She turned sharply left and almost fell off the floor. The floor, however, righted itself, and stairs formed a yard away from where she skidded—with the help of a wall—to a stop.

She cannot interfere here—

I think she probably can. Unless you want to tell her to stop, because I don't. She's only barely forgiven me for the last big argument we had—and I'm not having another one unless it's about the literal end of the world. Which pretty much summed up the previous argument.

She will not be coming overland. She will take the portal paths.

But—but that's how we lost the cohort!

Yes. And Kaylin, I believe the conspiracy that aided Terrano and his friends in their bid to escape the Hallionne the first time must still be active. Their goals at the time were unclear, but we can assume that their goals and the goals of the cohort overlapped. But they will now have some experience—

I know. They might have learned from their mistakes.

Yes. I am uncertain as to what they might have learned. Regardless, if the Consort does arrive, she will arrive at the portal gates.

"I don't think I've heard you swear quite so much. Ever."

"Lirienne thinks the Consort is coming by the portal paths."

"The portal paths on which the cohort disappeared?"

"The same." Even as she spoke, the ground—which had resembled stone beneath both of their feet—began to soften; the air thickened. "Is something on fire? Alsanis?"

"No. Alsanis is just upset." That was Terrano. Kaylin couldn't see him. "I've come back for the Shadow. What did you call him?"

"Spike. He didn't seem to notice."

"I noticed," Spike said. His voice was diffuse now, the syllables elongated; they no longer seemed to come from the spiky, silvered ball.

"I meant you weren't offended."

A series of clicks that might have been insects talking came from the ball. Terrano laughed. "He doesn't understand what you mean by offended. You can try explaining it. I'm not going to."

"Oh?" Bellusdeo asked.

"He'll ask what angry is. Or what fear is. It's going to be explanations all the way down, and I don't have the patience."

"Or skill," the Dragon muttered. She was visible, but sort of visually smeared. Kaylin lifted her hands to rub her eyes. It seemed that smoke—or mist—was creeping up from the ground in a way that obscured vision.

"Unlike the rest of you," Terrano snapped, "I don't spend my time doing nothing but pointless, boring, *political* talk!"

"That's what your friends are going to be doing when they arrive in Elantra."

Terrano shrieked in frustration. It reminded Kaylin of the sound Mandoran made when he got stuck in walls. The air grew more foggy as they began their descent.

"Bellusdeo?"

"Here."

"Do you see a lot of fog?"

"It seems more like smoke, to me—but yes, it's interfering with visibility."

Kaylin considered asking the Dragon to go back up the stairs, but decided against it; the stairs didn't seem particularly fixed in either form or shape. Whatever Alsanis was doing, he was doing in a rush.

"I do not see this smoke," Spike said. Terrano was unwilling to explain *offended* to Spike, but had no trouble with *smoke*.

"What do you see?"

"The atmosphere of the area which you are entering is not fully compatible with your species. This may cause difficulties with your perception of the space."

Kaylin ground to a halt. "My species? Or our species?"

He whirred a bit and then said, "You are human and Dragon. This area is not compatible with your kind."

"And him?"

"It's not a problem for me," Terrano replied.

"What exactly is his species?"

Spike whirred. She thought there were more sounds in it, but they didn't resolve into anything like language, at least not the languages she knew. "Alsanis?"

"Terrano has gone ahead," the Hallionne replied. "But there is an instability in the portal room, and I do not believe it will be possible to entirely contain its appearance. Please accept my apologies for the discomfort, Lord Kaylin."

"Will he help us?" Bellusdeo asked, her voice a rumble of sound.

"I am certain he will try."

The familiar squawked loudly, which was a warning. It wasn't a *timely* warning. The step on which Kaylin had leapt ceased to exist just as her left foot hit it.

Bellusdeo caught her before the ground—if there *was* ground—could. Gold-tinted claws grabbed both of her arms, and Kaylin, who could climb up the side of a building with a little bit of luck and equipment, managed—with effort—to twist her way up to the Dragon's back. Spike, on the other hand, didn't require rescue. If he no longer had wings, or what looked like wings, he seemed immune to simple things like gravity. He floated alongside Kaylin.

"I am going to be really displeased if I hit ceiling or walls," the gold Dragon said. She roared. In the depths of whatever it was that lay beneath her feet, something answered. This did not fill Kaylin with anything remotely resembling hope.

"Are you all right? Nothing's injured?"

"Well, I'm not bored."

"Where's Spike?"

"I'm not sure. I can't see him."

Kaylin shrieked and clung for dear life as the Dragon veered to the side. "Concentrate on driving—I'll look!"

Down was a long way away. Kaylin half doubted they would ever reach it; it felt as if they had been in flight for a long time. But the smoke—or fog, as there didn't seem to be a fire—that had made visibility so terrible seemed to clear as they descended. Beneath the Dragon, she could see what appeared to be ground.

It was, sadly, ground covered in trees.

A cursory glance at those trees didn't immediately surrender a clearing, and while the trees probably didn't pose a problem for Dragons, they weren't going to do Kaylin any good. She tightened her legs and clenched her jaw as Bellusdeo buzzed the tree tops, but the Dragon rose again, searching for somewhere convenient to land.

She settled, in the end, for inconvenient; the trees opened up around a lake, and the lake was possessed of something that might have been shore—if it had been longer and less rocky. Less inconvenient became hazardous as the rocks rose to impede the Dragon's skidding halt.

Bellusdeo corrected course and pushed up off the ground before impact, but it was close.

Squawk! Squawk! Squawk!

"You could *try* to be a little helpful!" Terrano shouted. A quick scan of the lake failed to expose his presence, and his voice seemed to be coming from the rocks.

"I think he wants us to stop right in front of the...rocks," Kaylin told the Dragon, who was now hovering. Hovering made the landing far easier, and she did as Kaylin suggested.

The rocks immediately fell, and Terrano climbed out of them, looking distinctly battered. "Honestly, the two of you. Could you not hear me screaming?"

"We heard the last bit," Kaylin said, before Bellusdeo could reply; Terrano looked frazzled enough that the inevitable sarcasm or condescension wasn't going to help the situation any. "What are you doing?"

"We're in trouble," he replied.

"Alsanis?"

"That's part of the trouble. He's not here. Or rather, we're not there anymore."

Severn?

Silence.

Kaylin swore.

The good news, such as it was, was that they were materially unharmed. The bad news? They appeared to be in the middle of nowhere. A kind of forest nowhere that reminded Kaylin of an insect-filled walk overland to the West March.

"*Don't* touch that," Terrano snapped. Since Kaylin hadn't moved, she felt this unfair. "It's not actually water."

"And the rocks?"

"Not rocks, either."

"So...this is like the portal paths."

He raised a brow at her, which conversely made him look younger than he usually did.

"The portal paths—at least at inception—could look like anything. The first time I walked the portal pathways, I entered a path that mimicked forest perfectly." Until it hadn't.

"It's not the same."

"How's it different?"

"When Alsanis creates the path, he does so deliberately. It's a narrow path—more like a tunnel through noise and chaos than an actual road—and it's sustained, in theory, by the Hallionne."

"How? It's not part of the Hallionne."

"It's—ugh. Everything in the outlines is supposed to be inert. It's supposed to be like the rest of his body, just outside of his absolute control. He does have some influence on the shape it takes. Inside the Hallionne, he can create anything he wants. The portal roads are not on the inside. He can influence the shape of the road, but it's as if he's made an object, say, a glass, that he's given visitors to take with them. He can't do anything about the glass if the visitor drops it and it shatters."

"So, he creates the path, and we walk it."

"Yes. But the path that he creates has layers. It's like—it's affected by weight. Sometimes some of those who walk the paths have different weights. It's like they sink to different levels. They all reach the portal's exit, eventually. In theory. He must have told you, last time, that portal paths were tricky if you needed to arrive at the Hallionne at the same time as your companions." He gave the gold Dragon—who was definitely draconic now—the side-eye.

"The last time we took these paths," Kaylin told her companions, "they disintegrated into shadow around our feet. By the end, we were *walking* on one of the siblings of Hallionne Bertolle. While he talked. He lay down, stretched out and made himself a road that the rest of us could more or less follow. And the stuff underneath that road didn't particularly want us there. Long story short, it sure didn't seem inert to the rest of us."

"It was. The Hallionne wasn't the only person trying to influence its shape or form. Or direction."

"That was you?"

"No, not directly. I was busy elsewhere." But he looked distinctly uncomfortable. "I may have taught some people a bit about how to manipulate it."

"May have."

He shrugged.

"*May* have."

"I didn't think it would matter!"

The Dragon breathed fire; it melted the ground a few inches to the left of Terrano. Kaylin hoped that his physical form currently represented the entirety of the space he chose to occupy, but even if it didn't, he didn't seem unduly bothered by the fire. He did, however, avoid the lake and its water.

"Spike," Kaylin said, to the floating, spiked ball to her left, "take a note of this. I am never coming back to the West March again." She looked at her familiar who, to her surprise, seemed to have slumped into his bored posture. "Well, we wanted to investigate the portal paths anyway."

Terrano snorted.

"And at least this way, my head won't be filled with people who are giving me constant advice."

Terrano stared at her. Something in the shape of his eyes, the brief tightening of his lips, made Kaylin think of…envy.

"What we need to know," Bellusdeo said, "is what you taught the people who might just be using that knowledge against us now."

"Could we learn it?" Kaylin added. The small dragon bit her ear. Spike was largely nonverbal, and he tended to move along at a steady pace. A *slow* pace. Even Hawks on patrol weren't this sluggish, and Hawks paid attention to everything. Ah, no. If she thought about it that way, Hawks didn't; not like Spike did. He was like an ambulatory recorder, like an external portable mirror.

"Spike."

"I am here." That had become his response to most uses of his name.

"You said that you were ordered to the edge of the fief—"

"I do not believe that is what I said. I can replay—"

"No, please." Spike's replay took a *lot* longer than the average Records response. "I don't need the exact phrase, only the gist of it. You met a man at the edge of Ravellon. You were supposed to stay with him. He was to carry you somewhere."

A long pause, which generally meant Spike was thinking. Or reviewing his own Records without sharing. "Yes."

"Fine. Could you ride with me the same way?"

Both Bellusdeo and Terrano said, "No."

Without the help of the familiar's wing, Kaylin couldn't see the Shadow's facial expression, but the sound of confusion was relayed quite clearly in its voice. "Yes?"

To her much less sluggishly moving companions, Kaylin said, "I have Hope. I can carry Spike. Hope doesn't even look worried. If we wait for Spike, we'll never get anywhere."

"Where, exactly, are we trying to go?" the Dragon asked, folding her arms.

Kaylin shunted the question to Terrano.

"I'm *trying* to follow the echoes of the path Alsanis created for my friends. It was," he added, "destroyed. It no longer exists as a functional path." Eyes narrowing, he glared at the Dragon. "I am *also* attempting to build a path that the rest of you can walk. *I* don't need it. If I weren't trying to do it without overwhelming the possible traces of what existed before, it wouldn't require so much *concentration*."

Bellusdeo shrugged, but fell silent. Watching her, Kaylin was grateful that the Dragon lived with Helen in the same house as Mandoran. Yes, they squabbled and took digs at each other across a dining table that never quite reached the level of battlefield, but she'd grown accustomed to the Barrani's attitude, his general nonchalance. An echo of that relationship formed the basis for her response to Terrano.

"Spike." While the Dragon and the Barrani were glaring at each other, the ball of silver floated toward Kaylin's outstretched left hand. "I'd really like it if you didn't actually make me bleed."

The Dragon pushed Kaylin's hand away.

"If a Barrani lord could carry it, I can carry it. Neither of us are Terrano."

"Even Terrano couldn't carry it for long, if you recall. He was bleeding."

"Was not."

"It was bleeding or disincorporating, which we happen to find more disturbing."

"Did I mention concentration?" To Kaylin he added, "Of all the companions you could have chosen, why a *Dragon*?"

"Among other things, she's never tried to kill me."

"I wasn't trying to kill you."

"The forest Ferals?"

"*They* were trying to kill you. It's not like I'm Shadow—I wasn't controlling their bodies *or* their minds."

"No, just conveniently leading them to us. Oh, and doing something to help them shift the shape of their bodies."

"I'm telling you—"

"Don't bother." Kaylin was torn between the strong desire to strangle Terrano and the desire to let Bellusdeo breathe on him. Terrano was unlikely to die, but if he got singed just a little...

He won't.

She blinked. This was a different voice.

Yes. It's mine.

She looked down at her hand. Spike had, apparently, passed through the less intimidating human draconic form to settle on Kaylin's left palm. She looked up at Bellusdeo, who was staring grimly at the ball, her eyes very orange. "Please don't breathe on it. Spike will survive. Probably. I'll lose my hand."

"You're right-handed."

Her familiar emitted a lazy squawk, and the gold Dragon surrendered. "Honestly, I'm beginning to understand why Tain is so attached to boredom."

Kaylin, however, was staring at her hand, because the lower half of Spike began to melt.

"I'm not sure that's a good idea," Terrano said, as if he had eyes in the back of his head.

"You focus on the cohort. I'll worry about me."

"You don't do a very good job of it." He stiffened, lifting his head. "Hold on tight."

"To what?"

"Anything."

Kaylin grabbed Bellusdeo—with her right hand. Spike was now half a ball; the other half had apparently become a thin, shining glove around her left hand.

I'm here.

"Tell me what he's looking at."

That is something you do with the eyes that you have, yes?

"Yes."

"Nothing." Spike spoke the last word aloud, so that Bellusdeo could also hear his reply.

Bellusdeo snickered at Kaylin's muted shriek. So did the familiar. "What is he *sensing*, Spike?"

"There is an anomalous fragment in the material." Hearing his voice, the Dragon stiffened.

Kaylin ignored her. "You mean the landscape?"

"The landscape? No. Terrano is shaping it as we walk."

"Bellusdeo?"

"Ahead of you," the gold Dragon replied, the sound of her voice shifting as she once again surrendered the human form for the draconic one. It was far easier to leap up on her back from flat ground than it had been from curved claws, and Kaylin did.

"The air isn't that much different," Terrano said, although he hadn't looked back. "Keep your feet on the ground unless you have no choice."

If Bellusdeo was reluctant to take orders from the equivalent of a Barrani child, it didn't show. "If we're swept off this path, can you find us?"

Terrano didn't answer.

Kaylin, however, said, "Probably not."

"No?"

"If he could find us, he would have already found the cohort. I'm not sure he knows where we are."

Anomaly was not the right word. Kaylin had traveled portal paths that had almost—but not quite—disintegrated beneath her feet before. She had retained her footing on increasingly unstable ground. Those of her companions who had not been as lucky had vanished; Kaylin had been informed that most of them had made it back to the Hallionne eventually.

Given that Bellusdeo was the only female Dragon, and given her importance to the Eternal Emperor, Kaylin understood that *eventually* was more than just career-limiting. And, if she were honest, Bellusdeo was her friend. She was part of Kaylin's daily life. If Bellusdeo were lost in the whatever it was, Kaylin firmly intended to be lost with her.

Yes, Spike said.

"Is something coming?"

Something is already here.

Terrano was cursing, now. Or at least Kaylin assumed that's what he was doing; she only recognized two of the words. "I'll teach you Leontine," she told him. "It's better. More visceral."

More cursing, but some of it was now aimed at Kaylin. She laughed.

He stopped.

"Bellusdeo."

"On it already," the Dragon said. She took two steps, and caught Terrano by the collar. With her teeth.

The land upon which he'd been standing reared up in a wave. It rounded, as if about to burst, and when it did, Kaylin was reminded of an egg, because something emerged from it. It had eyes, or what looked like eyes; it was hard to count them because they opened and closed at random. There was a least one mouth, but Kaylin had the queasy impression that mouths, like eyes, appeared and disappeared as they opened or closed. There were teeth, though.

She wondered, then, if this is what the cohort had faced.

Bellusdeo couldn't breathe fire without dropping Terrano. She didn't try. She lifted off, having secured him, and the moment her claws lost contact with the ground he had somehow created, the creature began to fissure and melt simultaneously.

Terrano was not familiar with Leontine, and unlike Mandoran or Annarion, couldn't hear Teela's internal voice; he hadn't learned it. Kaylin was therefore learning a *lot* of new Barrani words. "Land!" he shouted. "Land there!"

Bellusdeo's reply was muffled. Given she was speaking with full Dragon throat, this didn't mean inaudible. "There's no there!"

He didn't tell the Dragon to let him go. "It's not a danger—we need to land before we lose it!"

It's not a danger my butt, Kaylin thought. "Bellusdeo—"

"He's insane. That's a Shadow—"

The familiar squawked. Although in theory his throat and

jaws were much, much smaller, his screeching got through, and the Dragon immediately changed direction.

Terrano did not stop cursing when they landed; the landing was rough, but he managed to squeak out a single command: *stay on the ground!*

And ground still existed. It was the lake that had vanished. So had the creature, although something amorphous and foggy remained in its place; something smaller, with—thankfully—less visible definition. Terrano shook himself free of the Dragon's teeth; the Dragon was making spitting noises, as if he'd left something behind and she didn't want it staying in her mouth.

Terrano, however, didn't seem to notice. He raced across the ground, his stride almost unnaturally long.

The familiar squawked loudly, and Terrano shuddered at the sound, but his stride narrowed and although he didn't stop moving once, he slowed. Kaylin had no idea what he intended to do; she expected him to stop once he reached what her eyes perceived as the edge of the mass.

But no, that would have been too sensible. He did pause, but only to bend into his knees, readjust his weight, and throw his arms back to provide momentum.

He leapt into the shimmering mass, and disappeared from sight.

CHAPTER 21

"Should we be worried?" Bellusdeo asked; she retained draconic shape and size.

"You're not?" Kaylin replied, the words drifting over her shoulder as she ran. The familiar on her shoulder was sitting upright, and his squawk was shrill. He lifted a wing and smacked it across Kaylin's face, but didn't withdraw it. The wing did not reveal anything that her own eyes didn't see.

He bit her ear as she slowed. She could hear voices.

"Do you intend to follow?" Bellusdeo could move. Although the size of the form made her movements *feel* slower, they weren't.

"I don't know where he went. What do you see?"

"Haze."

Kaylin nodded. "Terrano!"

No answer.

"He really does remind me of Mandoran," the Dragon said, in a far more natural voice. "I want to strangle him."

"Stand in line." And then, casting a backward glance at her companion, Kaylin added, "You sure you want to lose the size advantage?"

"The ground is still here. Terrano, in some fashion, is still present. And I think he may need help."

"Will he need any help that *we* can give him?"

"True. Move over."

Kaylin rolled her eyes, but before she could respond, the eye that was covered by translucent wing caught movement in the haze. Something that looked like fog, but grayer, darker. It had no distinct shape, not immediately; it looked more like a body bag. She could not see it through her right eye. "I take it back," she told the Dragon.

"What's changed?"

"I think there *is* something in there."

"Terrano?"

"He didn't answer."

"Maybe," the Dragon said, glancing at Kaylin, "he couldn't hear you." It was just enough warning that Kaylin could bring both her hands to cover her ears. Or one hand; Spike was in the other and she didn't think attempting to jam half of him into her ears was going to help her hearing much.

Bellusdeo roared. Kaylin was vaguely impressed that the roar encompassed syllables. Something in the fog, however, was not; it froze. The Dragon's voice appeared to echo; the ground started to shift beneath their feet.

A head poked out of the haze. It didn't appear to be attached to anything else, but Kaylin recognized it immediately. She also recognized the expression. "Will you stop that *right now*? You're panicking everyone!"

Bellusdeo folded her arms, but fell silent.

"Step back," Kaylin suggested.

"No."

"I don't think he's bringing anything through that can kill us."

"Not us, no."

"Fine. I don't think he's bringing anything that can kill *me*."

"That is inaccurate," Spike said.

Her familiar hissed. The laughing hiss. "Nothing that *will* kill me, then."

"That is conjecture," Spike replied.

"Are you capturing this?"

"Yes. I am uncertain that you will be able to view it. Your vision is extremely limited, as is your ability to interact with the world."

Kaylin sometimes felt like companions were just a form of portable criticism, like portable mirrors, but less helpful.

"I believe Terrano is attempting to engage the layer that you occupy now. He is having some difficulty."

The small dragon withdrew his wing with a noisy, rattling sigh. He looked pointedly at his theoretical master, and she nodded. "Go."

He lifted himself off her shoulder as Bellusdeo said, "He should stay in contact with you." But there was a slight rise at the end of that statement, as if the sensible warning was uttered with some doubt.

If the familiar heard, he failed to reply; instead, he floated toward the visible haze. He didn't disappear into it, which was good, but inhaled as if he intended to breathe on it, which was less good. Maybe.

He exhaled a cloud of silver mist while she was still considering.

Where the mist hit the haze, the two combined. She had half expected the haze to freeze, but it didn't. It seemed to become more solid—and more silver—where the familiar's breath touched it, but no distinct shape emerged from the combination. He inhaled and breathed again. The mass became harder, reflecting a light that didn't have any obvious source.

As it did, Kaylin thought it looked like a cave, or a silvery, slightly melted version of a cave. And standing in its mouth, she could see Terrano. He had his left arm beneath the arms of another person, or at least something vaguely person-shaped, and as he approached the mouth of the cave, that person began to...cohere. She was a Barrani female, or rather, the ghost of one; she was transparent, but not in the way Kaylin's familiar was. Terrano's arm should have passed through her. It didn't. But Kaylin was certain he would be the only person present who could touch her.

The stranger lifted her head; her hair was ghostly, all color leached from it by lack of solidity. She lifted her chin, straightened her shoulders, but did not pull away from Terrano. Possibly because she couldn't. His grip was tight, his eyes the darkness of chaos or shadow. His form, however, did not waver.

He pulled her out of the cave.

She lost solidity, and he cursed; his grip appeared to tighten, but it tightened on smoke. Before he could shift it, she melted away again. Terrano sagged. "They never listened to me," he told Kaylin. "Mandoran did sometimes, but the others, not so much."

"Who was that?"

"Is," was his defensive reply. He looked exhausted as he turned, once again, to the cave mouth. To the familiar, he said, "Can you hold this space?"

Squawk.

"Good. I have to leave it in your hands. I don't think I'll ever be able to get them out of there if I don't."

It took Terrano three tries to free one of the cohort. But the third time she began to lose cohesion, she frowned, her eyes narrowing. Kaylin could practically see the blue in their ghostly appearance; she could certainly see the narrowing of lips and the determined tightening of jaw.

"Sedarias?" Kaylin asked.

The woman looked up at the sound of Kaylin's voice, her eyes changing shape. She caught Terrano's arm in her insubstantial hands, and as she wavered, Kaylin called her name again. The dissipation stopped; the ghost almost appeared to be sweating with effort. She began to walk, to take steps—all silent—as Terrano supported her.

Kaylin came face-to-face with Sedarias. Sedarias did not take on color, she didn't become solid. But she was, in as much as Kaylin thought she could be, here. She opened her mouth, but no words left her moving lips. And then her lips stopped moving as she caught sight of the Dragon.

To Kaylin's surprise, Sedarias bowed. She had expected a reaction similar to Terrano's, but remembered that Sedarias, unlike Terrano, was linked—or had been linked—to Mandoran, Annarion and Teela. What they saw, or at least what the first two saw, she also saw. She therefore knew Bellusdeo at least as well as the boys did.

Given what they said about Sedarias, probably better.

Bellusdeo returned the bow. Her eyes were a shade of orange that was probably about as close to gold as they could be, given her location.

Terrano exhaled and frowned. After a moment, he called Sedarias by name, and she turned to him, her own expression rippling. She spoke silently again, but he could apparently read her lips; he nodded and headed back to the cave.

One by one, he pulled the cohort out of it. Allaron was next; he was as large as Kaylin remembered, towering over the rest of his cohort by half a head. It was almost comical to see Terrano supporting him, but he didn't disperse as Sedarias had done. Sedarias, in turn, had come to stand slightly in front of Kaylin and Bellusdeo, and Kaylin was certain she was giving directions—to Allaron, at least. They were bound by True Name. Whatever she had done to breach the invisible threshold, she had clearly communicated to the rest of her friends. Whatever cut Kaylin off from the small host of people to whom she was likewise connected did not appear to affect the cohort. Then again, they were in this space together.

Valliant came next; his name in other circumstances still made Kaylin snicker. Fallessian, Serralyn, Torrisant, Karian and finally Eddorian, joined them. They were, to a person, as ghostly as Sedarias; none of them, however, looked as annoyed. No, Kaylin thought, she wasn't annoyed, she was angry. If her eyes had had color, they'd be midnight blue.

Terrano turned to Kaylin once the last of the cohort were as present as they were going to get. He glanced at the familiar, his natural suspicion and caution immediately obvious. The familiar generally glared at the former member of the cohort, but he wasn't doing that now; instead, he was surveying them all from Kaylin's shoulder—which, given the difference in height, should have looked ridiculous, but didn't.

The cohort couldn't speak in any way that Kaylin could hear.

They suddenly turned toward her, all eyes moving as one, which was kind of creepy until she realized they were looking at the familiar. He was squawking, but quietly.

"This is going to get complicated," the Hawk told the Dragon. "Spike?"

"I am here."

"Can you hear them?"

There was a very long pause as the spiked silver ball digested the question. "You cannot hear them?" he finally asked, with far more hesitance than he generally displayed.

"No. Neither the Dragon nor I can hear them."

"Terrano can?"

"Terrano," Terrano said, "can. But not clearly, and not well." He hesitated himself, and then added, "they can clearly hear each other." Again, Kaylin thought there was something wistful in his comment, but he spoiled it by adding, "Listening to Sedarias in her current mood, on the other hand, anyone sane could do without."

"She looks angry."

"She's beyond angry."

"What happened to them?"

"They encountered a trap."

"That thing we saw? The Shadow?"

He nodded. "It's not a complicated Shadow." Glancing at Kaylin's left hand, he added, "Spike is complicated. This one wasn't. But we spent centuries figuring out ways around Alsanis and his various walls and cages. Sedarias realized what was happening just before it did happen, and they all managed to avoid it."

"So…their state is voluntary?"

He winced. "None of them were as good at it as I was. And Sedarias isn't—wasn't—notably flexible. She and Annarion weren't the best."

Kaylin had seen Annarion alter his shape—without intent—before. She disagreed with Terrano, but kept it to herself.

He glanced at Kaylin again, exhaled, and said, "But she heard you when you called her name. They all heard you."

"Did they hear me because Sedarias heard me?"

He shook his head.

"You're certain?"

"They are."

"If it's possible," the Dragon interjected, "could we have the rest of this discussion somewhere else? I'm not entirely certain we're safe here."

Unfortunately for the Dragon, who was practicing common sense, Spike said, "If you desire it, I can translate for you. I did not realize your hearing was so inadequate."

★ ★ ★

Bellusdeo had had enough experience with Gilbert that she barely flinched when Spike spoke. And she had had enough experience with being a captive pawn to Shadow, or the Shadow in Ravellon, that she was willing—with effort—to see Spike as someone who was, when free, no threat to all of the rest of the living. But it was hard, and her eyes remained a steady, burning orange.

"If you'd like," Spike continued, "I can attempt to alter the range of your hearing; you would not require—"

"No, thank you," Bellusdeo said, her voice falling into draconic rumbling.

"Kaylin?"

"Could you do it safely?"

The question caused Spike to whir a bit as he considered it. Terrano clearly found this more amusing than pulling almost insubstantial people out of a cave.

"I do not understand the question."

"Oh?" the Dragon asked.

"I do not understand how you are using the term 'safely.' I cannot do so without making some changes in the actual mechanism, no."

"No," Bellusdeo repeated, making less effort to be polite since it was clearly wasted. "If Sedarias and her friends now exist on a plane with which we would never otherwise interact, the hearing—for our kind—is not required."

"But Kaylin desires communication."

Bellusdeo snorted. Small tufts of smoke were twined around the exhaled breath. The familiar also snorted, but then proceeded to squawk at Spike. Several times.

"I don't know about you," the Dragon added, "but I consider the possibility that there are unseen things living in the exact same space as I am extremely disturbing."

Kaylin shrugged. "If we can't normally see, hear, speak with, touch or otherwise be affected by them, I don't see why."

"You mean that?"

"For all intents and purposes, it's like they're not there." She shrugged again, uncomfortably aware of the Dragon's stare. "Look, you grew up in an Aerie, and you even remember a lot of it. I grew up in the fiefs. I had no fixed home; we had places where we squatted. Some were too exposed. I used to daydream of being able to live in a safe place—a single safe place—that we could call home.

"It's like—like there's a space, and more people can live in it. And they don't get in each other's way. They don't hurt each other at all." She exhaled. "That part's the important one. We're all minding our own business. We don't have to be aware of everyone else's."

"I am never going to understand mortals." The Dragon exhaled, and some of the tension left the stiff line of her shoulders. "Regardless, we need to get them out of wherever it is they are. I don't want Spike to play around with our ears."

"They're not quite anywhere," Terrano told them both. "They're in between states." When this clearly failed to enlighten either Kaylin or Bellusdeo, he added, "It's like they're stuck in a door between two rooms. They're not in one and they're not in the other."

"Was that the point of the trap?"

"No. The trap was probably meant to devour them."

"Was it Shadow?"

He hesitated, and then glanced at Spike.

Spike, on the other hand, said, "Yes. I do not believe you should remain here."

"And you're safe?"

"I am safe," he replied, without a hint of smugness.

This, on the other hand, caught Bellusdeo's attention. "There is Shadow here, or near here?"

"Yes."

"But it will not affect you."

"No."

"I think she wants a bit more of an explanation, Spike."

"It is not diverse enough to affect me. It was meant for you. Or for them," he added.

"Can you see it?"

The ball had no face, and therefore made no facial expressions, but Kaylin could almost feel frustration radiating from its core.

"I can sense it," Terrano broke in. He glanced at Spike and shrugged. "It's gathering over there." He lifted an arm and pointed into the distance to the left of where Kaylin was standing.

"And you're not in danger either?" the Dragon demanded.

"Not from this, no."

"Why?"

"I no longer have a name. Shadow doesn't seek to learn True Names; it seeks to change their essential structure. Where there are no names, it has more freedom to alter the base material."

"But if you—"

"My friends have more freedom than the rest of the Barrani have; more freedom, certainly, than Teela will now *ever* have. You encountered the Barrani who had reformed their bodies—they also had more freedom than Teela. And no," he added, "I'm not going to go into the boring details. If you're careful, the name isn't a cage."

"I do not understand why Barrani are so obsessed with their names," Bellusdeo said. "Dragons have them and we accept them. Attempting to somehow remove the dependence on True Names seems akin to suicide."

"It is by the use of that name that we can be enslaved, should a greater power discover it."

"But it's by the use of that name," Kaylin countered, "that you could speak with your cohort, even when you were nowhere near them. The name is a bridge between all of you. All of them," she corrected herself.

"It's not doing them any good here," he pointed out. She'd annoyed him. But he was right. None of the people who knew Kaylin's name could talk to her now. And she imagined that at least one of them would be panicking.

"We needed that bridge," Terrano finally said, "because we were trapped. We were prisoners. We needed it because we were weak. It's the reason mortals—and Barrani—congregate in a way that adult Dragons don't." It was the first time he had said anything positive about Dragons.

Bellusdeo, however, shook her head. "Dragons congregate. That's what the Aeries are. The only time a Dragon breaks away from his people is when he finds his hoard. It is considered the mark of true adulthood, among my kin. Or it was.

"And Terrano? Some Dragons find their hoard, and it drives them insane. They cannot exist among their own kind because they are terrified, possessive, obsessive; they no longer see their kin as anything but predators and encroachers. Barrani youth are, to my eye, very similar to mortals."

His brows rose into his hairline in outrage, but Bellusdeo held up one hand as he opened his mouth.

"It is not an insult. You exchanged names with your cohort. There were twelve of you. The cost to mortals of such an entanglement—were they able to make it—would be decades of their lives, at best. The cost to you—the cost to us—would be eternity, should even *one* of that number go rogue, go insane. You might, because of that one decision, exist as a slave to the will of another. You could make that decision as a gesture of trust—no, that's the wrong word. There is no word that describes it. You were not blood kin; you made that oath, and it brought you far, far closer than even ties of blood could.

"You say you did it because you were powerless, you were alone, you were being sent to a ceremony that might harm or even kill you in the worst case. You promised, if I had to guess, that you would put the cohort before any others, and the name was the way of proving that.

"It is entirely possible Dragons would have done the same, but we do not come into our names in the same way. Regardless, the desire for company, for companionship, is not merely the detritus of lack of power. I think everyone who lives as we do experiences isolation and loneliness." She had slowed down, and now seemed to hesitate. "I understand the fear of weakness. I understand what weakness means. Love is always a risk."

Kaylin had turned to stare at the gold Dragon.

"If we love, we open ourselves up to hurt, to pain. When we love, we allow people beneath the necessary armor of social interaction. I include war in that, by the way. And when we love, we hand those who would harm us their most potent weapon—because the loss of that love is profound and terrible, and we never fully recover from its absence. To us, then, love *is* a weakness."

Kaylin wasn't the only one who was staring.

"I was one of nine girls born to my clutch. We were sisters. We did not trade names as you have done, but we didn't require names, we knew each other that well. I am the only one who remains. The rest did not survive. I see the echo of their loss everywhere. In the end, in the life we lead, Shadow was the enemy, not you.

"I am *here* because of Kaylin. I am here because she brought Mandoran and Annarion back from the West March. I am here because I know what the cohort means to each other. It is an echo of what my sisters and I meant to each other, while they lived. I frequently have to stop myself from breathing on Mandoran. Or strangling him. But in some fashion, he and

Annarion remind me of my own youth—and my own losses. And I do not want them to suffer that loss.

"Because they are Immortal, they probably will. This is probably pointless. Love is a weakness. But…it is a weakness, in the end, that I value. Life without it is safer, yes. For us, it is safer." Silence again, weighted, heavy. This time Terrano didn't try to break it. "But I am not certain that survival without love or affection means all that much to me, anymore."

Standing in her plate armor, looking like the warrior queen she had once been, she did not evoke either love or affection. Terrano stared at her as if she'd grown an extra head. Kaylin tried hard not to do the same. But her familiar lifted his head and crooned.

"I am no longer queen. I am no longer ruler. In the beginning, it made me feel useless. But…because I am no longer either, I do not have to doubt. I don't have to be suspicious of Kaylin, or her friendship—which would, I think, have been impossible when I ruled. I don't have to doubt either Annarion, who I almost admire, or Mandoran. I don't have to sleep behind guarded doors. Yes, there are people who want me dead—there always were. But I have no reason to believe that the people who live with me are among them."

"And that makes up for the lack of power?"

The Dragon was honest. "I don't know. Perhaps, because I lack power, I huddle as the weak have always huddled. But I am not certain, now, that I would trade this life for the life I left behind." She exhaled a small stream of smoke. "We need to leave," she said, and turned away.

"Is she always like that?" Terrano whispered.

Kaylin blinked. "No."

"Do you remind her of her sisters, or something?"

"Her sisters, from what little I've heard, were…more bratty."

"She's…not what I expected of a Dragon."

Fair enough. "You're probably not what she expected from a Barrani. I know Mandoran isn't." She hesitated herself, partly because Dragon hearing was so acute. "But I think she'd go to war herself to protect Annarion and Mandoran from anything in the world except herself."

"She hardly knows them!"

"She has to live with them, and on some days, that's harder than others. She's fond of Teela, as well." Kaylin shook herself. "Right. Sorry. How *do* we get them out of here, again?"

Spike began to vibrate, which caused her entire body to tremble. "Kaylin."

"Is the Shadow moving?"

"It is moving."

"Toward us?"

"Yes. No."

"Which is it?"

"Bellusdeo!"

The gold Dragon nodded. Her body began to shift from the human to the Dragon form, flowing as if molten gold.

"I believe there is—or are—others of your kind here. The Shadow is moving toward them." Spike's words were interspersed with a type of clacking sound that made Kaylin think of chitin.

"My kind?"

"He means living people like you. Either of you," Terrano helpfully explained.

"Are they going to need rescuing?"

Both Terrano and Bellusdeo snorted in disgust, which Kaylin took as no.

"Can the Shadows sense you?"

"No."

"Can the Shadows sense *us*?"

"I do not think so. The ground here has been established across a spectrum." He whirred and clicked, and the spikes that were responsible for Kaylin's impulsive name choice began to extend, changing the space he occupied.

"Spike, do you recognize the person or people the Shadow is moving toward?"

A whirring, clicking noise was his only response.

The air in the immediate vicinity began to shimmer. Sedarias moved closer as an image coalesced from that sparkling air at Spike's unspoken command. Kaylin glanced at Terrano, who was fidgeting. She didn't expect to recognize whatever it was Spike chose to show them. The only person here who might was Terrano, whose left foot was now doing the equivalent of a nervous dance all on its own.

The man in the image was Barrani. The woman beside him was also Barrani. Nothing unexpected there. But the third person in the still tableau was human.

"There's a human here?" Kaylin all but demanded.

Spike whirred and the human faded from view, but not before Kaylin had gotten a pretty good look at his face. It was an older man's face, lines worn into the forehead and the corners of his mouth; he was clean-shaven, his nose was slanted slightly to the left of his face, as if it had once been broken. He was not otherwise well dressed, but something about his expression implied power. Very little of Kaylin's experience of power made that a positive.

"So, he's not here. Are both of the Barrani?"

Whir, click. *Squawk.*

"That's a yes," Bellusdeo said, in the quietest of her draconic voices. She tensed to leap and Terrano shrieked.

"You need to stay on the ground! The familiar can fly because he's not like the rest of you, but we'll lose you if you take to the air. You won't find the Barrani you're looking for, and you probably won't be able to find us again. Whatever was done to the portal paths has completely sundered them from the influence of the Hallionne at either end. Sometimes there are storms or environmental effects that will damage the path, but the path itself begins—and ends—at the terminal points."

"Which is not what happened here."

"Obviously. I think the path *does* exist as created, but neither my friends nor our group ever stepped foot on it."

"Did we even see it?"

"I don't see the way you see; I don't know."

"You were there, too."

A brief shift in expression that might have indicated guilt or humiliation chased across his face. "I was preoccupied."

"We all were. So...whatever we stepped on wasn't what the Hallionne created; it was something created by someone else."

"I...think so." He frowned. Like Mandoran, Terrano's expression moved the map of his face; not for Terrano the almost neutral subtlety of adult Barrani. "I think if things had worked out as intended, my friends would be lost, but the path itself wouldn't have been. It's like someone put a rug across the road, waited until someone stepped on it, and then rolled it shut and carried it off."

"Except for the Shadow devouring the people who stepped on it?"

"Except for that, yes."

Kaylin glanced at the Dragon. "Can *we* find that path if we clear away the Shadow garbage?"

Squawk.

"It's not that simple," Terrano began.

"Yes or no are pretty simple answers."

"And if you want to get devoured by Shadow, flip a coin and pick a random one," he snapped. He started to pace in a tight little circle; judging by the expression on Sedarias's face, she found this as frustrating as Kaylin did.

"What I want to know is why Mandoran and Annarion lost contact with the cohort. It's not the outlands path—they were in contact until the moment the cohort encountered the trap."

Terrano nodded.

"Well, we didn't encounter the same trap, but I've been cut off in the same way."

Silence. It was, judging by the contortions of Terrano's expression, a thinking silence. He closed his eyes. "We need to move," he finally said.

"Do you even know which way back is?"

"Yes." The word was resolute. "...But you're not going to like it."

"I don't like *any* of this. Which part in particular is going to bother me?"

"You're right."

"That doesn't bother me."

"You lost contact with your own people—"

"They're technically mostly your people, for what it's worth."

"—the minute we hit this path. We didn't enter it quite the normal way," he added. "So I could be wrong."

Sedarias appeared to be shouting in frustration, but her voice was inaudible. She was, however, mouthing something at Terrano, the movement of her lips slow and exaggerated. Kaylin caught some of it, but Barrani wasn't her mother tongue. She turned to Kaylin and made a second attempt at communication; Kaylin missed the first few words because Sedarias had switched languages.

Of course she had. Mandoran spoke Elantran like a native, and Sedarias knew what Mandoran knew—probably including the bits she wished he'd keep to himself.

"Sedarias doesn't think the Hallionne paths are safe—at all—for the cohort. If Terrano's right," she added, almost apologetically.

"Why?" the Dragon demanded.

"She thinks it's possible that Alsanis was instructed to create the path in a very specific way."

"Pardon?"

"She thinks Alsanis is partly responsible for what happened."

"What do you think?" Bellusdeo asked.

Kaylin had no immediate answer. When it did come, it seemed, for a moment, almost unrelated. "The Consort can speak directly to the Hallionne; she can clearly speak to the Hallionne from a distance. When we arrived—in Orbaranne—Orbaranne had been given specific instructions to house and protect my companion."

"But you didn't think the Consort knew that the companion would be me."

"I don't think it mattered. The Lady knew that we were gone—that we were somehow heading to the Hallionne. The water sent us, in a panic. I don't *think* the water was trying to save the cohort—I don't think the water was even aware of it. Something was done that upset the water—and I think it's bigger than kidnapping. Or murder. Sorry," she added, remembering that the intended victims were standing, in as much as ghosts could, around her.

"What could be big enough to upset the elemental water?"

"I don't know. I'm not an integral part of the existence of the world. But I'm afraid we're very likely to find out."

CHAPTER 22

Kaylin turned to Terrano. "When you broke into Orbaranne you said you weren't aware that you were standing in a Hallionne."

Terrano nodded, looking suspiciously at the familiar perched upright on Kaylin's shoulder.

"You didn't mean to slide under her defenses—but you said you had to push through to enter the safe space."

He nodded again, looking even more suspicious, although this time suspicion was aimed at Kaylin.

"What, exactly, were you running from that you needed the space?"

He paused to consider this. "It's not something that would harm you. Or could harm you. I don't think it's sentient the way we are—but there are predators in the outlands. Like wild animals, but hungrier. You get used to them," he added, shrugging. "I recognized the space Orbaranne occupies as a space that predators wouldn't go. They were avoiding it."

"Those predators wouldn't see me?"

"Not as you are now. I think."

"Could you lead us there?"

"To where? Orbaranne?" He looked doubtful, and glanced

at Sedarias as if for guidance. Which would have been ridiculous, except the ghostly Sedarias shook her head.

"I was thinking of Alsanis."

Terrano frowned. "I think so." The frown grew edges.
"Dragon lady, you said you had experience fighting Shadow?"

Kaylin glanced at the gold Dragon; her eyes were now a
deep blood red. "Yes."

"I think now would be a good time to prepare."

Kaylin, however, shook her head. "We need to get back
to Alsanis." She remembered, clearly, the way his Avatar had
begun to melt, its form lost to what Terrano had called anger.
And she remembered, as well—how could she have forgotten for even a minute?—what the cohort had tried to do to
Orbaranne. They had not intended to destroy her, although
that would have been the outcome of their goal; she would
have been simple, collateral damage.

No, what they had hoped to derive from Orbaranne was the
power inherent in the True Words at her heart. They required
that power to free themselves, fully and finally, from Alsanis.

The war band led by Lord Barian's mother had distracted
the Lord of the West March and Lord Barian. Neither man
remained within the Hallionne. Spike said there were two
presences toward which the Shadow was moving. He had
shown them two Barrani, with a human associate who had
not accompanied them here.

And here, she thought, was the outlands. Of course he
hadn't.

Kaylin had asked if the Barrani were in need of rescue.
What she hadn't asked was if those two presences were actually in *control* of the Shadow, if it moved at their command.
If it did, and if the Barrani Arcanists—and she assumed they
must be Arcanists—were here in the outlands, they might be
trying to do what Terrano had taught them, however imper-
fectly, to do.

She doubted very much they intended to approach Orbaranne. Not again. But she and Bellusdeo had fallen through the literal floor of Alsanis to land unceremoniously here. Here, where the cohort had been entrapped and almost devoured. They must be much closer to Alsanis than Terrano immediately realized.

"We need to go back to Alsanis," she said. "That's where the Shadows are heading."

This time, the words caught the easily distracted Terrano, and his eyes widened. He had spent centuries perfecting his escape from Alsanis's confines—but he did not hate the Hallionne. In some fashion, that Hallionne had become his only true home.

He was not the only one who felt that way; the whole of the cohort stiffened and turned. Sedarias spoke—silently, of course—but Terrano didn't bother to make the attempt to catch her words. Grimmer now, he seemed older as he turned. This time, he nodded.

"Bellusdeo—"

"Get on," the Dragon rumbled—at Terrano.

"The others—"

"It's your duty to drag them with us. It's your *only* duty." Kaylin didn't like the sound of that. "Kaylin—*you* find Alsanis."

What Kaylin wanted to know was the *how*. Given that Barrani—Lords of the High Court—were demonstrably involved, she understood the *why*. People in power wanted more power, and people in power often felt that the rules that applied to others could be safely circumvented, rules being meant for the powerless.

But she understood, from one glance at Terrano, that Bellusdeo's command would require the whole of his concentration.

"And you," the Dragon said, not to Kaylin, but to the translucent familiar, "make sure we don't get lost."

Squawk.

"Yes, I know. I'm searching for the Barrani I now suspect are infested. Kaylin is searching for Alsanis. When we find one, I think we'll find both."

In the end, it was not Kaylin who found Alsanis. Nor was it Terrano. He was literally sweating—which the Barrani of Kaylin's acquaintance did not do—with the effort of keeping his companions both together and in range, when he suddenly shouted.

"Sedarias, no!"

Sedarias, if ghostly and insubstantial, was not compliant and docile. She was angry, had been angry, since Terrano pulled her out of what was only metaphorically a cave, and she hadn't gotten any calmer. Bellusdeo had taken to the air; Terrano had started to tell her to stay on the ground when the familiar had snapped at him.

After that, he had offered no further argument. He didn't even have the energy to curse, so his expression had to speak for him. It spoke volumes, on the other hand. The cohort in their ghostly bodies walked—at speed and on air—alongside the fully aerial Dragon, until the moment Sedarias peeled away from the group. Allaron and Eddorian exchanged a telling glance; they looked to Terrano, miming action, before they followed her.

"Why," he demanded, through gritted teeth, "did I even come here at all? Why am I *trying* to rescue them?"

"They're your family," Kaylin replied. "Bellusdeo—"

"On it." The Dragon immediately corrected her course and headed in the direction Sedarias had taken, which was, in this case, to the left and down.

★ ★ ★

Before they'd even caught sight of what could only loosely be called ground, Kaylin's arms and legs began to tingle as her natural—and painful—allergy to magic flared up. She'd never quite figured out why some magic—say, Helen's magic—didn't cause that reaction, and at the moment, it didn't matter.

"We've got magic incoming," she told the Dragon.

Terrano had fallen utterly silent. Kaylin glanced at him, and then reached out and grabbed his arm; to her eye, he was becoming alarmingly translucent. "I need to go to where they are."

"We've got no way of fishing you out, if you do."

"Send your familiar."

"The one who *very recently* tried to kill you in a rage?"

"...Good point."

Hope bit her ear, but she didn't feel it; the tingling across the surface of her skin—the skin that bore the marks of the Chosen—became painful. This was both good and bad. Good, in that they probably wanted to go in the direction of the magic, and bad because: pain. Sedarias was only barely visible, as were the two who had followed her; the rest of the cohort stayed with Terrano, but they were all turned as one toward their distant leader.

Kaylin wondered if Mandoran had elected to accompany Annarion because it meant he could get away from Sedarias—but she was always in his thoughts anyway. Literally.

As expected, Kaylin's arms began to hurt; the sleeves of her shirt and the legs of her pants now caused acute pain if she so much as twitched. Given that she was riding a Dragon who wasn't exactly placid and still, there was a lot more than just twitching. But as she started to count in Leontine—one of the first vocal exercises she'd learned, to the great amusement of Marcus's kits—the ground appeared.

★ ★ ★

If she'd had any doubts about the speed at which Bellusdeo had been flying, they were shattered, because they couldn't have approached ground any faster if they'd been falling. But the gold Dragon was not a fledgling, and she veered what felt like inches from the surface, changing her angle to avoid collision. Kaylin's stomach still felt like it was hundreds of feet above them as the Dragon roared. And breathed.

Fire fanned out across the landscape, changing its color in a brief burst of orange and yellow. In the midst of those flames, a Barrani voice shouted a warning. It was a little late. Or maybe not; the fire had not consumed him and he clearly wasn't screaming.

Sedarias gave the Dragon the side-eye, but nodded grimly when their eyes met. Terrano slid off the Dragon's back—or tried. Kaylin's familiar flew at his face, and his instinctive backward movement resettled him.

"I don't think he wants you to leave. Whatever you're doing for the cohort is working—for them. But I think he's trying to tell you that the rest of us may need to move."

"I can't fight from here."

Kaylin shrugged. "Neither can I. But he clearly considers the possibility that you'll be lost—to us—more of a danger." Before he could reply, she added, "Without you, we'll lose the rest of them. You're what's keeping them here."

This mollified him, but only enough that he looked sulky and not as determined. "*They're* not staying put."

They weren't. Sedarias walked directly into the line of Bellusdeo's open jaw. She reached out to touch the underside of the Dragon's jaw; her hand passed through it, which seemed to satisfy some unspoken curiosity.

"The things that are likely to kill us—"

"Kill *you*."

"—kill the rest of us aren't likely to hurt them." But even

saying it, Kaylin wasn't certain. "And I think we've found our two Shadow controllers." She did not, however, see the Shadow itself. "Do you know where we are?"

He said nothing, and not just because he was sulking; his eyes had shifted to opalescent black, which was possibly her least favorite eye color, ever.

"Can you hear your namebound?" he asked.

Kaylin shook her head.

"That's unfortunate."

"We're at the Alsanis end of the portal path?"

"No. This is Alsanis."

Kaylin believed Terrano, but wanted to argue with him anyway, because she could not sense Alsanis at all. She expected the wild chaos of the portal paths by this point, but did not expect to find them within the Hallionne himself. Lifting her left arm, she rolled back her sleeve, almost weeping as she did; she felt as if she were peeling off the skin itself.

The marks across her arms were now an odd shade of gray blue. They were glowing, but the glow was faint and muted. On some occasions the symbols lifted themselves from her skin, as if they had life and will of their own; this time, they remained flat. She rolled the second sleeve up to join the first as Bellusdeo followed in Sedarias's wake.

"Is Allaron carrying a sword?"

"He is," the Dragon rumbled.

"So are the other two," Terrano added.

"What does he expect a sword to do, in his state?"

No one answered. Bellusdeo, however, spoke three sharp words, and Kaylin clenched her jaws to keep a small scream from escaping.

"Apologies," the Dragon said.

Kaylin barely heard her. Something had shifted in the wake of Bellusdeo's spell, and she could see both the ground and what lay across it far more clearly. Her heart, such as it was, sank, and if her stomach had finally rejoined the rest of her, she almost wished it hadn't. They were standing on stones; the stones were large, smooth and perfectly interlocked.

And there were words written across their surfaces.

As Bellusdeo continued her forward movement, those words began to rise, the flat inscription gaining volume as the lines, squiggles, and dots that comprised them asserted their existence in three dimensions. Kaylin sucked in air. Terrano was right, but in the worst possible way. Yes, this was Alsanis—but this was the *heart* of Alsanis. These were the words that defined him; the words that gave him absolute power within his own boundaries. The words that gave him life.

They were dark, not golden, and the edges of their various lines gleamed in a way that implied they were sharp enough to cut.

"I don't think this is a good idea," Kaylin told the gold Dragon.

"I'm willing to entertain better suggestions."

"I think we need to walk very, very carefully here."

"Implying that I can't."

"You can walk carefully at your size, yes—but the gaps between the words here aren't obligingly hall width. And I wouldn't bet on Dragon scale as a defense against those edges."

"How did the Barrani evade them?"

"Hells if I know."

The familiar squawked.

"We are *not* going to walk through this mess holding hands as if we were Kaylin's foundlings," the Dragon replied, in her iciest voice.

Terrano grimaced. "Can I improvise?" he asked the familiar.

The familiar snorted, the gesture a miniature version of

Bellusdeo's, with smoke. Except, of course, it wasn't. Terrano eyed the small cloud and grimaced. "Seriously?"

Squawk.

"Don't look at me," Kaylin said, when Terrano did swivel his glare. "I can't understand him."

The gold Dragon, however, could, and she collapsed once again into a gold plated warrior princess. "Next time," she told Kaylin, "I am bringing a sword."

"How can he even be your familiar if you can't understand him?" The gleaming field of risen words didn't seem to bother Terrano at all. The fact that those words appeared to be in the innermost sanctum of Alsanis didn't, either. No, the only thing that seemed to be of concern were the cohort and the distance that had grown between them.

"I can understand him some of the time," she replied, trying not to feel defensive.

"Well *now* would be a good time, don't you think?"

He spoke in Barrani, but spoke as if it were Elantran, which was a neat trick that Kaylin hoped never to learn; High Barrani forced her speech into more acceptable patterns. "Where are the cohort?"

"They've gone ahead a bit."

One, the tallest of the number, had jogged back. Although he couldn't interact with them physically, he nonetheless avoided the edges of the words that now formed columns. Kaylin thought they'd be deadly if they started to move. He spoke to Terrano, his lip movements slow and exaggerated.

Terrano made a face. "They want us to hurry," he finally told Kaylin. "Sedarias has reached the edge of the containment I've put in place, and she's not happy about being restrained."

"That's more words than he used," Bellusdeo observed.

"I filled in all the blanks."

★ ★ ★

Kaylin started to jog. She could maintain a slow jog for a very long distance, and could move into a sprint if the situation demanded it. Bellusdeo had no difficulty keeping up; Terrano seemed to resent the pace. Or at least being forced to keep it using actual legs.

But they didn't catch up with the cohort; Allaron hadn't lied. Sedarias was both angry and intent. The moment she realized she could safely proceed again, she did—and all of the cohort went with her.

Alsanis's words started to move. They were anchored in place, each to a very large stone, but they could, and did, cover the range of that stone; in places, they came together like a wall of blades.

"Should we try flying over them?" Bellusdeo asked; she clearly felt that Kaylin's directive had been the wrong one.

Kaylin shook her head. "I think they can move up and down at will. They seem to be confined horizontally." She glanced at her familiar; he nodded. But he didn't lift a wing; whatever she could see with her own eyes, he considered good enough.

The travel toward Sedarias grew much more treacherous; the stones into which words had been engraved were smaller, and the words themselves appeared to be more intricate. Bellusdeo managed to avoid them; Terrano, accustomed to a variety of traveling forms, didn't. He didn't instantly get turned into diced pseudo-Barrani, but he did get cut, and he did bleed. He seemed almost offended by the injury, and threw the familiar a baleful glare, but proceeded far more cautiously after that.

Caution, however, only carried them so far.

"That's a pretty solid wall," Kaylin said to the Dragon as she looked at the words that lay ahead of them. The stones upon which the words had been carved, and from which they'd risen, were smaller, which narrowed the space between what were effectively spinning blades.

The Dragon concurred. "Is flight still forbidden?"

The familiar nodded. As a small lizard, his facial expressions were limited, but he looked concerned, to Kaylin.

"How did the cohort get past this?"

"Don't ask me—I'm not one of them anymore."

Kaylin exhaled. "But you're here."

"Obviously I have an intelligence deficit."

"Fine. You recognized this as Alsanis."

"I spent most of my existence trapped here."

"So did the cohort. What did Sedarias do—if she managed to do anything—that allowed them safe passage?"

"Why do you ask?"

"Because my skin feels like it's being flayed off, and that's probably not a good sign—for Alsanis."

Terrano fell silent for one long beat.

"What are you doing?"

"Be quiet."

Bellusdeo shook her head when Kaylin opened her mouth again, and Kaylin closed it, missing Severn. He was generally content to let her do most of, if not all of, the talking. But as she watched Terrano, she had a feeling that he *was* talking, and in a way she couldn't. For perhaps the first time, she considered the advantages of being Terrano and Mandoran. She didn't much like the idea of getting stuck in walls, though.

The words spun slowly—and loudly—to a halt. And the air grew less heavy, the ground less hard. She couldn't hear Alsanis, and that still bothered her, but she now had a faint sense of his presence.

"What did you do?" Bellusdeo demanded.

Terrano grimaced. "When we were struggling to find our way out of our cage, we developed different forms of communication. There were layers to it; we could communicate almost entirely truthfully while obscuring small, but critical facts.

"It was obfuscation that was the important part, then. Of course, Alsanis was aware of our various attempts—he's a Hallionne. So it became a bit of a game. We have ways of communication that in theory shouldn't exist, and he created systems to hear that nonexistent communication. We had successes, but most of them didn't last long—it was always work to keep ahead of Alsanis."

"So you were—"

"Using one of the older secret modes, yes. If Alsanis has somehow been cut off from communication with us—I mean with you and the Dragon—there's a strong chance that the rest of the modes we developed were not considered when the interference was put in place." For a moment, he seemed highly pleased with himself, which once again emphasized his youthfulness.

"Did he answer you?"

Terrano pointed at the word forms. "He never used the undercurrent to speak *with* us; that would have made it clear, immediately, that he could. But he learned to listen."

"While he has this much control, let's get moving. Ummm, I don't suppose he could make the edges of those lines less sharp?"

Terrano snorted. "You might as well ask if he can make *you* less clumsy. If the edges are too sharp, don't touch them."

Bellusdeo's eyes lightened as she snickered, because clearly, that's what friends did. Kaylin forced herself not to reply, and began to navigate toward the distant cohort. She had questions, of course—but questions had to wait.

The tighter congregation of words did not diminish; neither did their edges. While it was easier to walk between them when they did not spin or move, following Terrano's advice was difficult, and became more so as they continued their awkward pursuit of Sedarias and company.

Three words in, Kaylin knew she was going to need a new shirt; the current one had been cut in three places, and the third cut wasn't small enough to patch. There'd been almost no friction; the slicing of cloth had made no sound. She glanced at Bellusdeo, but the Dragon scale was more hardy than simple cloth.

The fourth cut broke skin. It was a very shallow cut, more of a scrape or a scratch than a wound, and blood beaded from it slowly, welling up in uneven blobs of red. In the stillness, Kaylin didn't even curse.

She did curse the fifth time; the cut was deeper, and the blood, rather than beading, ran down her arm, as if it were trying to underline the injury. This time, that blood spread across her skin, running across the marks that lay there, flat and glowing a gentle gray. Her familiar squawked in her ear, in the tone of voice she imagined Terrano would use if he'd noticed.

And this time, the cut was deep enough that some of Kaylin's blood was left on the line of the word she'd been trying to circumnavigate. Terrano cursed as he turned to look, his eyes rounding, his jaw falling open. It would have been comical at any other time; now, it was vaguely terrifying.

"What—what did you *do*?"

It was the Dragon who answered, her eyes once again a darker orange. "She didn't manage to avoid the middle stroke on that word. I don't suppose you know what the word is?"

Terrano shook his head. "We weren't exactly trying to learn how to speak True Words." But even saying it, his gaze narrowed. "Well...not all of us. Eddorian might know. Or Serralyn."

The two names were names Kaylin didn't often hear at home. "Ask them," she said. Her thoughts caught up with her mouth only after the words had escaped. "...Sorry. I am so accustomed to Mandoran and Annarion. I forgot you can't."

Terrano said nothing. It was the wrong kind of nothing. He managed a shrug, turned away from the word and began to walk. Kaylin almost joined him, but Bellusdeo caught her by the shoulder. "Look at the word," she said, her voice the wrong kind of soft—the kind you got when you lost control of your voice and couldn't speak more loudly than a shaky whisper.

Kaylin had been looking at almost nothing else.

The word had started an odd shimmer the moment Kaylin had bled on it; she'd been watching because she was afraid it would start to move again, and if it did, she'd be shredded. But that fear was unfounded; whatever Alsanis had done, the word remained much more tightly anchored in space. What changed, now, was its color. Where the word had been dark, almost obsidian, something began to spread across its visible surfaces, until the whole was a pale, almost pulsing, gray. To Kaylin's eye, it was uglier, but she understood, as she watched, that the whole thing was transforming itself to better resemble the marks on her skin—marks that remained stubbornly flat.

"What have you done?" the Dragon asked, in the same soft voice.

"Nothing deliberate."

"You're going to have to do something about that. Accidentally tripping over the security precautions of a building that's like Helen, but on a far grander scale, is *not* something you should be doing carelessly."

Since Sedarias was the one who had chosen the direction, Kaylin thought this wasn't particularly fair. She was old enough now that she didn't bother to put the feeling into words, although in part this was because Terrano came running back. The sharp edges of these words did not cut him; he seemed to pass through them. Or they passed through him.

"Whatever you're doing, keep doing it!" He was almost breathless, which was unusual for a Barrani.

"Why?"

"...Sedarias said it's helpful."

The cut, which wasn't deep, was already drying, and Kaylin really didn't fancy shredding herself—deliberately—on the sharp, gleaming edges of these words. She wished, again, that she'd dragged Mandoran with her to Evanton's, rather than the Dragon; she was pretty certain if he were here with her, he could talk to Sedarias no matter how far ahead she was. Terrano couldn't.

But Terrano's trust in Sedarias had not wavered in his absence from the cohort, and if he could not entirely return to his friends, he had returned to that trust.

Kaylin gritted teeth, forced herself to walk to the next word, and cut the mound of her left palm.

"Are you choosing the words at random?"

"Yes," Kaylin said, as Spike said, "No."

She'd forgotten about Spike in the surge of adrenaline that accompanied the knowledge that the invaders were *inside* Alsanis. This wasn't the first time she'd encountered Shadow at the heart of a building, and they'd managed to repel those Shadows. The Shadows had been trying to revise, to rewrite, the words at the heart of a Tower, in the fief that was now Tiamaris.

But Terrano and his allies had been trying something entirely different, when they had almost destroyed Orbaranne. They'd been trying to absorb, to drain, the power of the words themselves. Kaylin understood that words had power—but that power was supposed to be metaphorical.

Here, it was not.

To speak these words one had to be Immortal. Or more. She remembered, dimly, the vision of one of the Ancients cutting into himself so that his blood ran into a basin—an ancient version of the mirrors upon which the city of Elantra now depended.

Her blood was not his blood. She was not a creator, not a god, if the word even applied. What she did here wasn't the same—but if her blood was mortal and thin and the wrong color—not golden but red—she bled anyway. She offered that blood, grimly, to Alsanis. Instead of avoiding the edges of words, she practically leapt between them, because she really did not want to cut herself every single time.

"What do you mean, it's not random?" she heard Bellusdeo ask.

Spike's words were underlined with a whirring; clicks broke the syllables as he replied. "Random implies that she is not making choices. But she is following a specific path; you will note it if you—"

"I can see where she's going."

"—read the words."

It was the Dragon's turn to be frustrated, and she wasn't above expressing it; the air at Kaylin's back grew much warmer. Kaylin was fairly certain that Dragon breath wouldn't harm these words. And she understood the frustration, because she *was* choosing words with no understanding of their meaning; she chose the ones with slightly wider forms while she picked her way across a nonexistent path.

But these words, like the first one, turned an even, almost glowing gray. She stopped once to look back, to see the path she'd taken. Terrano, however, had once again disappeared, running back to Sedarias as if afraid she would be lost here.

And as Kaylin cleared the last word, or rather, looked ahead to see an almost open space, she skidded to a halt so suddenly Bellusdeo ran into her.

The open space was a clearing, ringed in a circle of bristling, standing words, each bearing edges that could scar dragon scale. Kaylin understood that this was the heart of Alsanis, the heart of the words that defined his existence. It was in a similar space that Terrano and his associates had once attacked Orbaranne, seeking power.

Terrano was not the attacker here, but the space itself wasn't empty. Two very physical Barrani were at its center. They weren't dressed the way they had been in Spike's Records replay, but his images had been correct: one was male, one female. Their robes appeared to be dusty with travel. If they had come here through the portal paths, they had not found an entrance through the Hallionne—any of the Hallionne. Had they, the Hallionne would have been forewarned.

They were armed, and they turned toward Kaylin. She could see the glint of swords; the man was either left-handed or ambidextrous. Either way, he was Barrani, and Kaylin suspected that if he were here, in this room, he was also an Arcanist; the sword was almost irrelevant.

She ducked immediately behind the nearest word; she would still be visible, but the words themselves weren't lifeless architecture. As if he thought the same thing, he failed to cast anything resembling a spell—but against Kaylin, he wouldn't need it. The familiar sat up while Kaylin navigated, and plastered a wing across her face.

She didn't immediately realize why; the man looked no different viewed through the familiar's wing than he had through her unaugmented vision, and it wasn't always easy to move in a way that kept the wing firmly over her eyes. But he never smacked her face this way unless he thought there was something she should see. She looked.

Both the moving Barrani man and the woman who appeared to be standing sentinel remained unchanged. But through the wing, she could see the cohort clearly; she could not see Terrano. If he was here at all, he was hidden.

Bellusdeo was not.

The Barrani man stopped walking when the Dragon stepped out, gleaming in golden armor; he raised his sword as she inhaled. She didn't bother with warnings or threats; that wasn't her way. She breathed. The man spoke three harsh words, and the sword in his hand split the flame. Kaylin wondered, briefly, if it were one of The Three, the swords created by Barrani master smiths in a bygone age to kill Dragons. She lost that thought when the metal cracked and shattered. The shards flew out and away from the man, but the woman had seen Bellusdeo.

"Hold her off!" she shouted, although her hand was also on the hilt of a sword.

Kaylin noticed that the woman's sword, which she had assumed was in a rest position, was actually in contact with the stone beneath it. And she noticed that the tip—in the familiar-winged view—was glowing; it was a red glow, striped with gray, and it was dark enough that *glow* was not quite the right word to describe it.

But that reddish gray light was spreading; beneath the tip of the sword, Kaylin could now see a network of lines that made the rock beneath them look cracked or fractured, but not yet broken.

Kaylin knelt immediately to the side of Bellusdeo's battle, and placed one hand flat on the stone.

"What are you doing?" Terrano demanded.

The question half surprised her; she assumed, and had always assumed, that what she saw through the crutch of familiar wing, Terrano saw without effort.

She didn't answer the question, in the vain hope that the woman carrying the sword would fail to hear it. Terrano, on the other hand, was not exactly quiet.

Kaylin lifted only her head. "Bellusdeo—it's the other one you have to stop!"

The Dragon roared; the ground shook. Terrano, however,

was no longer bothering Kaylin. He headed toward the woman with the sword and checked his steps as Bellusdeo swung her head and sent the woman's partner flying. Unfortunately, that was literal, and if Kaylin had entertained the small hope that the man was not an Arcanist, it was dashed when he failed to fall.

The woman was not Terrano; she did not curse. The Barrani she used was clear and entirely recognizable. "Stop them!"

Kaylin once again bent her head. Beneath her hand, the stone over which she'd walked was warm; it had the give of muscular flesh. The word that hovered above her was not engraved into its surface, and Kaylin wondered if it had been, before the Barrani arrived.

Reaching up, she cut her hand and let the blood flow freely as she reached more gingerly for the sharp edge of a long, looped line. The word absorbed her blood, the shift in color obvious almost immediately. To Kaylin's discomfort, it was almost exactly the same color as the web pulsing beneath the woman's sword.

Terrano came back to Kaylin. "Hold on to something. No, not that—you'll lose a limb."

"What are you doing?"

"Talking to Alsanis."

"Is he replying?"

"I hope so." He turned toward the woman who appeared to be in charge. "I didn't come here planning to fight." There was a grimace in his voice; Kaylin couldn't see it, because he was now standing entirely in front of her, barring the way. "Whatever it is you're trying to do, do it *quickly*."

Kaylin was not under any illusion; she could be bled dry and she wouldn't be able to cover all of the words at Alsanis's core; he was far more complex than Helen. Her familiar didn't lower his wing, and as she bent once again to study the lines that seemed to travel like veins beneath skin made of stone from the tip of the Barrani woman's sword, she saw that they had spread, and were spreading, beneath her.

She didn't know what would happen when they stopped; didn't know what their purpose was. She assumed that it was... not good. Her familiar bit her ear, which, given the position of his wing, took real flexibility.

Kaylin put the bleeding hand flat against the stone, and pushed.

CHAPTER 23

A cut to the palm or the arm was nowhere near the worst of the injuries she'd sustained in the line of duty, but the only advantage her assailants got from those injuries was the hope that they might slow her down. This was different and she knew it.

Her blood seeped instantly into the stone, as if the stone itself were entirely illusory. It crawled—there was no other word for it that wasn't more disturbing—toward the web that spread from the tip of the sword, and met up with its strands, as if it were a small stream joining a large river. There was almost no visible difference between the two; only by tracing the lines back to their respective sources could Kaylin differentiate.

She'd hoped that somehow she would have control over her own blood, her own part of that moving web; she didn't. She started to lift her hand, but her familiar bit her ear again, harder this time.

Past her left shoulder, purple fire blossomed. It splashed across an invisible barrier. The Barrani woman shouted a warning, then; she was angry. Or afraid. With the Barrani, it was often hard to separate the two. It took Kaylin a moment, vision split, to understand what was happening: the woman was screaming at the man to stop using the purple fire.

"I'm fighting a *Dragon*!" he shouted back, dodging the very unpurple draconic breath. Which is more or less what Kaylin would have said had she been the person in midair without one of the three Dragon slaying swords to hand. But as the ground shuddered beneath her knees, almost knocking her over, the woman's concerns made more sense.

"She's afraid his actions will engage the interior protections," Terrano remarked. Both of his hands were in the air, palms facing out, as if he were intent on surrender.

"That barrier—that was you?"

"You're not a Dragon; the fire will kill you if you don't move out of its way. We should have help soon. And Sedarias will be really, really angry if you die here."

"Why?"

"Because then she'll have to deal with Mandoran and Annarion."

"It wouldn't be your fault!"

"You really haven't spent much time talking with Sedarias."

Purple fire gave way to purple rain. Terrano cursed and changed his position.

"Do you recognize them?" she asked.

"I'm a little bit busy now. Ask me later." He grimaced as some of that rain passed just to his left, and seared an ugly line through his tunic. Kaylin remembered that Terrano's current clothing was now much closer to Dragon armor than anyone else's. It was like another skin.

Bellusdeo took to the air. Although she was a much larger target, she wasn't much slower in full Dragon form than the Barrani Hawks; she made the most of her agility.

The Barrani woman moved as if the sword were a tether. But Bellusdeo's breath was a ranged weapon, and Terrano was right: something was happening within this room.

"Is Alsanis going to know that Bellusdeo isn't a danger?"

"You're watching her and you're telling me she isn't dangerous?"

"I mean it, Terrano."

"Yes. He'll know. Because Bellusdeo is a guest he's already accepted, and she's fighting to protect herself from intruders. Unless everything collapses here, he will not harm her." The last words were spoken in much slower, less frenetic Barrani. "Now stop talking and *do* something."

Kaylin opened her mouth to tell him that she'd already done what she could, but managed to snap her jaws shut before the words escaped. Terrano, not an Arcanist, could provide magical protection; Bellusdeo could provide the necessary attack. What Kaylin was doing—what she was supposed to do—could be done by neither. She didn't have to be a Dragon or an Immortal to be useful.

And Terrano was right. Useful had a short lifetime.

She lifted her hand to check the cut and the flow of blood while the familiar chittered like a bird trying to imitate an insect. The web came with it. She froze, staring at the strings that had been unmoored from beneath the surface of stone.

And she remembered the glove of shadow lace that had covered her hand during the defense of Moran's Aerie, hundreds of miles away. She remembered how it had come into existence: she had been attempting to prevent Mandoran from being possessed by Shadows that were worming their way into his body.

The familiar crooned.

She had prevented that possession by wrapping those strands around her hand, and in the end, those strands—inert—had remained. They reminded her, in some fashion, of the marks—but they had faded into invisibility. Bellusdeo, sensitive to all things Shadow, could not detect them, and everyone had assumed that they were gone. Even Kaylin.

Kaylin spent entirely too much time in wishful thinking.

Instead of laying her palm back against the rumbling ground, she raised it, and the strands of webbing that had looked so much like blood vessels gone bad elongated; moving her hand, she began to wrap those strands around her palm. The odd thing was, it didn't hurt. She felt almost nothing at the movement. Although she could see the strands as she gathered them, she couldn't feel them at all.

Nor did the woman holding the sword notice, at first.

The motion of the ground beneath Kaylin's knees had passed from tremors to waves—kneeling on it was like standing on the surface of moving water. But worse. The Barrani woman tried to drive the sword farther into the ground, and at first, it seemed she was successful. But Kaylin could see the way the ground itself moved around the swordpoint, as if avoiding it; what was no longer stone, although it still appeared that way, was creating a sword-shape pit, or sheath, for the weapon itself.

Three things happened at once.

Someone shouted her name—the words came at what felt like a great remove. The voice was familiar, but to hear it any more clearly, Kaylin would have had to tell Bellusdeo to shut up, which was never going to happen.

The Barrani woman realized that the sword was no longer penetrating the surface of the Hallionne's core.

And the cohort suddenly gained solidity. Kaylin noted the latter only because she could see them, now; they were standing much closer to the Barrani woman and her sword than they had been. The air in the room, which was thick and hazy, had all but rendered them invisible, at least to Kaylin's eyes; the color they seemed to be gaining as the seconds passed made them all appear more real, more present.

They wore no obvious armor, but three carried weapons—weapons that gained in color and substance as their bearers did.

The stranger looked up, instantly aware of them, although

her shoulders were still bent in the attempt to either withdraw the sword or push it through the impromptu casing. She
shouted for her partner, but her partner—while surprisingly
not dead yet—had a Dragon to worry about, and the Dragon
wasn't playing. Much.

Kaylin continued to rotate her hand, to wind thread by
thread of an ugly, terrifying web around it. She understood
that at base it was Shadow, that Shadow was transformative,
that it was poison—but she also understood that what she was
doing was having some positive effect. And if she couldn't
imagine what the Barrani would do with the power of a Hallionne, she was pretty damn sure she—and the laws she served
with her life—wouldn't like it.

Allaron, the easiest one to spot because he was abnormally
tall for a Barrani of any gender, stepped neatly in front of
Sedarias, as if Sedarias were in need of protection. Sedarias
said something—barely audible but sharp as a knife—and he
stepped to the side to let her pass, falling in beside her as if
they were partners of long-standing. When Sedarias lifted an
open hand in the region of Allaron's chest, Kaylin frowned.

She couldn't see what Allaron's response was until he
moved; he *handed* Sedarias his sword. It was a sword that had,
to Kaylin's eye, been scaled for his personal use; it looked far
too large for Sedarias, unless she meant to wield it in two
hands.

She didn't. If she dressed the part of a lady of the court, she
was nonetheless Barrani; arms that looked deceptively slender were perfectly capable of bearing that sword as if it were
a long knife. The Barrani Hawks didn't carry swords; none of
the Hawks did. Clearly the cohort had been trained to their
use. And of course they had. The entire purpose of their visit
to the green had been to somehow transform them into super
soldiers for use in the Draco-Barrani wars.

The Barrani woman let go of the sword she'd been so keen

on protecting; had she not, she would have lost her head; Sedarias didn't open with either discussion or negotiation. Or words. Kaylin had seen Barrani attempt to kill each other, and had always been surprised by the amount of *talk* that could happen before they got down to business. Sedarias didn't bother, and Kaylin both admired this and found it disturbing.

The cohort ringed the two; although other blades existed, no other blade was lifted, by which Kaylin understood that this was somehow personal; Sedarias recognized the woman, which made her very old, in Barrani terms. Well, as old as Teela, at any rate.

Given that the woman's sword was still buried in stone, this seemed unfair—but fairness of a certain kind had never been the Barrani way. And in truth, Kaylin's experience of life in the fiefs stopped her from being outraged. When faced with probable death herself, she'd never been one to stand on honor, either.

She shifted her opinion, however, when the woman spoke a lightning crack of a word. Purple fire rose beneath Sedarias, lapping at the material of her skirts, and probably at the feet beneath them. Sedarias leapt instantly out of the circle in which they burned, but some of the fire clung to her clothing. Someone—Eddorian?—shouted a warning; there was no way to know if Sedarias heard it.

And, come to think, it was unlikely that the warning had been shouted *to* Sedarias, which meant the incoming danger was aimed at someone whose True Name Eddorian didn't know.

She jumped up, her hand cocooned with strands of darkness, to see Terrano. Beneath his feet, as Sedarias's, purple fire blossomed. He lowered one hand, and kept one raised as rain of the same color fell. He was pale, his clothing was singed, and the fire seemed to struggle to entrap him, to cling to him. "Don't worry about me," he told her, although his gaze was drawn to the fire at his feet. It was a larger circle than the one that had opened at Sedarias's feet, and the color was subtly different.

As it spread, Kaylin realized why it was wider: it was also meant to encompass her.

Whatever she was doing was obviously having some effect—and if the Barrani woman considered it dangerous, it was positive, at least for Alsanis. Kaylin started to wind faster, and finally spared a frigid glare at her familiar.

Her familiar sighed. Loudly. He smacked her face with his extended wing, as if to drive a point home: he couldn't leave her shoulder to do anything else if she *wanted* to be able to do what she was doing, because she couldn't *see* the threads without his intervention. "It doesn't matter if I can see them or not," she snapped. "I'll just keep doing what I'm doing."

Terrano said, through clenched teeth, "You are an *extremely* unintelligent person. Do you honestly think that all he's doing is letting you *see*?"

Since the answer was more or less *yes*, Kaylin failed to give it. But she didn't glare at her familiar again, didn't demand to know why he wasn't helping Terrano shield them, and didn't send him buzzing off after the golden Dragon whose injury would probably end her career.

Bellusdeo was roaring between breaths, which meant she was still alive. She was conversant with magic and at least rudimentary magical protections, and she fought like the warrior queen she had once been, before the Shadows had finally devoured her world. If there was anyone deserving of worry here, it was *not* the Dragon.

She heard someone call her name again, and this time, her hand almost cramping because she hadn't stopped once, she recognized the voice. At any other time, she would have frozen; now, she worked *faster*, which shouldn't have been possible.

It was the *Consort*. It was the Consort's voice.

The thought that the Consort was *here*, that she was in the West March, or worse, in the embattled Hallionne, was almost terrifying. This was not the place for the only woman who could bring life to an entire race. And the cohort were here. Terrano was here.

Seething with fear and frustration, Kaylin turned to the familiar, but as she opened her mouth, the landscape suddenly changed. As if it had been shattered, the whole of the visual look of this enormous, open space broke, shards falling away to reveal something entirely different. The stones beneath her feet gave way, in an instant, to more earth-like dirt, and the giant, bladed words disappeared, to be replaced at random intervals by the trunks of looming trees. Above her head was sunlight, and beneath her feet, the greens and browns of the forests in the West March.

Voices—besides the voice of the Consort, which became distinct and much louder—filled her thoughts in a clamor of sound and emotion. She turned to look at Sedarias, who was carrying a sword that was, even at this distant, red with new blood.

"Terrano," Sedarias said, the word both a question and command.

"I'm fine." His voice was muffled.

Kaylin turned to look at him, and so did the more distant Sedarias. Terrano was *not* fine. His skin was livid with what appeared to be bruises, given their color; Kaylin, however, knew better. Looking down at her hand, she saw the frayed ends of what had been a web at the heart of Alsanis, and even as she did, her familiar finally withdrew his wing. He then shifted his head so his nose was pointed at Terrano.

"I know," Kaylin replied. As the wing left her face, the shadow left her palm; her hands were once again normal hands.

"You are *not* fine," Sedarias said. She returned the sword

to Allaron, without pausing to make certain he was in place to take it, and stalked across the forest floor toward Terrano.

Terrano took a step back as she reached for his arm; Kaylin could only see Sedarias's back. But as Terrano could see her face—which was, by Barrani standards, as expressive as the faces of most of the cohort—he stopped moving and allowed her to touch his wrist.

"We did not teach them this," she said. She turned to Kaylin, her hand still wrapped around Terrano's right wrist.

"I think you taught them that words have power," Kaylin offered.

Sedarias did not looked pleased. She did not, however, look guilty, either. "You understand why."

Kaylin did. She approached Terrano as well. "Yes. But my understanding—or not—doesn't change the consequences. It never has." She held out her palm, and Terrano examined it as if she were holding a live cockroach up for his inspection.

"Just let her examine you," Sedarias told him; she released his wrist and folded her arms. "We're about to have company. Significant company."

He deflated. "I don't want the Lady to see me."

"I understand. I am not looking forward to this meeting with any great anticipation, either. She's going to have questions."

"Are you two talking about the Consort? *Hand*, Terrano."

He grimaced and laid his palm against her own. It felt like a hand—a Barrani hand. "I don't want you to change anything."

"That's not how healing works."

"I saw what you did to the other Barrani. The Ferals."

"No you didn't—you were too busy talking to Teela."

"Yes," Sedarias said, "we were speaking of the Consort."

"There's no way she could reach us here—not in so little time."

The two exchanged a glance.

"Not entirely safely, no."

"Can you reach Mandoran, now?"

Sedarias nodded. "He is not the problem. Annarion is."

Kaylin, four voices said at once.

Give me a second. I just need to make sure Terrano doesn't get dissolved by whatever spell it was. She closed her eyes. Hand to hand, she could feel Terrano's physical form. To the eye, it resembled the Barrani, with a few notable exceptions. She had expected the appearance to be entirely superficial, and was surprised.

"What are you *doing*?" he demanded.

"Finding the fire," she snapped. "If you could shut up for a bit, I might even be able to make certain it doesn't dissolve you."

Sedarias repeated the sentence in much more precise— and elegant—Barrani. "Apologies," she said, dropping into Elantran. "He's not familiar with your tongue. Teela's concerned," she added.

"The entirety of the Elantran Barrani population should bloody well be concerned. I was *hoping* the Consort was speaking through a mirror or something similar. She can talk to the Hallionne from Elantra, and I *assumed* it was via mirrors."

"The mirror connections beyond your borders are nowhere near as complete as they are within your city. The Hallionne of old are very like your Helen; they distrust the networks required to maintain the connections."

"They're easier to maintain than a portal that passes from the High Halls to—here." She grimaced and closed her eyes. "Ummm, I need to concentrate on something other than fear or terror. Just—what in the hells *is* that purple garbage?"

"Teela says you've been taking lessons in applied and practical magic."

"Not in the last month or two." Ugh.

"She says it is, in her opinion, very like the fires that mages can master and use as weapons."

"Elemental?"

"Now she's annoyed. No, she says, like the fire itself."

"The fire *I* summon *is* elemental."

"She says, 'Fine, it's nothing like the fire that you summon, and more like the fire anyone else would.' But this fire does not, in her opinion as a former Arcanist, draw just from fire, but also from Shadow. She adds that you are now examining the possible fallout of such a summoning more completely than most of the Imperial Mages could, at least with regard to the effect on a living body." In the distance, one of the cohort burst out laughing. Kaylin grimaced; she could imagine exactly why.

"It's not you," Sedarias said, correctly divining the reason for the grimace. "She just made an observation about Terrano. And Mandoran. Mandoran did not approve."

"Terrano probably wouldn't, either." Terrano sounded waspish. "If you're all just going to talk about me behind my back, I'm leaving."

Sedarias frowned. "You are *not* leaving while you are injured." And to Kaylin, in more concerned Elantran, she said, "Teela's afraid that this will harm you in some fashion." There was a question in the statement.

Kaylin snorted. "Tell Teela that what's good for the goose is good for the gander."

"I'm uncertain that she understands."

"If I'm not allowed to worry about her, she's not allowed to worry about me."

"If it's acceptable to you, I will refrain from repeating her response."

Terrano snickered.

"It's fine. Annarion doesn't repeat much, either. Now—let me try to fix this. I'd personally rather not have Terrano become a mindless minion of Shadow."

"We are not mindless," Spike offered.

Kaylin shrieked in frustration, and Bellusdeo came over. She, like Terrano, looked like she'd been in a battle, and not necessarily on the winning side, especially her hair, which was decidedly ragged and singed. Normal fires, even elemental ones, were seldom much of a danger to Dragons.

"I'm fine," the gold Dragon said, in a tone that implied that it would be in Kaylin's best interests to accept the words at face value. Since she was standing beside Kaylin, and the Emperor—who would *not* be happy accepting those words at face value—was hundreds of miles away, Kaylin decided to be smart.

"What are you *doing*?" Terrano shouted.

Since Kaylin hadn't been doing anything other than examining the very unusual injuries, she said nothing.

"I mean it!"

"There's something in the wounds you took. It's not like whatever it was the Ferals did to the Barrani—but I think it *would* be, if you were actually physically completely Barrani. I am *trying* to remove it before it does whatever it's trying to do." But...she hadn't. She hadn't started. The last time she'd done this, she'd had to cut out the bad parts to stop the taint from spreading. And cutting out the bad parts meant cutting out the good parts they were attached to.

On the other hand, Terrano didn't seem to hate the idea of healers on principle the way the rest of the Barrani did, which was good because as Kaylin continued the contact with an increasingly reluctant Terrano, two things happened. First, behind the lids of her closed eyes, she could see the marks on her arm begin to shift color. Gray was more subtle than the gold they became.

And second: the infection began to retreat. She realized then that it, like whatever it was that had seeped into Alsanis, poisoning him, was being pulled out. It was being wound around her own palm, her left palm, even if she wasn't moving that hand at all. Terrano didn't suffer pain gladly, and the withdrawal obviously hurt. She wondered, gritting her teeth, if Alsanis had felt a similar pain.

"No, Lord Kaylin." It was Alsanis. Or his voice. Kaylin was surprised at the sting of relief she felt, but kept her thoughts focused on Terrano.

"I believe he feels that it alleviates some of the pain when he curses," the Hallionne added.

"Not *my* pain," Kaylin muttered.

What felt subjectively like hours later, she finished. Since Terrano's injuries were not severe enough to be life-threatening in the immediate future, she should have been fine—but she felt exhausted, and stumbled slightly when she rose. Terrano fell silent; he was glaring at her when she managed to open her eyes.

"Alsanis," she said, as Bellusdeo held out a discreet but steadying arm, "I thought I heard the Consort's voice toward the end."

"Ah, yes."

"Yes, I heard it or yes, I thought I heard it?"

The question seemed to confuse Alsanis. "Both? She is not physically present, if that is your concern."

"But I heard—"

"She is within Hallionne Kariastos's domain. She spoke to me from within Kariastos."

"I thought the Hallionne weren't connected?"

"We are not connected. We are capable of communication, should we be awake. And as of your first passage through the West March, the Hallionne are all awake. She intended to walk the portal paths directly to me."

Kaylin stopped breathing for one long beat.

"But she was convinced to wait."

"By who?"

"Kariastos, initially, although I believe it was Bertolle's word that carried the most weight. They could not reach me at all, and they were concerned about her eventual fate."

"And she decided to listen?"

"Let us say that while the Consort is powerful and clever, finding a path that would lead to me without their will and their aid would have taken much, much longer, and been far less safe. She is headstrong," he added, as if he were talking about the cohort and not the effective Empress of the Barrani. "She is not a fool. She was—and is—very concerned about the current difficulties facing my children."

His children.

Everyone else joined Kaylin in breath holding; Terrano exhaled first. "She doesn't want them to leave, either."

"Did you tell the Consort about the delegation sent to the Emperor?"

"Ah, no, Lord Kaylin. She is desirous of speech with you, and I believe it best that you convey your concerns in person."

"You said she wasn't allowed to travel here."

"You," he said, "will be traveling there. But not today."

Alsanis was kind enough to allow Bellusdeo to fly out of this vast and cavernous forest, which meant Kaylin could ride on her back without having to enter a portal. Terrano joined them, which surprised both Kaylin and the Dragon; he was silent for the entire flight. Given his reaction to riding Dragonback the first time, Kaylin was worried.

"You don't want to try flying yourself?" Bellusdeo asked, her voice a rumble of sensation beneath them.

"No. Alsanis doesn't like it."

"I have no objections," Alsanis said. Although his Avatar was not present, his voice was. Unlike Helen, Alsanis could exist, in Avatar form, anywhere simultaneously. He had chosen not to in order to spare Bellusdeo another passenger.

During the flight, Kaylin spoke with everyone namebound to her who had finally broken through whatever wall had existed between Alsanis and parts of himself. Ynpharion started, because while Ynpharion had remained behind in the High Halls instead of accompanying the Consort, he was still the Consort's servant; she held his name. And while he had been somewhat deflated about being abandoned, he had come to understand very clearly why she wanted him there: he was her eyes and ears in the Court and its many halls. It was not known to the Court at large that he had surrendered his name to her.

He was, regardless of the physical distance, also her line of communication with Kaylin. The Consort had left in a furious rush, taking little time to pack or arrange for more comfortable modes of travel. He did not believe the High Lord was pleased. Kaylin could well imagine. *But why was she in such a rush?*

Why did the elemental water deposit you within Orbaranne without warning?

We don't know.

Exactly. There has been some movement between the Imperial Court and the High Halls; the High Lord has taken the matter into his own hands. She felt the faintest edge of something that might be fear, but when she tried to examine it, she met wall. She didn't push. In theory she could—but if she did, it would cause her pain, and it would likely cause the Consort pain as well, if the Consort agreed that Ynpharion should not speak of it.

At the moment, Kaylin was exhausted enough that the thought of trying was beyond her.

It is not exhaustion, Ynpharion said, with his usual level of annoyance. *Even were you to be well rested and focused, it is not something you would attempt. You lack the will.*

She shut him out in as much as that was possible, and turned to the next in line, as if her mind were now a queue. Nightshade was largely silent. *Ynpharion is correct,* he said, when Kaylin complained. *But not for his own sake, nor for the Consort's. Your ability to lie is abysmal, and all of the politics of the realm require one form of lie or another. One must be able to feign delight, surprise or anger—and one must be able to hide those things when they are genuine at inconvenient times. Were you to understand the plans of the High Lord—or his Consort—anyone with eyes and ears in your vicinity would also understand them. Do not seek that information unless it is critical for your survival.*

Or the Consort's?

Or the Lady's, yes.

Lirienne merely wished to know that Kaylin was alive. He also wished to ascertain that Bellusdeo was alive, which surprised her.

Alsanis accepted her as guest. It is not our wish to antagonize the Hallionne. What happened?

There were two Barrani in the heart of Alsanis.

A pause. *Did you recognize them?*

While Kaylin was accustomed enough to Barrani that she could tell them apart, she couldn't do so as easily as she could with mortals; they had similar distinguishing features, were almost—Allaron was a notable exception—roughly the same height, with hair of the same color, except the Consort's. *No. I think Sedarias recognized the woman, though.*

More silence. This one, he didn't elect to fill. She could sense his brooding concern.

Do not mention the Lady to him, Ynpharion said. Kaylin, however, had figured that out on her own, and hoped that she had managed to contain enough information. What she needed was practice. She was used to clamping down on her own thoughts; she had reached a point where she could— usually—manage to keep her thoughts to herself. She didn't need to say what she was thinking, and didn't need to blurt it in anger or rage.

Keeping her thoughts to herself while other people were

part of them was far, far harder. Just another reason to hate True Names, but thinking this, she reached for the last one. Severn.

Did you recognize them?

I couldn't see them when you did. I did see the corpse of the woman when communication was reestablished; the man escaped?

Not exactly.

Bellusdeo?

Yes.

She wasn't injured?

Not according to her, and no, I'm not about to argue with her. She's in a better mood than she was, but not by enough. Not by nearly enough. Kaylin did, on the other hand, check Bellusdeo for injuries. To her surprise, most of the injuries she'd sustained were bruises and light, normal burns.

She roared and Kaylin instantly lifted her hand, flushing. She kept that hand to herself, and tried to come up with enough in the way of groveling apology that Bellusdeo wouldn't be tempted to bite it off when they finally landed.

But Severn was her partner, and Severn was fully capable of covering the ground she couldn't cover. If she were honest, he was probably better at it—he had contacts in the Wolves, and through the Wolves, that the Hawks had never fully developed.

He heard the thought; of course he did. She'd practically thrown it. *I'm going to start investigating on this end.*

In private?

Sadly, no. The Emperor has not traditionally concerned himself with the politics of the Barrani Court; he has turned a blind eye, except in cases where those politics spill into the open streets. Things are...tense. The Hawklord and the Wolflord have been closeted in an Imperial Tower; the Emperor is now very interested in Candallar, Teela, the cohort and the politics of the High Court itself.

Marcus?

He's been coordinating with the Lord of Swords in the Hawklord's absence.

Why?

People were understandably concerned when a Barrani war band, armed to the teeth, made their way to the Imperial Palace.

Ugh. Kaylin could just imagine the paperwork pouring out of the public facing office of the Halls of Law. And onto the Leontine's desk. *We'll be back as soon as we can.*

Come back in one piece. Come back, he corrected himself, *when you can be certain of arriving in one piece. Nothing less is going to calm the Emperor down.*

…He's angry?

He's beyond angry.

CHAPTER 24

Lord Barian was waiting inside the Hallionne when Bellusdeo finally landed and once again assumed her human form. Lirienne was not. Kaylin wondered if this was significant. The Dragon looked worse for wear herself, but most of that wear was survivable. There were no obvious burns or rents in the Dragon's armor; she was just incredibly rumpled. Especially her hair.

The familiar was once again slumped across Kaylin's shoulders; she thought he might be snoring. She offered Lord Barian a bow, certain for once that it was the correct one.

He returned it, and his bow was not—according to the Diarmat school of etiquette—the correct response; it was far too deep. This did not make her feel more respected; it made her feel instantly more paranoid.

As well you should, Ynpharion said.

Barian looked paler, his color off. "I regret to be forced to ask you to remain within the Hallionne," he said, before she could speak. She realized that he was actually injured; his color was off because he'd been bleeding. Etiquette did not cover what to do in circumstances such as this.

Wisdom should, Ynpharion snapped.

"What happened?" She was petty enough to ask the question just to hear Ynpharion's version of a shriek.

"There was a misunderstanding. The war band remains on the threshold of Alsanis. Its leader has asked Alsanis for permission to enter; he has failed to grant it."

"Why? If they try to harm Bellusdeo, he'll stop them."

Barian bowed his head for one long moment. When he lifted it, Kaylin could see that his eyes were blue—and narrow. He was, she realized, angry. Long years of experience as a Hawk stopped her from taking a step back, but he must have seen her stiffen; he held up one hand. "My apologies, Lord Kaylin. I am not angry with you; I am not angry with Lord Bellusdeo. Her...presence here has been explained to the satisfaction of both myself and the Lord of the West March. Neither you nor your companion have done anything to engender either anger or suspicion."

In him. Kaylin did not say this aloud.

Given the difficulties you just faced while in *the Hallionne, none of this should come as a surprise to you.*

Kaylin blinked. "You can't think that members of the war band are responsible for what happened in Alsanis?"

Because Ynpharion was not present in person, he felt free to continue to vent his frustration. Loudly, because no one else could hear it.

Barian's answer was clear in his expression, although he shuttered it immediately. He was angry at what must feel like betrayal; he was Warden of the West March, and one of his duties was the Hallionne Alsanis. This meant, on the other hand, that he was not responsible for what had happened.

Ynpharion told her not to be so certain.

Alsanis, however, said, "No, he is not. Your namebound fails to explain the concept of Lord Barian's duty—perhaps because he does not understand it himself. Regardless, no. Lord Barian was not responsible in any way for the intrusion."

But he had some idea who was, Kaylin thought.

"Yes, he does."

Barian looked distinctly less comfortable. "I am investigating," he said. "But at the moment, investigations are...fraught. The war band is not under my immediate control; nor is it under the immediate control of the Lord of the West March, which is the greater danger."

"Where is the Lord of the West March?"

"He is not within the Hallionne."

"He's not with the war band, either."

"No, Lord Kaylin," Alsanis said, when Lord Barian failed to answer. "He is, even now, almost in the heart of the green."

Bellusdeo, silent until that moment, turned to the Hallionne's Avatar. "Would we be expected to join him there?"

"Ah, no, Lord Bellusdeo. We believe that would be materially unsafe for you at this time." The Avatar bowed. "Forgive the deplorable lack of hospitality. Terrano has informed me of the possible weaknesses in my connections to the portal gateways, and I am attempting to repair them. If you would join me? Terrano's friends are waiting."

Kaylin glanced at Terrano. She wondered why he'd followed a Dragon and a human instead of joining his friends, and couldn't come up with an answer. But he did follow Bellusdeo and Alsanis as they traveled farther into the Hallionne.

Kaylin expected the dining hall to be noisy. It wasn't. Although the cohort were all seated—in various postures, most informal—around a large dining table, they didn't speak at all. Their faces implied speech—or rather, reactions to speech—but no words followed.

"I think," Bellusdeo said quietly, "that I would find Mandoran much more pleasant if he were this silent."

"He can't be," Allaron said, looking past his cohort to the

new arrivals. "If he were, he couldn't interact with the rest of you."

"And here I was thinking," the Dragon said in Elantran, "that the house would be much quieter with the lot of you as guests."

"Mandoran does not approve of that," Eddorian said, grinning broadly. "I will not, however, repeat what he just said."

"Can I?" Karian asked.

"No," Sedarias told him, frowning. "It was inappropriate. My apologies, Lord Bellusdeo, but—"

"He lives with her—and they're both still alive. How inappropriate can it be?"

Oh yes, *much* quieter, Kaylin thought. The presence of two people whose names did not exist in the mental space the cohort occupied had instantly added color and sound to the Barrani cohort. Kaylin glanced at Terrano, and found the answer to the question she hadn't asked him.

He stared at the table—at the cohort—his expression incredibly bleak. It was something she hadn't expected to see on his face, he was otherwise so much like Mandoran. But... he couldn't hear them, now. He couldn't be part of their conversation, except in the normal way: by speaking out loud. By putting his thoughts, such as they were, into words—and at that, words that were well chosen enough to make the thought understood to the rest.

He hadn't had to do that before.

He had come from wherever it was he'd so happily ventured because he had heard them in the wilderness of the pathways. He had come because he thought they needed his help—and they had. But he was no longer part of them. This, Kaylin thought, was the flip side of the freedom coin. He had desired nothing but freedom, and he had leapt into the unknown with both arms thrown wide to embrace it, almost literally.

He had seen things that the cohort had not seen; had done

things that the cohort had not done. But he had come home when he had heard their cries.

Alsanis, however, was not Terrano's home. They understood each other; their long struggle—the one to keep Terrano caged, and the other to be free of all cages—had bred the kind of affection and respect that only long rivalry could. Terrano was comfortable in Alsanis's confines because he understood the mechanisms of the cage; he understood it better than any other Barrani.

But his home, she thought, almost pensive now, was not Alsanis. It was not a place. It was there, at that table, surrounded by Barrani who had been brought to the green on the whim of the High Court in a desperate bid for power. Where they were, home was.

And he was discovering that he could not come home. Home no longer existed for Terrano.

As if they could hear the thought that Kaylin did not put into words, one of the cohort rose—Allaron, the giant—and crossed the room toward Terrano. Terrano stiffened, staring at that giant as if he were thinking at him, as if willpower alone could force the words he didn't say out loud to stop him.

Allaron reached out and cuffed Terrano on the shoulder, but caught him when he staggered. He didn't let go, either. Instead, he dragged Terrano to the table, pulled out an empty chair, and pretty much forced him to sit in it. He then sat beside Terrano, and dropped an arm around his shoulder which he didn't look like he was going to lift anytime soon.

Terrano flushed red. But Kaylin thought, beneath the embarrassment, he was pleased. Maybe.

"Now I *really* want you all to visit," Bellusdeo said, grinning. "I can only imagine what Mandoran would say if he were in Terrano's position."

"We don't have to imagine it. Sadly." Sedarias, Kaylin decided, was cut from the Annarion school of good manners.

Kaylin and Bellusdeo then joined the cohort at the table.

"We were just talking about what happened," Sedarias said.

"Which part?" Bellusdeo asked.

"All of it."

"Did you already cover the part about the two Barrani intruders?"

There was a full beat of silence, during which the temperature in the room seemed to plummet. Kaylin was certain the cohort were shouting up a storm on the insides of their own heads.

"We were waiting for Terrano," Sedarias finally said. "Alsanis believes he understands how they got in. It is not a method that they could use from the West March." She exhaled, her brows folding momentarily. "Do you understand what that is?"

When no one answered, Sedarias lifted a hand and pointed. At Spike. Kaylin had almost forgotten Spike was there.

"Not really. From what I've seen so far, Spike is like portable Records, only better."

"That is not all that he is."

"Do *you* know?" Kaylin asked, folding her arms and shifting her hips slightly. Before she did, however, she dislodged Spike, so that he was once again floating freely by her side.

Eddorian broke out laughing.

"You're talking to Mandoran again."

"Mostly listening," he said, in apologetic Elantran. "He thinks it unfair that we won't repeat what he's saying—but I told him that Sedarias is here, and he's across the continent."

Sedarias glared at him, but her eyes were almost green. Almost. "The intruders came by the outlands. They found the portal path. They could not have entered the Hallionne from above." At Kaylin's brief frown, she added, "In as much as direction makes sense in the confines of the portal lands, *above* is what we use to describe it. They couldn't have come in through front doors; I don't think they would have been allowed entry."

"They would not," Alsanis said. "Will Spike be remaining with you?"

"I don't know?" She turned to the floating, spiked ball. "Did you want to go back home?"

"Yes." The single word was spoken with far more vehemence than any other word that had left his—well, not exactly mouth.

"Lord Kaylin does not think she has asked the question you are answering," Alsanis then said. "I believe she means to ask if you wish to return to Ravellon."

"No."

"Ah. I believe her question implies a second question. If you do not wish to return to Ravellon, from whence she believes you came, where would you wish to go?"

Spike began to hum and spin.

Kaylin turned back to Sedarias. "You recognized at least one of the two intruders."

"I recognized the intruders as a serious threat to both my friends and the Hallionne."

"That, too."

It was Terrano who spoke, probably because he had to, to be heard. "She's going to find out who they were, anyway. We have one corpse. Lord Kaylin is *kyuthe* to the Lord of the West March, and the Lady is waiting in one of the Hallionne to speak with her. If you think you're keeping anything to yourself given events here, you are hopelessly optimistic."

"This is not a matter for outsiders; it is purely a matter for our people."

Terrano raised a brow. He really did remind Kaylin of Mandoran. "There's a war band on Alsanis's doorstep, waiting to kill the Dragon. There's a war band in the Imperial City because the Dragon in theory attacked the West March, and they consider this a racial act of war."

"The Dragon," Kaylin added, in case it was necessary, "did *not* attack the West March."

"It's already gone beyond the boundaries of the High Court, and if the West March is not beholden to the Emperor, the High Court *is*."

"Annarion doesn't want her involved in this."

"Annarion's in Elantra. *Kaylin* is here. She is definitively involved."

Bellusdeo cleared her throat. Dragon-style. This broke the discussion into smaller pieces. Hopefully, they wouldn't be picked up by the cohort immediately.

Kaylin then continued. "We need to know what, exactly, you taught to the Arcanists, or the Barrani of the High Court—the ones who were willing to ally themselves with you when you attempted to escape Alsanis last time. And if we don't, Alsanis and the rest of the Hallionne absolutely *do*. What were the intruders seeking, today? When they attacked—and almost destroyed—Orbaranne the last time, they were seeking power. Their needs and your needs coincided at the time.

"They're almost diametrically opposed, now."

"Mandoran wants it to be known that Annarion was against this from the very beginning."

"Which means he wasn't?"

"He says, 'What do *you* think?'"

"I think it's irrelevant. Having talked with Terrano a bit more, I think most of the planning was done closer to Alsanis. Sedarias?"

She grimaced briefly before composing her expression. "We wanted power in order to retrieve Teela. We did not mean to abandon her." Sedarias winced. Teela clearly had a word or two to say about that. "You know what we intended. You were there."

"It wouldn't have worked."

"We wouldn't have known unless we tried."

Terrano lifted his hand. "Could you all speak in Barrani? I don't understand more than half of what you're saying."

"Sorry—they learned it from Teela," Kaylin said quietly. "And they know I am much more comfortable speaking Elantran." She made the effort to speak in Barrani. "We need to know what you taught them."

"We didn't teach them how to walk into Ravellon and walk out again, carrying one of its occupants." Sedarias exhaled. "Terrano was the best of us. Mandoran was next, but he was not Terrano's equal. Terrano had a map of the interior layers of Alsanis, and even when those layers shifted, he could still see their edges in the new locations. He was capable of circumnavigating the Hallionne, by the end—he could leave. We could not."

Kaylin nodded; this much she knew from personal experience.

"Understand that we had given up on our kin, just as they had—long since—given up on both us and Alsanis. We understood that the Dreams of Alsanis—the eagles—had become blighted nightmares. We did not desire Alsanis's destruction."

"You didn't care about Orbaranne."

"Not as much, no. We could not speak True Words. Ah, no. We could not speak them into being, the way the Ancients could. We could recognize them, and we could—with effort—manipulate their shapes, but never enough. But we understood the theory: they are Alsanis. They are the Hallionne."

"They aren't all of the Hallionne!" Kaylin replied. She then flushed and repeated the words in Barrani.

"No. There is some core, some essential sentience, at the heart of the Hallionne; it is why they all differ. And it is irrelevant. If that core drives the Hallionne, if they command the power that resides within, they are nonetheless dependent on the shape of the words themselves for the almost limitless power they access within their own walls. I do not believe that the intent of the intruders was to destroy Alsanis."

"You think they were here to destroy you."

"Yes."

"You specifically."

Serralyn said, "That is not relevant." Which Kaylin took as a yes. Sedarias glared at Serralyn, who fell silent but obviously begrudged it. "The intruder was my older sister."

"The intruder you killed?"

"We have perfect memory, Lord Kaylin; you do not labor under that burden. But yes."

"Did Teela tell you that someone tried to assassinate her?"

Silence.

"...I'll take it that's a no."

"She's not happy with you," Eddorian said. "And yes, we knew something had angered her, and we had a few guesses. Teela doesn't like to share when she can avoid it."

"She can't avoid this." It was Bellusdeo who spoke.

"No. I believe she understands that. Mandoran says she has moved in with you, but adds, 'unfortunately, she brought Tain as well.'"

"More like she couldn't ditch him."

"Mandoran thinks Tain is devoted to Teela."

Kaylin said, "No comment."

"You don't agree?"

"I don't think it's safe for me—or anyone else, even you—to talk about Teela's personal life."

"We were talking about Tain," Eddorian pointed out.

"You were talking about Tain in relation to Teela. And she won't be happy about that. And regardless, what you can get away with, I can't. Tain is a Hawk. He's Teela's partner. When things get ugly, he has her back. That's what I know about the two of them, and that's really all I need to know."

"Have you no curiosity?" Serralyn asked.

Kaylin shrugged. "They were Hawks when I joined. They joined the force together. I once asked if there was something between them, and once was enough. They're partners and they're Hawks, and that's what really matters." She shook her head. "And you're distracting me. You killed your older sister."

Sedarias's shrug was cool. "This is not the first attempt she's made on my life."

"You spent most of your life here!"

"Yes."

"And you were all considered children when you were brought here."

"Indeed."

"So you're saying she tried to kill you when you were children?"

"No. I was considered a child; she was not. And before you ask, she was not the head of the line. Nor is she now."

"She's dead now."

"Fine. She was not the head of the line when she died, either." Sedarias rose. "Spike, will you accompany me?"

Spike failed to answer. The familiar glanced at Kaylin, and when Kaylin failed to do something—the nature of that something having not been communicated—squawked loudly in her ear.

Terrano stood and held out his left hand. "Spike," he said, in an almost aggrieved tone. "Will you accompany me?"

Spike whirred and clicked and floated through the air to land in Terrano's outstretched palm.

Sedarias glared—whether at Terrano or Spike was unclear—and pushed herself out of her chair. "I would like Spike to take a close look at the war band for later study."

"You said you have perfect memory," Kaylin pointed out.

"We do, yes. But we are not all magically inclined, and we

are not Records in any sense of the word. I think we'll want to be able to reproduce what we see in a more tangible way."

Kaylin shot Spike a dubious glance. "I'm not sure Spike would be considered entirely objective or acceptable as a legal source of information."

"We use what we have at hand," Sedarias replied, with an almost martial shrug. She started to leave the room, stopped, and turned back to Terrano. "Are you coming?"

Kaylin ate dinner when it appeared on the table. She became mildly self-conscious when the only people offered food were she and Bellusdeo. The Dragon, however, didn't seem self-conscious at all. She watched the cohort as they fell silent, and occasionally asked them questions. Having Mandoran as one of Bellusdeo's housemates seemed to have blunted the edge of their racial Dragon hostility. And given how often one of the cohort started a comment with *Mandoran says*, it was almost like they were at home.

Kaylin understood that Barrani families were not like mortal families, or at least not like the families of the mortals she personally knew, but still found Sedarias's attitude toward her dead sister disturbing. To be fair, she believed, as Sedarias did, that that dead sister had been trying to kill Sedarias—the rest of the cohort likely being collateral damage—so she didn't particularly judge Sedarias. If Sedarias had been obviously angry or obviously upset, it would have been easier. Sedarias, however, seemed to consider it the effective equivalent of bad weather—a simple fact of the life she had led before she had been brought to the green.

Kaylin had often daydreamed about having sisters and brothers of her own. The whole attempted murder element of family did not play any part in those daydreams. It was hard not to envy beautiful, healthy Immortals—but envy was not what she felt at the moment. She was therefore quiet while she ate.

Before Sedarias returned, Alsanis did. "The Consort wishes to speak with you now, if you are available." Although the phrase was politely worded, it wasn't really a request. Kaylin rose. She glanced at Bellusdeo, who shook her head. "I'll stay with the cohort."

The Consort was not dressed for Court, but her hair—a long, white drape that had parted to expose her face—was unique enough she could not be mistaken for any other Barrani. Her eyes, in the surface of the Hallionne's version of a mirror, which happened to be a pool of water nestled in an intricate, standing basin, were blue. The blue lightened the moment the Consort could see Kaylin.

"Why are you even here?" The Barrani Hawk demanded. "It's not safe, at the moment."

The blue darkened again.

Ynpharion was immediately present; his silence was almost scorching. It was also the silence of drawn breath; he meant to speak but could not find adequate words.

Don't shout at me, Kaylin told him, irritated. *Do something useful instead.*

I shudder to contemplate what you might consider useful.

Teach me how to think things that you won't be able to hear.

While I admit that actual privacy from the shoddy interior of your thoughts holds some appeal to me—

Thanks.

—I fail to see why I would teach you to lock the figurative door in my face.

It's not your face I'm worried about.

Silence. *You are worried about a different nameheld.*

I don't understand Barrani families, no. Most of the time Nightshade and Lirienne don't bother me; I can forget that Lirienne even exists. But...the Consort seems to have some suspicions about her brother.

Concerns, Lord Kaylin. Suspicion among my kin is different. But you are concerned about the Lord of the West March and Nightshade, and you are not concerned with me? This seemed to offend Ynpharion. Kaylin didn't care.

And that was the crux of the matter. She didn't care. There was no possible way to fall any lower on the ladder of Ynpharion's respect or regard; there was only up. He already despised her, barely tolerated her, and frequently shrieked—or the mental equivalent—at some perceived stupidity or other. But his anger or contempt was in no way equal to her anger or contempt for herself on the very bad days. With Ynpharion she had nothing to lose.

You might, he said, *have something to gain.* He was, predictably, annoyed.

I'm not sure anything I could do that would better your opinion of me would better my opinion of myself. And that's beside the point. I need to learn how to shield my thoughts and my life from the others.

I for one would appreciate less of your life in mine.

"Lord Kaylin."

Kaylin blinked. The *other* thing she needed to learn was the ability to have a full conversation on the inside of her head without bringing her external interactions to a dead halt.

"Sorry. My head is pretty noisy at the moment."

This got the glimmer of a smile from the Consort, which was probably as much as anyone could get, given current events.

It is, Ynpharion grudgingly said. *She is highly concerned. She is, I should warn you, not best pleased with the cohort at the moment.*

Oh?

Had they waited a handful of decades—perhaps a century at the outside—the entire High Court would be better politically equipped to deal with their presence. This is far, far too early.

Maybe the cohort didn't understand that, was Kaylin's uneasy response.

It is likely, given what you've witnessed, that most of them did not understand it; I do not believe Annarion considers it relevant. Sedarias, however, understood. She did not wish to take the risk that the preparations would somehow be either welcoming or positive.

And you know that how?

I do not. It is, however, what the Consort believes.

"If you would ask the committee in your head, as you put it, to allow me a few minutes of your uninterrupted time, I would be most appreciative. And while my brothers would agree that I was perhaps hasty in my attempt to reach you, I am far less likely to be lost—either in the Hallionne or on the portal paths—than you. And my presence, for better or worse, will not start a war."

"Bellusdeo had no intention of coming here."

"Oh?"

"The water dumped us inside of Orbaranne." If Kaylin expected this to make the Consort any more resigned, it failed spectacularly.

"You asked the water to bring you to Orbaranne?" Her tone was wrong; all edge. All steel.

"No. And the water didn't ask us for permission, either."

"Was the water operating under the command of another?"

Kaylin shook her head. "I'm almost certain that the water dropped us here of its own accord. And you knew something," she added, eyes narrowed.

"Ah, no. The Oracles have been troubled recently. You must know it is difficult to interpret their visions or creations. But the existence of the cohort has been much in my thoughts; one possible interpretation of the oracular message involved that cohort. And you. I thought there was a chance that you would be driven to the Hallionne. I interceded to ask that the Hallionne accept you and your traveling companion—" here she paused to eye the familiar, who snorted "—as guests. I did *not* expect that you would arrive with Lord Bellusdeo." She hesitated, and after a long pause, added, "I thought there was a possibility that you would have either Mandoran or Annarion with you."

"I don't suppose," Kaylin said in Elantran, "there's any way we can convince you to just go home?"

One perfect brow rose.

"Alsanis thinks we need to go to where you are. By the portal paths. Which hasn't really worked out well for us so far."

"Ah. Yes. I have been in discussions with the Hallionne about this problem. But the Hallionne are not extensible. They cannot simply extend their reach; they are limited by the words which harbor the entirety of their power. And you must understand the reasons for this."

Kaylin didn't, but it didn't take all that long to think it through. The Hallionne were sentient. They had desires of their own—desires that often caused conflict with the very reason for their existence. If they could simply expand their sphere of influence, they would become like gods; there was very little they couldn't do within their own space. She met the Consort's steady gaze and nodded.

"Sedarias thinks that the attack on Alsanis was motivated entirely by Barrani politics."

The Consort nodded again, her expression grave.

"You don't think so."

"Ah, no. I believe that Sedarias is materially correct. But I also believe there are consequences to the actions that have not been fully considered. It is the way of my kin to believe fully in their own power—and that belief does not often falter. Power is necessary for survival. We seek power in subtle ways, but where subtlety has failed us, we seek power in unpredictable places."

"I suppose Ynpharion told you—" The Consort cleared her

throat. Kaylin took the hint and started the sentence again. "I suppose you already know that one of the Barrani walked into Ravellon and came out carrying one of the Shadows with him. Literally with him."

"Yes."

"Into *Ravellon*," Kaylin repeated.

"Yes, Lord Kaylin. We are now aware."

"I think there's a chance that—" Kaylin faltered. She could not mention the High Lord in this context. She might have problems keeping her mouth shut when things got heated, but even she knew that there were some things that were never to be said out loud.

The Consort waited, as if testing that resolve, but when Kaylin failed to finish the sentence she'd impulsively started, she said, "We are aware of that, now. The situation is complicated. Will the cohort, as you call them, travel to Elantra?"

"I think there is no chance whatsoever that Sedarias will now remain here." Kaylin hesitated and then added, "I'm sorry about skipping out on dinner."

The Consort laughed.

Kaylin did not. "I know that everything with the Barrani is politics and misdirection. But—Mandoran and Annarion are part of my home, and the whole damn cohort comes with them."

"They are not kin."

"No—they're closer than kin. You don't get to choose your kin. But you do get to choose your *kyuthe*. And frankly, Sedarias killed her sister—who's tried to kill her before—and Teela killed her father. I'm not sure the Barrani really understand family the way the rest of us do."

"When you say 'us,' ask Bellusdeo about Dragon family, sometime. My brother will not be in favor of the cohort arriving in Elantra."

"You mean Lirienne?"

"I did, but actually, neither brother considers it wise."

"You don't think—"

The Consort lifted a hand. "I have spoken with the Hallionne. I am currently resident in Kariastos. Bertolle has sent his brothers to watch the byways, now that we are aware of some of the possible difficulties. But Kaylin, the portal paths are fraught. It would be safer if you traveled overland."

"That'll take *weeks!*"

"Yes."

"...And we've got Bellusdeo. We're not going to be safer overland right now—there's a war band camped outside of Alsanis. They're not going to just let us commandeer four carriages and leave with the Dragon."

"Do you have so little faith in the Lord of the West March?"

"Lord Barian went to speak with the war band. When he returned, he was bleeding."

Silence.

"He's not the Lord of the West March," Kaylin continued, uneasy with the texture of that silence. "He's the Warden. But...he *is* the Warden. And I think it might be his mother who's leading the war band."

The Consort looked once over her shoulder; whatever she was looking at was outside of the mirror's field of vision. The Consort then returned to the mirror, and to Kaylin. She was not wearing armor; she did not carry a sword or shield. But everything about her now seemed like the very essence of a warrior queen, not the mother of an entire race.

As if she could hear the thought, the Consort said, "When children are endangered, is there much difference between the two? Very well. The portal paths."

"I believe," Alsanis said, his voice a rumble, "that you should leave very soon. Sedarias and Terrano are returning, in haste; I believe Sedarias is injured."

CHAPTER 25

The mirror vanished. It wasn't that the image faded, as it did in mirrors in the Halls of Law; the entirety of the basin that contained the water disappeared. Kaylin turned to look over her shoulder; she could see the Avatar of Alsanis. If the Consort had somehow conjured the essence of warrior queen without bothering with the trappings, Alsanis had reformed his entire physical presence.

"Well it *was* stupid!" Kaylin heard someone shout.

"They were looking for *Dragons*!" Sedarias replied. Loudly.

Kaylin careened around the nearest corner; Alsanis had not bothered with subtlety, and had reformed the halls and the doors so that Kaylin was yards away from the room which now contained the rest of the cohort and Bellusdeo.

"It's not like someone, oh, just tried to assassinate you."

"I think it was a reasonable assumption that the war band that is *hunting Dragons* is not connected with the sister who was hunting *me*."

"Obviously not entirely reasonable, given the injury. You said it yourself," Serralyn told Sedarias. She looked up. They weren't speaking out loud for either Bellusdeo's or Kaylin's sake; they were speaking out loud for Terrano's.

Kaylin pushed them aside. "Let me see." Sedarias's arm had been slashed open. The cut didn't seem to be deep, but it was long.

"It would have been worse," Eddorian told Kaylin, "but Terrano pulled her back."

Terrano shrugged. "And for thanks, my ears are still ringing."

"Who did this?"

"One of the war band, and before you ask, no, I don't know which one; he was wearing a helm that covered most of his face."

"So...they mistook you for a Dragon?"

"I think the word was *traitor*."

Kaylin rolled her eyes so far back they should have been sprained.

"I'm not happy with it, either. Teela, on the other hand, is *blistering*. You should hear her."

"I've only seen her angry a few times—genuinely angry, not irritated. And I kind of like to avoid the hells out of her when she's raging."

"If it makes you feel better," Allaron said, "Teela's at least impressed that *you* weren't stupid enough to go out to take a look at the war band."

"Tell her thanks."

"She would have been annoyed had you gone. But...she kind of expects better of Sedarias."

Sedarias, however, was clearly angry at herself. Kaylin wondered if Sedarias was an anger-pointing-inward person or an anger-pointing-outward one. If the latter, she was going to be worse than a raging bear. And Barrani had long memories. On most days, Kaylin envied that, because her memory was a honed, mortal one. On days like today, however, she was grateful for the lack.

"Alsanis says—"

"It's time to leave, yes." Sedarias rose. Her arm had been bandaged by one of the cohort; Kaylin expected the work to be sloppy. It wasn't.

"Teela told us what to do," Serralyn said, by way of explanation. She glanced at Terrano. "We're heading to Kariastos."

"Shouldn't we stop at Orbaranne?" Kaylin asked.

They all stared at her.

It was Terrano, not connected to the cohort, who said, "Orbaranne does everything within the scope and limits of her power to aid the Lord of the West March."

"I highly doubt the Lord of the West March is involved with the war band."

"So do they." They. The rest of the cohort. "But doubting isn't the same as certainty. And Alsanis was breached here, in the heart of his domain. They don't want to take the risk."

Put that way, it was the smart choice. Kaylin nodded and glanced at Bellusdeo, who also nodded.

"Here," Terrano added. He handed Spike to Kaylin.

"You didn't need to carry him. He seems to be mobile on his own."

Terrano shrugged. "I didn't want to lose him. And I'm certain we would have. They have at least one Arcanist in the war band."

"Arcanist?"

"War bands have Arcanists, given what they were composed to fight."

"And you know they have one because?"

Sedarias said, "Are we talking or leaving?" Clearly, this was not a matter she wished discussed in front of a Dragon.

This irritated Kaylin, but it didn't seem to irritate Bellusdeo, who nodded in what almost seemed like approval.

"Are you *certain* you have control of at least this part of the path?" Kaylin asked Alsanis, for perhaps the thirtieth time.

Hallionne, or at least the Hallionne Alsanis, did not seem to be troubled by either the repetition or the worry.

"I did not lose control of the path the first time," he said. He'd only said this about fifteen times. "The path I created did exist; your friends could not find it. They stepped onto a layer that had been constructed deliberately over top of it, and it swept them away."

"And the Barrani who constructed that layer did so from within you."

This was the only point that seemed to trouble the cohort.

"Sedarias has some idea of how it was done," Alsanis said.

"Terrano should bloody well know."

"Terrano was not always a strategist."

"Meaning he didn't make the plans."

"Or follow them, half of the time. Were it not for the structure provided by the cohort ensemble, I highly doubt he would have been capable of troubling the Hallionne Orbaranne as he did. No, it is to Sedarias you wish to speak."

Fine. "Are *you* certain that the portal pathways will be safe for us?"

"We are aware of how they accomplished their attack."

Kaylin wanted to shriek. "Can they do it *again*?"

It was Sedarias who answered. "Not immediately and not without Alsanis's cooperation. He is aware of the avenue of attack used, and he has come up with an effective counter to it."

"They didn't have his cooperation the first time," Kaylin quite reasonably pointed out. "Look—from what I saw, they were carrying Shadow. Both of them. They didn't enter through the front doors, but they were standing *at the heart* of his power. How could he not have noticed that?"

"Why don't you ask him?" Sedarias said, throwing her hands up in frustration.

"She has," Alsanis replied. "I have chosen not to answer."

The cohort fell silent. Kaylin glanced at Bellusdeo and Terrano; Terrano was watching his friends as if, by strength of will alone, he could join what was obviously their discussion.

Kaylin then stared at the Hallionne's Avatar.

"It is best, Lord Kaylin, that you engage in discussions of this nature with care. Were you Barrani, it would be less unsafe, but your expressions give much away, even when your words do not. I do not mistrust your intent," Alsanis added, "but I have misgivings about your abilities."

Because that was *so* much better.

"This is how it starts," Bellusdeo said quietly.

The cohort looked toward her, even Terrano. "Those who seek power—the way one seeks one of the Dragonslayers—find power in Shadow. In small amounts, they consider it akin to the use of elemental magics, but small becomes large, because once one has broken certain taboos safely, there's no reason not to continue.

"Shadow has power. And in small quantities, if it can even be measured, it has no will; it is inert, in the way fire or water are when summoned to light or douse candles. Theoretically, even at that size, there is a trace of the living element, but it is too quiet, too slight, to be sensed. So, too, Shadow."

"And you know this how?" Terrano demanded. Sedarias kicked him; she knew the answer. She knew what Annarion and Mandoran knew.

"From experience." The Dragon's eyes were orange, but they were fixed at a point above and beyond the cohort's collective head. "Shadow can be used to combat shadow in subtle ways. In that fashion, it is very like the elements. If we summon fire in a large enough quantity, fire opposes us. The will of fire is to burn—at least when caged and summoned. The will of Shadow is different."

Kaylin glanced at Spike.

"I have now encountered Shadows who I would not consider enemies," Bellusdeo continued, speaking the words as if grudging every one of them. "And I believe that those Shadows have the same will—if not the same function—as the rest of us. But this creature," she said, indicating Spike, "was not under its own control when it ventured into the West March.

"And I believe that the members of your High Court who are being fed power—or absorbing it under their own recognizance—are in danger of becoming transformed and enslaved, just as it was. In the end, if they draw enough power, the Shadows have a doorway into the rest of Elantra. The Towers in the fiefs serve as a solid defense against a frontal assault. I do not believe Shadow can easily escape it.

"But the fieflords can—and have—entered Ravellon before, and emerged unharmed. Is it possible that the fieflords are allowing key Barrani Lords a path into Ravellon?"

"If the money was good," Kaylin replied, uneasy now.

"You may well find that Shadow has begun a subtle infiltration of your city in a way that the Towers cannot easily prevent. I believe it of utmost import that we return to the Empire."

"And put an end to the war?"

"As you've pointed out, your familiar appeared here without warning in the shape of a Dragon. No one who saw him believed that he *was* draconic, but it is a pretext for cessation of political hostilities." When Kaylin stared at her, Bellusdeo snorted. "It saves face."

"I'm not sure I *want* to save their faces."

Terrano snickered.

"Portal paths," Kaylin said.

The cohort were silent, which didn't really mean much except that Terrano couldn't take part in their conversation. Kaylin caught a few eye rolls, which meant the conversation was not all one-sided, and Sedarias did not notably cheer up. But Alsanis took them to the portal pathways without incident; the ground didn't fall out from beneath their feet, and Bellusdeo did not go full Dragon.

Kaylin was slightly surprised that the cohort accepted a Dragon in their midst so readily, but probably shouldn't have been. While they were holed up in Alsanis, Mandoran and Bellusdeo were bickering half a continent away. They had seen Bellusdeo as Mandoran and Annarion had; they'd seen her fight. They were aware that she had been injured in the defense of the High Halls.

And they were aware, as well, of her status, not as a member of the Dragon Court, but as a displaced person, a person who had been swept out of her life in the Aeries and deposited in an entirely different world. They were aware, as Mandoran was, that any old friends she possessed—those that had managed to survive three wars—were sleeping the long sleep of Dragons; she could not return to their sides.

War had scarred them all, destroying any lives they had planned before they were swept up in its currents.

Alsanis created a tall, rectangular arch; Kaylin watched as it went up, inch by inch, from both the left and the right, meeting at last in the unusual keystone at its height. There was a word carved out of the keystone that seemed to glow, and she looked at her arms almost automatically. Her own marks were flat.

To Kaylin's eyes, the portal resembled a mirror—a normal one. The central image it contained coalesced out of multi-hued, swirling fog, until it turned into a flat, almost empty plain.

"Yes," Alsanis said, to Kaylin's unasked question. "In general, we attempt to enforce a familiar landscape upon these pathways. It is far easier for those who choose to walk them not to stray."

"And today?"

"That shift in appearance requires more power, and more

planning. Some essential part of the path itself is diverted into maintaining its appearance." He did not need to point out all the reasons why that was a bad idea today.

Kaylin's gaze returned to the portal. Something was moving across the plain; it seemed to be running toward them. As it grew closer, she realized that it was not one thing, but two; they looked like long-legged animals, too light of foot and musculature to be horses. Only when they were almost at the portal did she recognize them. Or at least their faces. Grimacing, she told the cohort and the Dragon, "They're safe."

Bellusdeo eyed them dubiously.

"It's Winston and one of his brothers."

"And Winston and his brothers are?"

"The core of the Hallionne are people. Different races, but…people. I have no idea what Alsanis used to be; I suspect Orbaranne was once human. Bertolle was neither. When Bertolle chose to become a Hallionne, his brothers remained with him. They were sleeping. I woke them up on the way to the West March my first time through. They…don't really understand bodies."

"They do," Terrano said quietly. "They just don't understand *our* bodies."

Winston was delighted to see Kaylin. He was delighted to see the cohort. He was momentarily stunned at the sight of Bellusdeo, but not in the usual Barrani way. His passably Barrani head, attached to a much longer neck, swiveled from person to person until Kaylin felt queasy.

"Winston, please—just take a normal Barrani shape."

"Oh. Sorry. We had to move at speed and we were forbidden faster modes of transportation, so we had to improvise," Winston helpfully explained, while the rest of his body melted and reassembled itself beneath his face. "The Consort is waiting with Kariastos."

"Did you have any trouble finding us?"

The question confused Winston, who glanced at his brother. His brother had also disassembled and reassembled himself, and was blinking rapidly. When he opened his mouth to answer, he didn't use words; something very like a screeching insect buzz left his lips instead.

Spike whirred to life, and answered.

The two brothers exchanged a glance, and this time it was Winston who spoke.

"Can you understand them?" Kaylin asked Alsanis.

"Yes, Lord Kaylin."

"Can you translate what they're saying so it makes sense to me?"

A longer pause. "I am uncertain. Your friend is capable of communicating across species, and he may be able to explain the situation. I believe there is some concern."

"About Spike's presence?"

"About the portal paths."

"Were you two attacked on the way here?" Kaylin asked.

Winston blinked. "No."

"Why are you worried about Spike?"

"I believe that he'll be noticed."

"...And you weren't worried about being noticed yourselves."

"No—I told you, we avoided forms of travel that would be notable."

Bellusdeo coughed into her hand.

"There are hunters abroad," Winston continued.

"And that's different from the norm."

He nodded gravely. "Something is waking, Lord Kaylin."

She blinked. "Why are you calling me that?"

Winston blinked as well, but with more obvious confusion and less grimace. "We were told by Bertolle that that is the correct form of address. And that we must endeavor to use it."

"Bertolle was wrong. You can call me Private Neya, if you absolutely insist on using something that isn't my name." Which was irrelevant. Kaylin mentally kicked herself. "What do you mean, something's waking?"

The two brothers exchanged a glance, and the other brother then spoke, whirring and clicking at Spike. Spike replied in kind, and as he talked, Winston forgot about his eyes; they lost their resemblance to Barrani eyes, widening in his face until the upper half was a kind of black mess that resembled open eyes seen through a magnifying glass.

All of the cohort found this obviously disturbing, judging by their expressions. Bellusdeo, orange-eyed, turned to Kaylin. "You are *certain* they are safe?"

Kaylin nodded. In a much quieter voice, she added, "They're not quite used to having bodies like ours. I think. When they first woke, they reminded me of foundlings; they were extremely excited to see what these bodies could do. I think one of them grew both arms by several yards, and knotted them."

"That is...not comforting."

"It was very helpful when we were on the portal paths. They literally threw themselves down and became a road we could follow, which would occasionally open its eyes and mouths beneath our feet." Kaylin grimaced, remembering it. "But they were the reason we managed to travel in more or less the same direction. If you fall off the portal paths, you wander a lot."

"Do you think that was the intent with the cohort? That they fall off those paths and become lost?"

"It's a thought."

"Which means no."

"I think someone wants Sedarias out of the picture. I don't think they care whether or not the rest of the cohort arrives— but I could be wrong."

"You're wrong," Sedarias said. She glanced at Terrano, and her expression softened.

"Terrano, you said you ducked into Hallionne Orbaranne's space because something was chasing you?"

He nodded, his own expression uncharacteristically grim. "There are often things that will hurt you, off the pathways in the outlands. But most of them will hurt you unintentionally. They're just not equipped to interact with people like you. Winston—I'm going to assume you came up with that name— is a good example. He's flexible, and he can exist in a bunch of different states. He's more aware of the dangers out there because he can."

"Was the thing you were hiding from the same thing Winston's worried about?"

"It shouldn't be." Terrano frowned.

"Is it possible that you attracted attention while you were exploring? And now that you have, something that wasn't aware of us is now searching?"

The hesitation before the answer was longer than it needed to be. Kaylin chalked it down as *maybe*. She was therefore surprised when Winston said, "No. It is possible that he did attract attention; he is not like the others here. But what is hunting now is far more like him than we are. Something is waking," he said again.

"What? *What* is waking?"

Winston ignored this. "We believe that Spike should remain here."

"I think we need to have him at the Halls of Law when I report in."

Squawk. Squawk.

"If you want to risk it," Winston replied.

When Kaylin stepped through the arch, every mark on her body felt as if it had been slapped. Her eyes watered. But she took three steps and the pain faded, just as the pain of an actual slap did. She stared out into a vast expanse of nothing. No, not quite nothing; everything ahead of their group was a sprawl of gray. There were no trees, no sky, nothing that really resembled horizon. Beneath her feet, the gray was soft; there was a give to it that implied sand. Or flesh.

She went with sand.

She began to trudge across it; Winston was in the lead. In deference to Kaylin and the rest of the cohort, he chose to remain in his Barrani state. His brother, however, did not. Kaylin wouldn't have found the transformation so uncomfortable if, at the end of it, he actually looked like an animal. She'd seen Bellusdeo go Dragon enough times that the sight of shifting—and expanding—flesh seemed almost natural. In the case of Winston and his brothers, however, things like fur or obvious animal musculature were missing. He simply changed the shape and orientation of his limbs to better move ahead.

He ran off, and Winston turned to the group. "He will scout. I will lead."

"There's no path?"

"There is. You are walking on it. But it is almost in its base state. It will be far more difficult to shift or upset its construction."

"But not impossible."

"Nothing is impossible." Winston's eyes narrowed. "We can see the path. I believe that one or two of your friends are also sensitive enough to follow it without the visual cues that usually accompany it. What is important now is that you follow me. If you are falling behind, make certain that we know."

Walking on soft sand was far more taxing than walking on actual dirt or cobbled stone. Winston and his brother didn't tire at all; neither did Bellusdeo. But the cohort, with the exception of Terrano, appeared to find it as difficult as Kaylin did after the first hour.

If it had even been an hour. Without sun or light, it was much harder to mark the passage of time. There was little to break the monotony of the trek.

"Do you want to ride?" Bellusdeo asked.

"No. It's not hard, it's just..." Kaylin shrugged. "There's something about this place I don't like."

"I can't imagine what."

Kaylin continued, in spite of the obvious sarcasm. "It reminds me of the stuff between worlds."

"Between worlds?"

Kaylin nodded. "I think this is what exists when there are no words." She frowned.

Spike said, "Yes."

"Did you mean *words* or *worlds*?" the Dragon asked.

"Words. At their heart, even worlds have words. Big, complicated, messy words. I don't think you could know the True Name of a world—I don't think you could see it all at one time. Even the Barrani, with perfect memory, would probably be stuck just staring for centuries in an attempt to grasp it all."

"And in the absence of words, this is what remains?"

Kaylin shrugged. "You can ask the Arkon. He has old records. And opinions. *Lots* of opinions."

"Kitling, you are really going to have to do something about that memory of yours."

"It comes with the race."

"No, it does not. It comes with 'what Kaylin thinks is practical to know' or 'what Kaylin finds immediately useful.'" She eyed Spike. "Are you saying that this is similar to the space one would travel to arrive in a different world?"

"Yes."

"But the Hallionne can affect the space."

"Yes."

"Can you?"

"I do not understand the question."

"Can you affect the paths the same way the Hallionne can? No, forget that question. Winston looks as if he's about to turn green."

He really did. Kaylin would have asked, but his brother came racing back to the group before she could frame a question, and his expression drove all other thoughts away.

"We're in trouble," Kaylin said.

The cohort now bunched together as Winston's brother raced toward them. He came to an immediate and abrupt halt, as if momentum was irrelevant to him. He then spoke to Winston in a language that none of the cohort could understand. Kaylin glanced at Bellusdeo, who shook her head, her own brow furrowing. The brother was clearly agitated.

The familiar squawked loudly. He then lifted his wing and draped it across Kaylin's eyes.

The view behind the small dragon's wing was very different, and Kaylin almost pushed it away; what was gray and formless in her own vision was formless when seen through the familiar's wing—but that was the only thing the two had in common. Instead of gray, the landscape was an almost lurid splash of color, some harmonizing and some clashing badly. She had never seen blues so bright, reds so vivid, and had they not been moving, it might not have been so bad. But they were shifting constantly, as if seeking either position or dominance, and although there were no obvious objects—or people—in the mix, it made the landscape seem as if it was alive, and not entirely happy to be so.

A vortex appeared in that swirl of color; she could see it by the ways the colors began to move. As if they were liquid, they swirled in toward a point, elongating as they blended and vanished. What remained was Winston's brother.

No, Kaylin thought. Winston's brother had been invisible until that moment. Whatever had drained the colors of this land was not Winston's brother. She remembered, then, that he had been certain he would not be seen, and wondered if this was why. Behind Winston's brother was something defined by the lack of color that occurred as it walked.

"The good news is," Kaylin told her companions, "it's not yet another member of the Barrani High Court."

"Give us the bad news. Good news isn't likely to be a problem," Sedarias replied, in Elantran.

"I was afraid you'd say that. Something is following Winston's brother."

"Something?"

"Sorry. I can't see it clearly, so I have no idea what it is. Spike—do you recognize the thing that's following Winston's brother?"

Spike had already begun to spin, but he'd done so silently. Only when he began to emit a series of clicks that really did sound insectoid did Kaylin turn toward him, the familiar's wings fitted to her face like a second skin. He no longer looked like a spiky, floating ball. But she understood, looking at him, why Winston had been worried. Where Spike spun, colors were attenuated, stretched, absorbed; the landscape beneath the feet of the cohort was almost gray. It was a much larger patch of gray than the patch being created by whatever was chasing Winston's brother.

"Lord Kaylin," Winston said. "I believe we will be in danger if we do not move."

"Can you see the path? Because I can't."

"Yes," Winston said, grimacing. "I really hate this." He shouted something at his brother, whose breakneck pace had brought him much closer to the group than the thing that appeared to be pursuing him. It wasn't; Kaylin realized that now. It was heading in a straight path toward Spike.

She kicked herself.

You were not wrong, Nightshade said. *You will require what...
Spike...sees, if it can be trusted.*

I trust it.

*That goes without saying. I believe your Spike now apprehends
the danger.*

*Did you recognize what he was, when you first saw him? You've
crossed the border to Ravellon before.*

*No. But I would not have recognized your Gilbert, either. Shadow
is thought of as if it were fire; one does not need to place one's hand
within it to know that it will burn. Some revision to that thought is
underway, but...*

But?

*Castle Nightshade, as you call my Tower, is extremely reluctant
to allow any exploration.*

And Candallar's Tower isn't?

*If what you saw was correct, it was not Candallar who entered
Ravellon. But Kaylin, be cautious. It is clear, from your first meeting
with that fieflord, that he understands Imperial Law. I believe that
what he wants is mundane.*

And that?

To be repatriated, of course. He is, as I am, outcaste.

*There's something you're not telling me. I mean, something rel-
evant.* A thought occurred to her on the heels of that one.
Someone asked you for the same permission they got from Candallar.

Silence.

*It's not the first time you've had dealings with people of power in
Elantra. It's not the first time you've done favors.*

This time the silence was weighted—slightly—with approval.

We're not done with this, Kaylin told Nightshade, as Winston's brother arrived. He did not change shape, but he did
speak to Winston, his syllables thinner, higher and faster than
they usually were.

Understand, Kaylin, that were I to be repatriated, I would not be *the Tower's lord. I could not, and do what must be done.*

Is it because of the Emperor?

No. Lord Tiamaris retains his position in the Dragon Court. But he also retains and enforces the Imperial Laws within his fief. Not one of the rest of us do that. The Tower must have its lord. You have seen the Avatar of my Tower. Unlike the Tower of Tiamaris, it has a will that is ancient and not inclined toward mortals. It only barely accepts me—and I am not without power. There are, of course, those disinclined to have me return to Court. They would like Meliannos returned to the line; I have invited them to attempt to retrieve it.

If you came back, Annarion wouldn't have to take the Test of Name. The cohort wouldn't have to descend on Elantra. Things would be safer for everyone.

Is that what you believe of my brother? This time, there was both bitterness and amusement in the tone. *It is too late, regardless. The cohort, as you call them, are on the move. Even if they retreat now, Alsanis will only be besieged by those who wish to ensure that they do not move in future. Or did you imagine that the attempt came about only because of their decision? The attempt occurred now because of their decision. But it would have occurred, regardless. And Kaylin? Be careful. I cannot reach you. Lirienne cannot reach you; you have left your partner behind.*

I have a Dragon, and I'm not afraid to use her.

I am uncertain that a Dragon—even this one—will have much idea of how to deal with that.

CHAPTER 26

Kaylin let Nightshade's voice fade away; it was hard to listen to any thought that didn't concern their immediate survival. She had assumed that whatever was chasing Winston's brother was roughly his brother's size; she revised that. It wasn't; it had simply been much farther behind. Because the landscape was what it was, she couldn't correctly gauge anything about the creature; it seemed, aside from literally eating up the ground, more like an empty space whose clashing colors didn't hurt her eyes.

Terrano cursed. Loudly. He caught hold of Allaron. "Stick together!" he shouted, as if they needed to be told. Then again, given Allaron's position—ahead of, and in front of, the main body of the group, at least one of them did.

Winston, however, shook his head, grabbing Terrano's shoulder. "Let Spike act. Retain your current form."

"But—"

"The only thing the creature can see is Spike. If Spike is willing to hold its attention, the rest of you can move out of its way." He glanced at his brother.

"Spike's not really made for fighting," Kaylin pointed out.

"Why do you believe this?"

"He's kind of like portable Records."

This clearly made no sense to Winston, who glanced at his equally confused brother. In turn, they both looked at Spike. Or at least that's what she thought they were looking at; they were craning their necks—one attached to the body of a hairless animal—up, and up again.

The familiar squawked, but Kaylin had already turned toward Spike. She understood why the two brothers were now gazing upward. Spike—at least seen through the familiar's wing—was no longer all that small, nor was he particularly self-contained.

He was taller than most of the buildings in Elantra, and he didn't appear to be slowing down. Everything around him, including the ground beneath his feet, was now a uniform gray, which is what she'd first seen. In the absence of color, she could almost make out a form. It was not particularly pleasant; it was like Shadow—flexible, shifting and decidedly not mortal. Nor was it draconic, although something that trailed around its back implied the presence of wings.

And when it spoke—and it did—its voice sounded like a swarm of locusts, except gigantic and not particularly focused on agriculture.

"He's angry," Winston said, almost conversationally. He turned to Terrano and added, "Stay in that form, and follow us."

"But—"

"We've had to maneuver in the portal lands in *these* forms just to bring you safely to the Consort."

"And if you have to suffer, I have to suffer?"

"Yes."

Winston's brother grimaced and turned to Kaylin. "Can you ask Spike to move off the path?"

"But we don't want to lose him!"

Everyone stared at Kaylin as if she'd just grown two extra heads, both absent any actual brains.

"Spike—can you find us again? Can you find me?"

Is that what you desire? The voice shook the firmament, but sounded less insect-like.

"Yes!"

Something Kaylin could only perceive as absence lashed out. She felt a sharp pain down the length of her left arm, and realized that her shirt had been slashed open. And it wasn't just her shirt.

Terrano shouted, and Winston turned toward Spike, but Spike had already started to move.

"Do not bleed here," Winston told Kaylin.

Kaylin bit her tongue on the Leontine that often followed condescending and unhelpful advice. Winston didn't know any better. Probably. It was Sedarias who tore a strip off the bottom of her gown; she brought it to Kaylin and bound that arm. "Teela is *not* impressed," she said, as she worked.

"I've done worse."

Sedarias pursed lips and said, "I'd appreciate if the two of you had this argument in person, rather than through me." She finished binding the arm.

Spike began to move. Given his size, Kaylin had expected his movement to be lumbering; it wasn't. She could track his movement by the dimming of color, but didn't watch it for long. Winston retained Barrani form; his brother did not. The brother began to move as Winston marshaled the rest of the group. Winston watched the distant predator before nodding a hundred times. It was as if he'd set his head in motion and forgotten about it.

"Now," he said. "Run."

Running was part of beat training. The city streets were an obstacle course that generally impeded momentum. Stopping and starting, however, gave a person a chance to catch their breath; the current landscape didn't provide that. Even if it had, Kaylin was certain Winston wouldn't. But he appeared to be right: whatever it was that had caused Winston's brother to flee back to the group in a panic moved toward Spike.

"Are there always predators like that here?"

"No. That was highly unusual, this close to the Hallionne spheres," Winston said. He seemed to have dispensed with a need to breathe, and his syllables sounded exactly the same as they usually did. Kaylin's were more labored, their beat uneven.

"You think they're looking for us?"

"No. For your friends. Or for that one," he added, nodding in Terrano's direction. "Alsanis said you are aware that when your friends are careless they are easily heard, and easily found."

Kaylin cringed. She hadn't had this conversation with Alsanis, but was well aware that conversation—or volition—was not required. And it was true. She assumed, or had assumed, that Sedarias and the rest of the cohort had been learning the same lessons Annarion currently struggled with; that some of the cohort would be like Mandoran, and take them to heart more readily. And some would not.

"We were very lucky."

"Lucky?"

"You brought Spike. You were right," he added, without a trace of self-consciousness. "If we had left him with Alsanis, I'm not sure all of us would have escaped. They weren't expecting Spike."

"What *is* Spike, exactly?"

"You don't know?"

"We found him outside of Alsanis and did something to free him."

"Ah."

"He came from Ravellon."

Silence. Thoughtful silence. "When you say *we* do you mean *you*?"

"Yes."

Terrano cleared his throat. Loudly. "When she says *we*, she means *me*."

"Language is tricky. I see." He spoke again, but this time, Kaylin didn't understand the words.

Her familiar squawked. He had removed the wing from her face, and she could no longer see either Spike or the thing that pursued him, but she didn't look; she was too busy running and trying to squeeze a few words out of increasingly overworked lungs.

"Lord Kaylin, we believe that the predator might have originated in Ravellon."

"How? Something that size can't *leave* the fief. Unless..." Spike was from Ravellon. And Gilbert. And the Dragon outcaste. "Never mind." She asked the more important question next. "Why do you think that? What can you see that screams *Ravellon*?"

Winston's answer was unintelligible, but he appeared to be speaking to Kaylin. She frowned.

"I didn't understand a word of that."

He tried again. And a third time. When enlightenment failed to appear on Kaylin's face, he shifted his gaze to the familiar. Winston could run and rotate his head in a full circle, which was both disturbing and expected, at this point.

The familiar's squawking response was longer and louder this time.

"He's going to have to explain it to you later," Winston said, raising his voice over the familiar's. "But not *here*."

They reached what Kaylin assumed was Hallionne Kariastos without further incident or pursuit. Kaylin recognized their end point because it was a shimmering, standing arch. That, and Winston's brother had come to a full stop, finally condescending to change the shape of his body to better reflect the people he was escorting. Winston seemed relieved. He approached the portal and stuck his head through; half of his body seemed to disappear.

It reappeared more or less in the same place, but Winston's face now sported a frown, and his eyes had lost some of the Barrani cohesion.

"Is this the wrong place?" Kaylin demanded.

"It is the right place," Winston said, in the wrong tone. "The Hallionne, however, is not responding."

"Can we enter the portal?"

"I am not certain it is wise." He turned to his brother and spoke their unknown language, and his brother immediately returned to running form and headed back into the unknown.

Sedarias and the cohort were blue-eyed to a man, with the possible exception of Terrano.

"Do you think the Barrani could do to Kariastos what was attempted in Alsanis?" Kaylin demanded.

It was Terrano who said, "Yes. And they'd have more of a chance of success. Alsanis was accustomed to *us*. He couldn't keep pace with me," he added, without a trace of obvious pride, "but he was never that far behind. I'm not sure any of the other Hallionne would have the same experience."

"Terrano, you are going to tell me exactly what was done to enter Alsanis. Now. The Consort is there."

"The Consort will be safe," Sedarias interrupted. "If the portal is still standing, Kariastos is not yet undone."

"We need to do something—Winston thinks there's something wrong." She headed toward the portal, but Sedarias grabbed her by the shoulders, and met her gaze. "You don't understand the Consort's power. There's a reason she came to the Hallionne in person. A reason she came to this one." She turned to Terrano. "Can you find the way in?"

Since they were standing in front of the way in, the question made no immediate sense. Kaylin caught up with its meaning a beat after Terrano did.

Terrano did not look comfortable. Given Sedarias's blistering glare, this was not surprising; Kaylin didn't feel comfortable, either. "Kariastos isn't Alsanis. There's a reason we didn't come here the first time."

"And right now, that's good. But something's wrong, and we need to fix it," Kaylin told them both. Terrano looked at Sedarias. Sedarias looked at nothing for one long moment.

"Mandoran was right," she finally said. She looked at Kaylin as if she were an insect who had finally demanded her full attention. All of the cohort were now turned toward her, as if she were gravity and they were falling.

"Do not do that here," Winston said, his voice sharp. "We are not yet safe."

Sedarias laughed. In a bitter voice, she said, "There is no safety. Kaylin is mortal. If she can build safety, it only has to last decades. But you know, as well as we, that safety is an illusion. Trust is a lie we tell ourselves."

"Why lie?" Kaylin asked.

"Because if we didn't, we'd kill everyone in sight. If there is no safety, there are still variations on acceptable danger. Do you know what *trust* is, Lord Kaylin?"

Kaylin waited, lips compressing. It kept words from escaping.

"Trust is what we have when we believe the people surrounding us are harmless. It is the comfort we take when we are certain that we will survive anything they might do to hurt us. Do you understand?"

Winston looked confused.

Kaylin, however, was not. As if Sedarias were her thirteen-year-old self, she met the Barrani's blue-eyed glare. "You're wrong."

"Decades. Only decades."

"I've lived that way. I did it for the longest six months of my life, and at the end of that six months, all I wanted was death. Mine," she added. "I had nothing to offer anyone *except* death. Or worse. I looked at the future before me, and all I could see was pain and isolation and fear. I told myself that if I survived, I could change my life—and only if I survived. I did things *to* survive that I will never, ever forget. And on the bad days, if I could go back in time and eradicate myself, I *would*."

Silence. Sedarias finally broke it. "You're a Hawk."

"I went to the Halls of Law to assassinate the Hawklord."

"Teela says you are lying."

"She's wrong. It happens." Kaylin exhaled. "Fine. I went to make the *attempt*. I didn't expect to succeed. I expected to die. I expected to die, and if I'd had the strength, I would have saved everyone the trouble and drowned myself in the Ablayne. I didn't. I didn't want to live, but I couldn't end my own life.

"If survival were the only thing that mattered, I wouldn't be a Hawk. I wouldn't know Teela. I wouldn't understand the laws. I wouldn't understand that *no one* is perfect; that the laws can be both good and inadequate at the same time. I do my best. My best changes from day to day. But I *want* the Hawks. I want people who struggle to do more than just survive. I want people I can believe in.

"I *always* wanted it." Kaylin inhaled. Held her breath for five seconds and exhaled. "I trust Teela with my life. According to your definition, I can't." She glanced at Winston, who seemed to have calmed down a bit. "But...you wanted it as well."

Sedarias folded her arms.

"If you hadn't, would you know the names of the cohort? The True Names?"

"I did that, you foolish, foolish child, because it was the *only* way I could render them harmless. I did it *because* my will is the stronger, the greater, will. If I knew their names, I *could* defend myself against any possible attack. I did it because I had confidence *in my own power*."

Allaron placed a hand on Kaylin's shoulder. She glanced at him, and he shook his head.

But no. No. "Then why," Kaylin said, as Allaron's hand tightened, "did you attack the green? Why did you attack us when we went to perform the *regalia*? You almost destroyed an entire race—mine, incidentally."

"We did not—"

"Fine. Your advice and your plans almost allowed total idiots to destroy an entire race. Some of those idiots are *part of* that race. I'm not going to quibble specifics."

Terrano held up a hand. "Please talk more slowly."

Kaylin wanted to shriek. She wondered, then, what the inside of Sedarias's head sounded like. Hers was unusually quiet. "Fine. Why did you attack the green? Have you forgotten? Has your stay in Alsanis these past months damaged your Barrani memory?"

Silence.

"Because if it has, *I remember*. You wanted to *change the past*. It was impossible. It was always going to be impossible. But you did it anyway. Do you remember why?" None of the cohort spoke. Kaylin therefore turned to Terrano, the only member on the outside. "Terrano?"

His glance skittered off the ice of Sedarias's expression. "...To save Teela."

"Teela who abandoned you and returned to her home?"

"She didn't abandon us," he snapped. "You know what happened—why are you even talking about this?"

"You wanted to save Teela. Teela who was cut off from you. Teela who was no threat to you, and could never be a threat again. Teela, who you'd known for, what, months? At most?"

Allaron's hand tightened again. Kaylin turned her head and said, "I have no intention of shutting up. Give up. Or break my arm."

He actually reddened, but removed his hand.

"I understand who you say you are. I understand who you think you are. But there's more. You came back for Teela. You meant to escape—I don't know to where—but you didn't want to abandon Teela, the last of your number." She exhaled. "Nightshade never gave up on Annarion. Iberrienne never gave up on Eddorian. You all know this. Iberrienne almost destroyed us *because* he could be approached, could be manipulated. Why? He wanted his brother back."

"I am certain Nightshade is having regrets."

Kaylin's smile was almost a wince. "Possibly. He wouldn't go back, though. I don't know what family was to you," she continued, once again speaking to Sedarias. "But you could not have built this cohort if you hadn't desired more than the constant political struggle to survive. If the family you were born into was nothing but that, you wanted more. You made more.

"I trust Teela. She won't do what I tell her. She doesn't obey me. She doesn't serve me. We're not one person or one mind. But...neither are you. I know the cohort argues; Mandoran whines about it. I know that you've been arguing with Annarion at a distance. And I know that you've never even *tried* to exert the force of your will on his True Name. Could you? Yes. You could try.

"But it would break something, and you know it."

Sedarias glared at Kaylin. She transferred the glare to Eddorian, and then bounced it back. No, Kaylin thought, Sedarias's head was not a quiet place right now.

"I wanted," she finally said, "what Terrano wanted. I wanted to leave. I wanted to find a place that was not this one."

"But you stayed."

"I stayed because the majority of us wanted to stay. I knew what awaited me, and you are right: I did not want it." She exhaled and seemed to dwindle in size, although her anger was rawer and harsher. It would be. It was now pointed inward as well as outward. Or perhaps, Kaylin thought, it was always pointed in both directions. She knew quite well what that was like. "I was the one who suggested the exchange of names."

"You weren't," Terrano said—because he had to say it out loud.

"I was."

"You weren't."

"Who was, then?"

"Annarion."

The silence that followed was obviously an argument, but again, it was inaudible to anyone who was not a member of the cohort. Kaylin glanced at Bellusdeo, who had withdrawn entirely from all conversation. The Dragon shook her head as she met Kaylin's gaze; the motion reminded Kaylin of Allaron's.

"I agreed to it," Sedarias said, the majority apparently having gone against her, "for the reasons I stated. They were strangers, to me. We were twelve. We were meant to gain power, to become more useful tools for our families. In my house, we were not abandoned to the green—we were chosen *for* it. We understood the possible advantages. And we were people who desired power, because power was as close to safety as we could come.

"I won what was, in human terms, a very crooked election in my family line. And it was meant to be: we were meant to hone our power. We were meant to prove our worth." Every word was bitter. "Most of what you call the cohort *were* abandoned. They were not chosen as I was chosen. They were sent because of the chance—but their families valued their children in some fashion; they therefore sent those who would not otherwise be missed should the *regalia* fail. As it did."

Most, Kaylin thought. She wondered who the exceptions were, but didn't ask.

"We voted," she continued. "We had already started to form small alliances, but we had not yet hardened our lines of conflict. If it was not my idea," she continued, "I was the first to offer my name."

This, no one argued against.

"Why?" Kaylin asked.

"There are risks one takes. It was…a dare, if you will. I believed then—and believe, even now—that my name cannot be used against me." Even saying it, Sedarias did not look entirely comfortable. "I was first. But everyone took that risk. Everyone was willing to take it." She closed her eyes. "Yes. We came back for Teela. We knew what the *regalia* had cost her. I did not understand her mother. I did not therefore fully understand Teela. But I understood Teela's truth.

"I know all of our truths." Speaking thus, she looked to Terrano; he met, and held, her gaze. "I want us to be safe—and I don't believe in safety. Is that what you wanted to hear?"

Kaylin shook her head. "I don't believe in safety, either. But I do believe we can build something better. I didn't. For a long time, I didn't. I was afraid of having something to lose. I'm afraid of losing what I have, now. But…I'm willing to fight for it. I'm not willing to destroy it by pretending it doesn't exist."

"Teela says you're constantly willing to destroy it because you overestimate your ability to survive."

"Tell Teela that I'm not dead yet."

"She considers this proof of the miraculous."

Kaylin nodded, but continued. "If you feel this way about

the High Court and the Barrani, *why* are you going to the High Halls to take the Test of Name?"

"Because Annarion is going," Serralyn said. It was the first time she'd spoken out loud, and her answer overlapped Terrano's, but without his eye-rolling disgust.

"Annarion chose," Sedarias said, confirming Serralyn's words. "He was always more tied to this world than I. He wants his family line back. He wants his ancestral home. And he wants his brother free of the fiefs."

"I don't think his brother wants to be free of the fiefs."

"Not noticeably, no. I didn't say he was smart; I said it was what he wanted. It's what he feels his duty is. His upbringing was faulty," she continued. "He won't survive in the High Halls, even if he passes that Test." She winced. "I have not been idle since your departure from the green. My own contacts are a shambles, but I have sources of information; I have a better understanding of the current political structure, and I believe with our aid, he might survive."

"You seem to be more of a target than Annarion."

She inclined her head. "My sources will, of course, have other contacts as well." Her smile was slender and cold. "The sister I killed was not the head of our family, as the family is currently constituted, but she was not working on her own. I did not expect that she would be foolish enough to willingly take on Shadow elements in order to increase her power."

"For all the good it did her."

"For all the good it did her," Sedarias agreed. "We do not intend to disrupt the High Court; we intend to see Annarion through the Test of Name, and pass it ourselves. Becoming Lords of the High Court will provide us with options, should those options be required." She held up a hand as Kaylin opened her mouth. "We are aware of the risks. With the help of Alsanis, we have been taking the same lessons Helen has been forcing Mandoran and Annarion to take. We're aware of what happened with the ancestors; we're aware of what happened with the Shadows. We have been trying, with very limited success, to hear what the Shadows hear.

"And yes, Lord Kaylin, we're aware that whatever was sent into the outlands was sent hunting us. We believe they expected to find us as easily as they found Annarion and Mandoran. But Helen is a good teacher, if perhaps a bit too lenient; we could have walked these pathways without detection. We did not expect—I did not expect—to encounter either my sister or the High Court here. We did not expect to encounter a war band—I will confess that I am impressed.

"We certainly did not expect the Consort to come to the Hallionne. We did not expect—oh, many things." She then turned to Terrano. "We didn't expect to see you, either."

He was silent.

"We were happy for you," Sedarias continued, voice soft and almost—almost—pensive. "But there is a silence you once occupied that we cannot, quite, fill."

"I heard you."

Sedarias smiled. "You were listening. That would be a first."

"I gave you my name," he said.

She nodded. "And now, the risk is rendered irrelevant; you did not resume that name; did not choose to remain, bound and chained, to the world of your birth." She spoke in a tone that implied envy or yearning. "You should go. We can't take you with us. I didn't resent your decision. I didn't consider it a betrayal. What you wanted, you always wanted. We could see it. I can still see it now. It's bright, Terrano. It's shining. You at least escaped this."

"You could."

Sedarias shook her head. "Not anymore. Sometimes we are only offered one chance."

Winston was fidgeting. In his case, that meant lengthening his fingers and tying them into literal knots.

"What will you do?" Terrano asked of Sedarias. Of all of them.

"We will go to Elantra. We will go to the High Halls. We will take the Test of Name. In as much as we can, we will live as our people have lived for millennia. I will take my family. Annarion will regain his. Mandoran will do the same."

"Mandoran's not going to like that," Terrano said.

Sedarias raised a brow. "We will become what we were meant to become, before our lives were interrupted. And when it is time, Terrano, when it is *time*, we will turn our gaze and attention into the heart of Ravellon, and we will *break it*. We will reclaim what was lost to our people."

Terrano's brows had risen into the line of his falling hair. "How, exactly, do you intend to do that?" Clearly, this plan was a new one, made after his departure from the cohort.

"We don't know. But the Shadows appear to be hunting us—*us*—and I intend to make certain that they can never do so again."

He surprised Kaylin; he laughed. His laughter was almost joyful. He then crossed the distance that separated them, and threw his arms around Sedarias. Kaylin, even at her most comfortable, would never have dared. Sedarias was not a huggable presence.

"You really don't change," he said; she endured his embrace, but did not return it. On the other hand, she made no attempt to disengage, either. To Kaylin he added, "They didn't originally intend to take on Ravellon. Sedarias is angry at the thing that's hunting us, so it's become personal. No one can hold a grudge as long as Sedarias. No one, ever."

Kaylin didn't personally consider this a good thing, but kept that to herself.

Terrano let his arms fall away. "What I taught the Barrani

who were interested in forging an alliance with us, I taught here. Here in the outlands. It's not something that can easily be done in your world. I'm certain it can be taught there—but in spaces that draw on, that rely on, the much more malleable and amorphous environment. Places like the Hallionne. Or possibly Helen. Without the outlands, those buildings couldn't exist.

"Sedarias believed that without the outlands, the Keeper couldn't exist, either. This place is tied to all places in some fashion." His expression darkened. "The Shadows appear to be able to move here—but not all Shadows. They can't as easily leave it, either. But there were buildings in Ravellon that were the equal of the Hallionne, or so history tells us; I've never seen one, but even I know to stay away from Ravellon."

"You can see it from the outlands?"

"Yes. It's not safe to approach—not for me as I usually travel. It's a sticky web of strands and barbs, and it absorbs everything it can comfortably grasp."

"What does it look like, here?"

Terrano shrugged. "What does anything look like, here? I can't describe it to you because you won't understand what I see—you can't see it yourself, and you won't have the reference points. But if you could, I think even you might recognize it as a city. A congregation of cages, some taller than the Towers. I can," he added, "see the Towers that bind the fief of Ravellon in place."

"Right now?"

"Not right this exact minute, no."

"But you can see the Towers if you're in a different location?"

"Yes, why?"

Kaylin bit her lip.

"Winston, can you?"

Winston was frowning. "I do not approach the dark lands. None of us do."

"Because you might be lost?"

"Because we might be trapped and enslaved, or we might be contaminated. Bertolle is home to us; we have no other. That was the choice we made. But Bertolle would not have the flexibility of choice, were one of us to become infected. He would have to refuse us entry. In the worst case, he would be forced—by the words at his heart—to destroy us. We would not do that to him." He then said, to Terrano, "You should not play games so close to Ravellon."

"I didn't *know* it was Ravellon to start with, and I never approach anything that big carelessly. And before you ask, no. I haven't entered Ravellon. Had I, Alsanis would know, and I wouldn't be here. I'd be dead." He frowned. "Sedarias, don't do anything yet."

"Oh?"

"Winston is right. Something's wrong."

"That's *why* we're considering—"

"I don't think Kariastos has been compromised, exactly." His eyes began to spread across his face. Kaylin found such transformations acceptable in Winston and his brother, but found it disturbing in Terrano. And why should she? Terrano was not Barrani, now. He wasn't trying to be.

"Winston?"

Bertolle's brother was frowning as well.

And Sedarias said, "Everyone, be silent. Now."

In the silence, Kaylin thought. And in the silence, the crowd inside her head took the opportunity to speak when it wouldn't obviously distract her.

She is dangerous, Ynpharion said. The sentiment was echoed by everyone except Severn, who—as he usually did—said nothing.

Yes, but she's ours.

You are so certain. It wasn't a question.

Is Terrano right?

There was a glimmering of amusement. *Terrano is correct. The Consort chose Kariastos for a reason.*

All of Kaylin's worry, all of her fear, took shape and form, transforming as it did into a bitter anger. She had led the cohort—or almost led the cohort—into a trap. *Why didn't you say anything?* It was a stupid question. She knew it was stupid. But the anger had to go somewhere or it would overwhelm her.

Because she is not concerned about the cohort, as you call them; not in the fashion you are. If they are caught in a trap, it is unlikely that Kariastos will destroy them immediately. She can disentangle them afterward.

And me?

She did not—she does not—believe you are at significant risk. What Kariastos might build at her request will not harm you, because you have your familiar.

What is she trying to do?

Frustration. *What do you think?*

You do not wish to be involved in this, Nightshade said softly.

I'm involved anyway.

Limit your involvement.

I can't—I live with your brother. And Mandoran. The Barrani are trying to start a war because we have Bellusdeo, who had no intention of coming here at all. If I did nothing at all going forward, I would still be entangled in all of it.

Sedarias is dangerous.

Kaylin did not reply.

Lirienne did not ask her what she thought the Consort intended. And that told her something that she needed to know, and conversely, didn't want to. But that, she told herself, was life. *You know what they're doing,* she said, not bothering to hide the severity of either her tone or the disappointment she felt.

Yes.

It's beyond the political, now.

Nothing is ever beyond the political, kyuthe. *Nothing about my kin.*

Help us. Bellusdeo is with us. Bellusdeo isn't part of the cohort; she's a Dragon. If there's—if something was planned, she's going to get caught up in it, too. The Emperor will be enraged, and war is not in the interests of either of our people if Ravellon has somehow become involved. In fact, war is only of value to Ravellon; it'll split our forces. And it seems pretty clear that Ravellon is involved.

Lirienne said nothing. Kaylin let it go. She held his name, not the other way around, but she knew that she was not equal to enforcing her will. Not now, and probably not ever.

Kaylin lifted a hand and exhaled. Using her Hawk voice, she said, "No one enter the Hallionne."

"Oh?" Sedarias's voice was chilly.

Ignoring this, Kaylin turned to Terrano. His expression made clear that he thought anyone who gave orders to Sedarias—and expected to be obeyed—was so far beyond stupid they might as well be dead, which was what was going to happen when Sedarias was finished with them.

The ground beneath her feet—beneath all of their feet—began to rumble in a peculiar way. It did not feel like a tremor, exactly; Kaylin thought that standing *on* Bellusdeo's throat while she was attempting to roar would feel similar.

"Sedarias—" Terrano's voice was sharper and far less calm, but when she lifted a hand, he swallowed. "We're too close to the Hallionne, and I really don't think this is a good idea—"

"What is she doing?" Kaylin asked him. Her arms had not started to ache; her skin felt normal. But Terrano's queasy expression made clear that Sedarias, who seemed to be standing utterly still—as if she were a sword that had not yet been wielded—was doing something. Anything that could make Terrano nervous was bad.

"Sedarias—the Hallionne does not—"

Whatever she'd been about to say was lost to the sound of thunder, the flash of lightning and the buckling of the ground beneath their collective feet. Even Terrano's.

CHAPTER 27

"What did you *do*?" Kaylin shouted. She had to shout, to be heard; if Sedarias had not been not Barrani, she wouldn't have heard, regardless.

Sedarias might have looked smug, if smug had utterly lacked any sense of enjoyment. Kaylin searched for a word and came up with *vindicated* as the closest match for the Barrani woman's expression.

The portal that Winston had peered through changed shape as the thunderous cries continued. Kaylin remembered, then, that one of the Avatars of the Hallionne Kariastos was a dragon. A dragon made of water. She could hear his roar, absent the syllables necessary to make language of it.

"I tested the water."

"Kariastos does not sound happy with your test." Kaylin was disturbed; her skin had not informed her that magic was in use, and she had seen nothing but concentration—and suspicion—on Sedarias's face.

"You can't imagine, at this particular moment, that that has any relevance to us at all." There was, about Sedarias, a force of personality, a hint of danger, that made choosing one's fights essential. This was not the hill to die on—Sedarias had been suspicious, and Sedarias had been right to be so.

If Sedarias was right—had been right all along—that meant that the Consort was involved. The Consort had come here, not to save the cohort, but to more effectively entrap them before they reached Elantra. Before they passed beyond the Hallionne and their power entirely.

Bellusdeo's presence in the West March was outside of all plans. The cohort weren't responsible for the war band and its arrival at Alsanis's doorstep. What she couldn't be as certain of was Lirienne. Lord Barian had been injured. Lirienne was both alive and conscious, and he had not returned from his meeting with the war band.

Nor did he speak to her now.

She really hated this. She hated the suspicion, but why? She'd spent the first thirteen years of her life—or as much of it as she remembered—being suspicious. She'd called it caution, and it had been *necessary*. And when she had fallen into Barren, suspicion had become her only way of life. She assumed that everyone was out to kill her or sell her out, because that's *what she was doing*.

She'd walked away from that. At the time, she'd believed that the only way out of it—the *only* way—was death. Her death. And it had been hard, to change. She remembered. She had asked herself, almost constantly, *Why do I have to do this?*

She could still hear the answer—given to her by herself, but also by Teela, by Marcus, by Tain; by Caitlin and by Clint. *Because if you can't make* yourself *do this, you'll never believe that* anyone *can. You* make *the world you live in.*

And now she was a Hawk. She inhaled and exhaled as she balanced her weight over slightly bent knees in order to retain her footing. Suspicion was a useful tool. It was necessary in the life she'd chosen—but she had to be in control of it, not the other way around. She had, in her career as a Hawk, mastered a rudimentary objectivity.

Something was wrong, here. Something did not add up. She hated being suspicious, yes. But she hated being stupid *even more.*

"Sedarias. Terrano."

Something in her tone caught and held their attention. Sedarias's eyes narrowed. "What is it?"

"I think—for all of you—Kariastos is never going to be safe to enter." To Winston she said, "That's why we weren't asked to travel to Bertolle, who's closer. I don't think Bertolle would do whatever it is Kariastos has done."

Winston said nothing.

"We need to get out of here."

"But the path—" Winston began.

She told him, in descriptive Leontine, what he could do with his path. He looked dubious, and she said, "That wasn't literal. It was cursing. Terrano—"

Terrano had become a shade of almost green that meant he was distressed, or at least that's how she interpreted it. "That Shadow that Spike drew off was not conjured by Kariastos."

"No," she agreed. "And it doesn't matter. We'll be grateful to run into a Shadow, at this rate. Move. Winston—"

"On it," he said, mimicking Kaylin. He began to run, retracing the path they had taken. The cohort followed. So did Bellusdeo, but she held the rear, as if being a Dragon would be enough protection from the tendrils of a Hallionne. When they had run perhaps a mile in real world distance, Winston began to thin out, literally.

"I really hate this," he said, as he did. "Do you know where you're going?"

"Yes, and you're not going to like it. But you don't have to form a path for us all the way there."

Terrano, running alongside, said, "Please tell me you don't intend to walk the outlands all the way to Elantra."

"I don't see that we've got much choice. We could—maybe—head back to Alsanis. Or we could head to Bertolle, if Winston's brother manages to make it there in one piece to plead our case. But even if we reach Alsanis or Bertolle, we're not going to be able to leave again."

Sedarias said, "You're certain?"

"You're not?"

Sedarias did not answer the question, which Kaylin supposed was answer enough. "Why are you certain?"

"I have a couple of important True Names. I hold them. Start walking."

"...On Winston?"

"Does it look like we're going to be able to build ourselves another path?"

"Teela doesn't like it."

"Ask her for alternatives. Have her tell me—and you—that this is not actually some type of trap meant for you guys, and I will *happily* believe it."

"She says the Consort would never harm you. You'd be safe—"

Kaylin shrieked in outrage. "And Bellusdeo?"

"She does not believe the High Lord responsible for the war band."

"I would like to believe that. In fact, I *do* believe it. But I'm not willing to send the rest of you out into the outlands alone."

"Teela says—"

"You know how you said I should have these arguments in person, rather than through you?"

"Yes."

"It was a *great* idea."

It was Eddorian who picked up the thread of Teela's conversation. "Teela asks what in the hells do you think you're doing?"

"Tell her we're running to the outskirts of Ravellon."

Cacophony, then. If normal hearing had been the key to their detection, they would all be swarmed, by now. She started to tell them all to shut up, but Kariastos did that more effectively. He *roared*.

The cohort froze and turned to look over their shoulders, as did Kaylin. She could see what had once been a portal; it was no longer even a tiny bit welcoming. It was Kariastos, all right, but in a form that was much more like a Dragon—an enormous Dragon—than a building. Although Hallionne were not actual Dragons, Kaylin understood from his tone that he was not particularly happy. And as long as they could escape him, she didn't much care.

Kaylin.

Go away, she told Ynpharion.

Kaylin!

I mean it, damn you. Go the hells away right bloody now.

The Consort is waiting.

Kaylin struggled, hard, not to tell him where the Consort could go. She was upset. Angry. Possibly a bit confused. Mostly upset, though. *I am not about to turn around and betray them. They live with me. And you can tell her to forget dinner. Ever.*

Kaylin, you are not thinking. The cohort are dangerous—and you know why. You've seen why.

She said they might be able to help defeat the thing beneath the High Halls!

They will not help if they are not contained. She does not intend to destroy them; what she said to you was materially true. But she wants some guarantee that they will not become more of a danger to the High Halls than the Test in the tower.

I don't care.

Kaylin—do not do what you're considering. The Consort is against it.

If she hadn't been running, she would have shrieked for a good five minutes in fury and frustration.

She does not wish to lose you. Send the cohort on their way, if you must; she will guarantee—absolutely and unconditionally—your safety and the safety of your Dragon companion.

No dice.

Pardon?

No. Damn. Dice. And there's no point in guaranteeing their safety, either—I won't believe it. And I will never, ever speak to you again if you attempt to make me believe it. Now leave us alone.

She was practically leaking fury, and part of that was aimed at herself. She'd been stupid. She *hated* being stupid.

Kaylin. A different voice. She almost snapped at this one as well, but Severn had done nothing to deserve it. *What are you now doing? Teela has just turned a shade of ash and her eyes are practically black.*

You're with Teela?

We're all at Helen's, yes. Tain is worried about Teela. Mandoran and Annarion are indigo-eyed as well, but Mandoran's lost control of his eyes, so it's not as obvious. What's happened?

She told him. She told him everything, while running along a very flat Winston. She slowed only when she could see the distant city.

Structures rose in the distance, tall, pale, and slightly curved; they towered over the mass of what might be smaller buildings. The air was thick, hazy; the towers in the distance seemed to waver as Kaylin, Bellusdeo and the cohort approached.

Terrano had said that it was a city of cages, of traps, and Kaylin could see what he meant: the structures she thought of as towers seemed to curve inward, toward what existed beneath them; an odd light seemed to illuminate them from within.

In Elantran buildings, this would imply windows, lamps. This was not Elantra.

"Kaylin?" Bellusdeo touched her shoulder, a gesture that implied this wasn't the first time she'd tried to get Kaylin's attention.

Terrano was watching her as well. All of the cohort were.

She said nothing; they had slowed and she made no attempt to pick up the pace. Instead, she spoke a single word. *"Ravellon."*

It wasn't a city. It could be mistaken for one, as Terrano had said. But Kaylin had spent time in the morgue at the Halls of Law. She'd spent time watching Red at work. She had words for most of the parts of a body, although they didn't get much use.

Those structures weren't towers. They weren't buildings. That Shadows had somehow made a home of them didn't change the facts.

Kaylin.

If a giant had died in a desert, this is what they might leave behind. The towers were the great, fleshless rib cage of something far larger than Kaylin had ever seen in life.

Severn watched silently, as he often did. She felt his presence in the back of her thoughts and found it easier to catch her breath. *Well?*

He failed to answer the question she had asked. *Can you see the borders of Ravellon?*

She nodded; she could. But the borders seemed somehow mundane, slight; they were not the casket in which a body such as this should have been interred. *We need to reach the Towers in the fiefs. We need to find Tiamaris.*

You know the risk.

Yes, I know the risk. We're way *too close. But we can't go back to*

*Kariastos. The Consort promised that we'd be safe—Bellusdeo and
I—but promised nothing about the cohort.*

If you can, try not to be hurt.

I'm not hurt. I'm angry.

*The worst anger always comes from hurt. You trusted her. You
feel betrayed.*

Wouldn't you?

*I honestly believe that she intends you no harm. I believe she would
safeguard Bellusdeo against the war band, either in the West March or
in Elantra. I do not believe she had anything to do with that.*

But the cohort—

Teela is spitting fire, by the way.

So am I.

Yes, but not for the same reasons. I believe she is angry at Sedarias.

What? Why?

*She won't answer. Neither will Mandoran or Annarion. If I were
you—if I were exactly you—I would take the risk you're now taking.*

And if you were you, but in my position?

*I'm not you. I'm worried, but—do what you need to do. I'll meet
you there.*

No, wait!

Silence.

Severn—don't—

Silence.

She cursed in very loud and heartfelt Leontine, and turned
toward the city.

Toward Ravellon.

Winston pulled himself up from the ground. "This is as
far as I can safely go," he told Kaylin, his expression grave. "I
do not think I need tell you that Bertolle will be concerned."

"No, you don't. Tell him thank you."

"For what?"

"For sending you and your brother to help us. I'm not sure why he did it."

"He was worried about you." Winston smiled. "We would like it if you came to visit."

"I'm just wondering if there's any way you guys could come visit me. I live in a building that was once a little bit like a Hallionne."

"There are Hallionne in your city?"

"No, she's not a Hallionne. She's a sentient building, with the usual range of control over anything that happens within her borders."

"She was built close to Ravellon?"

"Yes, but she's not a Tower, either. Her name's Helen," she added. "And I think she'd be happy to meet you. You could—"

"Kaylin," Bellusdeo said, her voice a suspicious rumble. Kaylin glanced to confirm that she had gone full Dragon. "I understand that you wish to express gratitude, but now is *not* the time. Can you see the city?"

Kaylin nodded.

"It is Ravellon." Bellusdeo was the definition of grim, now. "And Ravellon exists everywhere."

"Can you see the rest of the city?"

"No. But Elantra is not Ravellon."

"Can you see the fiefs?"

"I can see the Towers," Bellusdeo said quietly. "And we're going to have a small problem, if I judge your intent correctly."

"What problem?"

"Look at the Towers."

Kaylin felt herself wilt as she obeyed. She *could* see the Towers. Terrano had been right: they were visible. But none of them looked like the Towers with which she was familiar. They were built around Ravellon, but seemed, to her eye, to stand at the very edge of that fief's boundaries. And they were absolutely identical.

"Does it matter which Tower?" Terrano asked.

"Yes. There's only one that isn't likely to immediately destroy us all, or make the attempt to do so."

"So...this was your plan?"

"I was kind of short on time."

The cohort were speaking among themselves. Sedarias turned toward Kaylin. "The Shadows are moving."

"I can see that." Kaylin glanced at Bellusdeo; the Dragon's eyes were blood red.

"You mean to approach Tiamaris."

"Tara, yes. I think there's a good chance she'll let us in through the back door. If we can find it."

"Castle Nightshade?" Bellusdeo asked.

"Will devour us whole. All of us. Without blinking. Nightshade can control the Tower, but I wouldn't put it beyond his damn castle to kill us in an eye blink, which would be about the time it would take Nightshade to assert control. His Tower really doesn't like Annarion, and I'm guessing by extension all the rest of the cohort as well."

You underestimate me, Nightshade said, clearly unamused.

"We'd rather avoid it, if we can," Sedarias told Kaylin. "We...know what Annarion encountered."

Kaylin cursed her lack of affinity with geography. Loudly. Often. There was very little in Records about Ravellon, and both the streets and buildings that made up Ravellon were known to physically change when people entered the fief.

There were seven Towers.

The most obvious landmark, the Ablayne river, was nowhere in sight. In fact, none of the streets beyond Ravellon were visible; nothing marked the location of the city she called home. Which made sense. In no way could they have reached Elantra from the West March by foot in so short a time. They couldn't have done it on horseback, either; Kaylin was less certain about riding Dragon-back, because Dragons could *move*. Regardless, Bellusdeo couldn't transport the entire cohort simultaneously.

Bellusdeo scanned the horizon, in part because there was something *to* scan, and in part because of what that something was. She had lived in Ravellon, albeit as a sword in the hand of an enslaved Maggaron.

"You are thinking too loudly," the gold Dragon said.

"Do you recognize anything?"

"Yes. And no. Ravellon changes from moment to moment. There's no certain sense of geography."

"Do you remember much about it?" This question, Kaylin asked in a much more hesitant tone. She didn't like to pry into the past—and the past pain—of others, because she hated it when people pried into hers. She wanted the past to be irrelevant. She wanted the present and the future to be the only things that mattered. And of course, that was impossible. Even now, the past defined so much of her life. But…if that past had brought her to this point—well, to the point of serving the Halls of Law, to be precise—it was the right past. It had led here.

Lord Kaylin.

Go away.

Ynpharion was frustrated. He was also afraid.

She's not going to blame you for this. This is not on you.

There is a danger.

Kaylin almost laughed out loud, but it would have been bitter, cynical laughter, and she didn't want to have to explain it to the cohort. *No kidding.*

You have not attracted attention, yet. The Lady asks—the Lady begs—that you come away while you have the chance. She is willing, and he clearly begrudged the word, *to guarantee the safety—and freedom—of your…friends.*

The astonishment must have shown on Kaylin's face, because Sedarias asked, instantly, what had happened.

"I'm indirectly in contact with the Consort."

Since Barrani eyes in this gathering were already all the bad blue color, Sedarias's didn't get any darker. "And?"

"She—she wants us to go back."

"And we'd like to be wealthy and powerful beyond all compare. What of it?"

"No, I mean—she says she'll guarantee your safety and freedom."

"Ours?" Sedarias glanced at Bellusdeo. This surprised Kaylin.

"She already promised that she wouldn't harm either me or the Dragon."

"Oh?"

"When we left Kariastos, and the portal path. She made it clear she had never had any intention of harming or caging us." At Sedarias's expression, she continued. "She didn't want us to come to Ravellon. She was afraid of what would happen."

"To you."

Kaylin shrugged.

"Are you a complete fool?" One of the cohort laughed. It certainly wasn't Sedarias, who had asked the outraged question. "We have historically *already* clashed at least once with the Consort and her forces. You must remember it—*you were there*. She has every right to be suspicious of us; she has *every right* to take *sensible* precautions!"

"And you wanted to be trapped in those sensible precautions? You wanted me to accept them without even knowing what they were? Without being informed, or asked for an opinion or anything?"

"Of course not! But there is no reason whatsoever why you—and the Dragon—should not have accepted the Hallionne's safety and hospitality!"

Terrano's attention was bouncing between Kaylin and Sedarias. "I think," he said, when it was Kaylin's turn to speak, "we should stop shouting. I'm not certain how much the Shadows in Ravellon are aware of, but we probably don't want to attract attention. Any attention. At all." He was glaring at the cohort, not Kaylin.

Sedarias was fuming. She was capable of the stony neutrality of her kind, but it had apparently failed to become her natural, normal expression.

It was Bellusdeo who came to the rescue, metaphorically speaking. She said, "I know where Tiamaris is."

The cohort looked at Kaylin as Kaylin turned to Bellusdeo. "How?"

"We lost our lands, and our world, to Shadow. But we fought it for a long time. Do you see the reddish glow there, in the distance?"

Kaylin's eyes were neither draconian nor Barrani. Terrano said, "To the left?"

Bellusdeo nodded. "Those are specific signal lights; we used them to mark decaying borders and areas of great concern. They are magical in nature, and they can be seen if Shadows envelope the land. The Norannir are there, and they keep those fires burning. They don't," she added, half-apologetically, "trust your Towers."

"Can you lead us there?"

The Dragon nodded. "I am ill-prepared for combat, but—yes. Can we assume that the Tower closest to the fires is the one we want?"

"I hope so."

Bellusdeo followed a circuitous route to reach the fires, which became visible to Kaylin only after they'd been walking for ten minutes. There was a direct path to Kaylin's eyes, and apparently to Terrano's as well, given the looks he was aiming at the side of the Dragon's face, but both were willing to trust Bellusdeo's greater experience.

Sedarias also said nothing. And that, Kaylin thought, was the benefit of living with Mandoran. His constant sniping—and to be fair, Bellusdeo's—had rendered the gold Dragon harmless. For a value of harmless that suited a very large, golden Dragon with blood-red eyes.

They didn't question her; even Terrano didn't put his growing unease into words. And to be fair, Kaylin felt no doubt at all. She glanced at her familiar; he was slumped across her shoulders, but lifted his head when she looked at him. His sigh was audible to everyone present, even Bellusdeo, whose much, much larger head turned toward him.

He remained silent, and Bellusdeo returned to the task at hand.

As they approached the fires, Terrano grew more agitated. Kaylin was worried about him. Not about what he'd do, precisely, but about Terrano himself. Without thinking, she slid an arm around his shoulders. He stiffened, and she withdrew it, but Sedarias had seen.

Sedarias surprised Kaylin; she substituted her own arm for the one Kaylin had withdrawn. Terrano also surprised Kaylin. He didn't look any more comfortable. "This is hard," he said quietly.

"What's hard?"

"This trying to be what used to be normal. It's hard."

Kaylin froze; Bellusdeo picked up the pace, forcing the Hawk to scurry to catch up. "You don't know what happened when Annarion and Mandoran came to Elantra."

"No, but I can guess."

Sedarias said something in a voice too low for Kaylin to catch.

"When I first headed out into the outlands, I attracted attention. Most of it wasn't harmful. Some of it could easily have killed me. When you're searching for something—and I wasn't searching for any specific thing—you almost vibrate in time with the world. It's hard to explain. You need to keep that to a bare minimum if you don't want to be eaten. But— it's hard. It's hard to do it *here*. If I were near Alsanis, I could just fall back into the places you live.

"But even if it was easy, it would be dangerous to do it here." He hesitated. "There's some part of me—of us—that is a little bit like Ravellon." As Bellusdeo turned again, her draconic ears missing nothing, Terrano rushed to continue. "It isn't about Shadow. That isn't what I meant. But Ravellon exists here. You can all see it. I can see it. Ravellon exists in your homelands. Ravellon existed in the world the Dragon ruled. Ravellon exists everywhere.

"We don't exist everywhere, but we exist in more than one place. We're here, but we're also there, where you two live. We spread. We changed. We grew. We had no choice."

"An interesting definition of choice," Bellusdeo rumbled.

"You would have done the same."

A small puff of exhaled smoke, and then the Dragon said, "I would have done more, probably."

This came as a relief to Terrano. The rest of the cohort expected it.

Dragon smiles—when the Dragon was in the scaled form— were not a comforting display of humor, but the Dragon smiled anyway, exposing very large teeth. "It's necessary for you to stay as quiet as possible. When we reach the city—"

"I'm not going into the city," Terrano said.

The cohort rustled; there was no other word for the wave of small movements that seemed to pass through them all. Terrano didn't seem to notice.

It was Sedarias who spoke. "Yes, you are."

"I'm not."

"You are."

The Dragon rolled her eyes and snorted smoke.

"I have no reason to go to the city."

"Are you here?"

"Here is not the city. Here is not the High Halls. Here is not the hive of buzzing politicians and the families that tossed us—that tossed *me*—away. I *hated* it, you know? I hated it. All of the life I remember before the green, before all of you, was nothing but anger and bitterness, nothing but criticism. I was too frivolous. I was too stupid. I was too unreliable. I was too childish.

"My past is littered with my constant failures. I was a failure—that's why *I* was sent to the green. And nothing's changed. Nothing. What I want is not what they wanted, if any of them still survive."

"They do."

"They have nothing to offer me. They have nothing I want. They have nothing I *ever* wanted. I thought all of life would be just that, and only that—an eternity of living a life I didn't want, until someone got lucky, or angry enough, and I died. I am *not going*."

Betting? Severn asked. Kaylin was surprised by his voice. He was reaching out to her when it wasn't a matter of someone's life or death. The subject was not an emergency or an investigation.

Depends. Are you betting that Sedarias wins?

Yes.

Not touching it.

Coward.

Breath held, they finally reached what Bellusdeo called signal fires. In the distance, it seemed a reasonable thing to call them; up close it was in no way accurate. They were a far more livid red, in a landscape that was otherwise so muted in color it could be safely called gray. Even Ravellon itself was faded and pale. The fires were not.

Nor were they hot; they weren't even warm.

"I would not touch those if I were you," the Dragon told Kaylin. "And I would *definitely* avoid them if I were any of the cohort."

Sedarias said, "Why?"

"You are not what we are."

"We're Barrani."

"I am willing to entertain that polite fiction. But at the heart of this debacle is the truth. You may, of course, choose to risk it."

"What do you fear it will do to us?"

"In the worst case? Destroy you. In the best case, injure you gravely. The fires were created as weapons against taint, against Shadow. And at the time, we did not know that there were Shadows trapped against their will in Ravellon, just as I was once trapped. You are not," she added, "Shadow, or of those Shadows. But there is, to you, a taint that would immediately render you outcaste among my own kin." She paused, and then added, "*Taint* is not perhaps the correct word.

"In our long history, we did not attempt to divest ourselves of the names that gave us life and form. But in Barrani history, there have been many such attempts. I would consider—pragmatically—that yours, as a whole, has been the most successful."

"We have our names."

"Yes. But whatever it was that the names gave you, you learned to exist without. Terrano does not have his name. He did not teach the others to do what he did."

"No. Just to change their form. I don't think the rest of our people could do what we did for centuries, unless they devoted almost all of their time to it. But even then, I am doubtful. What the *regalia* did, in the heart of the green, changed us."

Sedarias glanced at Terrano and exhaled. "We did not exist entirely without our names. Our names were within the Hallionne. He considered them to be abandoned, but they were present; they had not returned to the Lake of Life, as names do when the lives they sustain are extinguished. I do not know if knowledge of those names that were only barely ours would have allowed others to control us."

"Your circumstances were admittedly unusual."

"They were. And they will not occur again; it is now against Barrani law to expose children to the *regalia*, as we were once exposed." Sedarias looked at the raw, red splash of livid color, arms folded. It did not look like fire to Kaylin, and clearly Sedarias had her doubts as well. She held out her left arm just as Terrano began to move forward, and caught him. "I will strangle you myself," she told him, lips compressed.

"What? I'm trying to stand closer *to* the fire because there won't be Shadows near it!"

Judging by the expressions on half of the cohorts's faces, Sedarias wasn't the only one who didn't believe him.

"*Kaewenn*, I bid you welcome," a familiar voice said.

Kaylin turned. In the ether that existed in the boundary beyond Ravellon stood a familiar figure. "Tara!"

The Avatar of the Tower of Tiamaris stood in full armor, a sword in one hand, her helm in the other. Her eyes were a pale silver from which sparks seemed to fly when she blinked. At a distance, Kaylin thought she might not have recognized her.

Tara, however, was not addressing Kaylin, and when she bowed, she bowed to Bellusdeo. "My lord asked me to greet you, and to offer you and your companions the hospitality of Tiamaris." The words were stilted and formal.

The Dragon said, "A moment, Tara." Her voice lost some of its rumble as she finally slid back into her human form, losing the wings, the neck, the tail and the very impressive teeth. The scales reformed around her in the natural armor of her kin. Draconic faces didn't show a lot of expression that was easily recognizable to Kaylin. Human faces, like the one Bellusdeo now wore, did. "Who taught you that word?"

"The Norannir did. It is how they sometimes refer to you, even now."

"They should not use it."

"No? My lord did not think its use harmful; he said it was a sign of respect, or even reverence—and he believes that you are due that."

"Does he?" Bellusdeo's smile was weary; it held pain. "In the end, I failed them."

"If we judge all of life only by one moment, perhaps. But we do not, and they do not consider you a failure. You are here. They are here. And they light these fires in your name. Come. It is difficult for me to greet you thus, and I would speak with you at greater length from the confines of a safer environment." The red fire that was not hot and did not burn was reflected in the silver of her eyes, as if her eyes were mirrors.

Terrano was staring, openmouthed, at Tara. But to be fair, the rest of the cohort were staring only a little bit more discreetly.

"I am not Hallionne," Tara, said, her voice serene. "That was not my function. It is true that the full range of my power is only available within the Tower proper, but the fief *is* my domain—it is my duty to watch it, and to watch the borders. I see Ravellon no matter where I am; I see it no matter what form I take. I hear its Shadows, but they cannot reach you yet." She bowed, once again, to Bellusdeo. "I can contain the voices of your compatriots, but they are unstable here. It is not good for them to be here."

Bellusdeo nodded.

"And it's good for us?"

"You, Chosen, are what you are. The place in which you

stand does not change that. Bellusdeo is a known duality; she, too, is uninfluenced by her surroundings. But your companions are…" Tara frowned, and that expression was completely familiar. "They are fuzzy around the edges." The last sentence was spoken in Elantran. "I understand what your Helen has done for her tenants, and I can do the same. I understand the reaction of Castle Nightshade to Annarion, but I think it unnecessary."

"Why did Nightshade's Tower react that way?"

"Because he could hear Annarion's voice, and he believed— as I might once have—that it was a deliberate call, a deliberate beacon. My Lord is waiting, and he is perhaps not waiting patiently. He wished to come here himself."

"And he didn't?"

Tara smiled. "I judged it too great a risk."

"He really does trust you."

Tara looked surprised. "Of course." She smiled and added, "Severn is also waiting. He came to the Tower. It is how I knew that you would come here." She frowned. "Do not do that," she said, to Terrano.

"It's fine," Sedarias replied, before Terrano could. Allaron was standing closest to Terrano, and he slid an arm firmly around Terrano's shoulders.

"I don't need hospitality—"

"It is not a necessity," Tara told him gently. "But I do not think your friends are willing to part with you yet. There will be absence enough in the future."

When they turned to look at her—Allaron still firmly attached to Terrano—Tara smiled. "I am not a Hallionne, but I told you: the fief is my domain. I do not hear all thoughts or all voices unless I listen carefully, but I am capable of something as simple as this. And here, your voices are much, much clearer."

She turned and led them to the Tower.

CHAPTER 28

Tiamaris and Severn were, as Tara had said, waiting. They were waiting in a room that looked suspiciously like one of Helen's "isolation chambers," and they were silent as the company entered the modest door Tara opened for them.

Terrano and Allaron were the first through the door, which took a bit of navigating, because it wasn't really two people wide—not when one was Allaron's size. Terrano looked disgusted and demanded that Allaron let go, but as Terrano would not promise not to make a break for it, Allaron didn't.

Everyone else followed, Sedarias taking up the rear of the line as if she were mother hen and not captain of the cohort. To be fair to Sedarias, both Kaylin and Bellusdeo remained behind her, and although Kaylin wanted to be last through the door, the look Bellusdeo gave her at the implication that Kaylin's presence at her back would be of aid should anything go disastrously wrong was probably only a little bit cooler than Dragon breath.

So: Bellusdeo entered last, all golden armor, all warrior queen.

Neither Tiamaris nor Severn seemed particularly relieved; they waited as if waiting for the entire cohort were an everyday activity. Tiamaris took on the duties of a host, and did so with grace and wit; Diarmat would have been proud of him. Severn lingered as Tiamaris and Tara led the cohort to less martial looking rooms, and he fell in beside Kaylin as she followed the line.

She stopped walking, allowing the distance between them and the rest of their companions to grow. Turning to Severn, she hugged him. She didn't have words for him, because important words were often the difficult ones, but then again, he didn't require them.

"Sorry," she said, when she pulled away. "I didn't intend to leave Elantra."

"I know."

"Someone should probably let the Emperor know we're safe."

"I believe Bellusdeo has asked for permission to do just that. What are you going to do?"

"About what?"

"Everything."

"I'm going to eat something, and then we're heading to Helen, where we will hole up and discuss our various options. I think the Consort is going to be angry at me forever." This last was said glumly, Kaylin's anger having died somewhere on the long march.

She was surprised to discover that her anger was not the only anger in the room; Severn was angry. None of it showed. No one who was not connected to him the way she now was would have noticed it at all.

"Things will probably be ugly. I think we should skip the meal and head straight to Helen before the High Halls is aware of your presence here."

"They're already aware," she replied, thinking of Ynpharion.

"The Consort professed that she did not want any harm to come to either you or Bellusdeo."

"You don't believe her?"

"You do?"

Did she? She knew that she wanted to, and that that desire muddied the waters of objectivity. But Ynpharion had believed it. She nodded almost reluctantly. It was easier not to be upset with the Consort's anger if she believed that the Consort was somehow her enemy. But she held Ynpharion's True Name. He could keep things from her, but she was almost certain he couldn't lie.

But maybe that was wrong. The Consort also held his name, and she was not afraid, as Kaylin was, of using it. Ynpharion had known, when he had offered the Consort his name, that that was what awaited him. He hadn't offered it to Kaylin.

"I don't believe she ever intended to harm or cage either Bellusdeo or me."

"Then I doubt she'll inform the gathered war band that the Dragon has returned. But the Barrani have eyes everywhere."

Kaylin nodded. "We're going to have to sort that out before the Emperor attempts to reduce the High Halls to ash."

"He'll probably have help."

Kaylin winced. "Things have been bad?"

"Bad? That would be good, about now." He ran his hands through his hair, and she noted the circles beneath his eyes.

"I really am sorry. I wouldn't have gone without you if I'd had any warning." She certainly wouldn't have taken Bellusdeo.

"I know," he said again. "It was fine until—" He shook his head.

"Until?"

"We lost you. You've managed, against all odds, to survive, no matter where you land. But when you cut out, when I couldn't hear you and couldn't reach you at all..." Severn, so much better with words, even when he used far fewer of them, abandoned the attempt and again ran a hand through his hair. "I understand why Annarion, Mandoran and Teela became so upset."

"Is that why you went to Helen?"

He nodded. "I know as much about True Names as you do. I thought Mandoran and Annarion might know more. As it happened, Teela was there to answer questions."

"What was the general consensus?"

"...Not particularly good. Mandoran, however, said it was too sudden, too immediate; there was no hint of struggle. He would have expected the voices to die out singly, one at a time, otherwise. Mandoran assumed you'd found the rest of the cohort."

Kaylin could imagine just how much fun that conversation had been. "Sorry," she said again.

"Your own death has never truly terrified you."

"It has. But—not the same way. I mean, I won't be around after it happens." She shrugged, uncomfortable now. She understood Severn's fear—it was the fear that governed and shadowed her own life; the fear that had done so since the day her mother had failed to wake in the fiefs in the barely remembered past. She had nothing to say to that child, that other Kaylin, changed by the fiefs and by Severn and by deaths that she still couldn't think about without flinching; she had nothing to say to the girl who had run into Barren and become something darker, something far more dangerous.

And she found that she had nothing to say to Severn, either. The difference was that she *wanted* to. She wanted to say anything that would ease those shadows, visible across the whole of his expression.

Someone in the distance roared. In Dragon.

Kaylin reddened. "I think Bellusdeo wants us to hurry up."

A dress had been procured—somehow—for the Dragon. It was not a particularly fancy dress, but it was real, and it wasn't armor. Her hair had been plaited in a single braid that pulled hair off her face and made her look more severe. Or maybe it was just her expression. Her eyes were orange, but close enough to red to make conversation seem life-threatening.

The cohort were, unsurprisingly, blue-eyed. But the blue varied in shades, and two of the cohort were almost calm. Tara had led the cohort into a large room with various small tables situated across a carpet that absorbed all incidental noise. Terrano was seated between Sedarias and Allaron, but seemed to have given up on sulking; he was talking, in low tones, with the leader of the cohort.

Tiamaris stood at the center of the room, arms folded, eyes orange. "We have informed the Imperial Court that you have made a safe—if unconventional—return to Elantra. The unconventional will of course be a matter of grave concern. Lord Bellusdeo has claimed that the decision to take the path you took was hers."

"That's not—"

"Sedarias has likewise claimed the decision as her own. Do you have anything to add?"

"Yes. You're doing a damn good imitation of Diarmat."

Bellusdeo was surprised enough to laugh, which lessened the deadly color of her Dragon eyes. Tiamaris grimaced, which, given his demeanor, was unexpected.

"The Dragon Court is in an uproar," he said. "The Swords have been—I have been expressly commanded to inform you—working nonstop since your abrupt departure."

"By who?"

"Who else can give commands that I am obliged to obey?" Ugh.

"Bellusdeo has been granted conditional approval to remain with you—as long as you are situated within your own home. The Emperor trusts Helen."

Kaylin would have resented this, but given the circumstances, felt it unwise. She also happened to agree, and was being cowardly; she knew the Emperor would be blamed if Bellusdeo resented what might amount to house arrest, and the Emperor was in the Imperial Palace. Kaylin would be living with Bellusdeo under the same roof.

"And everyone else?"

"The Barrani are not the concern of the Dragon Court—or rather, these particular Barrani are not. The war band is. However, one possible benefit of a declaration of war is that the High Court and its lord are not in a position to make racial demands of the Emperor. Discussions and negotiations are tense enough that the Emperor would reject, outright, any attempt to forcibly repatriate your friends."

"You're speaking theoretically, right?" Kaylin asked, without much hope.

"He's not," Tara replied, before Tiamaris could. "Things have moved quickly, here, but nothing is on fire." She hesitated, which was unusual for Tara. "Ah, I forgot to mention something. You will not be able to speak with Lord Ynpharion, nor he with you, while you are within the Tower."

Kaylin folded her arms. "Thank you." She meant it. "Now that we're home and as safe as we're likely to get, we're going to have to visit Candallar. You're a fieflord, he's a fieflord. If you have any way of making that meeting safer, we'd appreciate it. His job as lord of a Tower is to stop Shadow from escaping to eat the rest of the city." To Tara, she said, "He apparently allowed a Barrani Lord—of the High Court—to enter and leave Ravellon. When he left, he was carrying a passenger."

Tara's eyes were obsidian.

"You let us in. You had that option. Could you let *me* walk into Ravellon and come out carrying Shadow?"

Tara's skin turned to stone. Literally. "No."

"Well, that's what the Tower of Candallar seems to have allowed."

"Impossible."

So not the word Kaylin wanted to hear. Before she could continue, Tiamaris lifted a staying hand. "We have been informed—by Corporal Handred—of Candallar's possible collusion with both assassins and...something at the heart of Ravellon."

I told him what you knew. If Shadows are leaving Ravellon and entering Elantra that way...

Kaylin relaxed. Marginally.

Tara said, "We are also investigating. My lord has begun the process of—"

Tiamaris coughed. Very, very loudly. Tara subsided.

Interesting, Nightshade said. Clearly not *all* Barrani had been forbidden communication.

"No," Tara said. "Lord Nightshade is a fieflord, and the possible problems with Candallar might affect us all. But you are tangled in too many names, and at the moment, we deem the information flow problematic. Lord Ynpharion and the Lord of the West March cannot hear you here; nor can you speak to them, unless it is absolutely necessary. We have not impeded the communication of your cohort." In a different tone, she added, "It is more complex, and the process would be more complicated; I am not entirely certain I would succeed. Has Helen tried?"

"I really wish you could visit and talk to Helen; I think you'd like each other. And no, I don't think she's ever tried. The cohort are part of Mandoran and Annarion. Losing that connection would be like losing a limb. She's not big on causing harm to her tenants."

"No. But her imperatives are not the same as the ones which bind me."

Tiamaris watched her, but said nothing, and Kaylin thought

that if Tara wanted to make the same adjustments that Helen had made to her own words, he might be willing to allow it.

"He would," Tara said, in a much softer voice. "But we were built where we stand for a reason, and while Ravellon exists, no such adjustments would be safe. I would not risk the fief he is building. I would not risk him." And she walked across the room to join him, losing, as she did, the armor with which she had greeted the cohort. Her clothing settled into the familiar, baggy gardening clothes that Kaylin privately thought of as the garb of her true self, and to everyone's surprise, Tiamaris gently laid an arm around her shoulders, and drew her toward him.

It was hard to tell if he was her support, or she his, and Kaylin watched with something that was almost envy. Almost.

"This place stinks," Terrano said, as they headed across the Ablayne. "It smells *terrible*."

Given the expressions of the cohort, most privately agreed, and Kaylin remembered Mandoran making a similar comment. Clearly, Mandoran was speaking to the rest of the cohort now. Severn was wearing his tabard. Kaylin was not wearing hers, as she had gone to visit Evanton after work hours. Although Tara could make clothing suitable for the Emperor himself, none of it persisted beyond the boundaries of the fief.

Kaylin did fall in beside Severn, regardless. He was alert. So was she. So was her familiar, who had perked up as they left Tara, and was now watching the streets like a hawk. There were no obvious threats; indeed, the threat seemed to emanate from the cohort, and Kaylin remembered, as a patrol of mounted Swords approached, that the Barrani war band had caused the Swords to go on full alert.

Severn, however, was uniformed, and was able to negotiate with the Swords; the cohort were not notably armored or armed. Their crime, such as it was, was being Barrani in highly concentrated numbers—and that was not, as Severn pointed out, against the edict of Imperial Law, which they all served.

The Swords did form up around the Barrani, more for the sake of the much more nervous onlookers than the Barrani themselves, and the cohort therefore had a more or less official escort through the rest of the Elantran streets. Kaylin found herself scanning windows in the taller buildings, but the usual street thieves and beggars stayed well away from the Swords, and as the neighborhood began to shift toward the high-end mansions that were common around Helen, they ceased to be even a passing concern.

I will inform the Consort that your lunatic plan was successful, Ynpharion said, the chill in his voice deeper than its usual frigid disdain.

You do that, Kaylin snapped back.

She points out that your dinner invitation is still viable.

Kaylin almost dropped her jaw. *You have got to be joking.*

No, Lord Kaylin, I am not. If you wish to withdraw that invitation—

I already did!

—feel free to send a message to the High Halls. Or better, deliver it in person.

There is no way *that she is coming here right now. We've just arrived, and she's already tried to harm the cohort. There is no way.*

Silence. She would have berated Ynpharion further, but sensed that he was no happier with the message he had conveyed than she was. If she wanted to shout at the source of her actual anger, she couldn't do it through Ynpharion.

She breathed again as they approached the gates that were Helen's actual boundaries, and smiled when the gates rolled open without assistance. Although this type of magic was not unheard of in the city, it was definitely unusual. But unusual, according to the mostly silent Swords, was the word of the very, very long day. Only when the cohort had been delivered to the property line did the Swords peel off and return to their regular patrol route.

Helen's doors were open long before the cohort reached them, and Kaylin noticed that the cohort became more martial, not less, with the loss of the Swords. She didn't tell them Helen was safe. If Mandoran and Annarion's experience hadn't made that clear to the cohort, nothing would. But she felt a bit bad for Helen, because Helen was social; she liked people, and liked guests.

Kaylin walked directly to Helen as Helen opened her arms, enfolding her in a hug that was simultaneously soft as comfort and rigid as armor. She looked past Kaylin to the cohort; Kaylin couldn't see her expression, but could hear it in her voice, anyway. "Welcome. The boys—I'm sorry, that's what we often call Mandoran and Annarion—are waiting for you in the dining room."

"Teela's not here?"

"Teela received a summons," Helen said, her voice flat and neutral, "and chose to honor it. She left some thirty minutes ago, heading to the High Halls."

Because if she went to the High Halls immediately, she could truthfully fail to answer most of the questions posed about the cohort's arrival.

"Yes, dear," Helen said. "I believe that was exactly her thinking on the matter." She paused. "Terrano?"

Kaylin withdrew and turned toward Terrano, who was pretty much holding hands with Sedarias and Allaron. Or at least they were holding on to his.

"I will not detain you or cage you. You are a guest, and in this house, guests are not prisoners. I won't deny that cages do wait—metaphorically speaking—for those who enter without invitation or permission, but you are not one of them. Ah, speaking of which," Helen added, "I believe you have a different visitor."

"Who?"

"I would tell you his name, but I don't think you could actually hear half of it. But I believe he said you named him Spike?"

She'd forgotten Spike.

"He apologizes," Helen continued, "but he could not follow you into the Tower; he could not approach it following the path you took."

"Wait, did you just say he's in a cage?"

"It is a comfortable cage, but yes. I have the ability to make decisions of my own, and his story, while *very* chaotic and jumbled, seemed to me to be true. He explained how he met you. I was slightly uncertain until he told me the name you gave him." She looked mildly disapproving.

"He—his form here—is a kind of floating, spiky ball," Kaylin explained.

"I'll let him out, then. He seemed to feel that you wished his company, and he owes you a great debt."

"Debt? Ummm, is he Immortal, by any chance?"

"I believe you would consider him so, yes. Why do you ask?"

"Because Immortals hate debt or obligation—it's practically a threat."

Helen smiled and drew Kaylin into the house, where she was no longer blocking the door. As the cohort filed into the foyer, Helen said, to Bellusdeo, "The Arkon has been using the mirror almost continuously. I believe he is concerned."

Bellusdeo snorted.

"And Maggaron is quite unhappy, at the moment."

The Dragon sighed. "Let me go talk to him. I shouldn't have left without him, but it might have entirely depleted the elemental water if he'd come as bodyguard."

Helen froze in place. Her eyes went the shade of color-flecked obsidian that was natural when she forgot to put effort into maintaining her appearance. "Have you spoken with the Keeper?"

"We've kind of been busy," Kaylin said. "Have you?"

"Teela and Severn did, separately. The Keeper did not, as we hoped, ask the water to intervene. Nor did the Tha'alani. The water acted entirely on its own."

Kaylin knew this.

"Understand that the Keeper exists for a reason. I do not know if all worlds have a Keeper, but I have often imagined they must. The Keeper harmonizes the elements; it is because they exist in his garden that the world is stable. Were they to range free, they would destroy each other, or try, and in the process, we would perish."

Kaylin nodded, because this was more or less her understanding.

"The water clearly feels that the danger is great enough to threaten them all."

"So: we have a Barrani war band, the threat of war, a High Court in revolt, Barrani Lords in collusion with a fieflord to enter Ravellon, and an elemental water that's terrified enough of *something* that she grabbed me and threw me at the West March. And at the heart of it all: Ravellon."

"Yes, dear. You forgot the cohort."

"No, I really didn't." Kaylin headed toward the dining room, followed by a quiet Severn. Bellusdeo, true to her word, had gone to apologize to her Ascendant.

The dining room was not silent, but Kaylin wouldn't have been surprised to learn that she couldn't hear a majority of the conversation. Allaron had released Terrano, and had pulled up a chair at the table; his posture was far more like Annarion's than Mandoran's. The table was the centerpiece of the gathering, but that was fair; it was the centerpiece of most of the discussions that took place while Kaylin was at home.

She was surprised to see that the cohort were very physical; there was almost always contact between the various members, even Sedarias. The stiff and very proper demeanor was shed in the presence of Mandoran and Annarion, and she sat beside Mandoran, an arm around his shoulders, her head tilted almost into his.

But she wasn't the only one. Two of the cohort were sharing a chair; several were holding hands or arms. They could have comfortably occupied half the space because they didn't seem to have any hesitation about how much they overlapped. Terrano was included in their number, but Kaylin noted that, after the brief hug he had offered a smiling Mandoran, he had pulled his chair to the side, out of easy reach of any of the rest.

She wondered, then, how much Mandoran and Annarion had adjusted their behavior as Helen's guests. Wondered if, when she wasn't in the room, they overlapped or huddled like this. This didn't look like a Barrani gathering; had Kaylin's vision been poorer, she might have assumed these people were Leontine kits, huddled in a pile near the hearth.

And she wondered if Teela's propensity for casual physical contact had been a memory of this, something she had lost for centuries—and that she had thought lost forever. She couldn't imagine Teela entwined with this mass of the cohort, though. And she grimaced when she thought of Tain's reaction.

Helen came to stand beside her as she lingered just on the inside of the doorway.

"They won't consider your presence a disturbance," Helen said. "If they need privacy, it comes built-in." Her smile was slender but warm. "I think they are surprised at how much they missed each other. They've relied on their names for so long, their names are like the Tha'alaan to them. But the physical presence has weight, as well. They are happy."

"I think Alsanis will miss them."

"I am certain, in a fashion, he will. They did not resent him, in the end. He did what he could for them, for as long as he could. But Kaylin, they are all aware that you carried them for the last stretch of that road. You are not of them, but they consider you one of theirs. It is part of the reason Annarion has been so aggrieved."

"Nightshade wanted me to do what I did. I mean, he didn't know precisely what it would be—but he wanted to rescue his brother."

"Yes. And I believe Annarion understands that. But you know better than anyone that there are some prices for rescue that you are not willing to pay."

Kaylin fell silent. Severn glanced at them both and then waded into the room. He pulled out a chair at the less crowded end of the table and took it, relaxing slowly into a seated posture that was very similar to Terrano's. On Severn, however, it didn't look unnatural.

Kaylin was about to join him when Spike came careening through the hall, like a ball thrown by an angry drunk. He came to a staggering stop inches away from Kaylin's face. Helen cleared her throat. Loudly. The familiar, however, looked bored and tired; he lifted an eyelid, looked at Spike, and let it close, his entire posture suggesting that nothing about this was an emergency.

"I am here," Spike said, as if the obvious needed to be stated. Kaylin stared at him, trying to figure out what he wanted. In the end, she lifted a hand—the left hand, because she was still capable of *some* caution—and let him settle into her palm, spikes and all. The spikes, however, didn't hurt, and he weighed next to nothing. She could probably injure herself if she closed her own hand, but Spike didn't seem intent on making her bleed again.

"He injured you?" Helen asked. Except that her voice was colder and harder, and the question came across as a demand.

"Probably my fault," Kaylin said quickly. "I asked him if he could find me again. We kind of—never mind. You can just read my mind."

Helen presumably did. Her eyes had gone obsidian again, but nothing else about her appearance changed; she was staring at Spike as if vision alone would answer any remaining questions she might have.

"Oh, it won't," Helen replied, although Kaylin had said nothing.

"I'm not sure why he cut me. I kind of wish he'd cut my hand, instead; I can patch up the shirt, but..." She shrugged. She was lying; she'd given up on salvaging this particular shirt, but had not yet done the math that would allow her to afford a new one.

"I understand why he cut you," Helen said. "He wished to be certain that he could find you again."

"And he can find anyone he—"

"Whose blood he has consumed, yes. He, by the way, is perhaps not the appropriate word. And no, he does not consume it the way your vampires would."

Kaylin flushed.

"He is evaluating the metrics of the blood itself in a way that means he can be completely certain of his identification."

"You don't do that."

"No, but it is not required. I have other methods of identifying you that Spike does not. If you would not mind, I would like to converse with Spike."

"Go ahead."

Helen's voice shifted; she lost words, or rather, words as Kaylin understood them. Here or there she caught a syllable, but in the end it became almost painful to listen to—it was like the droning buzz of a bee hive, except that as more words were added, more bees arrived. In the end, Kaylin lowered her hand from the underside of Spike's body, covered both ears with her hands, and retreated to the dining room.

She figured Spike wouldn't find the retreat insulting; she covered her ears whenever Bellusdeo spoke in native draconian—or at least she did if she had two free hands—and Bellusdeo didn't.

But the cohort were now craning their heads toward the door as Kaylin entered.

"Can you understand what they're saying?" Kaylin asked, as she retreated to the wall farthest from that open door.

Sedarias shook her head. "But I think, with time and Spike's input, we probably could."

"Can you ask for lessons when I'm outside of the house?"

Mandoran laughed.

Sedarias, however, took Spike's presence as a sign. It was time to get serious. Kaylin watched the transformation of the cohort's expressions. "Teela is at the High Halls," she said, which was not what Kaylin had expected.

"Is she under house arrest?"

"No. At this late stage, they would not dare. They are, however, very interested in our arrival."

"Interested in an aggressive way? Or politely, politically, *fictively* interested?"

"Our method of arrival has not been disclosed; questions are, of course, being asked, and possible explanations given."

"There are no good explanations."

"That just makes the proceedings more entertaining."

"Is Teela the one making stuff up?"

"No. Teela is very angry, and when she is angry she is on her best—her most exquisite—behavior."

"Is Tain with her?"

"Tain is with her. As one of four guards. He is not present

as a Hawk, and he has no standing in the High Court. Teela is there as a Lord, and she is surprisingly adept at it."

"Surprisingly?"

"Teela was always unusual." Sedarias turned to the cohort, although it wasn't necessary. "But while we were away, she grew. She's angry," Sedarias repeated. "And it's never completely safe for Teela to be angry."

"Safe for who?"

"Anyone, but mostly Teela."

Mandoran turned to Kaylin, his expression unusually grave. "We're here for her. We're here for each other. When our families threw us away—"

"I wasn't thrown away," Sedarias said.

"When the *rest* of our families threw away people *too sane* to demand the right to go to the *regalia*, we found each other. Teela doesn't want Annarion to take the Test of Name because she can't go. She's a Lord of the Court."

Kaylin frowned. "But that means—"

"Yes. You can't go, either."

Helen came into the room, Spike floating by her left shoulder. "I think," she told the cohort, "I should show you to your rooms. At the moment, Annarion and Mandoran are sharing. I was uncertain whether or not you would want to do likewise."

"Not if you let Mandoran design the room," Serralyn said, pulling a face. But the cohort rose almost as a single person, and followed Helen as she led them out of the dining room and to the room which would become their temporary home.

Terrano did not follow. He watched until the last of the cohort—Sedarias, as it happened—had exited the room. Only when she was gone did he sag in his chair, as if he'd been fighting to hold himself upright. Or together. Kaylin had no idea what to say to him; she only knew that she should say *something*.

People in pain often had this effect on her, if she cared about them at all. And clearly, she *did* care about Terrano, which came as a bit of a surprise to her, given how they'd first met.

"It is not surprising," Helen's voice said. The sound of it pulled Terrano from his thoughts, and he straightened in his chair again. "You have been living with two of his brothers. You've fought by their sides, more than once; they've come to your aid, and you've come to theirs, when there was no certain guarantee of survival. They are your friends. They are Teela's family. They live in your house.

"Terrano is one of them, to you." Helen's Avatar remained with the rest of the cohort; only her voice was present in the room.

"I'm not," Terrano said, voice low.

"They don't believe that," Helen countered. "They are waiting for you, and Allaron is about to leave the room to remind you."

"Remind me of what? That he's a giant, overstrong ox?"

"I heard that," Allaron said. "Look, I don't care if you don't want to stay. Sedarias is set on it. I never did understand why the two of you got along so well—you could not be more different." He lowered his voice as he approached Terrano who was, to Kaylin's eye, almost sulking. "You *know* what she's like when she's unhappy. Or maybe you don't. But she's been unhappy since you left."

"I can't talk to her," Terrano whispered. "I can't talk to any of you, anymore."

"You can. You can't do it the old way."

"I can't *hear any of you* anymore. I don't have—"

Allaron's large hand was gentle as he placed it firmly on Terrano's shoulder. "You did hear us," he said. "From wherever it was you went, you heard us. You came back for us. Without you, we would have been swept away. We understand. Sedarias thinks you've been listening with half an ear since you left."

"Half?"

"Well, she thinks you never listened before, so half is still impressive." When Terrano attempted to pull away, Allaron exhaled. "We are not suffering through Sedarias's deep, personal pain when we have a host of Barrani Lords bent on our destruction. Even if you can't speak to us and can't hear us the way you did before, you're part of our entire history. We're here because of you. If you'd never started your experiments, we would never have been free. So you're staying with us until this part is done. Got it?"

"You know you can't hurt me."

"Keep it up and I'll at least enjoy trying. Come on. Everyone's waiting." Allaron leaned down, lowering his voice. "Mandoran wants you to teach him not to get stuck in walls."

"In *walls*?"

"Seriously. He's gotten stuck twice now. Or maybe three times."

Terrano laughed, then, his expression brightening. "He's an idiot. I can easily show him that." And he straightened his shoulders and let Allaron lead him to their room.

"Well?"

Kaylin blinked. She had forgotten that Severn was in the room.

"You're worried."

"There's a lot to be worried about. The Consort. The Emperor. The Barrani attempt to start a war. The Arcanists who cooperated with Terrano and the cohort before they'd finally been freed. Candallar. *Ravellon*."

Severn nodded, raising a brow. Kaylin had practiced raising a single brow for years, and hadn't become proficient.

"Diarmat's report. If it's not at Evanton's, he's going to reduce me to ash." She would have continued, but Severn wasn't buying any of it, even if all of it was true.

It's all true, he agreed. *But it's not what you're worried about.*

It's what I should be worried about.

Yes.

Severn was right, of course. At the moment, she was worried about Terrano. Terrano, who had tried to kill the Consort on Kaylin's first visit to the West March. Terrano, who had abandoned his name and left his friends behind when Alsanis had finally released them all.

That Terrano occupied none of her thoughts. But this Terrano? He seemed smaller, frailer, and lonely.

"He's with family. They won't abandon him." He rose and held out an arm. "You need sleep. Tomorrow is going to be a long day, and if we all survive it, the day after isn't going to be much better." He hesitated for one long minute as Kaylin stared at his arm. "I don't know if Helen's mentioned it, but I'm staying."

She stared at him.

"Until the cohort leaves, one way or the other." He hadn't asked permission, but that would have just been awkward.

Kaylin exhaled heavily, but nodded. She didn't ask him anything either, for the same reason.

EPILOGUE

"I don't care if you read my mind," Teela told Helen, as she entered the foyer. "But at the moment, I do not care to discuss its contents."

"Not much to discuss?" A voice that was not Helen's said.

Teela looked up the grand, curving staircase. She had never had the heart to tell Kaylin that the younger Hawk's sense of appropriate, cohesive architecture was terribly off. Terrano was perched on the left side of the stairs, leaning into the guide rails. He rose as she headed toward him.

"Waiting for me?"

"It was quieter." Terrano hesitated. "You have your own room."

"Yes. I should warn you that I share it with my beat partner."

"He's not here."

Teela exhaled. "No. He's not here, at the moment. He had something else to attend." Her lips compressed in a *do not ask* line as she looked at Terrano, the lone member of the cohort who had elected not to return from the green. And yet, here he was, looking much smaller, and much younger—to Teela's eye—than either Mandoran or Annarion had, upon their arrival.

She headed up the stairs, and Terrano followed her. "I am going to change," she told him, without looking back. "I need, at the very least, a figurative bath."

"Spike arrived," he told her, as if he, like Helen, could read minds. "He's with Kaylin."

"And Kaylin?"

"Sleeping," Helen said. It was the first word she'd spoken since Teela's arrival. Teela appreciated the silence. Nor did Helen tell Teela that she should be sleeping as well; the Barrani were not a race that required sleep, although they did at times require rest.

She glanced once over her shoulder; Terrano waited, almost fidgeting. He would follow her to her own room if she did not tell him to leave.

She didn't tell him to leave.

Teela's rooms were open to light and air, and the floors and walls were wooden. Lintels were carved, tall.

"This looks like the West March," Terrano said, as he entered.

"What do your rooms look like?"

He made, in Kaylin's parlance, a face. "Like the High Halls. Or like Sedarias's home." Terrano didn't ask why Teela's rooms were different; he knew. These were the rooms in which Teela's mother had been happiest, and in which Teela had therefore been happy. At a remove of centuries, she could not recall the emotion of happiness; she merely knew that it had existed.

She wondered, then, about happiness, sorrow, hatred, love. She had Barrani memory; the slow decline of mortal memories did not plague her. She could remember every incident that led from the green to Helen. She could clearly remember her mother's face, her mother's voice, her mother's quiet presence.

But although she had those memories, she could not experience them as if she were, once again, that child.

Not even here. She headed to the room with the large bath. Water was—of course it was—warmed and ready; she divested herself of the court clothing that she had grown to loathe, and slid immediately into the soothing waters.

Terrano sat on the ground. The bath was built into the floor; it did not rise above it, as small mortal baths often did. He removed shoes—without actually touching them—and slid his feet into the water as well; his palms were flat to either side of him. He said nothing.

Teela understood that he would say nothing, until and unless she broke the silence. She therefore chose her words with care. "Thank you." Her voice was soft. She stared at the surface of the water, at the eddies that did not break the stillness completely.

"For what?"

"For waiting."

"You didn't seem all that happy to see me, that I recall."

"I was shocked to see you. I was—" Teela shook her head. "Understand that I am not considered young by *any* of the Barrani. A handful remember me in my distant youth—but it *is* distant, for both me and that handful." She bent her head. "Mandoran told me that it was you. You believed that you could find me. You believed that you could bring me…home."

Silence.

"I learned to live without you. I learned," Teela continued, her voice still soft, shorn of edge, "to live the life that was left to me after the green. I was angry," she added. "I hated my father, and I used the hatred to keep going. The first time— the first time I returned to the green, I had *hope*. I was chosen to play a part in the *regalia*. I believed—" She laughed, a brief, bitter bite of sound. "But you were still lost. Whatever role I was given, it was not, somehow, to free you all. I'm sorry."

"For what?"

"For failing you. For giving up. Because I did. I gave up on everything. I learned to live in isolation. I learned to live without your names and your voices. I made a place in the world that was my shape, and my size. But...I never forgot."

He was silent, lost in his own thoughts, his eyes becoming eyes that no Barrani naturally possessed; the color was wrong.

"You never forgot. But you never gave up, either. I don't approve of what you did, but at the same time, I am oddly grateful. You kept faith when I had all but lost it."

His expression was haunted. To Teela, he was the Terrano of that distant, irretrievable past.

"What was it like?" he finally asked.

And Teela, understanding the question he did not ask, said, "I think you're starting to know. Only the two of us, now, have lived outside of what Kaylin calls the cohort."

"You're not on the outside, anymore."

She closed her eyes. Opened them again, and gave up on the bath. Dripping water until she could reach towels, she held her breath, and when she chose to exhale, words accompanied it. "I am on the outside," she said quietly. Before Terrano could protest—and he seemed very much of a mind to do so—she lifted a hand. "I can hear them, now. If I listen. And they can hear me, if I so choose.

"You never did that. You never, ever shut them out."

He was staring at her as she turned fully to face him, his confusion evident on his face.

"For centuries, I woke to the remembered sound of your voices. I woke to my own nightmares. Losing you all was like losing the best and most important parts of myself. I thought I would die. I expected it would kill me. It didn't. It just caused pain." Wrapped in towels, she headed toward her bedroom, bypassing Tain's. "It caused pain and loss for a century. I think the reason I hated my father so much by the end was not just for his murder of my mother; it was for the murder of all the love that I had ever known."

His silence was textured now as he considered her words. She turned away from him, heading toward the bed, where she threw herself across its covers almost bonelessly, and rolled over to stare at the twining vines above her head.

"I am part of the cohort. Because of Kaylin, because of you, because of the choices made, I am part of it. My name is known—to them, to the people to whom I willingly surrendered it.

"But I am not the Teela I was when I did surrender my name. I didn't grow with the cohort—as you did. I didn't learn what the cohort learned. I didn't become so enmeshed in the thoughts of the others that I could not always separate their thoughts from my own."

"There wasn't any need to do that."

"No? Perhaps not. If all I was left, on the day my father pulled me from the Hallionne, was privacy, it's a cage that I grew to rely on. To even, in some ways, depend on." She held up an arm, and Terrano joined her. He was like a cat, she thought, or a puppy. She held him, as she would have held either. As she had sometimes held Kaylin on the nights when Kaylin's nightmares had been too harsh, too extreme. She had always told Kaylin that this was practical—Kaylin without sleep was an absolute misery for anyone who had to endure her—but Kaylin had not entirely believed it. Probably because it wasn't true.

He curled into the arm she had held out, and she lowered it around him. The child that Kaylin had once been was not quite gone, but almost, and so quickly.

"You didn't want to stay," she said softly, into his hair; he had buried his face, and therefore all traces of his expression.

"I didn't want to be caged," he whispered. "I thought—"

"You didn't think." She said it fondly; it was an echo of every word she had offered to one scrawny, angry, mortal. "You went out into the universe. You went out into the unknown. Sedarias wanted, so badly, to join you."

"She would have hated it," he said.

"Oh?"

"We would have been together, but only the way outsiders are. It's the name," he added. "It's the *name*. Our names bound us. Our names transcended everything else. We were never truly isolated, because we were always attached. I don't—" Silence, and tension, physical tension, in it. "I'm not part of them, anymore. They don't say it. But they don't have to say it. They try to make space for me—but I'm foreign now. I can't hear them. Can't think their thoughts; can't make my own clear to them. They're there. They're alive. They're like the people I knew—but it's almost as if I can't truly hear them, can't truly see them."

"They were part of you," she whispered. "They were only part of my dreams. I am not at home, in the end, with them, either. But Terrano—they're *here*. The part of them that you occupied is still part of them. That won't change."

"Did that help you?"

She tightened her hold on him. "And I'm here," she said quietly. "Outside in a different way."

"Can I stay with you, instead?"

"You'll have to put up with Tain." And he would only know what that meant if he could hear Mandoran's steady stream of complaints—and he couldn't. "Yes. If you want, you can stay here. Sedarias won't like it."

"She doesn't like anything," he murmured.

And the strangest thing happened, as she held him, wanting to shield him from a pain and loss that was so entirely internal she had no hope of doing so.

Terrano fell asleep.

* * * * *